SECRET WHISPERS

Virginia Andrews® Books

The Dollanganger Family Series
Flowers in the Attic
Petals on the Wind
If There Be Thorns
Seeds of Yesterday
Garden of Shadows

The Casteel Family Series
Heaven
Dark Angel
Fallen Hearts
Gates of Paradise
Web of Dreams

The Cutler Family Series
Dawn
Secrets of the Morning
Twilight's Child
Midnight Whispers
Darkest Hour

The Landry Family Series
Ruby
Pearl in the Mist
All That Glitters
Hidden Jewel
Tarnished Gold

The Logan Family Series
Melody
Heart Song
Unfinished Symphony
Music of the Night
Olivia

The Orphans Miniseries
Butterfly
Crystal
Brooke
Raven
Runaways (full-length novel)

The Wildflowers Miniseries
Misty
Star
Jade
Cat
Into the Garden (full-length novel)

The Hudson Family Series
Rain
Lightning Strikes
Eye of the Storm
The End of the Rainbow

The Shooting Stars Series
Cinnamon
Ice
Rose
Honey
Falling Stars

The De Beers Family Series
Willow
Wicked Forest
Twisted Roots
Into the Woods
Hidden Leaves

The Broken Wings Series
Broken Wings
Midnight Flight

The Gemini Series
Celeste
Black Cat
Child of Darkness

The Shadows Series
April Shadows
Girl in the Shadows

The Early Spring Series
Broken Flower
Scattered Leaves

The Secret Series
Secrets in the Attic
Secrets in the Shadows

The Delia Series
Delia's Crossing
Delia's Heart
Delia's Gift

The Heavenstone Series
The Heavenstone Secrets
Secret Whispers

My Sweet Audrina
(does not belong to a series)

Virginia ANDREWS

SECRET WHISPERS

**SIMON &
SCHUSTER**

London · New York · Sydney · Toronto · New Delhi

First published in the US by Gallery Books, 2010
A division of Simon & Schuster, Inc.
First published in Great Britain by Simon & Schuster UK Ltd, 2013
A CBS COMPANY

1 3 5 7 9 10 8 6 4 2

Simon & Schuster UK Ltd
1st Floor
222 Gray's Inn Road
London WC1X 8HB

www.simonandschuster.co.uk

Simon & Schuster Sydney, Australia
Simon & Schuster New Delhi, India

A CIP catalogue record for this book is available from the British Library

Hardback ISBN: 978-0-85720-203-1
Ebook ISBN: 978-0-85720-205-5

Printed and bound by CPI Group (UK) Ltd, Croydon, CR0 4YY

SECRET
WHISPERS

Prologue

NOT ONLY IN dreams but also in quiet moments when I was alone with my own thoughts, I would often hear a baby's cry. She sounded frightened, and I was confident she was calling for me. It was terrifying because when my mother had suffered a miscarriage and she and my father had lost their chance to have a son, she had gone into a deep depression and often thought she heard her baby's cry. My parents had already set up a nursery for the baby they intended to name Asa Heavenstone, after one of my father's ancestors who had fought in the Civil War. Daddy always wanted his Asa.

I had a different reason to imagine a baby's cry. I was afraid to tell anyone what I heard and have it get back to my father, but most of all, I didn't want to admit even to myself that a part of me was out there and would never know who I was and, perhaps more important, who she really was.

"Be still, my heart," I would whisper.

"Don't listen to the wind," I would tell myself.

If I was awake when I heard the cry, I would slap on my earphones and listen to my iPod or hurriedly turn on the television. Sometimes, I would simply start humming some song aloud. I would do anything to distract myself.

If I was dreaming, I would moan and then wake with a start and listen hard to be sure it had been only a dream.

The silence comforted me.

But it didn't make it all go away.

I knew what every mother knows.

It never goes away.

It only gets louder, and nothing would drown it out—not all the radios, all the televisions, or all the iPods in the world.

1

Birthday

"SEMANTHA! WHAT THE hell are you doing on the floor?" my dorm roommate, Ellie Patton, asked. She stood in our bathroom doorway with her hands on her hips, gaping at me with her black pearl eyes so enlarged that she resembled someone with serious thyroid problems. I realized she must have been standing there for a while calling to me and was getting upset at my not responding.

I was surprised she was up so early. Everything about her was usually frantic and last-minute. We had been together at Collier for my three years of private high school, but this was the first time she had caught me doing it.

For the last three years, I woke up on the morning of my daughter's birthday and secretly lit a candle. I would hear my sister, Cassie, whispering in my ear, reminding me of the date as well, not that I needed her to do that. Lately, however, I was even seeing her stepping out of a shadow or smiling back at me in a mirror.

Usually, I was home on my daughter's birthday because it occurred during a spring break. However, this year, the break occurred two days after her birth-day, so I was still at Collier, a private high school for girls just south of Albany, New York.

I hadn't expected to be sent to a private high school outside Kentucky, but Daddy had chosen Collier for me because it was so exclusive, which really meant very expensive and well supervised. My therapist in Kentucky, Dr. Ryan, had recommended it. It had a small but beautifully maintained campus. The main building was neoclassical and resembled a government office building, something you might expect to find in Washington, D.C. There were three dormitory buildings that looked like anything but dormitory buildings because of their elaborate landscaping and porticos. They looked more like private estates.

Our dormitory housed only twenty girls, and none of our classes had more than fifteen students in it. Some of my public-school classes had had nearly forty in them. It was impossible here to avoid being called on to answer a question or have your homework checked. Every teacher was well acquainted with all of his or her students, their work histories, and their families. The story circulated was that they had reports on us that rivaled FBI reports on terror suspects.

The school had a beautiful, technologically modern theater; two playfields, one for field hockey and one for softball; and a spanking-new gymnasium. The library was stocked with computers and had a separate audiovisual room for viewing information or listening to music. Our cafeteria reminded me of an upscale restaurant. The chairs were large and cushioned, and the tables were polished, rich, hard walnut.

Once a month, the school held a formal dinner for us during which the dean of students, Mrs.
Hathaway, delivered a report concerning the student
body's overall performance and her expectations for
the weeks to come. Attendance was mandatory. Every
violation, whether of rules or of the property, was
described, and the violators were sometimes publicly
chastised. Contrary to what she hoped, however,
making it onto what the students called Hathaway's
Hit List was viewed as some sort of accomplishment,
a respected act of defiance. I had yet to make the list.

Few private schools gave their students as much
personal attention, which meant there were more
eyes on us all day and all night than in most other
private schools. The restrictions on our comings and
goings were also far stricter than at other schools.
Our privileges were directly tied to our grades and
our on-campus behavior, as at other schools, but at
Collier, there was a hair trigger on punishment. It
wouldn't take much to put one of us in a cage, and,
of course, smoking, drinking alcohol, or doing any
drugs were reasons for immediate expulsion and for-
feiting all of the money your parents had spent, and
they had spent a great deal.

There was even a rumor that our rooms were
bugged and our phone calls monitored. Supposedly,
our parents received weekly reports about our behavior and our work. Some even thought it was a
daily report. Most of the girls believed the rumors,
because almost all of them had given their parents
cause to worry about them. It was almost a require-
ment for admittance that we were not to be trusted

or believed. The game played with incoming first-year girls was how quickly one of us could get them to reveal their embarrassing secrets, something that explained why their parents would want to pay so much more money for them to attend Collier.

The secret I revealed was probably the most boring for them. Ellie told me I was one of the longest holdouts, one of the most difficult to break, because I wasn't as desperate for their friendship. Finally, I revealed that I had been seeing a therapist regularly because of family tragedies and there was concern that I could have a nervous breakdown. Or, as my father put it to Mrs. Hathaway, "She's as fragile as a blue-jay egg."

Of course, nothing was ever said about my pregnancy and my giving birth, but when some people my age hear that you have deep-seated psychological issues serious enough to require regular therapy and you're on the edge of falling into a nervous breakdown, they look at you as if you have leprosy. I felt confident, however, that many of the others had been sent for counseling at one time or another as well. One or two looked and acted as if they had recently been released from a clinic, in fact. But unlike me, they felt that secret was too sensitive to reveal. They probably invented something else or told only part of their story. Ironically, they'd admit to getting pregnant and having an abortion before they'd admit to having been in psychological counseling for years, but that was not true for me. The Cassie living inside me wouldn't let me do that.

Even while I had attended my private high

school, I'd had periodic sessions with Dr. Ryan, when I was home for either an extended weekend or on holiday. It was really my father's younger brother, my uncle Perry, who insisted that my father arrange that in the first place.

"After all she has gone through, she has way too much emotional and psychological damage, Teddy," he told him right in front of me. "You can't just send her off to live in an unfamiliar environment with strangers. She needs support, professional support, and we both know you're too busy to provide it."

Of course, Uncle Perry had been right, and if it hadn't been for Dr. Ryan, I probably wouldn't have been this close to finishing high school, even one as insulated and protective as Collier. I certainly would never have had the strength to go off to college, not that I thought I would. I avoided filling out applications, but to satisfy my curious classmates, I pretended I had already been admitted to an expensive small college in Kentucky. They believed it. For the most part, everyone believed whatever I said because I said it with such conviction and nonchalance. I think that was because I made myself believe it first.

Even though I didn't see a therapist on a regular basis here, I had many informal sessions with Mrs. Hathaway. She obviously knew when I had a long break between classes and either casually came by my room at the dormitory or caught me walking on campus and invited me to her office for a cup of tea.

Her questions were always the same. "How are you getting along with your roommate, your classmates, and your teachers? Why aren't you participating in any activities like the drama club, chorus, or one of the athletic teams? You've got to expand your interests, explore, experiment, Semantha. Doesn't anything we offer interest you?"

Almost always, she'd tilt her head and smile softly before asking, "Have you met any nice boys at our social events?"

All of the girls thought little of Collier's social events. There were so many chaperones, and the security personnel hovered outside every entrance like killer bees ready to sting anyone for the smallest indiscretion. It was nearly impossible to go off and do something we considered more exciting. It was like being brought up in the mid-forties, when there were actually rules about how many inches apart a boy and a girl had to be when they danced together. And of course, if you wore anything Mrs. Hathaway considered inappropriate, you weren't even permitted to enter the auditorium for one of the official socials.

In general, the boys we met at these highly controlled gatherings came from brother schools for boys or nearby parochial schools. On very rare occasions, boys from one of the area public schools were invited, but they were usually what Mrs. Hathaway would call the crème de la crème, the honor students. Davina Bernstein said they were rented from Geeks R Us and at midnight would turn into laptops.

I told Mrs. Hathaway that I hadn't met any boy who remotely interested me or whom I interested. None of my answers to any of her questions really pleased her, but she wasn't pushy. Like most of the people my father had spoken to about me, she tiptoed and whispered and showed great patience and understanding. I was so tired of this so-called tender loving care that I wanted to scream, but instead, I turned myself into a sponge, absorbed what I had to absorb, and then squeezed it out of myself as soon as I was alone again or when Ellie was on the phone or out in the hallway talking to other girls.

Right now, she continued to stand in the bathroom doorway, impatiently waiting for an explanation for the lit candle and my sitting cross-legged on the bathroom floor talking to myself.

When I was at home on my daughter's birthday, I lit the candle in my bathroom with the windows wide open so no one would smell the wax melting. Softly, under my breath, I would sing "Happy Birthday" to her and pretend she was there, now almost four years old, sitting on the floor with me, her eyes wide with excitement. I even pretended to give her a present and watch her unwrap it. We would hug, and I would hold her and give her the security and comfort that came with knowing your mother is always there for you, loving you and protecting you. I cried tears of joy for both of us.

Then I would hear someone walking in the hallway or a door open and close, and I would quickly smother the candle flame and hide the candle again in the bottom of a sink cabinet. I knew how furious my father would be if he discovered I had done such a thing. Maybe for a few seconds, there was some awareness of the special day visible in his eyes on the first-year anniversary after I had given birth, but that candle burning in his memory was soon snuffed out. It was truly as though he had clapped his hands over the tiny flame.

I could never forget any of it, even though it was all so painful to remember. Of course, I tried to forget. I really did, and maybe I was making some progress. Maybe that was why Cassie was coming back to me in whisperings and shadows. She was afraid I would leave her in her grave forever.

"Semantha?" Ellie pursued. "Will you please tell me what you're doing in our bathroom?"

"It's just something I do in memory of someone I loved and lost," I told her.

"Oh," she said. "Sorry." I knew she thought I was doing it for my mother or my sister or perhaps both.

When Ellie and I were first assigned to room with each other, I didn't reveal anything about my seeing a therapist on a regular basis. I did that later, when it was clear to me that none of the girls would leave me be until I told them something negative about myself. It was almost as if they wouldn't tolerate someone who had nothing to hide.

However, I told Ellie the story that was so embedded in my mind that it was practically a recording. I couldn't avoid telling her, because I never had a mother call or visit, and the logical question was why not.

"My parents at a late time in their marriage tried to have another child, hoping for a boy," I began. "My father had always dreamed of having a son he would name after one of his famous ancestors, Asa

Heavenstone, a young man who fought and was killed in the Civil War. His portrait hangs on a wall in our house in Kentucky with the portraits of other Heavenstone ancestors.

"Not long after my sister and I were told that my mother was pregnant, it was determined that my mother was having a boy. The news brought my parents great happiness. They immediately began work on setting up the nursery, but my mother suffered a miscarriage and went into a deep depression. She took too many sleeping pills one day, and we lost her."

Of course, I didn't tell Ellie about the things Cassie had done to cause all of this. Only my father, my uncle Perry, and I knew the truth.

Ellie, like everyone else, looked devastated for me and nearly broke into tears.

"Less than two years later," I continued, "my sister, Cassie, tripped and fell down a stairway in our house and broke her neck. She died instantly."

When I added that, some people would just sit with their mouths wide open, and some would shake their heads and say, "You poor girl and your poor, poor father."

I would bear their sympathy like someone who had been beaten beyond pain and thank them.

Ellie didn't linger after I explained the candle. She nodded, backed out of the bathroom, and closed the door. She either fled from or ignored sad news and stories of family tragedies. It was one of the reasons I could get along so well with her.

I continued with my private birthday ritual and blew out the candle. Ellie never asked me anything else about it again, and, of course, I never mentioned it to her. I didn't like lying to her. I never liked lying to anyone, in fact, even though my sister, Cassie, had thought that was a weakness.

"There are very few people, Semantha, whom you can trust with the truth. The truth is naked, unprotected. Once it's out there, it's alone. Lying," she had said with that Cassie smirk I had grown used to seeing, "is simply another layer of protective skin."

I knew the other girls at Collier thought I was unusual in many ways, but my brutal honesty did the most to keep me from becoming very friendly with anyone else but Ellie. Despite what Cassie had told me about the value of lying, she had rarely bothered to do so even when it came to holding on to a friend. I had her way of simply telling other girls and boys whatever I really thought, no matter what the consequences. My quiet manner and my revelation about a potential nervous breakdown already had done much to create a deep, wide valley between me and the others at Collier. This characteristic of being coldly and factually honest at times was the icing on the cake. Even when I sat with them in the cafeteria or walked alongside them in the corridors, most avoided looking at me, and when anyone did, she usually turned away quickly. It was as if she was looking at something forbidden.

From the way the others whispered and sometimes hovered with Ellie in corners, I knew they were peppering her with questions about me. They surely wondered what it was like sleeping in the same room with someone as weird as I was. I never asked Ellie about it, but occasionally, she would reveal some of their questions—mostly, I think, because she was curious about the answers herself.

Naturally, they wanted to know what interested someone as offbeat as I was. *What does she like? Does she have a boyfriend? Did she ever have one? Is she gay? What makes her so quiet most of the time? What does she really think of the rest of us? Is she just a rich snob? Does she do anything strange, anything at all that frightens you?*

Most of all, they wondered why Ellie didn't ask to be transferred to another room. Of course, I wondered about that myself, but it wasn't long before I thought I knew the answer. I never did anything to make her feel uncomfortable. I didn't take up more room than I should. I didn't dominate our closets or dressers or bathroom cabinets the way some of the other girls did to their roommates. I was willing to share anything of mine with her. I certainly didn't keep her up at night talking in my sleep or complaining about the school and the other girls, which was what many of the girls suspected.

"After all, she's mental," I actually overheard a girl named Pamela Dorfman tell Ellie. "She confessed that she had and probably still has deep-seated psychological problems, didn't she? She's scary. Maybe she'll smother you in your sleep one night. I'd be afraid to room with her."

Natalie Roberts went so far as to nickname me Norma Bates, a play on the name Norman Bates from the movie *Psycho*. To her credit, Ellie always came to my defense, but not so strongly as to alienate herself from the other girls on my behalf. There was a limit to loyalty, especially loyalty to someone she had only met here and probably would never see again after graduation, which was now only a few months away.

There were other reasons she didn't desert me. Ellie was the youngest in a family with three other children, another girl and two boys. From the way she described her siblings, I understood that they usually overwhelmed her. "Trampled me," was the way she put it. She had had to fight to get a word in at dinner, had often been teased and criticized, and had always been the recipient of hand-me-downs.

"My sister would get new things, and I always got what she no longer wanted or what no longer fit her perfectly," she told me with bitterness. "'Nothing should be wasted' meant I got the used stuff."

Ellie came right out and confessed to me that she saw herself as Cinderella without the pumpkin and especially the glass slipper. "How would you like growing up in a family like mine?"

She claimed her parents always favored her older sister, Laura, and her two brothers, Jack and Ray.

"I was at the bottom of the totem pole when it came to anyone in my family caring about what made me happy," she said. "Sometimes I felt invisible. You know what I mean? I'd talk, but no one would pay attention. Actually," she added in a whisper, "I think I was the only one of us who was not planned, and you know what happens then."

"What?" I asked, interested in the answer for obvious reasons.

"The man blames the woman, and the woman resents it and the child as well."

I didn't openly disagree with her, but I didn't believe that was always the case.

Because I talked so little about my family and because she thought asking too many questions would only stir up my sorrow, Ellie talked for hours about herself and her family. In a few short months, I knew whom she'd had crushes on as far back as grade school, including teachers; what her first sexual experiences had been like; and a list of her favorites from ice cream to movie stars and singers. I quickly understood that I had become her longed-for audience. In our room, she did not have to fight to get a word in or dominate a conversation. In fact, she soon felt very comfortable spewing out her anger at and her unhappiness with her parents and her brothers and sister. We hadn't been together a full week before she revealed her secret, the reason her parents wanted her in a well-supervised school.

Ellie had been a kleptomaniac and had been arrested a number of times, but her secret mental diagnosis concluded that her compulsive behavior was not because of some uncontrollable obsession with stealing but because of her deep-seated need for attention.

"My parents were told they were lucky I hadn't turned to nymphomania instead," she said with that thin, evil little laugh she sometimes used to punctuate the ends of sentences. "Little do they know."

"I'm glad you don't live in Kentucky and frequent the Heavenstone Department Stores," I told her. "We'd be bankrupt." She loved that. I hadn't ever thought I was good at dry, sarcastic humor, but Cassie was at my ear prompting me. It was as if she had gotten into my head somehow and, like some traffic cop for thoughts, could direct and redirect ideas. Why I was so good at it didn't matter. I simply was, and Ellie enjoyed my biting remarks, especially when directed at some of the other girls.

So, with my unselfish manner, my willingness to be her audience and her sounding board, and my occasional witty remarks, Ellie was quite comfortable. As it turned out, that was fortunate for me in another, bigger way, too. She would point me at the first boy who sparked any romantic interest in me since my tragedies, but that wasn't to come without cost. Nothing came to me without cost, despite what everyone thought about my being from such a wealthy, powerful, and famous Kentucky family. In this case, the price was the end of my relatively close relationship with Ellie, the only person other than my uncle Perry and my father with whom I had become in any way close. I should have anticipated it. Cassie had warned me.

Feminine Gunslingers

ONE OF THE many lessons my sister, Cassie, had taught me related to what she called *feminine gunslingers*.

"Don't believe in this myth about your best girlfriend, Semantha. I'm your best girlfriend, because I'm not in any competition with you for any man and never will be. I'll never be jealous of your beauty, but every girl you meet will see you as a threat. When you walk into a room, they'll eye you up and down just the way gunslingers eyed their competition."

"Why?" I asked. "I won't try to steal away their boyfriends. I would never do that."

Cassie laughed. She loved to laugh and raise her arms as if we were having these conversations in front of a big audience, and she could turn to them and say, "Do you all see this? See how much she needs me?"

"You don't have to want to steal away their boyfriends, Semantha, but that won't stop their boyfriends from looking at you with more interest and excitement than they look at their girlfriends. You're beautiful. But more important, the girls won't believe you're not trying to steal their boyfriends away. They'll watch every move you make, and I mean every move—the roll of your eyes, the swing of your hips, and the softness in your voice. They'll compare themselves to how you wear your makeup, what outfit you have on, shoes, jewelry, everything!"

"Well, what should I do?" I asked her.

"Nothing. There's nothing to do. I'm telling you all this so you won't expect any real favors from any so-called best friend, Semantha. Just don't be naive, and above all, never trust any other girl but me."

I had swallowed what she told me and reluctantly digested it because I didn't want to believe these things. Surely, there was someone out there, maybe a number of girls, who would be like a sister to me someday, a girlfriend I could trust and who really cared about me. The world Cassie was describing was far too lonely for me. She was comfortable in it, but I knew I would never be.

However, in my private high school, Cassie's warnings seemed justified. I did seem to be threatening to some girls, and not only because of any psychological history. I'd really never had a best friend in the public high school I'd attended. I suppose I could easily explain my low level of popularity now by saying I was still fresh from all the tragedy and still quite emotionally wounded. Dr. Ryan said I was simply and clearly terrified of any relationships. Cassie's betrayals had wounded me too deeply and left large scars. A friendly word, a soft touch or smile, actually frightened me. I fled from friendships and especially avoided relationships with boys.

"None of this will ever completely go away, Se-mantha," Dr. Ryan said. "What we have to work on with you are ways to help you live with it so that you can assume a somewhat normal life."

I always wondered what he meant by "some-what." How far from normal would I be? And who would want to be with someone who could never be completely normal? Who would put up with my introverted ways, my fears, my unexpected and un-explainable cloudbursts of tears? What man would want someone who never held his hand as tightly as he held hers or returned a kiss without some skepti-cism? I would surely grow old wearing the invisible banner that read: *Teddy Heavenstone's Emotionally Crippled Daughter. If you know what's good for you, stay away.*

Despite Cassie's warnings, I had been roommates and close friends with Ellie Patton during all of my time at Collier, and I had yet to feel that she viewed me as any sort of feminine threat. She was quite at-tractive, with her tall, slim, fashion-model figure, her thick and rich licorice-black hair and stunning pearl-black eyes. Her facial features were as diminutive as mine. If I had anything over her, it was my higher cheekbones and more shapely bosom, but to my way of thinking, that would hardly tip the scales in my favor when it came to competing for boys. Not that I ever did.

In fact, it was only at her insistence that I at-tended any social functions at all. Whenever I did, I looked for the warning signals Cassie had taught me, but none of the young men who showed interest in Ellie showed any interest in me. I knew a few of them actually felt uncomfortable in my presence, and one of them, according to Ellie, stopped calling her because of me.

"In other words," she said, "you spooked him. I told him that was just too damn bad. We were room-mates, and if he didn't like it, he knew what he could do." She shrugged. "I guess he did. He stopped talking to me."

I started to apologize, but she wasn't upset about it. She wasn't particularly fond of him. In fact, Ellie was as flighty about her male relationships as I was indifferent. Her problem was quite unlike mine, though. She was always worried that she was settling too soon or too low, and consequently, she was always looking over their shoulders at the next possibility or someone else's boyfriend. I couldn't imagine Ellie thinking of me in Cassie's *feminine gunslinger* terms, but that was about to change.

About two weeks after she had walked in on my secret birthday ceremony in the bathroom, which was about a week after we had returned from spring break, Ellie told me I had to do her a big favor.

"And don't pull a Norma Bates on me," she said before she got specific. "Don't come up with any of your weird excuses this time, Semantha."

She had come back from a late tutoring session with Mr. Schooner, our math teacher. Ellie rarely got better than a C or C-plus, whereas I rarely got a grade below B-plus. I thought for sure she was going to ask me to do one of her final research papers or some extra math assignments Mr. Schooner had given her.

From time to time, I did help her understand things, but there was no secret about her lack of interest in education. In fact, she thought most men disliked very intelligent women. She based her opinion on her own father and her brothers and how they thought of women. She would say, "I don't know why you care so damn much about your grades. You're rich, and your father will get you anything you want anyway. And it might stop someone wonderful from falling in love with you."

Maybe she was right, but I didn't really care, not that I was hung up on being a very good student. Most of the time, I was just going through the motions. I even walked to and from my classes like a zombie, or at least that was what Ellie had been told and told me in the hope that I would change. She was always trying to get me to change. She never gave up on me during our years together. It wasn't that she felt sorry for me so much as that she wanted to take credit and get more recognition. I was positive that I was a topic of conversation at her family dinners now. At least, I had given her something, a way to be heard, I thought.

"What is it?" I asked timidly.

"What's that face you're putting on? Don't act like I'm asking you to contribute a kidney or something, Semantha."

"Okay, what?"

"Remember Ethan Hunter?"

I thought for a moment and shook my head. She sighed deeply and then plopped onto her bed.

"I did speak about him so much before we left

for spring break that I thought you would puke, Semantha. I remember telling you about all the times he called me to beg me to go out with him and those supposed coincidences when he appeared at the shopping mall when I was there. You have to remember me talking about that."

I nodded, even though it was quite obvious that I still didn't recall. That wasn't her fault, but she could surely tell now that I often listened to her with what my father would say was half an ear. She babbled so much about one boy or another that I didn't pay too much attention to their names. There were times when she talked after we had gone to bed and I was sure she was still talking long after I had fallen asleep. I could hear Cassie complaining inside my dreams.

"Oh, forget it, already. It doesn't matter," she said. "I'll tell you about him again. Ethan's a senior attending SUNY Albany. I met him at that fraternity mixer you wouldn't attend."

"We weren't supposed to go," I reminded her. "It was a school night, and Mrs. Hathaway specifically forbade us to go to college social events without specific parental permission."

To violate that rule was almost serious enough to justify expulsion. We were on our honor when we went shopping or to a movie at the mall, but Mrs. Hathaway had her ways of finding out things. Some of the girls thought she even had undercover detectives, and others always talked about the so-called plant, a girl who was older but pretended to be one of us.

"It's how they break terrorist groups," Emerald Fitzgerald declared. "They infiltrate them." She was successful enough to spread rampant paranoia. Sometimes I thought they believed I was that girl and that my sessions with Mrs. Hathaway were reports about them. I became a logical suspect, but Ellie went out on a limb reassuring them all about me. Otherwise, she wouldn't have taken the risks she took.

Ellie and two other girls from Collier had snuck off campus to go to the forbidden college fraternity party. Although the dormitory doors were locked to prevent anyone from coming in after hours, they couldn't be locked to prevent anyone from going out. There were fire regulations. To get back into the dorm later that night, they crawled through an unlocked window. I knew she would talk my head off, so I pretended not to hear her enter. She made as much noise as she could without alerting Mrs. Hingle, our dorm mother, and then gave up and went to sleep, but she began describing the adventure the moment my eyes opened and didn't stop until we entered English lit class.

"Oh, right," I said, pretending to remember now. "Ethan Hunter. Yes."

Whether she believed me or not didn't matter. She was on a roll, and nothing except a call to evacuate the building would stop her, and even then she would talk all the way out.

"I didn't have a particularly fabulous time with him that night, but he was persistent, and as you might recall if you strain your brain a little, I've seen him and spoken with him a number of times since.

He's very good-looking, and I can tell he really likes me. His father is a very successful accountant in Buffalo and . . ."

"So, what's the favor, Ellie?" I didn't want to seem impatient, but I had about four hundred pages of outside reading to do for anthropology.

"I'm on probation because of my grades, which means I'm grounded."

"What? When did this happen?"

"I just found out. And this weekend, there's a big party at his fraternity, like the biggest party of the year."

I stared at her for a moment. This was a long pause in an Ellie Patton speech. What was coming next? It looked as if I would have to pry it out of her.

"I still don't see how I can . . ."

"I never told you that Mrs. Hathaway called me into her office to discuss you," she blurted.

I sat back. "No. I wouldn't have missed that if you did. Why did she do that?"

"Why? You know how much she likes to turn everyone into a little spy around here."

"And?"

"And . . . and you never ask permission to go off campus on a date. You never go to any social events on campus, even the geeky ones, unless I force you to go with me." She leaned in. "I think she was really trying to find out if you were a little . . ." She moved her hand like some bishop offering a blessing.

"A little what?"

"Gay, not that anyone could be a little. You

either are or aren't, I think. You know some of the girls thought that from the day you came to Collier. I told you they did."

I looked away. She had told me that, but I was sure there was a great deal she hadn't told me.

"Of course, I told Mrs. Hathaway no way, but she was concerned. Some other bigmouth told her mother that she thought you definitely were, and her mother called Mrs. Hathaway and gave her an earful, I guess."

"Who?"

"I don't know for sure, but I suspect Amanda Crowley. She's in the next room. Maybe her mother thought she'd get infected or something through the wall."

"I don't care," I said. "I'm leaving here soon, and I don't intend to see any of them again, especially Mrs. Hathaway."

"Yes, but about the favor . . ."

"Christmas trees, Ellie!" I cried. It actually felt as if Cassie was now talking and not me. That was her favorite expression of frustration. "What is it, already?"

"I think—in fact, I feel pretty confident—that if you've been invited to a social by a boy from one of the so-called approved high schools and you won't go unless I go with you, I can get a pass on this probation. I'll make it look like I'm doing you a favor, which will please Mrs. Hathaway, get it?"

"But I haven't been invited."

"Yes, you have," Ellie said. She reached into her purse and pulled out a small envelope.

"What is that?"

"Your invitation, silly. Take it," she said, thrusting it at me.

I took it, looked at her suspiciously, and then opened it and pulled out the card. It was an invitation from someone named Clark Kelly Morgan. I had no idea who that was, of course. I shook my head and looked up at her.

"Why would someone I never met invite me, Ellie?"

"Guess." She waited a moment and then exclaimed, "He's Ethan's best friend. I told Ethan about you and what I thought might work and . . ." She turned her hand in the air. "So?"

"But this is a college fraternity party again, and that's off base, Ellie. We could both be expelled."

"I thought you didn't care about school that much. I've stuck out my neck for you plenty of times, Semantha," she whined. "Don't worry. I've got it all figured out. I asked this boy at Pine View, that school that attended our last function, to pretend he's asked you out. That's what Mrs. Hathaway will hear, and if she checks up on it, he'll say it's true. Of course, I had to promise him I would really go out with him sometime soon, but I won't. Well?"

I didn't know what to say.

"Look. I got the impression from Mrs. Hathaway that your father was concerned about you not having any social life," Ellie said.

"My father? I don't think so. My uncle Perry, maybe, but not my father," I said. "That wouldn't be at the top of his agenda." She had no idea why, of course, but she could see I knew she was exaggerating. "In any case, he certainly wouldn't approve of me breaking a serious rule here."

"C'mon, Semantha, can't you do me this little favor? Say you'll accept the invitation. I'll go speak with Mrs. Hathaway and work on her. You won't even have to talk much with this boy if you don't want to. Please. My God, don't you ever want to do anything exciting?" she added with frustration.

"Okay," I said. It was the fastest way to get her to leave me alone.

"Terrific. Leave it all to me." She jumped up and rushed out.

I couldn't help being so reluctant and appearing so disinterested. Going to parties, dancing with boys, even simply talking to them now gave me goose bumps. On the other hand, I did want to do something exciting, but I was afraid I was about to make some terrible new mistake and somehow add more sad weight to the load my father carried on his shoulders.

"Why did you agree to that?" I heard Cassie whisper. *"If Daddy finds out . . ."*

Mrs. Hathaway would turn down Ellie's request, I thought. Surely, she didn't trust her. But less than an hour later, she returned with a smile across her face that could light up Times Square in New York. I didn't have to ask how it went.

"Start thinking about what you'll wear," she said.

I felt my heart start to thump as if it were trying to break out. Forget about the violation of one of

Hathaway's cardinal rules. This would be the first date I'd had since I was in public school.

"We're both going to look really hot." She went to her closet.

I looked at the invitation again.

Clark Kelly Morgan? He sounded as if he came from some aristocratic family. For the first time in a long time, I wondered what a boy might be like. Ellie saw me staring at the invitation.

"He just happens to be quite good-looking," she said.

I looked up at her.

"He's supposedly a pro-quality tennis player, and, not that it matters to you, he comes from a well-to-do family. They're probably not half as rich as yours but, according to Ethan, nothing to turn up your nose at."

"I'm not a snob, Ellie. I don't care if his family is wealthy or not. Besides, I'm sure I won't have much to do with him after this. I can't carry on with a college boy and keep it forever from Hathaway."

"Maybe not," she said, and then paused and smiled. "And then again, maybe you will like him so much you won't care."

"*No!*" I heard Cassie cry inside me.

I tilted my head and shook it as if I were trying to get water out of my ear.

"What are you doing?" Ellie asked.

"Nothing," I said quickly, but I could see it in her face. Despite how well we got along, she was counting the days until we parted. I certainly couldn't blame her. If I could part from myself, I wouldn't hesitate. Of course, rejection of a Heavenstone for any reason would infuriate my sister, Cassie. I didn't have to imagine what her comment would be. She was there, eager to make it.

"Don't give it a second thought. Good riddance to her," Cassie whispered. *"Good riddance to them all. We don't need anyone else but ourselves."*

3

Ethan

"Well, that's very nice, Semantha. I hope you have a good time," Daddy said when I told him I had a date to a school party.

Of course, I didn't tell him it was a college party, but I didn't doubt for one moment that Mrs. Hathaway had already called him to report my sudden interest in doing something social. Despite what I had told Ellie, I thought the news might please him, and that was more important than telling him the whole truth.

"Thank you, Daddy."

"I have a little breaking news for you, too," he said.

"You do? What?"

He laughed and then said he was going out on a real date himself.

"You are?"

"I feel like a teenager calling it a real date, but you know how it's been, Semantha. So many people have been trying to fix me up with this woman or that woman. I've gone to functions and met women who were deliberately placed in my path, but it's not been easy. Not a day goes by when I don't miss your mother. I've tried to bury myself in my work. Your uncle Perry drives me crazy about it, but he's not completely wrong. I am a young man yet, don't you think?"

"Yes, of course you are, Daddy."

"No one will ever replace your mother, but it's very lonely here without her and you."

"I'm coming home soon, Daddy."

"Yes, I know, and we'll talk about what you should do or want to do, but you have your own life to lead, Semantha. You don't want an old guy like me weighing you down."

"You just said you were still young, Daddy."

"Young for my age, not for your age. Anyway . . ."

"Who is the woman—your date, I mean? Have I ever met her?"

"No. Her name is Lucille Bennet. She's the daughter of Martin Spears, president of the Lexington Home Bank. Her husband passed away four years ago. Heart attack. They never had any children."

"How old is she?" I asked. Something in his voice told me I'd be surprised.

"She's just turned forty," he said.

She's nearly twenty years younger than he is, I thought.

"But," he continued quickly, "you'd never know she was that young. I don't mean she looks older. She's quite young-looking and attractive, but she has the demeanor, personality, and wisdom of a woman at least twenty years older."

"How do you know if you haven't been on a date with her?"

It wasn't like me to cross-examine my father about anything, ever. That was something Cassie had been good at doing and something he had tolerated her doing. There was no question in my mind that if Cassie were alive today, she would be at Lucille Bennet with a microscope. Maybe she had put the question in my mind. I was surprised at myself for asking.

"Well, we have had occasion to see each other at events, and I did have lunch with her. Besides, I think you know how good a judge of character I am, Semantha," he added with a trickle of annoyance. "I employ hundreds of people."

"Yes, Daddy, I do. I was just curious. I'm happy for you," I said quickly.

"Well, you let me know how your date goes and how things are, will you? Your uncle keeps threatening to pay you a visit, but I told him to let you be. You don't have all that much longer to go, and we'll be there for graduation. Am I right?"

I wanted to say no, to say he should please come with Uncle Perry immediately, but I just said yes.

"Good. Well, otherwise, things are going well at the stores and here at Heavenstone. I'm very happy I hired Mrs. Dobson to run the house. She continues to do a fine job of it. She's reliable and efficient."

During the first year I attended Collier, Daddy had decided to find someone who could not only prepare his meals but also oversee the care of the mansion. He had taken the recommendation of a business associate in London and hired Patsy Dobson, a fifty-five-year-old widow who had been working in what she called "posh homes." She had been between jobs and was excited about living and working in America. Daddy had made all the arrangements to get her over, and although she was nowhere near the gourmet cook my mother or Cassie had been, she was, in Daddy's words, "quite capable of feeding a team of hungry lumberjacks."

Mrs. Dobson took firm control of the house and had gone through four different maids and maid services before settling on Doris Cross, a forty-five-year-old divorced mother of two sons who had married and lived far away, one in Texas and one in Oregon. Mrs. Dobson said Doris had the proper respect for antiquities and, like her, believed that dust was a sign of disrespect. I had to admit the house and everything in it had never looked better under Mother's and Cassie's care. I knew Daddy believed that, too, even though he never said it in so many words.

"I'm glad, Daddy. She is very nice," I said.

I did like Mrs. Dobson. She was always pleasant to me whenever I was home for holidays and over the summer. Often, she was even quite funny, especially when she used some of her English expressions. She knew our family's tragic history the way I had explained it to Ellie and nothing more. If she ever overheard anything, however, I was confident she would make herself forget it. Sometimes I felt she was treating us like British royals. She was continually after me to smile more and always called me Miss Semantha. Even Doris Cross had started calling me that.

"You okay, Semantha? You sound a bit down. You're not doing too much, are you?"

"I'm fine, Daddy. Maybe I'm just a little home-sick."

"Well, it's not long now. Take care, and call if you need anything," he said. "I've got to rush off to a meeting."

"'Bye, Daddy," I said. Although he hung up, I held the receiver. I would have sworn I heard Cassie talking, as if she had picked up one of the phones at Heavenstone and had been listening all the while.

"She has the wisdom of a woman twenty years older? He knows how to judge character? Don't believe it. Well, we're going home not a day too soon. Lucille Bennet . . . twenty years younger than he is. He'll make a fool of himself. Daddy always needed to be looked after. He's brilliant when it comes to business, but when it comes to his personal life . . ."

"Why are you holding the phone like that?" Ellie asked, snapping me back to the moment. I hadn't heard her open the door to our room and had no idea how long she had been standing there watching me.

"Oh. I just finished talking to my father."

I hung up the receiver.

"You didn't say a word for the longest time. Were you talking to yourself?" she asked, and closed the door.

I started to come up with an answer, but she waved at me to ignore her question. She was carrying two big bags. "I have something for you for tomorrow night," she said, rushing over to slap the bags onto the bed. She reached into one. "This is your size."

She pulled out a slinky, deep-V-neck black satin dress and held it up against me.

"Yes, this is terrific for you. I looked through your wardrobe. You have nothing as sexy as this. Naturally, you'll need this black clutch to go with it." She reached into the same bag to show it to me. Then she went to the second bag. "You don't have a pair of these, but they'll look terrific with the dress." She opened a shoebox and held up a pair of red peep-toe pumps. "Come on. Start trying it on," she said, tossing the dress at me. "Oh, I almost forgot." She reached into the second bag again and took out a pair of chandelier earrings. "I just thought these would look darling on you."

"How much was all this?"

"Not much," she said.

I saw there were still tags on everything. "Ellie, you didn't . . ."

"What?"

"Shoplift again?"

"Just try everything on and stop worrying, Semantha. At least have one great night before graduation without analyzing it to death, will you?"

She went into the bathroom. I looked at the dress and the shoes and felt a little excitement. Maybe Ellie was right. Maybe I needed to loosen up and try to enjoy myself for a change. Daddy was doing that, wasn't he? I slipped on the dress. The shoes fit perfectly. Then I opened the closet that had a full-length mirror and gazed at myself.

"*Well, that doesn't leave much to the imagination,*" Cassie whispered.

"Hot, hot, hot!" Ellie cried. "Put on the earrings, too, and let's do something different with your hair and makeup, Semantha. You look too dowdy these days."

Did she really want me to have a good time, or had she made promises about me that she wanted to fulfill? *There's a Cassie question,* I thought, but I let her go on to show me how she thought I should wear my hair and do my makeup. The Semantha Heavenstone I saw in the mirror the next evening looked like a totally new person, who was arguably brighter, far sexier, and, dare I think it, even happy about herself.

My legs were actually trembling when we were called down to the lobby to greet our dates. I didn't realize I was walking with my head down, my eyes on the floor to hide my nervousness. Ellie nudged me, and I looked up to see our dates waiting. I wasn't sure which one was Ethan. One of them was about six foot one or two, with a slim build and light brown hair trimmed in a traditional style, the way my father and his business associates wore their hair. The other young man was short and stocky, with longer dark brown hair not that neatly kept. It was over his ear on the right but not on the left. He had harder facial features and a cleft chin.

"Hi, Ethan," Ellie said to the taller one. I felt a glob of disappointment settle in the base of my throat. Ethan's eyes shifted quickly toward me, and I looked down again.

"Hey, Ellie. This is Kelly Morgan," he said.

Why did he have to introduce his best friend to

her? She had talked about Kelly as though she had
met him.

"Kelly, this is my roommate, Semantha."

"Yeah, hey," he said. "You look terrific."

I smiled a thank-you, but I couldn't keep my
eyes from drifting back to Ethan, who wore a small
smile that tucked in the corners of his lips slightly.
The softness of it touched me. I once read a romance
novel—one of the books Cassie had mocked, in
fact—in which the main character said she fell in
love with her boyfriend first through his small ges-
tures, the movements in his face, the way he tilted his
head just slightly when he looked at her, and the way
the tips of his fingers moved ever so gently over her
arm and into her hand. She said she knew she was in
love with him the moment she saw him and claimed
she discovered what was meant by falling in love at
first sight.

*It was the magic he had only for me. Only I
could see it telegraphed in a movement in his lips, a
turn of his eyes.* Those words had seemed like over-
the-top romantic drivel to me then, but suddenly
seemed possible, real, now.

"I think we should get going so Kelly and Semantha can get to know each other a little before we get
to the party, Ethan," Ellie said sharply.

He snapped to attention and reached for her
hand. Kelly reached for mine.

"Usually, I don't believe in blind dates," he said
as we followed Ellie and Ethan out to the car. "Who
else but losers need to go on blind dates? But I can't
see you being a loser."

I wanted to say thank you, but it seemed dumb, and I heard Cassie whisper, *"Ask him what he's talking about. You're going on a blind date. I guess that means you're a loser, then, huh?"* Of course, I didn't say it, but my silence surprised him. He opened the rear door for me and smirked.

"Thank you," I said.

"She speaks!" he cried. Only Ellie and he laughed. Ethan looked back at me and started the engine.

Kelly got in and slid over the seat to be close.

"Okay, so let's go through the required questionnaire," he said. "What's your favorite subject? What do you want to be when you grow up? What kind of music do you like? Seen any movies lately?"

"Try not to be yourself tonight, idiot," Ethan said.

Kelly laughed. "Just kidding," he said. "You like this school?" he asked, looking back and jerking his right thumb at the campus.

"It's all right," I said.

"She hates it. We all do," Ellie said. "All it needs is bars on the windows. Graduation will feel more like parole."

The boys laughed. Because of his closeness to me, I could smell the whiskey on Kelly's breath.

"Well, forget about it," he told Ellie. "We'll have a great time tonight and make up for the week or weeks or months. Okay, Semantha?"

"Even a great New Year's Eve couldn't make up for all of that," I said. This time, only Ethan laughed.

"Well, the night's young," Kelly offered, sounding as if I had wounded his ego. "And you haven't given me a chance to show you a good time. I don't get many complaints from the girls I date."

I gave him a small, courteous smile. Then he began to talk about himself, how he had decided to go into the navy after he graduated from college and how that was driving his father nuts. He said his father had pushed him into going to college. He had told his father he wasn't going to be a lawyer or a doctor or even go into business with him, but his father had insisted he give college a chance. I quickly understood that he was just barely passing his subjects. I didn't know much at all about Ethan, but I began to suspect that he wasn't really best friends with Kelly, and later, at the fraternity house, Ethan confessed that he had asked him to double-date only because Ellie had told him there was no other way she could get out.

"My roommate is practically engaged, so I couldn't ask him," he said.

By now, it was pretty clear that Kelly wasn't having a good time with me. I danced with him, but I wouldn't drink his liquor or pop any of his Ecstasy. He carried the pills in what was supposedly a pack of gum. His bragging about himself began to bore me, too, and he eventually began drifting off, spending more time with other boys, and even flirting with other girls right in front of me. So far, I wasn't that impressed with a college fraternity party. I think Ethan saw that more than either Ellie or Kelly did. Whenever Ethan had an opportunity to step away from Ellie and come to me, he did. At the moment, she was with some other girls.

"Sorry about Kelly," he said. "Ellie was so desperate to get out and made it sound as though you were just doing her a favor and didn't care who your date was. She made you sound as if . . ."

"What?"

"You don't have any interest in boys."

"Did she? I suppose she really believes that, but I'm not what she's making me out to be."

He smiled. "I had a feeling she didn't know what she was talking about, but I can see you're not a happy camper here, and you're not the sort of girl who doesn't care who she's with as long as she can get out."

"She wouldn't take no for an answer, but it's not important," I said.

"It is to me. I don't like doing things like this, especially to someone I can see is quite nice."

"Thank you," I said.

He smiled, and when he did, to me it looked as if he tilted his head just slightly, just the way the character in my romance novel said her lover tilted his head.

"I'll find a way to make it up to you," he added quickly as Ellie approached.

"What's going on?" she asked, pulling her lips back tightly and showing her teeth like some snarling alley cat.

"Far as I can see, not much," Ethan said, nodding toward Kelly, who was practically slobbering over a girl in a tight knit dress. "Or nothing unexpected, I should say. I was just apologizing to Semantha."

"Well, your party isn't as exciting as I had hoped," Ellie muttered. "Maybe we should go somewhere else."

"Where would we go, Ellie? We're taking a big enough chance as it is coming here," I said quickly. "We have to indicate our destination before we leave the campus, and we've already lied about that," I explained to Ethan.

"Oh, brother. Relax, Semantha. I'm sure Mrs. Hathaway didn't follow us," Ellie said.

"Why make her feel any more uncomfortable than she is?" Ethan asked.

She looked at him and then at me and shook her head. "You don't have to feel so sorry for her, Ethan. She's not a baby or something. She can handle it."

"You don't have to be a baby or something to be unhappy with this situation, Ellie." Again, he nodded in Kelly's direction.

She glanced at him and shrugged. "Right," she said. "I guess I'll just have to make the best of it."

For the rest of the evening, Ellie spent most of her time with other girls and some other young men, and Ethan spent most of his time talking to me. He even asked me to take a walk with him outside. I looked toward Ellie, but she seemed quite distracted, so I agreed, and we went out.

Ethan had a soft, gentle manner about him that helped me relax. I wondered how much of what Ellie had told me about him was true. He didn't seem to be the sort of boy who, in Ellie's words, practically stalked her. I was beginning to get the feeling it was Ellie who had been stalking him.

"Ellie's okay," he said when our conversation drifted to how she and he had met, "but she has a way of making me feel like I'm more of an escort than a date, if you know what I mean. I always feel she's looking at everyone else to be sure no one's ahead of her. Does that make sense?"

"Yes," I said.

"I can see you're not comfortable talking about her behind her back. It's not important," he said. "I doubt that I'll see her much after tonight."

I was pleased to hear it, but I didn't say so. He talked about himself, his interest in getting into business, the excitement of developing a company. He envied the young men who had been so successful with dot-com companies, but he said he liked more traditional business enterprises because he liked contact with people, all sorts of people. He assured me he wasn't going to put himself into any office where he was shut away from the world. I envied him for his interest in people, in being social. From my answers to some of his questions, he quickly gathered that I was more like a hermit. He thought it was just my shyness.

"There are ways to overcome shyness," he said. "It's like anything else. You have to get your feet wet, push a little, maybe, but in the end, you'll see how easy it is. You have nothing to be shy about, anyway, Semantha. You're a very attractive young woman, and I'm sure you're as bright as, if not brighter than, most people."

Before I could thank him, Ellie appeared. It was clear she was really angry now. She had what Cassie would call "the gunslinger eyes."

"Who's your date tonight, Ethan, or did you forget?"

"You seemed pretty occupied," he said in a quick defense. "And Kelly's practically deserted Semantha. I feel bad about bringing him along."

"I feel bad about being here, period," Ellie said. She wobbled a bit, and we could both see she had drunk too much of the vodka I had seen being passed around. "Let's get out of here, Semantha," she told me.

I looked at my watch. "We've got to get back anyway," I told Ethan.

He nodded. "I'll go look for Kelly," he said, and hurried off.

"Well, you're doing all right for someone who had to be talked into going out with college boys," Ellie told me. "Ethan looks quite smitten with you, which was just the way he looked at me the first time. College boys," she said disdainfully. "They're not very dependable."

"He's just being nice, Ellie."

"Right," she said. "Looks like I dressed you up too well," she added bitterly, and went back inside.

I followed, and we met Ethan, who said Kelly was too drunk to put in his car.

"I don't want him along, if you don't mind, Semantha."

"Why should she mind?" Ellie said sharply. "She's been well occupied."

We left the party, and Ethan drove us back to

the campus. I saw that he didn't even kiss Ellie good night on the cheek. She was sullen and sulked the whole trip back and hurried out when we stopped, not even waiting to walk in with me.

"Sorry about the night," he told me, looking after her. "I'll make it up to you." He smiled and got back into his car.

Reluctantly, I followed Ellie to our room. I wished I had somewhere else to sleep tonight. I wasn't in the mood to hear her ranting. Whenever she drank, she had a runaway tongue. To my surprise, this time, she was simply sulking.

"What's wrong with you?" I asked her after a while.

She sat on her bed staring at the floor. "Nothing."

"Why did you spend so much time away from Ethan? I thought you were dying to be with him?"

"He turned out to be boring," she said. "I really didn't know him that well, Semantha. I think you got to know him better than I know him, in fact."

She went into the bathroom and closed the door. I could hear that she had definitely drunk too much alcohol.

"*What did I tell you?*" Cassie whispered. "*Gunslinger. All girls resent each other, except for us. We're sisters, real sisters.*"

Ellie went right to sleep without saying much else. In the days that followed, she spent more time away from the room than she did in it. On Thursday night, Ethan called, and I happened to be alone in the room. I thought he was calling for Ellie, maybe to apologize, and immediately told him she wasn't there.

"I'm not calling to speak with her," he said. "I'm calling to see if you would like to go to dinner with me tomorrow night. I'll come by about six-thirty. What sort of food do you like?" he asked even before I had answered. I could tell he was very nervous and was just trying to get it all said. I was too embarrassed to explain that we weren't permitted to go on dates with college-age boys unless we had special permission from our parents. Thinking that suddenly gave me the idea.

"Really?"

"Yes, really," he said, laughing. "What do you say?"

"Give me your phone number, and I'll call you back to let you know."

"Sure," he said, and gave it to me.

As soon as he hung up, I called my father. Mrs. Dobson said he was out to dinner, but she would give him the message to call me. I waited an hour and then grew too impatient and called his cell phone. When he answered, I could hear he was in a busy restaurant.

"Semantha? What's wrong?"

"Nothing's wrong, Daddy. I want to go out with a boy who is in college, and Mrs. Hathaway wouldn't approve of that without your approval first, so if you can call her . . ."

"A college boy?"

"Yes, Daddy. He's very nice."

From the muffled sound, I realized he was putting his hand over the mouthpiece and talking to someone.

"Where are you going with this college boy?" he asked.

"To dinner, Daddy. It's a dinner date."

"I see. Well, I'm sure you now know to be careful, Semantha."

"Yes, Daddy."

"I'll call Mrs. Hathaway first thing in the morning."

"Please don't forget," I said.

"I don't think I forget things yet, Semantha," he said, more for whomever he was with than for me, I thought. I heard a woman's laughter.

"Thanks, Daddy."

"Right. Take care," he said.

After he hung up, I called Ethan and told him I would go out with him. Ellie wasn't talking about him anymore, and pleasing her didn't matter to me much anymore, either.

"I guess I like Italian food the best when I go to restaurants," I said. Cassie never had. She'd always thought the food was too blah or too spicy.

"Perfect. I have just the place. I'm looking forward to seeing you again."

"Yes, me too," I said.

Even though I didn't care about Ellie becoming upset, I didn't want to tell her about my date just yet. I was happy that Ethan had ended the call before she returned. When she did, I said nothing. She was talking now about a different boy she had met at the fraternity party, but she wasn't sure how she was going to get out this weekend. She couldn't use me again as an excuse, and as it turned out, her teachers had complained to Mrs. Hathaway even more about her grades. I could see the writing on the wall as Friday drew near. I held back as long as I could, and then on Friday afternoon, I announced my date and said I didn't have to be deceitful about it, either.

She stood there staring at me for a long moment in shock.

"You had your father call Mrs. Hathaway?"

"Yes."

"Great. Now she's going to wonder how you met him, and she might figure out that we violated her rules."

"I don't think she'll want to do anything to discourage my socializing, Ellie. Remember how she called you into her office to discuss me?"

She bit down on her lower lip and nodded. I had always known she was lying about it or at least exaggerating.

"Why would you want to go out with him? You saw what a dull boy he is."

"I didn't find him dull. I thought he was very nice," I said.

She shrugged. "If that's what makes you happy, go for it."

She tried to make it seem as though she didn't care, but when I began to dress and fix my hair, she left in a huff and slammed the door.

When I looked back at myself in the mirror, I saw Cassie standing behind me. She wore that Cassie look of self-satisfaction.

"Well? Have I ever given you bad advice?"

I tried to ignore her. I finished fixing my hair

and doing my makeup, and then I rose and went to my closet. I was determined to wear something a lot more conservative than the dress I let Ellie put on me last time.

"Don't get your hopes up, Semantha," Cassie said when I took one last look at myself in the mirror. *"When he finds out about you, he'll disappear faster than I do."*

I took a deep breath and went to the door. Ethan would be arriving any moment. I opened the door and looked back. I could see her in the mirror.

"Do me a favor, Cassie," I whispered. "Stay here."

I walked out and closed the door behind me. Down the hallway, I could see Ellie holding court with a few of the girls. They all looked my way and were silent. I waved to her, but she didn't wave back. She turned away to start talking again. *At least she has a new audience*, I thought, *but only for a little while*. After school ended, she was going home, and I knew how unhappy she was there. For the first time, I actually felt sorrier for her than I did for myself.

Ethan was right on time.

"I hope you're hungry," he said. "These people who run this restaurant feed their customers as if they were members of their immediate family."

"I'll do my best," I said, and he laughed.

"Don't worry. There's no way you can do badly with me." He took my hand, and I held his tightly, something I hadn't done since I was in public school. He smiled as if he knew, and we were off.

The restaurant was small and family-run. Because he went there so often, everyone knew Ethan. The husband and wife who cooked and oversaw the place greeted us as if we really were members of their family. Almost before we sat down, a basket of fresh homemade Italian garlic rolls was brought to the table. Ethan introduced me, and they talked about their grandson, who was attending Yale. They said they had heard of my family's department stores. They asked me about Kentucky and how I liked New York. I told them what I really felt. Kentucky was just in my blood. I couldn't imagine anyplace else ever being home. Then they described their specials for the evening, and Ethan ordered for us both.

"I can see they really like you," I said.

"They're good businesspeople. They know how to stroke their customers."

"I didn't feel anything phony about them," I said.

"Oh, no. I don't mean that. I just mean they know how to run a business. Restaurants are the most difficult, I think. So many fail. My father is an accountant and handles many big restaurants where we live," Ethan explained. "It's through him that I became interested in business. By the way, I loved the way you described your family's department stores. You made it sound more like an institution than a business."

"I suppose it is, in Kentucky. As my father says, there's a lot of history. If you saw what was in our house, you'd think it was some kind of museum." I described the portraits, the old books, and the awards my family had won from business organizations, chambers of commerce, and the like. "There are plaques everywhere you look, practically," I said, and then suddenly realized how much I had been talking. During the last five minutes or so, I probably had said more than I had at school in a month. He sat with a faint smile on his face.

"I guess I'm babbling," I said.

"No, no. You do sound proud of your heritage. I don't hear much of that. I imagine you people in Southern states have it more."

"If you met my father, you'd understand," I said. "He used to teach my sister and me our family history as if it were a subject in school."

"You didn't tell me you had a sister," he said.

I looked away toward the window in front of the restaurant. There was Cassie looking in at us.

"She died in a tragic, freak accident," I began, and pushed the button that played my programmed explanation of my mother's death and Cassie's.

Like everyone who heard it, he looked sorry that he had asked. But then he said, "So, there's only you and your father now?"

"And my uncle Perry, my father's younger brother."

"He's not married?"

"No." I paused and added, "And won't ever be, to a woman."

He raised his eyebrows.

Our food was served, and he quickly changed the topic of conversation, describing his plans to go to graduate school for business—but first, he thought he might get out into the real world and experience some of it firsthand.

"That way, when I learn theory, I can either accept or reject it and explain why."

"That sounds very smart, Ethan."

"And you?"

I shook my head. He was surprised I had no plans, no ambitions, and hadn't even applied to any colleges.

"You're going to work in your father's business, then?"

"I don't know. I'm not sure what I could do."

"Sometimes it's good to take some time off to think things out carefully," he offered. "You can do it, so you should."

After dinner, we went for a walk and talked some more. Actually, he did most of the talking, but he was always interested in what I thought about something he had said. On our way back to my campus, he told me he had enjoyed being out with someone who was not an airhead. When we drove up to the dorm, he got out quickly to walk me to the door.

"How about we go to a movie tomorrow night?" he asked.

"All right," I said. "As long as I get permission."

"Permission? To go to a movie? What kind of school is this? Ellie might not have been exaggerating when she said there were practically bars on the windows."

"They take guardianship seriously," I said as an abbreviated answer. I certainly didn't want to get into why Collier was populated mostly with girls who'd had serious problems at one time or another, and I especially didn't want to mention my own.

"Well, you'll let me know. I'll come by at six so we can grab a quick bite to eat at the mall first. Is that okay?" he asked when I didn't respond.

I nodded. This was beginning to feel more like a dream I wished would never end. I'd stay asleep forever to keep it going.

He looked at me and smiled. "You're a very beautiful girl, Semantha. I'm glad you're shy," he said. "That way, no one got to you before me and stole you away."

I started to laugh, when he kissed me. My first reaction was that fear that always lay just under my heart whenever a boy had looked at me with interest or had gotten too close since my pregnancy, but those feelings seemed to recede as he held me longer and then kissed me softly again. I felt myself relax and then respond. It surprised me more than it surprised him. He pulled back but held me.

"Good night," he whispered.

I watched him walk back to his car, where he paused to wave before getting in.

As he drove off, I felt Cassie at my side. She had been trying to step between Ethan and me all night. I had refused to let her get a word into me and, except for when I had seen her looking in the window, had avoided looking at her wherever she was.

I could feel her rage. At the moment, she was very angry, too angry to say a word, which was very unusual for Cassie. She always had something to say.

But I really didn't care.

"I thought you would never be jealous of me," I said. "I thought we would never be those gunslingers you described," I added.

Which only made her angrier.

4

Exposed

I NEVER BELIEVED the friendship between Ellie and me would last much longer than our time together at Collier, so her indifference and coolness toward me as the school year drew to an end weren't particularly upsetting or surprising. Ethan and I were seeing each other every weekend now. Mrs. Hathaway not only approved but commented about my improved disposition. Ethan and I went to movies or to dinner and often spent entire weekend days together, having picnics or going for drives.

The New York spring this year was far warmer than the previous two I had experienced. The trees and foliage were lush, and the lawns actually compared in rich green color to some Kentucky grass. When I told that to Ethan, he laughed and said, "I can see you'll measure the rest of the world against your precious old Kentucky home." He quickly added that he thought there was something wonderful about having such a sense of home and admitted he wished he had the same passion for the world in which he had been raised.

I really enjoyed and looked forward to being

with Ethan. At times, I felt as if he knew my deepest secret and skirted and avoided anything that might upset me. We kissed and held each other, but he never pushed me to have sex with him. Anyone might have thought he was someone who lived in an earlier time, when relationships were more formal and women held on to their virginity.

On the weekend before graduation, however, we went for a ride and came to an out-of-the-way motel. We were about twenty miles west of the city. He didn't drive in, but he pulled the car to the side of the road in front of it. For a few moments, he didn't say anything.

"What's wrong, Ethan?" I asked.

"I don't want to lose you," he said.

"Why do you think you might?"

He turned to me with as serious an expression as I had ever seen on his face. "Women have always been a puzzle missing a few pieces for me," he began. "So, I'm not quite sure what I should do next, what you expect of me."

"I don't understand, Ethan."

"On the one hand, I don't want you to think I want to be with you for a short, sexual affair and then never see or care about you again, but on the other hand, I don't want you to think for one moment that I don't desire and need you more than anything or anyone."

I smiled. I was expecting something far worse. "I don't think either one, Ethan."

He reached for my hand. "I haven't felt this way about any other girl, Semantha. I hope you believe that. Unless I'm reading an assignment or doing a paper or taking a test, I'm thinking about you. No matter what other girl crosses my path, I see you. When I close my eyes, I hear your voice only and smell the scent of your hair. I'm sure this is what they mean when they say someone is possessed."

All I could do was smile. His words were like soft butterflies finding and weaving their way into my heart.

"In a little over a week, we're going to be very far apart," he continued. "Of course, I'll come see you whenever I have a chance, if you want me to."

"Of course I do. I'll look forward to it, more than I'll look forward to anything else."

He drew closer to kiss me.

"I guess what I really mean to say right now is that I'd like to spend more intimate time with you," he said softly. "I mean, before we part. Would you like that?"

I sat back. His gaze was on the motel. It wasn't hard to imagine what he meant.

"We'll be safe," he said, seeing me look at the motel, too. "I have what's necessary."

"Don't believe him," Cassie whispered.

If she hadn't, I might have said we should wait, but I didn't. I wanted to defy her, to prove her wrong, so I said, "Yes, I would like that."

He smiled and drove us up to the motel office. I waited in the car. I could feel Cassie in the backseat, glaring at me.

"You're going to make another dreadful error."

"I never did," I said. "You caused it. You were totally responsible, so don't dare blame me."

"Nothing happened that you didn't want to happen. It takes a willing garden to let a flower grow."

"Shut up," I said. I shook my head and put my hands over my ears.

Ethan came out and got into the car. He saw how upset I was getting.

"You okay? Something wrong?"

I looked back. She wasn't there.

"No, nothing. I'm fine."

He drove to our room. When I started to get out, I felt her holding my arm, holding me back.

"Daddy would be very upset," she whispered. *"Very, very disappointed."*

I pulled my arm away and got out, slamming the door behind me. I saw her face pressed against the rear window. Ethan opened the motel-room door and stood back. I was still looking at the car.

"Is something wrong, Semantha? You can tell me."

"No, nothing's wrong."

"If you would rather we didn't . . ."

"No, I'm fine, Ethan."

I entered quickly, and he closed the door.

"I wish we had a more romantic setting," he said as he put on the light and then closed the curtains, "but as long as I'm with you, any place is romantic."

I can't say I didn't want to change my mind. That thought zigzagged in my brain, but I held it back. I had never been more attracted to any other man, but I was also curious about myself. Would I shut myself off completely? Would I welcome his caresses and kisses and return them as passionately? Was I capable of loving anyone anymore? Had Cassie destroyed all that in me forever and ever? Was that what Dr. Ryan had really meant when we'd concluded our last session and he had said "somewhat normal"?

Ethan stepped forward and kissed me. Then he brushed his hand through my hair and went to the bed to pull back the spread. I watched him do everything as if I had stepped out of my body and was observing. He undid his shirt, and then he unbuttoned mine, pausing to kiss me again. I stepped back and slipped out of my skirt. He smiled and undid his belt. We were both quickly naked. He kissed me again and lifted me into his arms to bring me to the bed.

"Semantha," he said, "I don't know if it's really possible to fall in love with someone as quickly as I've fallen in love with you, but I'd argue forever that it is."

"Yes," I said. "It is. I know, because the same has happened to me."

He kissed me and very gently began to caress me. Suddenly, a shocking train of images began to travel on the rails of my memory. Once again, I saw Porter Andrew Hall, the young man Cassie had brought to our house, hovering over me naked. I could hear him talking to someone, but his voice was distorted like a recording being played way too slowly. I turned to look to my right and saw Cassie standing there, smiling and nodding. "Yes," I again heard her tell him. "Yes, do it now."

For a long time afterward, I had wondered if it had all been a dream, a dream Cassie had said was more of a fantasy. When it had turned out not to be, she had claimed, as she was doing in my mind even today, that it had been something I had wanted very much. Yes, he had been very handsome and charming, but I hadn't wanted that; I hadn't fantasized about him the way she'd claimed I had. Later, of course, I found out I had been given what is called a date-rape drug.

"Stop him!" I was suddenly screaming. "Stop him, Cassie."

"What?"

I opened my eyes to see Ethan holding himself above me. He looked down at me with confusion.

"What did you scream? Cassie? Wasn't that your sister's name?"

I shook my head and turned away.

"What's wrong, Semantha?"

"I'm sorry," I said. "A memory . . ."

He sat back and gazed at me. "What memory?"

Cassie had once told me that no matter what the facts were, people would always blame me. If they didn't believe it was something I really wanted deep inside me, they would accuse me of being too careless or too stupid. Somehow, it would end up being my fault, no matter what. I had used to think she was saying all of this so I would not reveal what she had done, but I had seen accusation on the faces of those who saw me pregnant afterward. Even if I were a victim, I was stained forever in their eyes.

I had successfully kept anyone at Collier from knowing what had happened to me, but it was foolish of me to believe I could hide it from someone who fell in love with me. Eventually, he would know, and my worst fear was that he would think he had been somehow deceived, tricked, and betrayed. What had become loving and wonderful would turn into something distasteful, and it would end badly.

I turned back to Ethan, took a deep breath, and said, "I was date-raped."

"What?" He grimaced as if it had happened to him and not me. "When?"

"A little more than four years ago."

I waited to see what he would say, but he just stared, waiting for more information.

"It happened in my house. My sister, Cassie, made it happen," I quickly added. "She arranged for it all, planned it all, had me drugged."

"*You traitor!*" Cassie screamed from the doorway.

"Your sister?" He shook his head. "I don't understand, Semantha. What do you mean? Why would your own sister do something like that to you?"

"It was after my mother had died. Cassie wanted a baby for my father. She was hoping for a boy, of course, only she couldn't get pregnant, so she bribed a young man who had begun working for us and arranged for him to sexually assault me when I was under the influence of a drug. It was powerful. I wasn't even sure it had happened, and when I . . . realized I was pregnant—"

"Pregnant? You got pregnant?"

"Yes."

He thought for a moment and then rose off the bed and walked to the window. Cassie stepped toward me, smiling.

"Ethan?"

He turned slowly. "Did you give birth? I mean . . . did you get an abortion?"

"No. My sister tricked me. She paid someone to pretend he was a doctor who could diagnose me with something called pseudocyesis."

"What's that?"

"With pseudocyesis, women have symptoms similar to true pregnancy. They have morning sickness and tender breasts, gain weight, suffer abdominal distension, and many actually claim they experience the sensation of fetal movement, known as quickening, even though there is no fetus present. Some actually go into false labor."

"You're kidding. This really happens?"

"The most famous case of that is Mary Tudor, the queen of England, who believed she was pregnant more than once when she wasn't. She needed an heir. I read up on it all once I was diagnosed with it."

"And you really believed this was what was wrong with you? How could you believe such a thing?"

"I told you. My sister brought a doctor to me. I was hearing it from a man I thought to be an honest doctor."

He shook his head. "This is fantastic. So, eventually, you realized you were really pregnant, didn't you?"

"Yes."

"And you really gave birth to a baby?"

I nodded. "A girl."

"Well, what happened to the baby?" he asked.

"My father arranged for her to be given to distant cousins. I've never seen her since she was born," I said.

"So, you have a four-year-old daughter? Will they ever tell her the truth?"

"I don't know. I don't think so. I think that was part of the arrangement my father had made. He gave them money for her, of course."

"Yes, I'm sure he did. And this sister, Cassie? She had the fatal accident on the stairway?"

"Yes."

"Well." He wiped his face and shook his head. "I guess all of that helps to explain why you're so nervous when we're together and I'm a little aggressive."

"I'm sorry, Ethan. I don't want to be. Don't say you're aggressive. You're just doing what any normal man would do and should do."

"Right." He thought a moment as he stared at me. "Exactly what happened just now when we . . . when I was about to make love to you?"

"The memory of the date rape was so vivid for a moment that I got confused."

"You mean, that's what I did, caused you to relive it?"

"It's not your fault, but yes, that's what just happened. I'm sorry."

"Does that happen often? I mean, not with other men, but just happen?"

"Not often, but . . . it happens sometimes in the middle of the night."

"Have you been seeing someone about this sort of thing, a therapist?"

"Yes."

"Recently?"

"The last time I was home, but the doctor, Dr. Ryan, didn't think I needed to see him again."

"Maybe he's wrong. Maybe you're not quite . . . ready," he said. "Maybe you should still see this therapist, especially if this thing still happens to you."

I nodded, close to tears. I could feel the distance growing between us. Cassie was smiling wider and nodding her head. I wanted to scream at her, but I was afraid of what that would do to Ethan, so I kept my eyes down. He reached for his clothing.

"Ethan . . ."

"I'll take you back so you can rest," he said. "We'll try again some other time," he added, but he didn't sound sincere.

I said nothing. I got dressed quickly, too. We left the motel room in silence. When I looked back, Cassie was standing in the doorway, with her arms folded over her breasts the way they were when she was planted firmly in a thought or a decision.

"You want to get something to eat?" Ethan asked.

"No," I said. "I'm not hungry."

He nodded and drove us away. After a few minutes, he began asking more about the date rape.

"Who was the man? Was he arrested or anything?"

"Not arrested. My father handled that. As I said, he was working for us, and Cassie had promised him a promotion. My father liked him. It was a shock for my father to learn what my sister and he had done."

"I'll bet. Your sister was quite a piece of work, I guess."

"She was very intelligent, always far ahead in her schoolwork."

"Lots of crazy people are intelligent," Ethan said.

I was afraid of his thinking Cassie was crazy. Most people believe that if there's one mentally ill person in the family, there is the possibility of another or that the mental illness will poke its ugly head up sometime in the future. It makes you more self-conscious about everything you do, wondering always if it will cause people to think you, too, are showing signs of some psychological problem.

Later, when we pulled onto the Collier campus, I asked him if he was still planning on coming to my graduation ceremony. He had said that he wanted to meet my father and my uncle Perry. I told him that I had told my father about him. There was no conflict with his own graduation ceremonies.

"Sure," he said. "You take it easy this week. I'll call you during the week. I don't think I can get over here, because I still have lots to do myself."

"Okay." I held on to his hand. "I didn't mean to keep it all a secret from you, Ethan. It's not easy for me to tell anyone about it."

"I understand."

He leaned over to kiss me. It was already a different kiss, the sort of kiss a friend gives a friend or a relative gives a relative. There wasn't even a trace of passion in it. His lips flicked on mine and were gone. I hardly had time to close my eyes and savor the taste of his love.

I got out quickly. He waved and drove off. My heart felt like a brick of lead in my chest. With my head down, I walked into the dormitory and toward my and Ellie's room. I was immediately surprised by laughter and loud music. When I paused at our doorway, I saw Pam Dorfman, Natalie Roberts, Ellie, and Cara Allen smoking what was clearly pot. Natalie was drinking something obviously alcoholic from a paper cup and dancing. Cara was standing on my bed, and Pam was wearing my beret.

"What's going on?" I asked.

"Party time, Norma," Natalie said, laughing.

"My name's not Norma. Ellie, what are you doing?"

"Mrs. Hingle's brother just died. She had to leave for Delaware, and Mrs. Hathaway has no one to assign. She was here an hour ago to tell us we had better behave and follow all the rules until Mrs. Hingle returns or she finds someone qualified. So . . ." She held out her arms. "We're behaving."

They all laughed.

"Are you crazy? Someone will tell Mrs. Hathaway what's going on. Why are you doing this in my room?"

"It's my room, too. If you don't want a joint, I've got some other good stuff," she said showing me the two bottles of tequila. "It wasn't difficult to get, if you know what I mean. How was your day with Ethan? You're back early, aren't you? Are you going out again? You're Mrs. Hathaway's new darling, so you're on the honor system. Just sign the clipboard on the desk out front," she said. "I'm still confined to the barracks but making the best of it." They all laughed.

"No. I'm not going out again, but I was hoping to do some studying. We have two finals on Monday, Ellie."

"What?"

"Turn down the music."

"What did she say?" Pam asked Ellie, pretending not to hear me. "Something about Monday?"

"Take off my hat!" I shouted at her. She shrugged and tossed it like a Frisbee at the closet. "I want my room back."

"Chill out," Natalie said. "Or we'll have to commit you. Where is the nearest psycho ward?" she asked Pam.

"Ask her. She probably's been there."

They all laughed again.

"Get out!" I screamed.

"Relax, Semantha," Ellie said. "It's the end of the year. We're entitled to some fun."

I turned and started away.

"You better not squeal on us, Semantha!" Ellie shouted after me.

I had no intention of doing that, even though I was fuming. After I marched out of the dorm, I kept walking. Ethan's reaction to my deep secret and now this wild party in my dorm room were too much. I felt like walking back to Kentucky. I didn't realize I was crying, too, until I heard someone call my name and turned to see Mrs. Hathaway standing with Mr. Kasofsky, our history teacher. They were talking by his car. I had wandered all the way to the main building.

Oh no, I thought as Mrs. Hathaway started toward me. I looked back at the dormitory.

"What's wrong, Semantha?"

"Nothing," I said, wiping my cheeks quickly.

"Why are you crying?"

"I'm not. Something got into my eye," I said.

She stood there looking at me. "Didn't you sign out earlier?"

"Yes, ma'am."

She looked at Mr. Kasofsky and then back at the dormitory. "Is something going on that I should know about back there?" she asked.

"No," I said, too vehemently.

She tightened her lips and walked back to Mr. Kasofsky. My heart began thumping. They got into his car and drove toward the dorms. *They're surely going to blame me,* I thought. I started back slowly. By the time I arrived, Mrs. Hathaway and Mr. Kasofsky had obviously been to Ellie's and my room. The hallway was dead quiet. I heard Mrs. Hingle's office door open and Ellie and Natalie Roberts came out, both, as my father might say, looking like death warmed over. I could see the other girls were still in the office.

"I didn't tell her anything," I told them.

"Right," Natalie said. "She just happened to come rushing back here after you left."

"How could you do this to us?" Ellie asked me.

"I didn't. She saw me walking and saw I was crying. I didn't even know I was crying, but . . ."

"You're such a phony," Ellie said. "I bet you made up that whole story about your mother and your sister. That whole candle thing in the bathroom was probably some kind of voodoo ceremony or something. You pretended to be such a wallflower, but you managed to steal away my boyfriend. Now you put on this act for Mrs. Hathaway and got us all expelled just before our graduation. We had to sit in there while she called our parents to tell them. Congratulations."

They started away.

"None of that is true!" I screamed after them. They didn't pause or turn around.

I backed up and sat on the small sofa in the lobby. I was too frightened to return to our room. Minutes later, the other girls, looking just as devastated as Ellie and Natalie, emerged from Mrs. Hingle's office. They glanced at me and continued down the hallway.

Mrs. Hathaway came to the open office doorway and looked out at me.

"Come in here, Semantha," she said.

As soon as I entered, she closed the door. Mr. Kasofsky was sitting on the settee, looking just as upset as she did.

"Sit," Mrs. Hathaway ordered, nodding at one of the chairs. "I'm happy you didn't participate in their debauchery," she began.

"They think I turned them in," I muttered.

"So what? They're certainly not good friends of yours. They said some nasty things about you in here," she revealed. I looked at Mr. Kasofsky, who nodded. "I don't imagine you'll ever have anything to do with any of them again, either."

"But the rest of the student body . . ."

"Are you running for president of the student council or something?"

"No, but . . . they'll blame me!" I cried.

"They have only themselves to blame for what's happened. However, I don't imagine they'll make things pleasant for you until they leave. I have arranged for taxicabs to pick them up in less than an hour. I'd like you to go to the library and wait there until I call for you. I can't imagine you'd want to return to that room while Ellie Patton is still here, and I want it fumigated anyway. It reeks of marijuana. They are lucky I didn't call the police. That has been my standard procedure for such behavior. I'm calling your father, and I want you to be present while I speak with him."

"Why? I didn't do anything."

"Whenever a student has any significant changes in her living or schooling here, we inform the parents immediately."

She picked up the phone and called my father. I sat and listened as she described the events, emphasizing how I had been made uncomfortable and placed in danger. I couldn't help but wonder how he was really feeling and what he was really thinking about all of this. In my heart of hearts, I had always believed that he thought I would do something or something would happen that would make my graduating impossible. He had often said about other things Cassie and I had done, "I'm waiting for the second shoe to drop."

"Your father would like to speak with you," she said, holding out the receiver. She stood. "Mr. Kasofsky and I will see to the girls and make sure they do not do any more damage, especially to your things."

I rose and took the phone. She and Mr. Kasofsky left the office, and I sat behind Mrs. Hingle's desk.

"Hi, Daddy," I said.

"Well, that does sound like quite a disaster there. I'm glad you're on the right side of all this, Semantha."

"I didn't tell on them," I said. For some reason, I felt that was important for him to know. "Mrs. Hathaway just guessed something was wrong when she saw me. I was upset and had left the room."

"It doesn't matter. None of that matters. What matters is your being comfortable and safe until your graduation. Perry and I will be there. Just listen to Mrs. Hathaway, and do whatever she tells you to do."

"Okay, Daddy. I'm sorry."

"There's nothing for you to be sorry about, Semantha. What you can learn from this is how important it is to be careful about the friends you make, even mere acquaintances. Call me whenever you want," he said.

After I hung up, I saw Cassie standing in the doorway.

"*I didn't tell on them,*" she mimicked. "*Don't you realize how pathetic you sound, and to Daddy?*"

Everyone is going to hate me here, I thought. I didn't have to say it aloud for her to hear me.

"*Hate you? Nobody here likes you anyway. Go home, and stop feeling sorry for yourself. Self-pity is unbecoming for a Heavenstone.*"

The moment Mrs. Hathaway returned to the office, Cassie evaporated.

"Follow me," Mrs. Hathaway said. "I want

you to get your books and notebooks to use in the library."

I got up quickly and walked back to my room with her. Ellie was putting her things in her suitcases and didn't look at me at all until I started to gather my books.

"Where are you going?" she asked.

"I don't want you speaking to Semantha. What she does and doesn't do is no longer your affair," Mrs. Hathaway said. "I'm this close to changing my mind about the police," she added, showing her right thumb and forefinger closing against each other. Then she went down the hallway to check on the other girls.

Ellie continued to put her things together in silence. Suddenly, she crossed to my closet and took the black satin dress off the hanger, picked up the red shoes and the clutch, and stuffed it all in her suitcase. She closed one suitcase and stood there a moment, looking out the window.

"You know, you really owe me a lot, Semantha. I never told the other girls how you talk to yourself. I heard you say your sister's name, too. I know you talk to your dead sister. I ignored it because I felt sorry for you, but you're crazy for sure, and you'll really end up in some nuthouse."

She rushed to finish packing her other suitcase and bag when Mrs. Hathaway returned.

"There seems to be an additional problem," Mrs. Hathaway said. "Miss Patton, leave your things as they are and follow me to Mrs. Hingle's office."

"Why?"

Mrs. Hathaway didn't reply. She turned and walked off. Ellie spun on me.

"What else did you say?"

"Nothing. I never said anything. Maybe one of your new best friends told her something," I said. I could see the possibility lighting up her eyes.

She went to the doorway and looked down the hall to her left. Then she looked to her right. I could hear the footsteps, too.

I stepped up beside her. Down to the left, Pam Dorfman was talking to Mr. Kasofsky. Coming down the hallway from the lobby was one of the campus security men. Ellie's eyes widened, and she rushed back to the suitcase she had closed and opened it to dig under the garments and bring out a gold necklace. She rushed into the bathroom. I heard her flush the toilet just as the security guard appeared. He went right to her suitcases and began to rifle through them.

She stepped out of the bathroom.

"What are you doing? Those are my things. You can't do that. It's against the law."

"We have the right to search any room and anyone's things," he told her. "It's part of the agreement your parents signed when you were admitted. If I were you, I'd move along. Mrs. Hathaway is waiting for you."

She looked at me with such desperation my heart actually ached for her. The security guard began to pull things out of her suitcase. When he turned to her again, she hurried out of the room.

"If you know where she's hidden stuff that she

has stolen, you'd better tell me," he said. "Otherwise, you could be considered an accessory to a crime here, Miss."

"*Tell him,*" Cassie whispered. "*For Daddy's sake. Tell him!*"

"She brought these things to me once," I said, and took the dress, shoes, and clutch out of her suitcase. I opened one of my dresser drawers and handed him the chandelier earrings.

"What else?" he demanded. "There's more," he said. "I'm sure."

"I don't know anything except . . ."

"What?"

"I think she threw a necklace down the toilet."

He went into the bathroom and then came out. "Don't use it," he said.

I looked out the doorway into the hallway. Mr. Kasofsky was walking by with Pam Dorfman. She glanced at me with a look of satisfaction on her face. She had saved herself. It had become rats deserting a sinking ship.

But who was I to talk? Look at what I had given the security guard. I was twisting up inside with all of my mixed feelings. They hadn't liked me before; they'd hate me now.

"*Stop thinking about them. You don't want to be on this ship anyway,*" Cassie muttered. "*Let it sink.*"

5

Sinking Ship

LESS THAN AN hour later, I looked out my room window and saw the police car. I stood mesmerized by the sight of it. This was far more than just being expelled and having to face your parents. Ellie was going to be in very serious trouble now. This was no longer some silly prank her parents would eventually excuse. Moments later, the campus security guard and a patrolman escorted her out of the building with her hands behind her back in handcuffs and put her into the rear of the vehicle. I knew all of the girls were at their own windows, watching in shock. Mrs. Hathaway stood on the steps talking to another patrolman for a few minutes, and then he got into the car, and they drove Ellie off. I caught a brief glimpse of her face in the window. She looked like a little girl, really terrified. It brought tears to my eyes.

"Stop that pity. Good riddance," I heard Cassie whisper. *"Just think of the trouble she could have gotten you in and what this might have done to Daddy."*

"I'm not as hard as you are, Cassie," I whispered back. "I don't think I ever will be."

"Yes, you will," she insisted. *"Someday, you will be just like me."*

Not long after the patrol car left, two taxicabs arrived. Natalie Roberts got into one, and Cara Allen got into the other. I watched them drive away as well. Then I went to my doorway and looked down the hall to see Pam talking softly with some other girls. She glanced up at me and quickly turned her back. Despite what I knew Cassie thought of this, I couldn't help but feel even more pity for Ellie. I felt sure that the biggest disappointment had been learning that her so-called good friend had turned her in to save her own neck. But to my surprise, Pam went into her room and came out with her suitcases, too. She marched down the hallway, where the security guard waited to take one of her bags and escort her out. I followed curiously and saw her stop to talk with Mrs. Hathaway before she went out to a third cab.

I was confused. If she was being forced to leave, too, why had she turned on Ellie?

"She's letting her take her exams a week after graduation," Amanda Crowley said, as if she could read my thoughts. She had come up beside me. "If she passes everything, she graduates. That was her deal."

"Oh."

"You're getting away with a lot, too, aren't you?"

"Me? Why?"

She smirked. "She stole things for you. Everyone knows it. She told some of the girls. You're an accessory. You should have been in that police car sitting right beside her. But not Princess Heavenstone." She walked away.

"*Den of vipers,*" Cassie muttered.

When I returned to my room, I called Ethan.

"Hey," he said. "What's up?"

I described the events that occurred after he had dropped me off. He listened in silence and then said, "Wow. What a terrible scene. I'm sure you can't wait to get out of there."

"Yes, but I can't help feeling sorry for her, Ethan. You should have seen her in the police car."

"Well, I feel sorry for her, too, but I'm not surprised that something like this has happened to her," he said. "Best we both concentrate on what we have to do to finish things up and not let any of this bother us."

I wondered how much he was including in "any of this." Did it include what had happened at the motel?

"Okay. Call me when you get an opportunity," I said.

He promised he would, and I hung up.

Not a day passed when I didn't wait for his call, but none came. On the Friday before graduation, I finally called him again. His roommate answered, sounding annoyed to be interrupted. He blurted something about Ethan going home on a family matter. He wasn't sure when he'd return. He hung up before I could ask him to be sure to tell Ethan I had called.

That Sunday, Daddy and Uncle Perry arrived after noon. They had flown in on the private jet

Daddy rented. To my surprise, Lucille Bennet was with them. I had been waiting at my dorm-room window and saw them driven up in a limo. The driver opened the door, and Daddy stepped out first, turned, and offered his hand to a tall woman who looked only a few inches shorter than he was. She had light auburn hair in a medium cut, layered in a semistraight style I couldn't help but think was very attractive.

There was something elegant about her. Dressed in what looked like an expensive bright white designer outfit, a cardigan with three-quarter-length sleeves and a skirt, she had a very self-confident posture. The cardigan had black piping and a floral pattern at the left shoulder. Daddy wore one of his black suits with a ruby tie, and Uncle Perry, who stepped out quickly behind them, looked as handsome as ever in a light blue suit and tie.

I rushed down the hall to the lobby to greet them. Daddy opened the door for Lucille and Uncle Perry and followed them into the dorm.

"Hey, Sam," I heard Uncle Perry cry. As far back as I could recall, he had called me that.

"Hi," I said, and moved quickly to embrace and kiss Daddy and then him.

"Our graduate," Uncle Perry said, smiling.

"Semantha, I'd like to introduce you to Lucille. She was nice enough to want to travel with us to attend your graduation," Daddy said.

"*Nice enough?*" Cassie whispered. "*What a sacrifice. She traveled here in a private jet and a limousine. It's clear what she's after.*"

"Hi," I said, and she held out her hand very slowly, her eyes scouring my face as if she were looking for some blemish. Of course, I had no idea how much, if anything, Daddy had told her about me and what had happened. Of course, she had to know about my pregnancy, but what details had he told her?

"I'm so happy to meet you, Semantha. Your father has told me so much about you. Congratulations on your graduation."

"Thank you."

Because of how hard she was looking at me, I shifted my eyes quickly to Uncle Perry, whose obvious excitement at seeing me warmed my heart and helped me feel more at ease.

"You do look wiser," he said, smiling.

"I don't feel wiser."

"You will," he insisted.

"You all packed to leave immediately afterward?" Daddy asked.

"I bet she's been packed for days," Uncle Perry said.

I laughed and nodded. I didn't have to say it. He could see in my eyes how true it was. Then I glanced at my watch and looked at the front, hoping to see Ethan drive up. I still felt Lucille's eyes on me, studying every movement in my face. She was making me feel very self-conscious.

"*Look right back at her,*" Cassie whispered. "*Don't let her intimidate you.*"

I looked at her, trying to be as hard as Cassie would be, hardly blinking.

But that didn't drive her eyes from me. She had

almond-shaped grayish blue eyes that telegraphed self-confidence reinforced with her firm but feminine lips. She was not as pretty as Mother was, but she was very attractive and had a beautiful, stately figure. I hated to admit it, and Cassie certainly never would, but she looked as if she complemented Daddy well. It was easy to believe that people would see them as a power couple. Everything about her said, "I take charge, and I support the man I'm with."

"I'll never forget my college graduation ceremony," she said. "I had partied so much the night before that I nearly fell asleep on the stage."

"Then how can you say you'll never forget it? How do you remember anything about it?" Cassie urged me to ask.

"Well, I hope we have time for some lunch," Daddy said, looking at his watch. "What time do you have to be in the auditorium?"

"Three-thirty."

"That gives us a few hours. Know somewhere nice not too far away?" he asked.

I thought of the coffee and sandwich shop Ethan had taken me to just last week and nodded.

"Wasn't there someone you wanted us to meet?" Uncle Perry asked with an impish grin.

"I was hoping he'd be here early, but he had an urgent family matter, and I'm not sure if he's going to make it," I said.

"Too bad, but you have me," Uncle Perry added, offering his arm.

"Should we put her things in the limousine now, Teddy?" Lucille asked. "To save time?"

"Good idea. Let's do that, Semantha," he said.

I glanced at Lucille and saw how pleased she was to have her suggestion followed. I led them back to my room. Some of the other girls looked with interest at my family. None of them had much to do with me after Ellie and the others were expelled, so I didn't introduce anyone to my father. They turned away quickly anyway, showing me their backs and acting more interested in themselves. Actually, they weren't acting.

"Sorry you had such an unpleasant finish to your school years," Lucille commented, looking toward the other girls. "I can only imagine how difficult it was for you to have a roommate like that."

"What doesn't Daddy tell her?" Cassie whispered.

I said nothing and continued leading them to my room.

"How nice," Lucille said. "I can tell you this is head and shoulders above what I had at my finishing school."

"We paid enough for it," Daddy told her. "One year here is equivalent to my whole college education, and that's not just because of inflation."

"She deserves it," Lucille said, smiling at me.

"Oh, brother, give me a break," Cassie whispered. *"She probably slides instead of walks half the time."*

I put a few more things into my carry-on bag. Uncle Perry went for my two suitcases, and I took one last look through the closets and dresser drawers. When I looked into the bathroom cabinet, I saw the birthday candle. I stared at it a moment and then closed the cabinet.

Lucille came up behind me. It was as if she didn't want to miss a thing I did.

"Have everything?"

"Yes," I said quickly. Had she seen the candle?

"Despite how cozy and well furnished this is," she said, "if you're anything like me, I'm sure you don't regret leaving."

"I'm looking forward to going home."

"Have you thought about what you want to do next?" she asked as we walked down the corridor to the lobby.

"No," I told her.

"If you had, you wouldn't tell her before you told Daddy and Uncle Perry anyway," Cassie whispered. *"What nerve!"*

Lucille slipped her arm through my father's and said, "Young people today take so much longer to settle down than we did."

"That's because we were always in a rush," Uncle Perry offered.

"I wouldn't call it a rush, Perry. I'd call it a sense of responsibility, ambition."

"Semantha is one of the most responsible young women I know," he said. "I'd trust her with the keys to the kingdom any day, hey, Sam?"

I simply smiled. If I were Cassie, I thought, the keys to the kingdom would fit neatly in my hands, but I doubted I knew more about our business than the average customer.

"How sweet," Lucille said. "You have quite a cheerleader in your uncle."

"And her father," Uncle Perry said. "Right, Teddy?"

"Absolutely. She's my girl," Daddy said.

I hope so, I thought. How I hoped so.

I anticipated some complaint about the restaurant because it wasn't anything special, but even Lucille thought it was "delightfully quaint," whatever that meant. I was surprised at how much control she had over what Daddy wanted to eat. She seemed already to know what agreed with him and what didn't, what was good for him and what wasn't.

"She's after me to lose the ten pounds Dr. Moffet wants me to lose," Daddy told me when she advised him not to have the heavy garlic-bread club sandwich and fries. He ended up eating the same salad she ordered. Uncle Perry and I had the hamburgers I told him the restaurant was well known for. When I explained that I had been there with Ethan Hunter, Lucille began to ask questions about him. She wanted to know where he came from, what his family was like, what he was going to do after graduation, and what sort of student he had been.

"She's acting like your mother already," Cassie whispered angrily.

I could see that my answers were quite vague and unsatisfactory to her.

"It doesn't sound like you were all that involved with him," she said.

"I was involved with him more than I've been with any other boy," I snapped.

Daddy looked up sharply, surprised at my tone. I could almost read his thoughts. *You sounded just like your sister just now.*

"Well, I don't imagine you'll see him too often

now, anyway," Lucille said. "If there is one thing I'd advise young women today, it's not to rush into romantic relationships. That was my mistake."

"You're too hard on yourself, Lucille," Uncle Perry told her. I couldn't tell if he was serious. Uncle Perry always had that way about him, balancing what he really thought with what he had to say and therefore never sounding completely sincere. Cassie hated it.

"Maybe," she said, "but I still give any young women I know that advice, even William's nieces, who still talk to me more than they talked to him."

"They're lucky to have you as a mentor," Daddy told her.

"He's drooling over her. We have a lot of work to do," Cassie whispered.

When we returned to campus, I looked for Ethan in the crowd of relatives and close friends that was gathering. I didn't see him, but I still had high hopes. I went backstage to get my cap and gown and listen to last-minute instructions from Mrs. Hathaway. It wasn't going to be a long ceremony. There were only thirty-four of us graduating, and that included some early graduates as well. The speaker was Helen Fleming, a graduate of the class of 1995 who was now a New York State senator.

My eyes panned the audience as we marched down the aisle to take our seats on the stage. Ethan was still nowhere in sight, so my expectations dwindled, and even though this was supposed to be a very happy day for me, I felt a thick cloud of disappointment drift over me. I barely listened to any of

the speakers and nearly didn't hear my name called
when it was time to go up and get my diploma. Mrs.
Hathaway held my hand a little longer than she had
held the hands of the others.

"You can be very, very proud of yourself, Semantha," she said. "You overcame a great many obstacles
to get to this place. Good luck, dear."

"Thank you," I said, and looked out at Daddy,
Uncle Perry, and Lucille. Uncle Perry was waving.
Daddy looked lost in thought, and Lucille looked
pleased and kept whispering something in his ear.
Daddy finally nodded and smiled at me as I walked
around to return to my seat. Only Uncle Perry
snapped a picture.

Afterward, I introduced the three of them to
some of my teachers, and then Lucille reminded
Daddy of the time. With one more desperate search
of the crowd, I looked for Ethan but didn't see him.
If he had been there, he would have come over, I
thought.

"Forget about him," Cassie said. *"We'll find
someone worthy of a Heavenstone."*

"So, how does it feel?" Uncle Perry asked when
we were all in the limousine heading for the airport.
He reached for my hand and gently squeezed it.

"Not much different," I said.

It was true. It was almost as if someone else had
been on that stage. I didn't have any girlfriends to
hug and cry with. Other than my times with Ethan,
there were no great memories, nothing about the
school to cherish and tell my children about in years
to come. Now my years at Collier and even these past

weeks felt more like a dream. Soon I would wake up and find myself back in my own bed at home.

Maybe it had all been a long, bad dream. Maybe when I woke up, I'd hear Mother coming down the hallway to wake me up and Cassie complaining that she was babying me too much.

"If she's late for school, it's her own fault," Cassie would say.

And Mother would respond, "That's why I'm here. To make sure she's not, and you should be, too, Cassie. We have to look after each other in this world."

"There's a limit to that, Mother. She'll become too dependent on us and weak."

"Nonsense," Mother would tell her with a short but soft laugh. "A Heavenstone can never be too weak, remember?"

"She's not a Heavenstone yet," Cassie would reply and leave it at that, whatever it meant.

I could hear them bantering so clearly. It really was as if no time had passed.

Oh, please, please let it be true, I prayed.

"Don't be an idiot," Cassie muttered in my ear. *"Open your eyes and look at Daddy and his Lucille. We have no time for dreaming."*

Cassie was right. They were behaving like two teenagers, giggling and whispering and sitting so tightly against each other that they could surely feel the blood moving in each other's veins. I looked at Uncle Perry to see what he thought of them. He smiled and shook his head. Then he leaned over to whisper in the ear Cassie favored.

"Your dad's finally coming back to life, Sam," he said. "That's good. Things will be better for you, for us all, if he's happy again."

I looked at him with surprise. Didn't he see what I saw? Didn't he see how controlling Lucille was, and how self-centered?

"*See?*" Cassie said. "*I told you he was a lame-brain.*"

For most of the remainder of the trip, Uncle Perry was the only one talking to me. Daddy was on the phone with some of his store managers, and when she wasn't talking with him, Lucille read fashion magazines. Uncle Perry described some of the changes he had been making in the Heavenstone fashion line. Despite some cutbacks Daddy had made when Cassie was working with him, Uncle Perry had held on to what interested him most and eventually brought it back to where it was.

"Maybe you'll come work with me," he suggested a little before we landed. "I always welcomed your opinion and advice, Sam, and it's a lot more interesting than the work your father does."

"Maybe," I said.

I really hadn't given much thought at all to what I would do now. Once I had thought I might go into teaching, but the idea of facing so many different personalities and dealing with them all had turned terrifying. I didn't want to be in front of any audience, no matter how small or how young.

I thought Uncle Perry might stay over after we landed, but he said he had work to do in the morning and promised he would try to get up on the weekend.

I expected Daddy would want to take Lucille home first, but nothing was said, and he didn't give any other directions to our driver.

I was tired from the day and the journey, but the sight of our historic family home silhouetted against the night sky bright with stars filled me with new energy. Daddy wasn't exaggerating when he carried on about our heritage and our ties to our past through this grand house, our Heavenstone. It was comforting and safe, a world unto itself. The voices, laughter, and even tears of sadness and tears of joy still echoed within, as did the footsteps of our grandparents, great-grandparents, and what Cassie used to call our triple great-grandparents.

Growing up there, I often felt as if the house were truly alive, beating with a heart of its own, its lifeblood flowing through the pipes and wires. Every light was another eye, every creak in the stairways or floors another moan. Both Cassie and I had always felt guilty and ashamed if we scratched a wall or a floorboard, broke a dish or a glass. Repairs were like medical treatments. It was never permissible to injure Heavenstone in any way. Few, if any, of our peers had similar feelings about their homes. Most families in our school moved from place to place, house to house, periodically, their parents viewing their homes as investments and not gardens in which to grow families.

I always felt closer to Mother and even to Cassie in the house than I did at the cemetery. I vividly remembered where my mother had stood or sat when she had said something wonderful or when she had looked beautiful and happy. I loved to sit in her favorite chairs or look out the windows she had looked out to see the world through her eyes. Being there, touching things she had touched, holding things she had held, and using things she had used helped me to feel her presence even now. She was still in our mansion and still giving me a sense of security and a sense of great love. I could never, ever be alone in Heavenstone. The memories would always surround me and comfort me. Lucille Bennet wouldn't understand this, I thought. Cassie wasn't all wrong. How could anyone but a Heavenstone understand?

Of course, there were other, darker memories that were continually resurrected in our house. After Cassie had made sure that Mother overdosed on her sleeping pills, she had tried to erase any and all traces of her death by changing our parents' bedroom. She could replace the furniture, the flooring, and the curtains, but nothing would ever erase the image of Mother asleep forever in her bed. Nothing would drown out my screams and tears. I could never look at the stairway to the attic and not see Cassie tumbling down. And it was certainly impossible for me to fall asleep in my own bed and not, as I had told Ethan, occasionally revisit my rape.

Once, when Daddy and I had one of our painful conversations after it was all over and done, he said, "As hard as it will be, Semantha, we must face our demons here. We cannot let them drive us from our home and our history. We'll never be who we really are if we leave. Be strong. Face them down."

I promised I would, and I was confident I could,

but that was before Cassie had returned from her grave to haunt me. That had become more and more intense this last year of private high school, so I couldn't help being a little more apprehensive than usual as we approached Heavenstone.

"Home sweet home," Daddy said as we drove up our long driveway.

Our Gothic Revival mansion had been built in the Bluegrass region of Kentucky because this was where Daddy's ancestors had come to live when they left England. The house had ten rooms. Five were downstairs: the large living room with the original fieldstone fireplace with stone up to the ceiling; a large dining room with a grand teardrop chandelier that had been imported years ago from France; a kitchen that had been renovated five times to provide for more modern appliances, twice alone after Daddy and Mother married; a dark oakwood den that was our entertainment center; and Daddy's home office with its library of leather-bound first editions.

Mrs. Dobson, anticipating our arrival, was at the door even before we got out of the car. Our limousine driver grabbed my suitcases, and we started up the steps. I imagined Daddy wanted to get me settled in first and then would take Lucille home.

"Welcome home, Miss Semantha," Mrs. Dobson said. She reached for my carry-on bag.

"It's all right, Mrs. Dobson," I said, keeping it. Ever since she had come to work for us, she had pampered me. My father swore he hadn't given her any special instructions regarding my needs. She was more like a sweet grandmother to me now.

"Oh, but you must be tired, Miss. All that traveling and excitement were surely enough to wear you down."

"It's nothing, Mrs. Dobson. Really, I'm fine."

"She's still young enough to handle this short a trip," Lucille said almost curtly. "We didn't exactly travel in what you would call steerage."

Mrs. Dobson glanced at her without speaking.

Daddy took my suitcases from the driver. "I'll take it from here, Jeff. Thanks."

"Very good, Mr. Heavenstone."

He turned and headed back to the limousine. I looked at Lucille. Why were they sending the limousine away?

We entered the house.

"Should I prepare something to eat, Mr. Heavenstone?" Mrs. Dobson asked.

"We ate on the plane. Thank you, Mrs. Dobson," he said, and then turned to Lucille.

"I'll just get her set and come down. Pour me a scotch and soda, will you?"

"Of course. Welcome home, Semantha," she told me, and went into the den.

"Oh, I can do that, Mr. Heavenstone," Mrs. Dobson said, reaching for the suitcase.

"They're not too heavy?"

"Hardly," she said. "I've carried heavier up steeper hills than this beautiful stairway."

It wasn't like Daddy to let her carry suitcases, but he gave in quickly.

"I'll take one," I said sharply.

"Okay," Daddy said. "After you settle in, come

to the den. We'll talk and catch up. Unless you are too tired."

"Oh, no, Daddy. I'm fine."

"Good. See you soon," he said, and hurried after Lucille.

Mrs. Dobson and I began to go up the stairway.

"How was your graduation ceremony?" Mrs. Dobson asked.

"Fine," I said.

"Despite what you just told your father, I imagine you are tired," she said, hearing the tenseness in my voice.

"No, no, I'm fine," I said. It had been so long since Daddy and I had had any sort of face-to-face conversation, I was eager to get back downstairs.

Mrs. Dobson, however, had gotten to know me well over the years. She looked at me closely when we turned at the top and started toward my bedroom.

"I imagine there are a few surprises for you here now," she said.

I paused and turned to her. "Yes, there are."

She nodded, and we went to my bedroom. No matter how short or long the interval between my being here and somewhere else, I always felt a little numb when I first set foot in my bedroom again. Daddy tried to make changes for me after the date rape. He had replaced the carpeting with a darker color, bought new bedding and comforters, and re-done the curtains and had the walls repainted, but when I looked at my room, I always saw the old room, the room in which Cassie had arranged for my pregnancy. It made it hard to take that initial step, but of course, I did. Daddy's words resonated: "We must face our demons here."

"I can unpack everything for you, Miss Semantha. Go ahead and shower and change if you want. I'm sure you want to join your father and Mrs. Bennet."

"Is she here often?" I asked.

Mrs. Dobson paused. I knew it was against her nature to gossip, but my question apparently struck a deeper vein in her thinking. In fact, she looked surprised by it.

"Maybe you should let your father tell you, Miss Semantha."

"Tell me what? If she's here often? I don't care. I just wondered why—"

"Miss Semantha, Mrs. Bennet's moved into the Heavenstone house," she blurted. She put her hand over her mouth as if the words had escaped.

"Moved in? When?"

"About two weeks ago. Oh, dear me, dear me. I really wish your father had been the one to tell you this. I'm not sure he'll like it that I'm the one telling you. Maybe they're preparing to do just that right now. Oh, dear."

"Don't worry, Mrs. Dobson," I said, squeezing her hand gently and leaning in to whisper. "When they do, I'll act as if it is the first time I'm hearing it."

She nodded and smiled. "Here we are like two conspirators in Buckingham Palace," she quipped.

"Do you like her moving in, Mrs. Dobson?"

"Oh, it's not my place to have an opinion about such a thing, Miss Semantha."

"Nevertheless, I'm sure you do have an opinion," I said.

She glanced at me, but she didn't respond. It would be cruel to force an opinion about it out of her, I thought, and went to take a quick shower and change. When I looked at myself in the mirror just before going downstairs, I saw Cassie behind me.

She didn't have to say a word.

We were sisters. From the look on her face, I knew exactly what she was thinking.

Lucille Bennet might have moved in, but she would never take our mother's place.

Not if we had anything to say about it, and with Cassie always beside me, I was sure we would.

6

Facing Demons

I HEARD DADDY and Lucille's laughter as I walked toward the den. They were standing beside each other, hovering over the bar. Then they kissed. I stepped back out, not wanting them to see I had walked in on them. I waited a moment and then walked in. They both turned as I entered.

"Well now, officially welcome home, Semantha," Daddy said. He stepped forward to give me a kiss. "How about a drink? You're old enough. What do you like?"

"Just some white wine, maybe," I said.

"Very wise," Lucille said, holding up her wineglass to show me that was what she was drinking.

Daddy poured me a glass, and I sat on the ruby leather settee. I remembered when Mother had decided to buy new furniture for the den. It was always a major decision to replace anything in the Heavenstone mansion, no matter how worn or damaged it might be. Daddy used to say it was like burying history when we changed anything.

Lucille sat in what had always been Daddy's favorite heavy-cushioned leather chair, and he remained standing beside her. They both looked at me for a moment with identical silly grins on their faces.

"I suppose," Daddy began, "you're wondering why Lucille is still here."

I shrugged. "No."

She looked at him and smiled, and he took her hand and held it as he turned back to me. "Lucille has moved into Heavenstone, Semantha. It was on a trial basis, and I do believe the trial is over and the verdict is in."

While he spoke, Lucille continued to look up at him with admiration. I remembered how Cassie would look at him that way. It always made me feel as if I weren't paying enough attention to him or showing him enough respect and love.

Suddenly, he put down his glass of scotch and reached into his jacket pocket to produce what was clearly a box holding a ring. I held my breath as he opened it to show Lucille.

"Oh, Teddy!" she cried, putting her wine down and carefully plucking the ring out of the box. Even from where I was sitting, I could see it was a very large diamond. She slipped it on her finger. "Perfect fit."

He knelt to kiss her. Then he turned to me. "Well, Semantha, you witnessed it, the moment Lucille and I got engaged."

I saw he was waiting for me to say "Congratulations," but it was as if Cassie had her hand over my mouth. I struggled to offer a smile.

"Semantha?"

"It's a bit of a shock to her, I'm sure," Lucille said. "And it's been a very long day."

"It should be your day," Cassie whispered. *"Not her day. You graduated!"*

I nodded, still speechless. I had known this woman less than twenty-four hours, and she was soon to be my stepmother, my father's new wife. This was unfair. Why couldn't it have waited until I had spent some time with her? Why hadn't Daddy thought of that?

Daddy started to turn a shade of crimson, which was a clear indication that he was becoming angry. Cassie would have said, "Here it comes! Hold your ears."

"You're a young lady now. We brought you up to know the social graces. You could have the sense to offer us your congratulations, Semantha."

"I'm sorry. I was just about to, Daddy. I was taken by surprise. Congratulations, Mrs. Bennet. And you, too, Daddy," I said, forcing a wider smile, but he still didn't look satisfied by my reaction.

I couldn't help that it must have looked forced. I was second in line again! I had always been jealous of the affection Daddy had for Cassie. I had always known Cassie was his favorite, the more perfect daughter. After all of his discoveries about her and her death, I thought he would really get to know me, really look at me. We would finally get to be a real father and daughter.

Just when I thought all of that would happen now, Daddy inserted Lucille Bennet between us. I recalled when he had first told me he was going on a date with her. It didn't seem that long ago. How could he make such an important decision as marriage so quickly? Daddy was never impulsive. Was it simply because of his loneliness?

And why couldn't Daddy see what bothered me

and understand? Weren't fathers supposed to be able to understand their children more easily than anyone else? What did I have to do to get him to see my pain? Burst out in tears?

"Please, call me Lucille, Semantha. I do hope you and I will be on a legitimate first-name basis. I'd like to be more your friend than just a stepmother."

"And you'll be a lucky girl to have a friend with Lucille's wisdom and experience," Daddy said. "I hope you have the sense to appreciate it," he added firmly, his eyes beady with angry authority. It was the same as his saying, *You had better appreciate it, or else.*

"She will, Teddy. Give the girl a chance."

He relaxed but still shook his head and continued to look annoyed with me. I felt my eyes tearing and looked down as I sipped my wine.

"Why don't I leave you two for a little while to talk?" Lucille said, rising and putting her wineglass on the bar. "I'd like to take a hot bath and relax anyway, Teddy."

"You don't have to go," he told her. "We're not going to keep secrets from each other ever, from this day forward," he declared. From the way he looked at me, I could see that was a comment made more for my benefit than hers. It sounded more like a threat, too.

She smiled and looked at me as someone who had just won a serious argument might.

"I'm sure we won't," she said. "See you in a while. Good night, Semantha."

"Good night."

She walked out, and for a long moment, the silence that followed echoed in my ears.

"I'm very disappointed in you, Semantha," Daddy began. "I was hoping another year of private school would have matured you. I realize you've been through quite a lot, but you can't wallow in the misery of the past forever. Heavenstones don't give up, don't surrender. Every one of them up on these walls either was heroic or had the grit to make a better life for his or her children. It's in our blood.

"For a long time after all that happened, I was almost like you, so depressed and unhappy I could not enjoy anything or anyone. My footsteps echoed in this house and riled up the bad memories constantly. I didn't give in, but I wasn't making any progress, either. Oh, I don't mean with our business. Our business is an animal in and of itself. It has its own life, and it will overcome every economic downturn and survive. If anything, we feed off it, and I don't mean just on the income. I mean on the reputation, the history, the very essence of it. When I go to work, I'm energized, and I hope, if you don't decide to do something in education, that you will find a comfortable place in our company. I know Perry wants you to work with him.

"Now," he continued, pacing a little, "although my relationship with Lucille comes as a bit of a surprise to you, I hope you will have the maturity to understand that she is responsible for something important being brought back to me. I can't simply work, eat, and sleep, you know. I have to have a life, too. I want to travel, go to the theater, take pleasure in grand parties and dinners again. In short, I'm not ready to crawl into my grave, and Lucille, bless her soul, saw my needs and loved me for them immediately. She's made the gray skies go away and driven the cobwebs out of my brain. I'm a happy man again, Semantha, and if I'm happy, you'll be happier, too.

"So, for the present, I'd like you to try to stop thinking only of yourself. Think about all of us, about our Heavenstone heritage, and become a pillar of support. It won't be easy for Lucille, either, you know. She has to adjust, to make sacrifices and compromises. It's not easy for a woman to step into the shadows left by a previous wife, especially someone who was as wonderful as your mother was, but she's more than willing to do it, and one of the priorities in her life, she has said, will be you."

"Me?"

"Yes, you," Daddy said, pausing in front of me. He had his hands behind his back and was looking down at me. For a moment, he seemed even bigger and taller than he was in my eyes normally. "Lucille knows about the baby, of course, and now she knows how it came about."

"You told her about Cassie, what she had done?"

"There can't be such deep secrets between a man and a woman who are going to become one in marriage, Semantha. If and when you meet the man of your dreams, you must make sure he's willing to open his heart and soul completely to you." He paused again and looked at me. "Otherwise . . . otherwise, it's not a marriage; it's a civil union, a legal merging of two financial entities. It's not a complete and solid thing built on a foundation of love, as I once had with your mother, God rest her soul."

He paused, took a deep breath, and returned to his chair. He looked at me while he finished his drink. It took a few moments for all he had said to sink in.

"Are you saying she even knows what Cassie did to Mother, Daddy? I mean, with the sleeping pills?"

"We were never certain she deliberately emptied all of that sleeping powder into your mother's drink. She might have . . . prepared the powder for your mother that way because your mother wanted it that way, and then . . . then she was ashamed or feeling guilty, so she hid the bottle in the attic. She knew she would be blamed."

I stared at him, my mouth slightly open.

"Don't gape at me like that, Semantha. It's not an attractive thing for a young woman to do."

"But what about what she did to me . . . the rape?"

"That was very wrong, of course, but I understood her motives. She had a great desire to please me, greater than she should have had, but nevertheless, I don't think she wanted to hurt either of us. She simply went overboard."

"No, Daddy. She threw me overboard. She didn't go overboard."

"Whatever, Semantha. I don't like us to dwell on it!" he practically shouted. He realized it and calmed. "It's not doing either of us any good. In short, no, I did not tell Lucille about your mother and Cassie, and I insist that you never mention it to her. That's a dark part of our past that would only depress her, and at the start of a new life for both of us, there's no point in it. What good will it do, anyway, to bury Cassie any deeper than she already is buried?"

I wanted to tell him that Cassie had not remained in her grave and maybe never would. In fact, she was standing right beside him now, looking at me and smiling. But I said nothing. I looked away. It was as if he had driven a nail of ice into my soft and already quite wounded heart. Denying what Cassie had done, ignoring it, or searching for a new, more comforting interpretation diminished what had happened to me and to Mother. Daddy was still thinking more about Cassie than he was about us, and especially me now, even after all that had happened. But what was I to do about it? It made me sick even to talk about it, and I didn't want to get him any angrier at me than he was already. I turned back to him.

"When are you and Lucille getting married? Next week?" To me, it wasn't a foolish question. Look at how quickly he had gotten engaged to her.

His grouchy, old-crumpled-sock face softened into a new smile. "Oh, no, not next week. It's not going to be something simple and quick. We're planning a grand wedding that we will hold here on our grounds. She's already begun a good deal of the work. She won't do anything shoddy, that's for sure. She says protocol requires eight weeks normally for the invitations, but we're planning on taking the honeymoon suite on the Ecstasy Cruise the last week of August, so she's agreed to what she says is the absolute minimum of six weeks. The invitations will go out in two days."

"Two days? So, you already have the invitations and the wedding list made up?"

He smiled. "You'll find that Lucille is like me in that regard. When there's something to do, she goes at it body and soul until it is done and done well. She's a woman of action and will be quite an asset to the Heavenstone management. She basically ran her husband's four car dealerships and after he died worked a very lucrative deal for herself in their sale. She's not just the daughter of a bank president; she is as capable as a bank president. You'll learn a great deal from her. And I mean about everything in life."

He leaned forward.

"I won't say I was any real help to you during your own difficult period, Semantha. You needed the wisdom of a mature woman, and with your mother gone and no one close enough to us to trust, you had to sink or swim on your own. Oh, I got you all the medical and psychological attention I could and sent you to the best private high school I could find, but it would have been much better for you if there had been someone here who could have understood things from a female viewpoint. Well, now there is." He slapped his palms down on his knees and stood. "I don't know about you, but I'm very tired, and tomorrow's another big day. We're going through some major changes in the Lexington store."

He crossed to me and reached for my hand. I stood up, and he hugged me and kissed my cheek.

"Welcome home, Semantha. I hope your life is much, much better in the days, weeks, months, and years to come."

With that, he turned and walked out of the den. I stood there a moment and then sat.

"*Did you ever hear such a crock of crap about any woman?*" Cassie muttered. I shook my head. I could feel her standing beside me, looking toward the doorway. "*That man has changed. He would never sugarcoat anything. He wasn't afraid of the truth and would certainly never invent lies to make himself happy. Our ancestors must be squirming in their graves, their bones rattling. I know mine are. That woman must be a witch to have put such a spell on him so quickly. And what about that business with how organized she is? If she ordered the wedding invitations already, she shouldn't have been surprised by the engagement ring. The whole thing was an act.*"

Yes, I thought, Daddy had changed, and the engagement ring and the announcement did feel like an act put on for my benefit.

"*Of course it was. You certainly can't trust or like Lucille Bennet. She gave me a bad feeling, a cold feeling, the moment she appeared. I could see it in her eyes when she looked at you. She knows you're the only thing between her and Daddy, the only person who could in any way get him to deny her something.*

"*I bet if you investigated, you'd find out she somehow was responsible for her husband's heart attack. She's bad for you, Semantha, and she'll be very bad for Daddy. It's up to you to stop her. Stop her!*"

How was I supposed to do that? *I'm not you, Cassie,* I thought. *I'm not going to put sleeping powder into her drink.* I rose and started out.

"You heard him. Mother did it to herself. I was just being cooperative. You heard him!"

Yeah, right, I thought. *Now who's sugarcoating?*

I walked away quickly and hurried up the stairs, chased by Cassie's laughter. Finally, I was exhausted. It had been my high school graduation day, but I had suffered some very serious disappointments. Ethan was obviously gone from my life, and my father was becoming someone else's husband.

Welcome home, I thought. *Welcome back to the demons.*

I wasn't in my bed two minutes before I fell into a deep sleep. I tossed and turned with a mixture of images and memories, sometimes seeing Cassie on that stairway and sometimes seeing Lucille Bennet. I'm sure I groaned and moaned in my sleep, but I didn't wake until I heard a knock on my door. I rubbed my eyes to drive away the distorted visions and sat up. There was a second, louder knock.

"Yes?"

Lucille opened the door and stepped in, smiling. She was in a beautiful emerald-green silk robe and had her hair swept back. What, did she sleep with her makeup on? She continued across the room and pulled the curtains apart on the window to my left to let in the bright sunshine.

"What's going on?" I asked.

"Plenty," she said with a short laugh. "It's a beautiful day in the neighborhood. You don't want to miss a minute of it."

She opened the curtains on the second window and turned back to me.

"I told your father you would sleep late this morning. He was hoping we'd all have breakfast together, but he's gone off to work. He couldn't wait any longer. I promised him I would look in on you after another hour or so. How are you feeling after having such a big day?"

Confused and disappointed, I wanted to say, but I said, "I don't know. Exhausted, I suppose."

"Of course you are. I've asked Mrs. Dobson to prepare your breakfast and bring it up to you. She said she knew exactly what to make you, what was your favorite breakfast. We should spoil you for a little while. You deserve it. You had some very nice grades and must have worked hard, harder than most of those girls from what I saw of them, I'm sure."

"I didn't do anything special. I didn't win any awards."

"Nowadays, from what I can see of young people, graduating with decent grades or graduating at all is truly an accomplishment."

I shrugged. I wasn't eager to accept her compliments. Compliments from someone put you in debt to them. That was something Cassie had taught me, and it had stuck. I didn't want to be in debt to Lucille, not in any way, but she wasn't easy to refuse. She gazed at me a moment with that studied look, narrowing her eyes and then relaxing her lips, almost smiling.

"From what I understand, you didn't really have much of a social life at school, at least until the final weeks. You didn't belong to any club or team?"

"No."

"Didn't you do any sort of extracurricular activity at all? That's the best way to make friends."

"Nothing interested me enough."

She nodded and sat on my bed. "I know your problem, Semantha. You simply won't let yourself enjoy anything. You feel guilty when you do, correct? You think because your mother died so young and tragically and your sister . . . your sister did the things she did and died so harshly, it's wrong for you to be happy."

She reached for my hand. I wanted to pull it back, but it was as if Daddy were in the room, too, watching, studying my reactions.

"I know how difficult it must be for you to forget all that. Maybe it's impossible to really forget, but what I do with bad memories is pile on good memories, deliberately do things to please myself, to create happy times, and after a while, the weight of all that drives the bad memories farther and farther down until they don't come back at you so often, and even when they do, they're easy to push away. Doesn't that sound like a good plan?"

"I suppose, but I don't know if I can do that."

"Of course you can." She patted my hand. "Now, tell me about this young man who didn't show up for your graduation. I could see at lunch that you didn't want to say much about him. You gave such vague answers. But from what you had told your father, it sounded like you were developing a nice relationship."

Daddy had told her that? What hadn't he told her other than what he wanted me never to tell her about Cassie and Mother? He was already sharing my private life with her, even before he had become engaged. It angered and disappointed me, but what was I to do about it now?

"We were going out for a while, yes," I said.

"Well, tell me more details about him. You said his name was Ethan?"

"Ethan Hunter. I did tell you he's graduating from SUNY Albany, and he was interested in business."

"Is he enrolled in a graduate school? Which one?"

"No, he's not. He plans to spend this year actually in the working world. Why do you want to know so much about him, anyway?"

She smiled. "When it comes to men, I have good instincts. That's evident by the fact that I'm with your father. So, tell me, really. What sort of a young man is Ethan? I don't mean tell me about his grades. Think about your impressions of him as a person. Draw a picture of him for me so I can visualize him."

"It's no longer important."

"Humor me," she said. "Please."

"He's very intelligent, ambitious, and mature," I said quickly. I described his physical features and added that he had a very nice smile.

"And his family? You didn't say that much about them at lunch."

"I told you his father is an accountant. I don't know how rich they are," I said, now letting some Cassie bitterness into my voice.

"Oh, I'm not impressed by people with money,

Semantha. As you can imagine, because of my father's position in the bank, we have always known wealthy people. In my view, money often makes potentially interesting people boring."

"Really? Money does that? Why?" I asked, surprised.

"They get too comfortable, rarely do spontaneous, interesting things. All sorts of advisers manage their lives. I know people who don't even know their own net worth. They leave it up to some hired hand to decide if they can buy this or that, and often when they want something, they get talked out of it because it isn't as financially wise as something they don't want as much. For some people, money is freedom, but for most, as far as I can tell, it's another form of imprisonment.

"So, getting back to my question, I wouldn't judge your boyfriend one way or another based on his family's income. Money doesn't make your character, but your character can help you make money. That is, if you're sincere and trustworthy. Is your boyfriend sincere and trustworthy?"

"I guess he's not really my boyfriend," I said. "I mean, we never said we wouldn't see anyone else, and no promises were made for the future."

"And most of all, he didn't show up for your graduation, which I know was very upsetting for you," she added, nodding in sympathy. "Do you have any idea why not? He hasn't called since?"

I had an idea, but I wouldn't tell her. That was for sure. I had the feeling, though, that she saw it in my face.

"No, he hasn't called."

"Well, whatever. I just wanted to assure you that one disappointment in love has nothing to do with what might come later and also to assure you, without even knowing any more, that it's not something for which you should blame yourself, no matter what. My goodness, look at you. You're a bright, beautiful, healthy young lady from a historic family that is the envy of everyone."

She patted my hand again and stood.

"The worst thing to do is wallow in disappointment, and I have just the solution to prevent that."

"What?"

"I'd like it very much, Semantha, if you would participate wholeheartedly in your father's and my wedding plans. I have a great deal to arrange—music, menu, flowers, dresses for the bridesmaids, the first of whom I hope you'll be. I'd like your opinion about it all, so I'd like you to accompany me to the various venues. Starting today."

"Today? What about your mother?" I asked.

"What about her?"

"Won't she be participating?"

"My mother passed away nearly five years ago."

"Oh."

"And I have no sisters. So, you see, it's just the two of us women now. I really do hope we can become close, and there's no better opportunity for us to do so than planning my wedding, don't you agree?" she asked with a wide, warm smile.

"Yes," I said.

"Good."

Mrs. Dobson came in with my breakfast tray.

"I could have gone down for breakfast," I said, more for Mrs. Dobson than for Lucille.

"I told you we're spoiling you a little. Let us do it," Lucille said. "You agree, don't you, Mrs. Dobson?"

"Miss Semantha's not an easy young lady to spoil, ma'am. She's always thinking of others," she replied without looking at her. She set the tray on my bed table and moved it over to me.

"Yes, well, that's the sort of person we want to spoil, then," Lucille insisted. "Why don't we plan on leaving in two hours?" she told me. "I have an appointment at my dressmaker's to confirm my gown and review the gowns for the bridesmaids. There will be three others besides you. One of my best friends from college, in fact, is flying in from Monaco. Claire Dubonnet. She works for the prince."

I saw how Mrs. Dobson was studying me for my reaction.

"Can I count on you, then?" Lucille pursued when I didn't respond.

"Yes," I said.

"Excellent. And as you can now see, it's a beautiful day, a wonderful day for a new beginning for us both, Semantha. Once again, welcome home," she said, and walked out.

"I made those scrambled eggs just like you like them, Miss Semantha, with the cheese."

"Thank you, Mrs. Dobson. Did you know my father was intending to marry Mrs. Bennet?"

"The birds were chattering about it, yes," she said.

"Were they happy or sad?"

She just looked at me and started out, pausing at the door. "Call me if you need anything else, Miss Semantha."

I started on my breakfast.

"*Why were you so nice to her?*" Cassie asked.

"I have no choice. I don't want to upset Daddy. Maybe . . . maybe she isn't that bad. She sounded like she was really interested in me, and I liked what she said about rich people."

"*You always have been stupid when it comes to seeing people for who and what they are,*" Cassie muttered. "*Whether it was those idiots in public school or Ellie or Ethan. Don't you see? She's using Daddy's happiness as her shield and her armor. As soon as they're married, she'll set out to destroy you.*"

"No," I said.

"*Yes,*" she insisted.

"No!" I screamed, loudly enough to blow her out of my mind. I thought my cry would bring someone to my room, but apparently no one had heard me. I was no longer hungry but continued to eat what I could so Mrs. Dobson wouldn't wonder why I had lost my appetite.

After all, the last thing I wanted anyone to know was how much Cassie spoke to me from beyond the grave.

And how much that upset me.

Wedding Plans

LUCILLE HAD DADDY's limousine and driver at her disposal. When we got in, she handed me a catalogue of wedding cakes.

"I'd like your opinion on them," she said. "It has to be a rather big cake. We've decided to pare down the guest list to eighteen hundred. Of course, we could invite many more, but we want these eighteen hundred to feel special on our special day."

"Eighteen hundred people?"

"Yes," she said, laughing. "I suppose that sounds rather large, but this is a huge property, and your father and my father have made so many important acquaintances over the years, it would be difficult to invite fewer. Notice I said acquaintances, not friends," she added. "That's something I want you to digest for a moment, the difference between a friend and an acquaintance."

Although she was acting like a teacher, I didn't feel she was being condescending.

"A real friend," she continued, "is even more important than a relative. Relatives are too often envious of each other and easily persuaded to believe that this one or that one was handed everything on a silver platter, especially siblings who are always feeling their parents favored the others."

That was Ellie, I thought, and when it came to Daddy and Cassie, I had certainly used to believe that. Lucille was right. Maybe I should listen to some of what she said.

"Now, a real friend, who is so rare, is someone who is genuinely, sincerely happy for you when good fortune occurs. She or he doesn't resent it or feel more envy than happiness. A real friend is selfless when it comes to doing things for you, especially at your time of need, and if you're a good friend, you'll do the same for him or her. Have you any real friends, Semantha?"

"Not like that," I admitted.

"Precisely. I have only three, maybe four, I'd consider real friends out of all of the acquaintances I've made over the years, and as you can see, that's a lot. With real friends, time and distance don't matter. We never stop being true to each other. I hope someday you'll have some real friends, too, even if it's no more than I have.

"Of course," she continued, "no one can be more of a friend to you than your husband, as you are to him. Your father and I became real friends, in fact, before we became lovers. Did you feel this was possible eventually with this boy you were seeing, this Ethan?"

"I don't know," I said. "We really didn't see each other that long, Lucille."

"Still, you might reserve your judgment about

him until you find out what his reason was for not attending your graduation and meeting us. We'll see."

Why was this so important to her?

"How?"

"Time will tell," she said.

"What if I never see or hear from him again?"

"Well . . . then time told, didn't it?" she said with a grin. "Now, look at those designs for wedding cakes. I'm anxious to see what strikes your fancy."

I gazed at the book. There were multitiered cakes with all sorts of flower decorations. The traditional cakes were round, but there were also hexagon- and octagon-shaped cakes. The variety was dazzling. I had no idea how any bride would go about choosing, until I saw a design that resembled the cake in Mother and Daddy's wedding photographs. It was shaped like a richly wrapped present with the silhouettes of the bride and groom airbrushed.

"You like that one?" she asked, seeing me spend so much time gazing at it.

"Don't dare recommend the cake that our parents had at their wedding," Cassie warned.

I shrugged and turned the page.

There was a huge hexagonal cake with a jade topper of an angel. At the bottom of the page was an estimate of one hundred dollars per serving. I started to turn the page.

"That's my favorite," she said.

I quickly did the multiplication.

"That's one hundred eighty thousand dollars for just the cake," I said.

She laughed. "Well, one thing I never expected

to hear from you was a comment on the cost of anything. Bravo. That shows you do have a bit of a head for business, but your father and I intend to be married only this one time more, Semantha. It's a wedding for a lifetime," she said. She pointed to the cake. "What I was thinking of doing is having the Heavenstone Store emblem on top of this cake in jade like that or maybe silver. The Heavenstone Stores are so much of who your father is, and I will be so much of who he is now, too. When you marry someone, you marry all of him, all that is important to him. What do you think?" she asked, nodding at the cake. "Should I have that one made for us?"

"I guess that would be nice."

"Oh, it will be more than just nice. It'll be the pièce de résistance, Semantha. Can't you just imagine the guests circling and admiring it, taking pictures?" She laughed. "It will be the most expensive dessert most of them have ever had. This will be a wedding no one will forget. We're having a twenty-six-piece orchestra. Your father is having a two-thousand-square-foot dance floor built, with multicolored lighting strung above it. We'll have tents with tables all decorated according to the theme of love and union, and we're going to provide the guests with a memento they will cherish and not just put into some box to forget. I have lots of ideas for that. We'll be going to the wedding planners after the dress designer to work on that and see his suggestions for the menu. Of course, we've hired not just a wedding photographer but also a professional movie director to film the entire event.

"Regarding the menu, here's what I was think-ing." She turned fully around to me. I smiled to myself. She was like a little girl turned loose in a toy store and told not to worry about any costs.

"There'll be caviar and champagne, of course, a variety of at least three special soups, lobster in cream sauce with chopped truffles, as well as beef and pork filets and chartreuse of pheasant. Of course, there'll be sherbet to cleanse the palate between courses, a wide variety of red and white wines, any possible liquor, and very expensive port for after din-ner. I'm getting advice about the wine from a famous French sommelier. I think it's important to provide a good variety at a wedding like this, especially with such a big guest list, don't you?"

I nodded, but I saw she wanted a more enthusi-astic reaction.

"Isn't this exciting?"

"Yes," I said, widening my eyes. "It's very excit-ing, Lucille. I can't imagine any wedding grander, except maybe the wedding of a king or a queen."

She laughed at my obvious attempt to match her enthusiasm.

"I'm sorry. I'm overwhelming you with my pas-sion. You must feel like you're under a waterfall or being swept along in a great tidal wave."

"Yes, I do," I said, trying not to sound unhappy about it, but the more she talked about how she and Daddy were going to become one, the more left out I felt.

"Just try to ignore me when I get this car-ried away." She squeezed my hand. And then she exclaimed, "Oh, it's so wonderful to have you with me for all of this!"

She leaned over and hugged me, and I thought, *Shut up, Cassie. None of your sarcasm and meanness.* I'd love to be as happy as Lucille. Would I ever be? Maybe sharing Daddy and Lucille's joy was as close as I would ever come, and if Lucille was willing to let me share, then maybe she wasn't as bad as I had first thought.

Despite my fears about my losing interest and being dragged about, there was little or no time to be bored when I was with Lucille. We spent hours at the dress designer's showroom. She had me try on the maid of honor gown immediately and told the tailor to make mine fit absolutely perfectly. I thought none of his suggested alterations would ever satisfy her. This was too tight; that was too loose. Why was she spending so much time on me? She answered that for me by telling me that any imperfection or mistake would reflect on her. "But," she added, "I want this to be just as perfect for you as well. You'll be in so many wedding photographs, memories forever."

Finally, after one more adjustment, she gave him her approval. After that, we went to lunch at a French restaurant to explore some other possible choices for the wedding menu. She did most of the talking, describing all of the places she had been in the world, especially the famous restaurants in London and Paris and Rome, and some of the sumptuous meals she had experienced. I couldn't imagine anyone having a more glamorous life, and most of that even before she was my age. Why had she been so blessed?

She saw the envy in my face, and I immediately felt guilty for having a face that Cassie said was so easy to read that it should be in a library.

"Don't be discouraged," Lucille said, reaching for my hand. "You'll do all these things someday, too, Semantha. I know you will. I'll make sure you will," she added, pressing her lips together and nodding.

"What does she mean by that?" Cassie whispered. *"Make sure? Whose life is this, anyway?"*

I didn't ask. As soon as we were finished with lunch, Lucille marched us down the street to her beauty salon to get her hairdresser to study me and come up with a more attractive style. She ran through some pictures and then pointed to one and asked what I thought. It surprised me at first, because I would have thought it was more daring, sexier, than what she would like. When I agreed, she scheduled my appointment.

"Don't mess this up," she warned him. "What's done to her is done to me."

He looked sufficiently terrified.

Moments later, we were rushing to the wedding planner's office to review suggestions for the menu and wedding mementos. She settled on Waterford flutes, which would be almost as expensive as the wedding cake. My mind was reeling with the costs, despite what she had said about this being a one-and-only second wedding for both of them. She wanted to think more about the menu, so she didn't agree to as much as a single hors d'oeuvre.

After that, she surprised me by taking me to her favorite jeweler, where she had a graduation present waiting for me. I was speechless when the saleswoman brought it out to show me. She unwrapped the wax paper and placed it on the counter. All I could do was stare for a moment. My throat closed up, and my eyes burned with tears.

Lucille had obviously gotten Daddy to find her one of my better baby pictures with Mother holding me. She'd had it put in a solid gold oval frame that was connected to a solid gold base with the words *A mother's love can never end* inscribed on it.

"Is it all right?" she asked me when I didn't respond.

"Oh, yes, thank you, Lucille."

"Good."

When I turned to her, the tears began streaming down my cheeks.

"Oh, dear," she said to the saleswoman. Then she hugged me and held me and whispered, "She's passed her love on to me to give to you, and that is exactly what I intend to do. It's a big responsibility, but I accept it openly and willingly forever and ever."

I said nothing. Cassie was groaning and moaning in the back of my head, but I kept her from invading my thoughts. I wasn't often strong enough these days to keep her words boxed up. I held on to Lucille, and then I let go and waited off to the side while the saleswoman put my gift in its box. I held it in my arms and followed Lucille back to the limousine.

"Thanks for putting up with me today," she said as we started back to the Heavenstone mansion. "I'm sure you would have had more fun doing other things."

"Oh, no. It was fun, Lucille."

"Was it? I was so afraid you would be bored. Good." She smiled and then giggled as if she were my age before squeezing my hand. "Won't your father be surprised at all the decisions we made today?"

We? I thought. She was really including me.

As soon as we arrived, I ran up to my room and found an ideal place for my graduation gift. It would sit on the table beside my bed so I could see it as soon as I woke up every morning. I sat on my bed and stared at it. I was ashamed at how little I had thought about Mother these past months. Memories about her frightened me because I feared they would make me too sad to go on, but that was selfish of me, I now thought. My mother didn't deserve to be forgotten. I was sure she had loved me as much as any mother could love a daughter. It was a sin to push her away just to keep myself from being upset. *Face our demons here,* I chanted to myself. *Don't let them win.* Wasn't that what Daddy told me? The most difficult battle would be with Cassie. Even in her grave, she was stronger than I was, and I feared she always would be.

There was a knock at my door.

"Yes?"

Mrs. Dobson came in with a look of surprise on her face.

"You ran into the house and upstairs to your room so fast I couldn't even call to you," she said. "Is everything all right? Did you enjoy your day with Mrs. Bennet?"

"Yes, I'm fine. I'm sorry I frightened you. What is it, Mrs. Dobson?"

"This came for you," she said, and handed me a

small, gift-wrapped box. A card was taped to it. She started to turn away.

"Oh, no, stay. Let's see what it is," I said. I opened the card. It was a graduation card with *Good luck, Guess who?* written in it. Ordinarily, I would have let my thoughts flow quickly to Ethan, but I knew this was the way Uncle Perry always signed his birthday and holiday cards to us. Cassie used to smirk and say he was ashamed of his own name or something.

I opened the gift and took out a woman's Rolex watch.

"Oh, how beautiful," Mrs. Dobson said.

"Look," I said, showing her. "It's inscribed with the date of my high school graduation."

Here, Uncle Perry had written his name. Despite what she had thought of him, I was sure Cassie would be green with envy. He had never given her anything half as beautiful or half as expensive.

"It's a real gem of a watch, Miss Semantha." Mrs. Dobson's eyes drifted. "That's your mother with you there, isn't it?" she asked, nodding at my graduation present from Lucille.

"Yes."

"What a beautiful frame." She read the inscription. "Very nice, Miss Semantha. Your father get you this?"

"No, Lucille bought it for me. She gave it to me today."

"Really? Lucille," she muttered.

She looked at the frame and photograph more closely, as if she was more surprised than I had been. Maybe she had misjudged her, too, I thought.

Now that I was in my room, I had been waiting to hear Cassie complain, but there was only silence. In fact, I was struck by how little of Cassie's voice I had heard in my mind the whole day. Maybe that wasn't simply my keeping her still. Perhaps Lucille had overwhelmed her as much as she had overwhelmed me.

Mrs. Dobson nodded. "Well, it's very pretty, Miss Semantha. And that's a lovely watch. Both meaningful gifts." She smiled and left.

I went to shower and dress for dinner, feeling far happier than I had yesterday.

Daddy and Lucille were already at the dining-room table when I arrived. I had taken my time with my hair and makeup, admittedly because of Lucille's influence and comments during the day.

"Well, who's this beautiful woman?" Daddy asked. "I don't recognize her."

"You look lovely, Semantha," Lucille said. As soon as I sat, she began to describe our day. He kept looking at me to see if I agreed and was just as enthusiastic as she was. I saw how much pleasure it brought to him. He didn't mind any of the costs and seemed to approve of every decision.

"My two girls," he declared, looking from me to Lucille. "You're getting me more excited about a wedding than I ever thought possible."

"As far as that goes, Teddy," Lucille said, "I have a surprise for you to add to the excitement."

"More?" He raised his arms. "I don't know if I can stand it. What?"

"The governor's office called. He and his wife will definitely attend."

"Well, I'll be. What do you say to that, Semantha?"

"He should attend, Daddy. You bring a lot of tax money into the state."

"What? Hear that, Lucille? Is she a Heavenstone after all or not?"

"She's definitely a Heavenstone," Lucille said, looking at me and smiling.

If I hadn't had my hands on the table, I think I might have risen and floated with new pride, but when I looked across the table at where Cassie used to sit, I saw her looking as angry as I had ever seen her.

She wasn't angry at my increasing friendship with Lucille or my embrace of their wedding. She was angry that I was finally beginning to replace her.

"You'll be sorry," she mouthed, and disappeared.

"What's that on your wrist?" Daddy asked, finally noticing the Rolex.

"A graduation present from Uncle Perry."

"Really? That sneak. He wasn't supposed to beat me to the punch."

We heard the doorbell.

"Well, now, here's the punch," Daddy said. "Mrs. Dobson," he called. "We'll get the door. Hold back serving for a little while," he told her when she appeared. She nodded as though she already knew.

"What is it?"

"Just follow me," he said. I looked at Lucille, but her face betrayed no knowledge. In fact, she looked more surprised than I was. He and she rose, and I went with them to the front door, now more curious and excited. A young man waited with a large manila envelope.

"All the paperwork is in here, Mr. Heavenstone, and the keys, of course."

"Thank you, George."

I stood back, waiting nervously. Before Lucille, Daddy rarely pulled off surprises. He had always lectured about the importance of a foundation, preparation, for anything.

"Well, come on, Semantha," Daddy said. "Your graduation gift is impatient."

I stepped up to the doorway and looked out at a red Aston Martin convertible with a huge yellow ribbon tied around it. Daddy reached into the manila envelope and handed me a set of keys.

"Congratulations," he said.

"My God, Teddy, that's almost a two-hundred-thousand-dollar automobile!" Lucille said.

I turned to her, now really surprised that she hadn't known what he was giving me and that she was so overwhelmed, perhaps even more than I was, because I didn't know that much about cars.

"What of it? She's the only Heavenstone left to spoil," Daddy told her. He looked intently at me. "And besides, we're very proud of her accomplishments, considering what she has been through."

"Of course we are," Lucille said quickly, and hugged me. "Good luck with it, Semantha. You're certainly going to turn heads when you're driving that."

We all went down the steps to look more closely at the car. Daddy undid the ribbon and had Lucille and me sit in it so he could take a quick digital photo.

"I hope you understand that this is more than just any car. It's a work of art, Semantha," Lucille

said, running her hand over the fine leather. There
was a note of real envy, even anger, in her voice, but
then she quickly smiled and added, "I'm sure you
do. You're far from too spoiled to appreciate nice
things."

"Now that you said how much it cost, I think
I'm going to be afraid to drive it. It will attract lots of
attention."

"So what?" She narrowed her eyes. "Never,
never let anyone make you feel guilty for having expensive and beautiful things, Semantha. Believe me, if
they could, they'd have them, too. Rich people who
feel that way diminish not only their own meaning
and identity but the hard work and effort their fathers and mothers have put in to get them to where
they are in the world. I'm with those who say if you
have it, flaunt it." She laughed. "Although, I can
tell you, I didn't learn that from my father. After all,
he's a banker, and bankers hoard money rather than
spend it."

"What are you two gabbing about?" Daddy
cried. "I'm starving. Let's eat. There's time enough
for you girls to ride around and show off."

"Oh, we know. There'll always be time enough
for that, Teddy," Lucille said, winking at me.

We got out. I looked back at my car and then
down at my watch and thought, *Lucille is right. I
won't be ashamed of what I have or who I am.* I was
sure I could do that and still respect people who had
far less. At least, I hoped I could.

We returned to the dining room and the conversation about their wedding. Even so, I could

see Daddy's surprise graduation gift seemed to have taken some of the wind out of Lucille's sails. I couldn't help but feel a little sorry for her, sorry I had taken away the spotlight. I think he realized it, too, because as soon as we finished with our entrée, Daddy said, "I hear Lucille gave you your graduation gift today as well, Semantha."

"Oh, yes, Daddy. You must come up to my room to see it."

"That I will," he said. "Mrs. Dobson, we'll have coffee and dessert in the den in ten minutes," he told her, and rose. "Lucille?"

"Why don't you two go up and look at it, Teddy. I'll meet you in the den. I want to check on something in the office," she said. "I'm waiting for a fax from Senator Brice's office. His secretary told me she was confident he would attend our wedding, but I want to see it in writing."

Daddy nodded.

"She's not checking on anything," he whispered to me as we started for the stairway. "We already heard from Senator Brice. See how sensitive and considerate she can be, Semantha? That was just an excuse. She wants us to have some father-daughter privacy. You're going to come to appreciate Lucille as much as I do. I'm confident of it."

I wondered if he could hear Cassie's scream as clearly as I could. It seemed to echo down the hallways and bounce like a ping-pong ball against every door and window.

When we stepped into my bedroom and he saw the photograph in the frame, he stood looking at it so long in silence I thought I would burst into tears before he said a word.

"It's a beautiful frame, perfect," he said softly. "Your mother loved you very much, both of you. Back then, I couldn't imagine life without her. It seemed our love for each other had built a divine wall of protection around us."

He took a deep breath, drinking in air like someone who had just come up from being underwater. Daddy wasn't one to show his emotions so easily, especially with me. He could be angry, yes, but a face of sorrow wasn't something he permitted himself often. He nodded and smiled, quickly regaining hold of himself. I could almost see him seize his emotions around their necks and set them down.

"I think it's a terrific sign of self-confidence for Lucille to think of such a gift for you. She believes, as do I, that you will come to accept her as a close friend, if not a mother. You did a nice thing today shopping with her. She told me when we first met that she regretted being an only child and not having an older or younger sister. I guess you'll be more like a younger sister to her than a stepdaughter, don't you think? At least, I hope you'll be."

He turned to me and realized I had been staring at him the whole time he spoke. Then, without further comment, he put his arm around me and held me close. Together, we cried in silence. We finally cried together, both of us, out of happiness and sorrow. Lucille had done this. She had brought Daddy and me together the way I had hoped we would be.

"Come on. Let's see what Mrs. Dobson has for

dessert. She told me she was doing something special for your first dinner home after your graduation."

She had done something special. She had made her famous English white cake with the words *Congratulations, Miss Semantha* in chocolate. Daddy led our applause. I could see how much pleasing him meant to Mrs. Dobson. Lucille had probably been sucking up most of his compliments these days, with sparingly few going to her.

"This is my own mum's recipe," she said proudly. "We had it only on very special occasions."

I thanked her and hugged her, which embarrassed her, so she fled.

Later, the three of us sat in the den and talked. Actually, Lucille did most of the talking, mainly continuing the discussion about their wedding and the high-profile guests they were expecting. Every once in a while, she would turn to me to support her opinion of something we had seen or ordered for the wedding. Daddy looked happier than I could ever remember. Normally, that would have upset me. Normally, it would have seemed sinful for him to be happier than when he was with Mother, but tonight I could deny him nothing.

How different I felt when I went to sleep this time. Something Lucille had advised appeared true. She had said that the way she handled bad memories was to pile on good memories, deliberately do things to please herself, to create happy times, and after a while, the weight of all of that drives the bad memories farther and farther down until they don't come back so often, and even when they do, they're easy to push away.

Today was certainly proof of that. I hadn't thought much about Ethan or Ellie or any of my unhappy experiences at school. I wondered if I could do it tomorrow and the day after as well. I wanted to. For one thing, Cassie still had little or nothing to say. She was mute in her grave, and my mind danced with all sorts of wonderful and delicious new possibilities. Maybe I would go to work with Uncle Perry. Maybe I would find someone better than Ethan. Maybe we would be a family again.

Like a dying ember in a fireplace, the image of Cassie's angry face dwindled and went dark. I could sleep, and for once I would not be afraid of my dreams. The Heavenstone house sighed with relief. There were no moans and groans of age in the pipes, floors, ceilings, and walls. Downstairs, our ancestors opened their eyes again. Maybe Daddy was right. We were too powerful a family. Fate would pause at our gates with her bag full of trouble and disaster, look up our driveway, and quickly move on to the homes of weaker and more vulnerable families.

I imagined a sign on the lawn: BEWARE OF THE HEAVENSTONES.

I smiled to myself and fell asleep, no longer afraid of the morning to come.

But before morning, I had a terrible nightmare. In it, Lucille was shoveling dirt into Cassie's grave, covering her coffin.

And Cassie was screaming my name, pleading with me to stop Lucille.

I let her keep shoveling.

8

Beware of the Heavenstones

THIS TIME, I was grateful for the morning sunlight rushing through the opened curtains to wash the nightmare out of my head. It popped like a bubble, and I rose quickly to shower and dress to go down to breakfast. Uncle Perry had left a message that he was coming to have lunch with me. I was surprised he would make the trip during the workweek, but I knew he was very concerned about me and my adjusting to Daddy's marriage to Lucille.

During the dark period after Cassie's death, when Daddy was so withdrawn and sullen, it was Uncle Perry who had spent hours talking with me, taking me for rides, eating dinner with me, trying to help me recover from what anyone would have thought was an impossible series of tragedies. He had always been a candle in the darkness for me.

Although I could never put it into the proper words the way Cassie could, I had always seen Uncle Perry as the softer, kinder side of the Heavenstone family. It wasn't that I thought Daddy an unkind man, but he was more of what Cassie liked to call *man tough*. She said Daddy had inherited far more of the pioneer spirit of rugged individualism than Uncle Perry had. She didn't imply that it was because Uncle Perry was gay. She said that had nothing to do with it. There were many strong and successful and even ruthless businessmen who were gay. No, she said, it was simply that the independent, courageous, and determined spirit that had made our ancestors so successful had seeped into Daddy's genes more easily than into Uncle Perry's. Uncle Perry, she said, was more his mother's child than his father's. Although she never quite came out and told me so, she surely believed that was true for me as well. She had always thought she was more of a Heavenstone than I was, and that this was why Daddy would never love me as much as he loved her.

"However, Uncle Perry loves you more than he loves me," she had told me, "but believe me, Semantha, I can live with it. I couldn't care less if he respected me or liked me. He's all yours."

Uncle Perry realized that, too. I knew he had never been very comfortable in Cassie's presence and had welcomed spending as much time with me, without her, as possible. He never even mentioned her name now. It was on the tip of my tongue to tell him I wasn't as able to forget and avoid any references to Cassie as he was. I wondered what he would think if I told him she was still there, still inside my head—I still heard her. He might want me to go back to regular psychiatric therapy. I certainly didn't want that, not now. So I decided against even suggesting anything about Cassie.

I was surprised to learn that both Daddy and

Lucille had left the house before I went downstairs. Mrs. Dobson said they rushed out "as if the house was on fire." She didn't know why, either, but she did say they appeared more excited than frightened about anything. I could see she was more curious than usual, which made me more curious, but I told her I didn't have a clue.

For the first time since I had returned from school, I was alone at home. Mrs. Dobson and Doris had their work, and besides, neither really ever spent time socializing with me. Of course, I had been home alone often while I had attended Collier and returned for the holidays. Daddy rarely took a day off besides Sundays, and often, since Mother's death, he didn't even do that. Most of those times, I'd had schoolwork to do. With what I could do on my computer and in our own wonderful library, I hadn't had to leave the house.

Now, however, all that schoolwork was behind me, and I had little to occupy my thoughts. Any future plans and ambitions remained vague. I really had little to look forward to and little to do, which was why I was now so eager to participate in Daddy and Lucille's wedding. Of course, that stirred up dreams and fantasies about my own marriage and wedding ceremony. I didn't want it to be as grand and as elaborate as Daddy and Lucille's. I imagined a wedding in a small chapel followed by a family banquet and then a wonderful honeymoon. All I needed was a groom, someone to fall in love with me, someone with whom I could fall in love, but I didn't even have a date with anyone. None of the boys who once knew me when

I was in public school ever called or wrote e-mails. I was sure for them it was as if I never had existed.

The thought depressed me, but for the moment, at least, I could look forward to Uncle Perry's visit. I told Mrs. Dobson that he was coming for lunch and asked her to prepare her chicken salad. Uncle Perry really enjoyed it the way she made it with apples and pears. I knew she liked him very much. She referred to him as "a refined gentleman," someone who reminded her of her last employer in London. She said she would set up the table on our back veranda and would put out flowers and dress it up "like a Sunday high tea."

While I waited for him to arrive, I went on a tour of our home. I was curious to see what, if any, changes Lucille had already accomplished or begun. The door to the room that had been going to be little Asa's nursery was still locked. I was happy to see that. And aside from the way Lucille had set up her vanity table in the master suite, nothing there had been changed. I went into the room and, feeling a little like a voyeur perhaps, opened her closet and looked at her fine clothes and shoes. There was already far more than what Mother had had in it. There was a different scent in the room, too, although the room itself was still the way Cassie had rearranged and redecorated it.

I recalled how she had done it without Daddy's permission, planning and scheming with the decorator. Even I hadn't known what she was up to until the day she'd had it all done. I'll never forget the look of surprise and shock on Daddy's face when he entered the room that day. It had driven home that Mother was gone. I knew that was why Cassie had done it. She never had trouble facing reality and had expected the same of everyone else, especially Daddy.

I had told her that I thought it was cruel and I could never do such a thing. She had said that was why she was more of a Heavenstone than I was. She could do the hard, necessary things without emotions dragging her down.

"You don't lower yourself and your beliefs to fit the inferior ones. You force them to rise to your standards, whether it's painful for them or not. That's what Heavenstones do," she had lectured.

I thought to myself, if she was right, I wanted to change my name.

I hated the idea that Mother was completely erased from existence. Even the traces of her in her own bedroom were gone. Cassie had put away their wedding photos and photos of us with Mother as well. Daddy had put them back, at least, but I suddenly realized as I gazed around now that they were gone again. That was obviously because of Lucille.

"*Of course it is,*" Cassie whispered, seeing her opportunity to open the floodgates in my head again. "*You fool. She gave you that photograph to seduce you. It's only the beginning. By the time she's through, you'll think you were always motherless.*"

I put my hands over my ears and rushed out. After I calmed down, I continued my exploring. Everything was the same in all of the guest bedrooms, and I already knew that nothing had been altered in the rooms below. As far as I could tell, not a thing downstairs had been moved, not even an ashtray in the den. Lucille must really respect and admire Daddy and the Heavenstone family, I thought. It was either that, or she was afraid to challenge anything. Somehow, however, I couldn't believe Lucille was the sort of person who would put up with anything she didn't like. I guess she and Daddy were really a good fit after all, I concluded.

"Despite what you think," I muttered at a shadowy corner in which I could see Cassie hovering like a ghost made of cobwebs.

Uncle Perry apparently had arrived at a similar conclusion. After I thanked him for my watch, all he talked about again at lunch was how changed for the better my father was since he had met Lucille. I had to agree.

"Sometimes he looks younger to me."

"Exactly," Uncle Perry said. "Sorrow ages you."

Then he told me things about my father that he had never told me.

"There were times after your mother's death when I thought he might really take his own life, Sam. I'd find him sitting and staring out the window in his office with a pile of work left on his desk. Most of the time, he didn't even hear me enter, and when he realized I was there and turned to me, I saw how vacant his eyes had become. He looked like a shell of the man he had been. Almost nothing interested or excited him. He was simply going through the motions.

"And then that day, that fateful day when Cassie fell down the stairs, he put on a good performance for everyone, including you, but he was truly like

someone running on fumes. I was doing things at the
company that I had never had to do before. Employees were coming to me for answers and instructions
about things that were, frankly, quite unfamiliar to
me, but because he hadn't given them answers and
there were deadlines, I had to become a quick learner.
Somehow, I made the right decisions, and we sur-
vived, but after you went off to your private school,
he grew so depressed I was even more convinced that
he was seriously contemplating suicide."

"After I left?"

"Yes. Alone in this big house, with all of the happier memories echoing and fading, I'm sure it looked
to him as though everything was gone, his whole
family gone. You can't even begin to imagine how he
would brag and boast about the three of you before
all this tragedy came raining down upon him."

"Mostly Cassie, I'm sure," I said.

Uncle Perry didn't deny it. He shrugged and
drank his lemonade. "He thought she was a good
influence on both you and your mother. 'They'll both
be happier and better because of Cassie,' he would
say if I uttered even the smallest criticism or concern
about her. To think that he had to face the reality of
that not being true but in fact its being the exact opposite," Uncle Perry said, shaking his head. "It really
destroyed his self-confidence. That was when he was
afraid to make the smallest, most insignificant decisions, especially about personnel. And then . . ."

"What 'and then'?"

"And then he met and began seeing Lucille Bennet more and more. I swear," Uncle Perry continued

with his young boy's smile, "whenever he talked about her, he sounded like some lovesick teenager. I was actually embarrassed for him at times, especially when he gushed with compliments about her, making her seem like some sort of gift from the gods. Here was my older, wiser, stern, and correct brother behaving like a schoolboy with a crush, thinking and doing the silliest of things, like putting on two different socks or saying good morning to the same person three times. The employees didn't know what to make of it, and many were worried he was losing his mind, until, of course, the word spread that he was in love. That seemed to be the excuse they'd accept for anything, and I saw, Sam, that they actually began liking him because of it."

"What do you mean? Why would they begin liking him? Didn't they always like him?"

He shook his head.

"Most of our employees respected your father, but they all feared him. I would never have said they liked him, but I can say it now."

"Even when Mother was alive?"

"Maybe in the early days, but my brother can be and was quite a stuffed shirt. He had to live up to that image of what he believed a Heavenstone should be. He hardly ever smiled or made small talk with an employee. He quickly began to resemble some of the men in those portraits on the walls in there. I'm glad your mother resisted sitting for one of those portrait painters. Anyway, as you admit, you see a big difference in him now, too."

"Yes, I do."

"Well, then, I guess we should both count our blessings and be happy that Lucille Bennet's come into his life, which means our lives, too, eh?"

"I guess, Uncle Perry."

He tilted his head a bit and smiled. "You don't sound as convinced as I am."

"I am," I said. "It's a little harder for me because . . ."

He nodded. "Once you fully accept her, you feel you've betrayed the memory of your mother?"

"Exactly." I smiled. I'd never deny that Cassie had been right about me. I was so easy to read I really should have a library card for my face.

"It's *Hamlet,* only reversed," Uncle Perry said. "Right at the start, we learn he felt that way about his father and about accepting his uncle as a replacement."

"I know. I love that play."

"Well, then," Uncle Perry said, leaning toward me, "beware of ghosts, Sam."

"Mother doesn't haunt me like that, Uncle Perry. She would never be the one to take away any of Daddy's happiness."

He studied me a moment, and then, again leaning toward me, said, "But Cassie haunts you?"

I was shocked. I had debated with myself about telling him. How did he know? I was sure I hadn't given him any reason to think so. Was she haunting him as well?

"I can't help thinking about what she would think, Uncle Perry. She never hesitated to give me her opinion about anything."

He waved it away. "Fight it, or don't care, Sam. I don't like speaking ill of the dead, but I never had trouble believing what you told us Cassie had done. Cassie was an evil child, no matter what your father thought. I even saw that when she was no more than four, saw how she clung to your father but not your mother. I could see how she recoiled when she touched her. Why, she wouldn't even let her brush her hair."

I didn't speak. I had no doubt Cassie was listening. He saw how I gazed about the veranda, and he raised his eyebrows.

"You're worried someone will overhear me? Don't worry. I don't say these things to your father. I'll stop talking about her. I can see it makes you uncomfortable. All right." He changed his tone and folded his hands on the table. "Let's talk about you instead. Have you given any thought to working with me? You've got that fabulous new car now. You can drive yourself, make your own hours, and get as involved as you wish. What do you say?"

"What would I do, actually?"

"Lots of things, Semantha. We're constantly evaluating the new clothing lines, and you know how much I rely on your opinion about that, especially for the teenage market, and then there is the advertising, dealing with the magazines, newspapers, television, and radio. We're also working with an Internet firm to dress up our Web site and start linking to our products everywhere. There's a lot for you to do. It's important we keep the younger perspective on everything."

"Okay, Uncle Perry. I'll really think about it."

"Maybe you can start after the wedding. They'll be off on their honeymoon, and it will be pretty lonely and quiet around here."

"Yes, that sounds like a possibility," I told him.

"Mission accomplished, then," he said, clapping his hands.

"What mission? So, that's why you wanted to have lunch with me, isn't it?" I asked, teasing him with narrow, suspicious eyes.

"Hey, I'm still a little bit of a Heavenstone, shrewd and conniving. But for good things."

I laughed. No matter what, I would always have Uncle Perry there for me whenever I got too low or simply needed a shot of energy and hope. There weren't many occasions when he wasn't a bright light. Sometimes, I thought, even Cassie had to admit it to herself, if not to me.

He looked at his watch. "I've got to get back," he said, rising. "There are still a few things I want to do today. Tell Mrs. Dobson she outdid herself again."

I rose and took his arm. He never wanted to walk with me without me doing so. How that used to annoy Cassie, I thought. "It's the blind leading the blind," she would tell me. "That's what the two of you look like."

Only to you, I thought. *Only to you.*

"I hear you're really involved in this wedding planning now," Uncle Perry said as he opened the front door.

"I'm not really that involved. Lucille wanted me to go along with her to review the dresses and choose some things at the wedding planner's, but I think she pretty much had everything already chosen. She says she wants me to help arrange for the flowers, the altar, chairs, food kiosks, be with her every moment, not that I know anything about it. I mean, I'll do whatever she wants, but I know she just wants to give me the feeling I'm involved."

"See?" he said. "You're pretty sharp and never to be underestimated. You know exactly what's going on around you. Everything's going to be fine, Sam. You take it easy and start planning on coming to work with me. I'm surrounded by too many old biddies."

He kissed me and held me a moment, which was something he always had done. Most relatives kiss each other the way they would pat each other on the hand and move on, but Uncle Perry always gave me the feeling that he wanted me to believe he loved me. It was as important to him as it was to me.

"See you soon," he said, then went to his car, pausing to appreciate mine. "It's truly a magnificent-looking driving machine."

"I'm scared to drive it!" I shouted.

"Nonsense. You have to break in this baby, Sam. No car can be a virgin in the Heavenstone collection."

I laughed and watched him drive away. I stood on the portico until he was gone, and then I felt a chill and embraced myself. I needed to be in the sunlight and decided to go for a walk. I strolled slowly, lost in my own thoughts for more than an hour, but when I was on the pathway and almost at the end of our garden, something made me turn. It was as if someone had tapped me on the shoulder, and I looked back at the house.

I saw her up in the attic window, looking down at me. *She won't retreat to her grave*, I thought.

"Leave me alone!" I screamed.

She smiled and backed away. My heart began thumping. She knew if there was one place in our mansion where I would never go, it was the attic. It was up there in the old dresser that I had found the emptied sleeping-pill capsules and realized what she had done to Mother. It had been our struggle over that evidence at the top of the attic stairway that had resulted in her fall and death. Even though I didn't need anyone to tell me, I had once overheard Mrs. Dobson tell Doris that the dead haunt the place where they died. They retreat to it like vampires retreating to their coffins, only to rise again and again.

It all gave me the chills, and I started back. I was in such deep thought about it that I didn't hear the limousine come up the drive and stop right behind me.

"Semantha?" Lucille called as she stepped out.

"Oh, hi," I said. I felt the wide smile sit on my face, thinking how Mother had never looked this fashionable during the day and had never really been a designer-clothes person. She had been far more conservative, which both Cassie and I had thought fit the image for a Heavenstone wife, especially Daddy's wife.

But here was Lucille in a salmon silk shantung suit. A tie cinched the waist of her button-front jacket with short bubble sleeves. It had a narrow pencil skirt. With the luminous silk scarf topping her wide-brimmed hat, she truly looked as if she had just come from modeling at some high-fashion show. And with her height and figure, there was no way she wouldn't stand out anywhere she went.

"Your father and I had a most exciting morning and lunch," she said. "We were both in a panic this morning and had to rush out to get over to Frankfort for lunch with the governor. Your father rented a helicopter. Can you imagine? He's going to tell you when he gets home for dinner tonight, but I can't hold it in," she said, looking as if she would burst with excitement. She was so buoyant I couldn't help but get excited myself, even though I had no idea why.

"What is it?"

"Your father has been chosen as Kentucky Citizen of the Year, and just think, the same year he and I are getting married! I guess we're really good luck for each other, and," she quickly added, "I'm sure for you."

"That does sound wonderful, Lucille."

"The formal ceremony won't be until we return from our honeymoon. He'll be in all the newspapers, on television. There's a grand ballroom dinner with a guest list that would make the queen of England envious. We'll have to buy you something special to wear." She paused for a breath. "So, how was your lunch with your uncle?"

"Very nice."

"He's quite fond of you," she said as we started into the house. "And worried about you," she added.

"I know. He wants me to come work with him."

"Yes, I heard him ask you on our way back from New York. I guess he really meant it. Well," she said pausing at the bottom of the stairway, "there is no reason for you to rush into anything. Why not just enjoy the summer first and wait to see what you want to do? I'd hate to see you buried in some back room with department-store employees and not having the opportunity to meet people your own age. Maybe you should think about a group trip to Europe or reconsider your decision not to attend college. You know we could get you into any school you wanted to attend, especially here in Kentucky. I certainly wouldn't be in any rush to do anything uninteresting." She started up the stairway before I could respond.

"Uncle Perry's work is interesting," I called up to her.

She turned, shrugged, and shook her head. "Whatever, Semantha. All I'm saying is, don't do what got you into unhappiness before, make impulsive decisions. Let everything ruminate . . . as with any life-changing decision. Nothing is too small when it comes to our happiness." She laughed and looked out at our property. "Speaking of happiness, isn't this paradise? Look at where we live and what we have. Aren't we the luckiest people in the world?" Before I could respond, she added, "I've got to change, stop being a wide-eyed teenage girl, and start on some important phone calls."

"Well, she made your precious uncle Perry sound like a stick-in-the-mud, offering you a job in a closet.

Still think she's so wonderful?" I heard Cassie whisper. I spun around but didn't see her.

Then I started up the stairway to go to my room. I was a little more than halfway up when I heard Lucille scream. It was such a piercing screech my heart did flip-flops, and Mrs. Dobson, who was just coming out of the den where she and Doris had done some furniture polishing, paused as though she had been instantly frozen.

"What was that?" she asked me.

I shook my head.

A moment later, Lucille appeared at the top of the stairway.

"Who was in our bedroom and at my vanity table?" she demanded.

Neither Mrs. Dobson nor I spoke. Doris came out and looked up, too.

"Well?"

"Doris made the bed and cleaned the bathroom this morning as usual," Mrs. Dobson said. "We had no other reason to go into your room. Laundry and dry cleaning don't get done and put back until tomorrow, as you know, according to the schedule, and . . ."

"Don't lecture me about the house! Someone was in my room!" Lucille shouted, her words falling like thunder over us.

Mrs. Dobson turned to Doris, who, despite her diminutive size, a little more than five foot three, was a tireless worker, unafraid of any chore, no matter what she had to lift or do. She wasn't easily intimidated.

"I never touch anything on your vanity table, Mrs. Bennet," Doris said firmly. "There's no reason to shout at us."

Lucille relaxed her shoulders and quickly seized control of herself to speak in a calmer but still coldly measured tone.

"Well, someone did. I get this special facial cream from France," she said, holding up a piece of glass. "It comes from a very special small organic factory. Each four-ounce jar costs seven hundred and fifty dollars! I just found it on the floor, the jar broken, the cream spilled out and useless. I'd never put anything that could have pieces of glass in it on my face. This jar is lost, seven hundred and fifty dollars lost."

"I assure you that I didn't touch anything, Mrs. Bennet," Doris said.

"Well, what did it do, jump off the table? I'm very disappointed, Mrs. Dobson. Very disappointed," she said, and spun on her heels.

For a moment, no one spoke, and then Mrs. Dobson asked Doris if she might have accidentally brushed against the table or something on it.

"Absolutely not," Doris said. "You know I don't rush my work."

"Well, perhaps she knocked it off the table herself just now. She's always in something of a rush, but far be it from the likes of me to accuse her," Mrs. Dobson said. She looked up at me and then followed Doris into the kitchen.

I turned to start up again and saw Cassie smiling at me. A moment later, she was gone, but when I turned into my room, she was there standing by the window, looking down at the entrance to our property.

"You did that, didn't you?" I asked.

She didn't move and didn't answer for a long moment. Finally, she turned, a dark, angry smirk on her face, that same look of rage that used to send me off crying for Mother.

"*You don't have the courage to do anything, Semantha. You never did. I want you to know that although you didn't see me there, I heard all that garbage Uncle Perry told you, by the way. I'm not surprised, and I'm not surprised that he thinks Daddy is better because of Lucille. She's killing the Heavenstone in him. Soon, he and Perry will be indistinguishable, two lapdogs cowering under Lucille's shadow.*"

I started to shake my head.

"*That is, if I let it happen,*" she added, and slipped away in the whispering breeze that came through an open window.

Maybe it was time I should tell Daddy about Cassie, I thought. Maybe he should know she was still there.

What I feared, however, was not that he wouldn't believe me.

I feared that he would.

And that he would be happy about it.

Politics

LUCILLE COMPLAINED TO Daddy about her skin cream as soon as he returned that afternoon. After he had spoken to both Mrs. Dobson and Doris, he came to my room to speak to me. He was upset and paced because he thought one of them was lying. I couldn't let him think that.

"This is all simply a silly mistake, Daddy. I know it is."

"What do you mean? How can you be so sure?"

"After Lucille and you had left and I had my breakfast, I did a little tour of the house. I wanted to see if any real changes had been made since Lucille had come to live here. I didn't mean to spy on you or anything, but I went into your bedroom. I was thinking about the changes Cassie had made, and I was thinking about Mother."

He stared at me a moment and then took a step toward me. "Did you knock that jar off her vanity table? Is that what you're telling me?" he asked.

"No," I said, shaking my head vehemently. "I didn't touch a thing on her table."

"Then what are you saying, Semantha? Why did you say this is silly and you're so sure?"

"I didn't see any broken jar on the floor, and Mrs. Dobson and Doris had already been in there to do whatever had to be done, just as they do every morning. When I was up there, they were already busy with the downstairs."

He thought a moment and then shook his head. "I saw the jar. It was broken. I don't understand what you're saying, Semantha. Speak directly. Exactly what are you saying?"

"I think Lucille must have knocked it off herself when she returned and not realized it."

At first, when he opened and closed his mouth, I thought he was simply going to get even angrier at me, but he surprised me by smiling.

"Lucille knocked it over herself? You don't know how ridiculous that sounds, Semantha. First, if she knocked off a jar like that, she would surely hear it shatter on the floor, and second, if there is one thing we'll never accuse Lucille of being, it's flighty and absentminded. It's just not possible for her to have done something like that and not realize it, not her. I've never met anyone who pays attention to detail as much as she does."

"I'm just telling you that I didn't see anything broken, Daddy, and—"

"Obviously, Doris or Mrs. Dobson returned to the room when you didn't notice and one of them had the accident. Maybe Doris refilled the tissue box or replaced something."

"Neither of them would hide something like

that, Daddy. They would have admitted it immediately."

"There's no other possible explanation, Semantha. I've already put them both on notice. They know I'm very upset. I want honesty in this house. To me, this house is a temple, and no deceit or dishonesty is going to be tolerated within it."

Where were you when Cassie was alive? I wanted to say, but didn't dare.

"For now, we'll put it aside, but if anything else like this occurs, I will depend on you to step forward and let me know. I want you to think of the three of us as one now. What happens to any of us happens to all of us, understand? Do you?" he asked, punching his words at me sharply.

"Yes, Daddy."

"Okay. I've already ordered her a new jar. It should be shipped overnight and be here tomorrow. I don't want to hear another word about it."

"Good," I said. He nodded and started out. "Daddy."

"What?"

"With all of this excitement, I forgot. Congratulations on being chosen Kentucky Citizen of the Year. Lucille told me."

"Oh, she did, did she? Well, thank you, Semantha. It will be a wonderful occasion for us all." He smiled. "I think Lucille was more excited about it than I was." He lowered his chin and raised his eyes and whispered, "I think she and her father had a little to do with it. Whatever. It makes for a nice wedding present. We'll talk more about it at dinner, I'm sure."

As soon as he left, Cassie appeared in the door-way. She watched him walk away and then turned to look in at me.

"He's such a man fool now. If she had anything to do with his getting the honor, it wasn't for him; it was for herself. She'll do anything to climb the social ladder, even stand on his back. And you don't have the courage to tell him so. He's acting more like a worshiping servant than a fiancé. You—"

I stepped forward and closed the door on her.

Later, when I went downstairs, I saw Lucille sitting on the rear patio by herself. She was sipping a glass of wine and reading a large notebook. I wasn't going to join her, but she turned sharply as if she could sense that I was standing there looking out at her. Not wanting her to think I was spying on her or anything, I continued out the French doors and joined her. It was a particularly beautiful twilight, with patches of milk-white clouds so still they looked pasted over the darkening velvet sky. Mother used to call these Angel Nights and told Cassie and me that the bright stars that appeared and grew even brighter were their eyes looking down on us all to decide whom they would help.

"If you look really hard," she said, "you can see them."

Cassie thought it was ridiculous, but I would swear even today that I did see angels.

Lucille smiled. "I'm glad you came out, Semantha. Please," she said, indicating the seat across from her.

When I sat, I saw that the notebook was from the wedding planner. She closed it quickly.

"I'm sorry you saw me so angry today," she began. "Believe me, that's not my usual manner when addressing servants or any employees, for that matter."

She took a sip of her wine. I wasn't sure what she expected me to say, so I remained quiet.

"I think it's admirable that you feel you have to defend Mrs. Dobson and Doris. After all, they've been with you much longer than they've been with me. Loyalty is a good thing when it's directed to the right places."

I realized Daddy must have told her what I had told him. It wasn't a big betrayal, but it hammered home how serious and determined he was when he had said we would be keeping no secrets from each other. I realized he wanted to show me clearly that it would never be he and I on one side and Lucille on the other.

"Mrs. Dobson and Doris don't break things, and if they did, they wouldn't lie about it," I said.

She shook her head and smiled again. "Semantha, Semantha, I envy you your innocence, especially when I consider all you've been through already in your young life. I, too, was eager to live in a world full of candy canes and lollipops, a world in which people were honest and true. It's earth-shattering when you realize how few people you can really trust. Some people can't deal with it at all and spend their entire lives with their heads buried in the sand. I always imagined them old and tired and alone, unable to rationalize or turn the other cheek any longer. It has to be far more difficult for them than for the rest of us who mature and become realistic early enough in our lives to avoid the pain."

She tilted her head and changed the tone of her voice as if she were now talking to a very young child.

"Do you think your father got to where he is today by being naive and avoiding reality? Hardly. He is one of the most emotionally centered and one of the strongest men I have met, and it's for that as well as his other wonderful qualities that I love him so dearly."

"Neither Mrs. Dobson nor Doris ever lied to my father or me about anything," I insisted. I would never even consider the alternative, no matter what she said.

She kept her smile, but the warmth left it so that it looked more as if she wore a photograph of her face.

"Whatever you choose to believe you can believe," she said. "I simply want you to understand your place in this historic and important mansion and family. It's one thing to treat your servants decently and fairly but quite another to place yourself on their level. There has to be a professional distance between you, me, and your father and them, Semantha. Some servants understand that distance well, and there's never a problem. Some really resent being servants themselves, and no matter how they smile or speak to you, they really hate being at your beck and call."

"But . . ."

"And there are some who don't even realize themselves how much they resent being servants.

Mrs. Dobson and Doris strike me as like that." Her face hardened, her eyes more steely cold. "Now, I grew up with house servants, too, and most of my friends did the same. I know a quality servant when I see one. I'm not sure Mrs. Dobson and Doris are up to what's required in a home this prestigious, working for a family this important."

"Oh, but they are!" I cried. "Mrs. Dobson has worked in the homes of lords and ladies in London."

"Titles are bought, and some are so thin they border on the ridiculous."

"Whatever. Mrs. Dobson has been more like a grandmother to me, and—"

"Exactly. That's my point." She pounced. "A servant is not a member of your family, Semantha." She relaxed her shoulders and smiled again. "However, let's not talk about this right now. There are too many far more important things to discuss. We've got to lay out the wedding and reception as intelligently as we can on these grounds." She looked at her watch. "Mr. Manglesthorpe, my wedding planner, is arriving soon. There's enough time before dinner. We'll walk the grounds and design everything. I'd like you to walk with us. Here," she said, sliding the notebook across the table. "You can look over the set pieces, and if you have any suggestions, don't hesitate to make them. I love seeing things through younger eyes. Sometimes innocence has a refreshing point of view."

"How come you don't ask my father to help with all this?"

"How come? Simple. He's thrown the whole

thing in my lap, which is fine," she said, smiling. "I only hope I live up to his expectations. Your opinions are very important to me, Semantha, not only in relation to the wedding but also for how the house will be run."

"The house?"

"We'll have to make changes to keep up with the times and our needs, won't we?"

"I suppose," I said, though I had no idea what she meant by "our needs." It seemed that my father's and my needs were very well attended to as it was. "Daddy doesn't like to change much in the house, though."

"Nothing will be so dramatic a change, something that would detract from the Heavenstone image or anything, but a house is more than a furniture collection, statuary, and paintings. This is like a living, breathing animal." She narrowed her eyes. "That's why I really want you to take your time deciding what to do next, why I suggested you don't rush right into working at the stores. I'll have a great deal to do in and out of this house, and I'll be depending on you to be involved and alert about what goes on within it."

Now what was she talking about? Involved and alert about what? Neither Daddy nor I nor even Cassie thought the running of our house was so complicated.

She finished her wine. "In the meantime, peruse the wedding planner's book. I want to run in and change these shoes. We have time before it gets too dark, but I'm sure I'd break a heel traipsing over the lawn."

She rose and leaned over to kiss me on the cheek.

"I'm so glad we had this little chat. I look forward so much to our intimate little chats to come. We'll be each other's trusted confidant and in no time be comfortably revealing the deepest secrets in our hearts."

She turned and hurried into the house. A moment later, I felt Cassie standing beside me. I didn't look at her and spoke before she could.

"That's the sort of woman you would have become," I told her.

When I turned around, she was gone.

Not ten minutes later, I heard Mrs. Dobson greet Mr. Manglesthorpe. Lucille came down the stairs quickly and introduced him to me.

"I asked Mr. Manglesthorpe to come now, which will be about the time we begin the reception," she explained. "It's the best way to see how it will be."

"Let's hope we have a night as beautiful as this one's promising to be," he said, more to me than to Lucille. "However, I have provided for large tents."

"It won't dare rain. Semantha and I won't permit it, right, Semantha?"

I nodded. Ordinarily, I'd have thought that was a really silly thing to say, but Lucille sounded and looked as if she actually believed she had the power to control the weather.

We began the tour. I felt a little silly walking behind Lucille and Mr. Manglesthorpe, even when Lucille would turn around to me and ask, "Don't you agree?"

To me, it didn't seem to make much difference if

the soft-drink kiosk was just down from the second bar or not. I certainly wasn't going to disagree with their decision to form a U with the tables so that more people could actually view the dais, and what was so complicated about where the altar should be so as not to have the guests looking into the sun?

She surprised me, however, when she told Mr. Manglesthorpe that the dance floor should be in front of the dais so I could feel more involved in the activity.

"I don't want any of us shoved off to the side, especially the younger people at this wedding. We want to be right in the thick of it, right, Semantha?"

"Yes," I said quickly, even though I had no idea how I would be in the thick of it. She smiled at me as if she knew something I didn't.

Afterward, at dinner, Lucille described the wedding arrangements to my father, again making it seem as if I had been an integral part of the decisions. Daddy was in a much better mood and applauded every decision Lucille had made. The only moment that gave him any hesitation was when she asked if he was certain he wanted my uncle Perry to be his best man.

"Of course I do. He's my brother," he said, holding his smile. He glanced at me. I was sure I looked quite shocked that she would even think to ask.

"Well, I was just thinking . . . I know how close you have been with Senator Brice. Just imagine what it would look like, how impressive it would be."

"What? You mean to have Captain Brice be my best man?"

"He was a war hero, and I know he would wear his uniform for the occasion," she said. "What a picture that would make in the newspapers."

Again, he glanced at me, and then he smiled. "It sounds as if you've already broached the subject with him."

"Not him, exactly. You know I've been friends with Meg Brice for years."

He was silent. I said nothing, but I was sure he could feel my eyes on him.

"I wouldn't want to hurt Perry's feelings," Daddy said.

I was grateful for that and stopped holding my breath. I didn't think Lucille would go on with it, but she surprised me.

"Perry is a pretty astute man. He would certainly see the political benefits, I'm sure."

"Political?" I asked. The word just shot out of my mouth, as if Cassie had propelled it. "I mean, it's a wedding, not an election."

Lucille smiled that smile she gave when she wanted me to feel like a much younger girl, someone who needed doors and windows opened so she could see what was going on in the real world.

"When you reach your father's and my social level, Semantha, everything we do has political implications." She turned back to Daddy and gazed at him with admiration as she slipped her right hand into his left. "Your father knows I have secret ambitions for him."

"What secret ambitions?"

"Oh, Lucille," he said. "Let's not talk about any of that now."

"No, Teddy, she should know. She's a grown woman now, and besides, she should be part of every important family decision." Lucille turned back to me. "There's been some serious talk about your father running for governor at the end of the present governor's term. He has a little more than two years left, and he's made it clear that he won't run again."

"But . . ." I turned to Daddy. "How can you be governor and still run the Heavenstone Corporation?"

Lucille looked to him for his answer, too.

"Well . . . Lucille is coming aboard to assume, assist, and take on some of my executive responsibilities," he replied. "In time, she can take on more."

It had the sound of a rehearsed and memorized answer, one she had planted in his head.

She nodded, released Daddy's hand, and turned back to me.

"Which is why I urged you earlier to give second and third thoughts to your getting yourself involved with your uncle in a rather minor part of our business right now. As I assume more business responsibilities, it will fall more and more on your shoulders to manage this great house. I'll help you gain more of the needed experience as soon as we return from our honeymoon, but don't underestimate how important this is to the Heavenstone image and reputation.

"And," she added, reaching across the table to take Daddy's hand again, "how important this house and its history are to your father. I'm sure he would want someone he could trust, someone who understands the heritage, to take charge while we're off doing our work. Naturally, after your father is elected governor, we'll all move into the governor's mansion, but we won't let a single dead lightbulb go unchanged here."

She looked at me again.

"Unless, of course, you're romantically involved with someone and perhaps still living here. Then all our problems are solved."

I stared at her, stunned. She wasn't only planning her own future with my father. She was planning mine as well.

Daddy widened his smile. "She's quite an executive thinker, our Lucille," Daddy said. He patted her hand. "Okay, I'll have a talk with Perry and smooth it over. You go forward with Senator Brice."

I felt the breath get caught in my throat again. Of course, if Daddy asked him, Uncle Perry would step aside, but I knew in my heart that he would be terribly and deeply hurt. How could Daddy not realize it, too?

"That's wonderful, Teddy," Lucille said.

They stared at each other lovingly for a moment, and then Daddy stood up.

"I've got some work to get back to at the office," he said. "There were a few things I had left to do and would rather have done before morning."

"I'll walk you out," she told him, and put her arm through his. When she looked back at me, I thought she wore an expression of utter self-confidence and power. It was as if she said, *See, he's putty in my hands.*

I watched them leave and then went out to the

rear patio again and looked over the grounds toward where the altar was to be set up for them to take their vows. The bottom of my stomach felt full of worms. I took some deep breaths and stepped down to walk toward the pool and cabana. Cassie stepped out of a shadow cast by one of our great old oak trees. She said nothing at first. She just walked along with me.

"Still want to close doors in my face and shut me up?" she finally asked. I said nothing, just walked. *"When a man makes that much of a fool of himself over a woman, you can't depend on him for anything. The fact is, Semantha, you'll have to become Daddy's eyes and ears. It will fall to you to wake him up."*

I continued walking, even though she paused.

"You're going to need my help!" she shouted after me. *"Do you want my help or not? I'm not going to beg you, Semantha. Well?"*

I paused, thought a moment, and turned around. "Yes," I said.

She caught up with me, and we walked side by side, neither of us saying much. It was like the old days before everything terrible had happened, the time when I used to think we could be wonderful sisters, the Heavenstone sisters, the most famous two sisters in all of Kentucky, with our picture together in the newspapers and magazines. Underneath, the caption would read *Beauty and Brains*. We would be thought of as two parts of one wonderful person.

I felt Cassie slip her hand into mine. *"Don't worry,"* she whispered. *"We'll save him and save ourselves."*

"What about my little girl?" I muttered. "Who will save her?"

My hand felt empty, and when I turned to look, she was gone.

But the stars were bright now, and when I looked up and studied them, I saw my angel. That sight, more than Cassie, buoyed my hopes for tomorrow.

I returned to the house, intending to go up to my room to watch some television, but when I entered and started toward the stairway, Lucille called to me.

"Is that you, Semantha?"

I went to the living-room doorway. She was sitting in the living room in Daddy's favorite chair.

"I went looking for you after your father left. Where were you?"

"Just taking a walk," I said.

"Now, listen to me, Semantha," she began. "Come in here," she ordered. "Sit."

"What do you want?" I asked, but walked in and sat across from her.

"I don't like it that you spend so much time alone. It's not natural for a girl your age with all of your attributes to be so withdrawn. And don't tell me about your therapy and all the rest. I have eyes and ears and can see and hear you. There's nothing wrong with you. You can be happy, too.

"Now, I know you were a little upset at dinner, but you must believe me when I say I'm looking out for all of us now, including your uncle Perry. Don't you think he would be proud of his brother if his brother was elected governor? Don't you think his life would improve and he would benefit, too? Well?"

"Yes, I suppose."

"Good. So don't sulk about this little change in the wedding plans. He'll be fine with it."

"I'm not sulking," I said.

"You're not exactly a secret wrapped in a riddle, Semantha. You wear your heart on your sleeve, so to speak. I haven't lived with you very long, but I can see and feel your emotions almost as well as your father can. When he left, he was upset that you were upset."

"He was?"

"Yes. He asked me to talk to you a little more about it. He's very sensitive to your feelings and what bothers him bothers me. Don't you want him to be happy?"

"Yes, of course."

"So make an effort to see things our way. Don't make any petty displeasures so obvious. When you show your hand, you lose the game. My mother gave me that advice, and I never forgot it. Will you try?"

"Yes," I said quickly. At this point, I just wanted to get away from her.

"Don't tell me things I want to hear just to get rid of me, Semantha. I want to do what's right for everyone, including you. I want you to be happy, too, very happy. I'm determined to help you have a full and productive life. It will please your father, and he'll be happier as a result. Now, it's not good that you have no friends your own age and you are not doing things girls your age should be doing."

"I went to a private high school for three years. I've lost contact with anyone I knew here."

"Well, maybe we can fix that."

"How?"

"Give me time to think about it. I'll come up with something. You'll see. Just give me a chance to be all I can be for you. Give me a little trust, okay?"

I started to nod, but it was as if Cassie had her hand under my chin and wouldn't let me dip my head. Lucille looked displeased at my silence.

"Okay," I finally managed.

"Good," she said. "You can go up to your room if you like."

"*Dismissed,*" Cassie whispered.

I rose and walked out slowly. My head felt as if it had turned into a hive filled with angry bees. Thoughts, feelings, memories spun around, twisting and turning everything into tight knots. I felt like screaming to rid my ears of all the voices I was hearing.

One of the voices I heard was real, but I didn't realize it for a few moments.

Mrs. Dobson was standing in the kitchen doorway, calling to me in a whisper and beckoning. I looked back at the living room to be sure Lucille wasn't watching and then went into the kitchen. Doris was sitting at the kitchenette, her hands wrapped around a cup of tea. She looked up. Mrs. Dobson stood beside her.

"We want you to know we absolutely did not break Mrs. Bennet's jar of skin cream," she said.

"I know you didn't," I replied.

"We just wanted you to know we wouldn't do anything to hurt your father or you, Miss Semantha, and we're both quite upset that your father is so upset with us."

"I know, Mrs. Dobson. I spoke to him about it. He said we should forget it all for now."

"We thought you'd stand up for us. Didn't we, Doris?"

"Yes, thank you," Doris said. "I'd hate to lose this work over something I didn't do."

"You won't," I promised. I smiled at them and started out.

Mrs. Dobson followed me to the stairway. I turned to reassure her again, but I could see there was something more.

"What is it, Mrs. Dobson?"

She looked toward the living-room doorway first and then leaned in to whisper to me. "I saw Mrs. Bennet looking at the mail and taking an envelope that was addressed to you," she said.

"When?"

"Yesterday. I thought she might have taken it by mistake, but I wanted to be sure. Did she give it to you?"

"No. I've received no mail."

She nodded. "I had a suspicion. Your father told us how he doesn't want any deception in this house. It's a very special house, and you're special people. I didn't think it was my place to say anything about your mail, but I don't like us being unjustly accused of things, either."

"No, you shouldn't like it, and you shouldn't be accused," I said.

"If you tell her I told you, she'll be very upset

with me, I'm sure, and probably go complaining to your father, but I haven't lived this long and worked this long for good people to end up sneaking about and tiptoeing around so as to make myself invisible. If someone can't stand the sight of you, you don't wish them to be blind. You just walk off. That's what me mum taught me," she said. "Sorry to disturb," she added, and returned to the kitchen.

I looked toward the living room again.

Why would Lucille take my mail? Who would write to me?

After the talk we had just had, I didn't think this was the time to ask about that letter addressed to me and accuse her. I started up the stairway, telling myself I would find out why, if she had taken it by mistake, she hadn't yet given it to me.

Little did I know how quickly that would be and what an impact it would have on the future Lucille so wanted to design for me.

10

The Letter

I INTENDED TO confront Lucille about my letter the following day, but she was gone before I went to breakfast, and then she and Daddy went to dinner with some people after work. When they came home late that evening, they were together laughing and enjoying a nightcap in the den. I didn't want to bring it up in front of my father, anyway. However, the following morning, I deliberately rose earlier and waited for Lucille to come out of the bedroom. I saw my father leave first, and then, when she emerged, I pretended to be walking out and down to breakfast at the same time.

"Good morning, Semantha." She waited at the top of the stairway.

"Good morning."

"What are your plans for today? I'm going to Lexington to meet the governor's wife for lunch," she said before I could reply. "I'd take you along, but it's not proper to surprise her with a guest."

"That's all right. I'm going to do some reading, relax at the pool. Uncle Perry is sending some design proposals over for me to look at. They're for girls my age. I used to give him input all the time."

"How nice. I took a brief look at that sector of the business. He could use something to boost sales."

We started down the stairway.

"He wanted me to come to his office today, but I asked if he could just send them over."

"Good. I like you here to babysit the house," she said, smiling. "You know that old expression: When the cat's away, the mice will play. What are you reading these days? My father was so critical of whatever I read. I had to be sure it had some intrinsic value and wasn't simply entertainment."

"*The Magic Slipper.*"

"I don't know it."

"It's a modern-day version of *Cinderella,* which even your father might think has intrinsic value, as you say."

She laughed. "I doubt it. I had to bribe my mother to get permission to see *Beauty and the Beast.*"

"How sad. Speaking of reading, however," I said as we reached the bottom of the stairway, "I was wondering if you might have picked up some mail for me accidentally."

"Mail?" She paused. "When?"

"Yesterday, maybe?"

"Oh. You know, maybe I did. I just scooped up the pile and brought it to your father's office. I haven't gone through half of it," she said. "Are you expecting mail?"

I shrugged.

"Well, why would you think I accidentally picked up something addressed to you?" she asked suspiciously.

"I just wondered," I said. "Some of the girls mentioned they'd keep in touch."

I knew Mrs. Dobson had told me she wasn't afraid of my mentioning her seeing the envelope addressed to me, but unless I had to do it, I saw no reason to get her on Lucille's bad side.

"Oh, I see. Well, you're quite welcome to go to the office and look through the pile yourself," Lucille said coolly. "I'm just grabbing a little breakfast and then leaving. I've been on such a merry-go-round with the wedding preparations, business issues, and social events, I haven't had a moment to think about the mail. I do hope there's something nice there for you," she added, and walked on to the dining room.

Either she was a great actress or she really had accidentally taken a letter addressed to me, I thought as I walked to the office. Cassie was already there, standing behind Daddy's desk.

"Accidentally? Or she's a great actress? Take a wild guess which it is," she said.

I ignored her and went to the mail stacked on the desk. I was only halfway into it before I found the letter. It was from Ethan.

"She read it," Cassie said. *"She steamed it open and read it."*

I turned the envelope over and looked at it carefully. The edge of the seal was slightly torn and when I brought it into more light, it did look as if some glue had been reapplied. But unless I had a forensics expert check the fingerprints on the letter inside, I really couldn't be sure. I opened it, took out the letter, and sat behind the desk to read it. I saw from the date that it was nearly a week old.

Dear Semantha,

I was sorry to have missed your graduation. The fact is, I even missed my own. I was called home because my father had a heart attack. It was touch and go for the first few days, and then the doctors decided to operate and do a triple bypass. It went well, but I remained here during his first weeks of recuperation. Naturally, I put my own life on hold. He's doing well now.

I hope your graduation went well and your family enjoyed being there. I know how hard it was for you the last few days at Collier, and I wish I could have been there for you.

Perhaps we'll see each other again in the near future. Despite the craziness toward the end, I really did enjoy our time together. Let me know how you are doing.

Love, Ethan

He'd added his e-mail address at the bottom. I folded the letter and put it back into the envelope. How unexpected this was. When Ethan hadn't shown up or called the day of my graduation, I had assumed that after all he had learned about my past and all of the commotion because of Ellie, he wanted no more to do with me. I had all but written him out of my life, fighting back any nice memories that tried to rise to the surface like bubbles in a pond. Even Lucille's questions didn't raise any new hope in me. I waited to hear Cassie say something sarcastic or nasty about Ethan's letter, but she was silent.

"Anything there for you?" Lucille asked when I entered the dining room. She was looking at the newspaper's society page and sipping her coffee, sitting, I noted, in Daddy's seat.

"Yes." I put the envelope in front of me on the table.

"Oh. I do apologize. I've been rushing about these days and simply missed it."

Mrs. Dobson came in to bring me my juice and a bowl of my favorite cereal and fruit. Lucille waited for her to leave.

"Well," she said, nodding at the envelope, "did it bring you some good news at least?"

"Sort of. It was from Ethan Hunter."

"The young man you were seeing?"

"Yes. He explained why he didn't attend my graduation. His father had a heart attack, and he had to go home to be with his mother."

"Did his father live?"

"Yes, but he had to have a triple bypass."

"Well, then, that is good news," she said, smiling. "I remember I told you to reserve your judgment about him. We're all so impulsive when we're young. We haven't the patience to let things jell a bit. It's nice that he wrote you. Is he going to call you?"

"I don't know," I said, starting my breakfast. "He wants me to write to him first, I think. He added his e-mail address."

"I won't tell you what to do, but he sounds very thoughtful and not like the sort who would waste his time," she said. She snapped the paper and finished reading, occasionally announcing the names she read and explaining how she knew them. There didn't seem to be a charity or entertainment affair to which she had not gone in her life. After she had her breakfast, she told me she had a number of things to do before meeting the governor's wife. She also said that she and my father would have dinner out again tonight.

"I do hate to see you all by yourself so much, Semantha," she said as she rose to leave.

"It's all right."

"No, it's not. I know what you've been through, and I worry you're going to ruin all the progress you've made with your therapist. I promise I will try to devote more time to you as soon as I can. Perhaps you should send Ethan a quick note to let him know you don't hold a grudge or anything," she added, flashed a smile, and walked out.

She's so confusing, I thought. Sometimes she gave me the feeling she was totally into herself and would eventually hurt the family, or what was left of it; and then sometimes, like now, she seemed really concerned about my welfare. Could she really be like an older sister to me, a tried-and-true, trusted friend? Should I give her the chance?

Across the table, sitting in her seat, Cassie simply stared at me and shook her head as if I were a lost cause. She had done that more times than I had strands of hair on my head. Mrs. Dobson came in to clear off Lucille's dishes.

"She did pick up a letter that was for me," I told her, and showed her the envelope. "I didn't mention that you had seen her do it. She said she had scooped up a pile of mail and told me she hadn't yet gone through it all."

She paused. "And?"

"I went through it and found my letter. She said she did it accidentally."

Mrs. Dobson continued to clean up, but then paused, looked at the doorway, and then looked at me. "I've known many fine people in my time, Miss Semantha, people of high quality, some quite decent, some quite the opposite. Money and prestige don't guarantee anything. That woman," she added, nodding at the doorway, "never does anything accidentally."

She went into the kitchen.

Across the table, Cassie broke into a wide smile.

"Think what you like," I told her, "but if there's anyone who knows what it's like for people to think badly of you without real proof, it's yours truly."

She mocked me with a face of exaggerated sorrow and pity. I left quickly.

That afternoon, before I did anything else, I went on my computer and wrote a quick note to Ethan, just as Lucille had suggested. I thanked him for his letter, wished his father well, and clearly indicated that I would love to hear from him whenever he had a chance to e-mail back. I described my graduation ceremony and told him a little about my father and Lucille and the plans being made for a grand wedding. I also told him about my father's new honor, but I didn't tell him anything about Lucille's political ambitions for him.

Afterward, I changed into my bathing suit,

scooped up the novel I wanted to start, and headed for the pool. Downstairs, I found that Uncle Perry's designs had been delivered. I took them with me and sat on a chaise.

We had a nearly Olympic-size light-blue Pebble Tec pool, deep enough at the far end for a diving board. There was a cabana with bathrooms and five changing rooms with showers. Daddy had installed a large-screen television under the roof of the shady patio, where we had a beautiful blue and white ceramic bar behind which was a full kitchen. To the right of that was a built-in barbecue. Spaced around the pool were a dozen tables with umbrellas, and to the sides was some more outdoor furniture with tables.

I sat back and thought about the grand pool parties with live music that Mother and Daddy had had years ago. I was permitted to stay until ten o'clock, but afterward, I would keep my bedroom windows open so I could hear the music and laughter flowing through the night. Nothing like that had happened around this pool since Mother's death. I imagined Lucille would plan some parties after she and Daddy were married, but no matter what she did or how elaborate those parties would be, they just couldn't be the same for me.

I began studying Uncle Perry's new ideas for teen fashions in the Heavenstone line. Some of the drawings reminded me of outfits the girls wore at Collier. At the end, he had a list of possible magazines in which he wanted to place advertisements. He wanted me to check those I thought would be most effective.

I didn't read any of them, but I had seen a number of them at the dorm. He added a little note, once again telling me how much he hoped I would come to work in his department.

I was thinking that I would do just that when I heard the phone ringing. I saw it was my private line. I assumed it was Daddy calling and quickly answered.

"Hey, thanks for the e-mail," I heard Ethan say. "Sounds like a lot going on at the Heavenstone estate. How are you?"

"I'm okay," I said. My mind was reeling. How had he gotten my phone number? I didn't recall putting it into the e-mail or ever giving it to him when we were seeing each other in Albany. I didn't want to sound annoyed about it, so I didn't ask. "How's your father?"

"Oh, he's doing really well since the bypass. Finally, we got him to stop smoking. We're all our own worst enemies when you get right down to it. So, what have you been up to? Planning on college or what?"

"I might go to work for my uncle Perry. He's in charge of a number of things, including teen fashions under our trademark."

"Sounds very interesting. I always had a feeling you'd get involved in your father's empire one way or another. Can't blame you for that."

"What about you?"

"Oh, as I told you, I'm taking my time, looking at my options," he said. "With all that happened, I feel like I need a bit of a breather before looking at possible employment."

"I'm sure you need to catch your breath. Sometimes it all seems to happen so fast."

"Absolutely. Which is really why I was so happy to hear from you."

"Oh?"

"I was thinking of taking a drive out there. I've never been to Kentucky. Maybe I could spend a few days nearby and see you. What do you think?"

My heart began racing with the possibilities. After what Cassie had done and the birth of my daughter, I thought the chance of my ever having a relationship was slight to none. Ethan's initial reaction to my revelations had convinced me that was true, and when he hadn't shown up or called for my graduation, that belief had been solidly confirmed, which was probably why I was so reluctant to get back into any social scene, no matter how much Lucille prodded.

Now I wondered, could I be wrong? Could I get past Dr. Ryan's comment that I might become "somewhat" normal? Was there a chance for me to have a life full of happiness, too? If Daddy, after all of this family tragedy, could resurrect his optimism and hope, why couldn't I?

"I think that's a wonderful idea, Ethan. In fact, I think you should stay here. We have plenty of room."

"Are you sure? Would your father approve?"

"I'm sure he will," I said. "But if you like, I'll ask him as soon as I can and call you."

"That's great, Semantha. I'm really looking forward to seeing you again."

"And I'm looking forward to seeing you."

"Okay, I'll wait for your call," he said. " 'Bye."

"Wait."

"What?"

"You forgot to give me your telephone number."

He laughed. "I guess you got me so excited I can't think straight," he said, and gave me the number.

When I hung up, I realized how Lucille's accidentally burying my letter in her pile might have led Ethan to believe I wanted nothing to do with him. I had Mrs. Dobson to thank, but I was too excited to dwell on being angry or annoyed. I quickly tried to reach my father at work. He was in a meeting, so I had to wait almost an hour, but he finally called, obviously worried that something was wrong. When I told him what I wanted, he laughed.

"Sure, he's welcome," he said. "I can't wait to tell Lucille. She was more worried about you than I was. She'll be happy to hear that you're doing something social."

"Thanks, Daddy."

"See you later," he said.

As soon as he hung up, I called Ethan.

"That's great," he said when I told him my father had said he was eager to meet him, too. "You know what? I think I'll fly instead of drive and get there tomorrow by late afternoon. I'll rent a car at the airport."

"You will?"

"Absolutely. I'll e-mail you my arrangements so you'll know exactly when to expect me. I can't wait to see you and meet your father."

As soon as I hung up, I went into a little nervous

frenzy. There was so much to do to prepare for Ethan's arrival. Which bedroom would he use? What sorts of things should we do? What could I show him? *Wait until he sees my car,* I thought. Of course, I would let him do the driving.

So excited now that I thought I would burst, I gathered my things and hurried back to the house to talk to Mrs. Dobson. When she heard Ethan was coming and I described who he was, she was very excited for me.

"He sounds very nice." She thought a moment. "I'd say the guest bedroom down from yours would be the best one for him. It has the nicest view of the rear of the estate. Doris and I have to get in there, though. We haven't worked on that one for a few weeks, not that there's anything but some dust here and there, I'm sure. We'll get right on it, Miss Semantha. And I suppose you would want to plan on a dinner, too."

"A dinner? Yes, a dinner. Can you make some Italian dish? Ethan loves Italian food."

"My employer who had a house in Mayfair in London used to rave about my lobster Alfredo. I got the recipe from the chef at his favorite Italian restaurant. He said I did a better job of it, and he wasn't the sort who handed out compliments freely. That's about all the boasting I'll do," she added.

"Sounds perfect."

"But maybe you want to check with your father and Mrs. Bennet first."

"Daddy loves lobster. I'm sure it will be fine. When they're not around, I'm the one to make those decisions," I said, thinking of what Lucille had told me. This was what she wanted, my taking charge in the house so she would be able to devote her attention and time to the business, wasn't it? Besides, I felt good taking charge, especially when it involved Ethan.

"Okay. I'll have to go to the market, so if you're sure."

"I'm sure," I said.

"We'll have something special for dessert, too," Mrs. Dobson said.

"Thank you."

"I must say, Miss Semantha, this is the first time since you returned from school that I can see some color in that pretty face of yours. I think this young man means a lot more to you than you let on," she teased.

Now I felt myself blush.

"You just go on and be as excited as you want," she added.

"I've got to start planning what I'll wear tomorrow!" I cried, and hurried out with her laughter echoing behind me. I charged up the stairs, feeling as if I had returned to age twelve, when everything that happened in our mansion had been exciting for me. Until Cassie got to me, that is. Then she would do or say something to bring me back to earth.

"Try not to be so flippant and shallow," she would say. "We're the Heavenstone sisters."

She had a way of sending my most joyful and exciting moments into retreat. Even Mother would criticize her for it whenever she heard her on my case.

"Let her be young," she would say.

"Young is one thing; stupid is another," Cassie would retort. She was never intimidated, either by our mother or by our teachers. Only Daddy could clip her wings or staple her tongue. His approval or disapproval were the only adult reactions that mattered to her.

Well, I was determined that she wasn't going to intimidate me now. I would ignore her if she appeared, and I would shut my ears to her if she spoke. She must have known, because she didn't so much as whisper the rest of the day. Right before dinner, I found Ethan's e-mail on my computer. He was leaving early enough to get to the Heavenstone house by three in the afternoon. I was eager to tell everyone at dinner, including Mrs. Dobson, who assured me that everything was ready in the guest room.

Daddy seemed amused by my excitement and happy for me. I saw how he and Lucille exchanged conspiratorial glances and didn't understand until Daddy announced that at Lucille's suggestion, he'd arranged for me to take Ethan on a tour of our store in Lexington the day after tomorrow.

"You two can drive out yourselves. I've already told Perry about it," he said, "and he's eager to show him his department. Lucille suggested we take the two of you to Wally's for dinner when you visit the store."

"That all sounds wonderful, Daddy. Thank you."

"I wish I could take credit for thinking of it, but it was Lucille's entire idea."

"Thank you, Lucille."

"Not at all, dear. I'm happy things worked out

for you. It is so devastating to have a romantic disappointment when you're as young as you are."

"Are you telling us you had some?" Daddy teased.

"Let's just say I caused a few," she replied, and they laughed.

There was so much inside me resisting it, but I couldn't help but feel happy for them, for the way they looked at each other, held hands, spoke softly and laughed, and just simply looked at each other. Had it been like this with Mother? I felt terribly guilty even wondering.

That night, I went to sleep expecting to dream of Ethan, of his eyes, his smile, his wonderful kiss, imagining us behaving just like Daddy and Lucille. I hadn't had a single Cassie-like thought since I had heard from Ethan. She was so sure that was over, that he was unworthy of a Heavenstone. Perhaps I was acting a bit too smug, too overconfident now, and it was annoying to her, but after I had gone to bed and lowered my head to the pillow, which I hoped would become a well of good dreams from which to draw, I was sure I heard her whisper, *"Don't be so naive. Something is rotten in the state of Denmark."*

Out of the corner of my eye, I saw her kneeling beside my bed, but I didn't respond. I turned my back to her instead and dove headfirst into my fantasies.

I was running around like someone with her pants on fire from the moment I woke up. My excitement stole away my appetite, but Mrs. Dobson insisted that I eat properly. She winked at me and said, "Something tells me you're going to need your energy."

I tried to keep myself busy. I read a little, but my eyes kept sliding off the page, and my ears were open to any sounds that even suggested someone had arrived. We had deliveries often during the day, and because of the size of the estate, there were men constantly at work on the landscaping, the pool, and basic maintenance. Twice I ran upstairs and inspected the guest room Ethan would have, to be sure there were enough towels and washcloths. Mrs. Dobson was too competent to forget a single thing. She even had new tubes of toothpaste in the cabinet and new unwrapped bars of soap at the sink and in the shower.

I forced myself to eat the chicken salad Mrs. Dobson prepared for my lunch, and then I took a long walk just to slow down my beating heart and pounding anticipation. All sorts of questions raced through my mind. Had I changed in any way? Would he look at me and think, *What was I thinking of, coming here to see her?* Would all of this, the Heavenstone estate, intimidate him and turn him away from me? When I was younger, most of the other girls and most of the boys thought we were too high on the social ladder. The girls thought I would look down on them and their homes, and the boys thought I viewed myself as some sort of princess. No matter how nonchalant I acted about our fame and fortune, they couldn't get past it. Of course, Cassie thought that if they couldn't, they weren't meant to, and I should have little or nothing to do with any of them anyway. She never stopped hounding me about our responsibility to the Heavenstone reputation. Whether I liked it or not, she forced me to think that I was better than most people.

It was one thing for Ethan to have met me and been with me at Collier, far away from the Heavenstone estate and the Heavenstone Department Store empire, and another for him to drive through our grand entrance and up our long driveway, with its elaborate landscaping and beautiful lanterns, his eyes surely fixed on the immensity of our house and its grandeur. I was suddenly afraid to show him my expensive birthday gift. That car would eclipse his rental. What if the shoe were on the other foot? Surely, when I met his father, I would naturally think that he would think I was not good enough for his son.

My wave after wave of elation and excitement waned. I fell into one of my characteristic depressions and flopped on the chaise at the pool, staring at the water and thinking, *He'll be in and out of here, making all sorts of excuses for a quick retreat. This is going to be a disaster.* Just as I was at the bottom of this dark pit, the phone rang. I was never so happy to hear Uncle Perry's cheerful voice.

"I can't wait to meet this guy. I saw how anxious you were at your graduation and how disappointed you were when he didn't show up," he began. "Anyone who can put that sort of light in your eyes is a winner in my book."

"I wish you were here tonight, Uncle Perry."

"I would have come, but a good friend of mine

is celebrating his fiftieth birthday. It's very special
and . . ."

"Oh, I understand."

"And you're going to see me tomorrow, right?"

"Yes."

"Well, you try to get here early enough for me
to take both of you to lunch. I know your father and
Lucille have made dinner arrangements, and I thought
it would be better if that was just the four of you."

"You're more a part of my family than she'll ever
be," I said.

He was silent a moment. Then he said, "I appreciate what you're saying, Sam, but don't ever let her know
you feel that way. She's going to be your father's wife."

"I know," I said.

He laughed. "It's good to hear you sound so nervous over a boy. I mean, a young man. What about
my designs? I bet you haven't looked at them."

"Yes, I did. I love them. I'll bring them along
tomorrow with the list of magazines I know girls my
age read."

"Thanks, Sam. Have a great night tonight,"
he said. "I love you very much and want you to be
happy."

Tears came to my eyes. I thanked him and hung
up. His call was just the right medicine, however. My
enthusiasm and excitement came galloping back. I
was up and at it again, rushing about the house until
Mrs. Dobson gently suggested that I might want to
freshen up. It was nearly three!

I ran up to my room and did just that. Then I
went to my window and watched our front gate.

When people are nervous, they claim that they feel butterflies in their stomach. To me it felt as if I had swallowed a bag full of marbles and they were all rolling about.

When I saw the gate opening and a strange car coming through, I gasped and for a moment couldn't move. Then I shot out and down the stairs so quickly I nearly twisted my ankle on the last steps. I heard Mrs. Dobson's laughter but kept going, opened the front door, and rushed to the steps of our portico. Ethan pulled in behind my car and got out slowly. He was wearing a thin yellow cotton short-sleeved shirt and jeans. He wasn't gaping at everything stupidly, but it was obvious he was quite overcome, and he turned slowly to look at it all. Finally, he noticed me standing there and laughed.

"Hi!" he cried, walking toward me.

I came down the steps slowly. I didn't speak. He smiled, and then he just kissed me as if we were in the last scene of a romantic movie, the kiss long and warm.

"You look great," he said. Then he laughed again. "What happened? Did you lose your voice?"

"I can't believe you're really here."

He nodded, looked up at the house, and said, "Neither can I. I guess you weren't exaggerating about any of this. It's like a palace or something."

"It's just where I live," I said.

"Well, something tells me it's a little better than the motel I was thinking of checking into when I arrived. But I like the way you put it," he added. "Let me get my bag."

I followed him back to the rental car. He took out his suitcase and paused to look at my car.

"This is an Aston Martin," he said. "Someone else visiting?"

"No, this is my car. It was my graduation gift."

"You're kidding."

"Don't make a big thing of it," I said, pretending to be annoyed. "You're driving it tomorrow. We're going to Lexington to visit the store and have lunch with my uncle and dinner with my father and Lucille."

"Well, I'll cancel my appointment with the president in that case."

"You'd better," I quipped. He laughed and put his arm around my shoulders as I led him up the steps and into the Heavenstone mansion.

I didn't notice it until after I had introduced him to Mrs. Dobson and Doris and after I had shown him his room, but it was something I had been feeling all day.

Or, rather, something I had not been feeling.

Cassie was gone.

And in my heart, I harbored the hope that it was forever.

11

Arrival

IT WAS MRS. DOBSON who told me, "For goodness' sake, let the young man catch his breath, Miss Semantha."

I had immediately been dragging him through the house and was about to show him the grounds as well. She leaned over to add in a whisper, "He hasn't even unpacked."

Ethan laughed, but I realized I was overdoing it and insisted he march back up to his room and get his things out of his suitcase.

"Just leave anything on the bed that needs ironing," Mrs. Dobson called after us as we started back up the stairs. "Doris will stop by in an hour."

"You always live with this sort of service?" Ethan asked as we turned to go to his room.

"No. Before my mother passed away, we all worked on keeping the house and our things in order. Cassie was probably the best at it and the most dedicated. Despite the size of this house, my mother wanted to be in charge of its maintenance. It was a lot of work, but she wasn't at all involved in the Heavenstone business, and she enjoyed our privacy, our intimacy."

"I'm sure that was hard to do, considering how famous your family is in the state. She must have been quite a woman."

"She was," I said. "And she was very beautiful. I'll show you albums and pictures later, unless Mrs. Dobson thinks I'm overwhelming you again."

He laughed and pulled me closer to him. "I like it when you overwhelm me, Semantha. Don't stop," he said, and kissed my cheek.

"My father and Lucille should be home soon. Why don't we both shower and change and get ready to meet them for cocktails before dinner?" I said.

"Sounds like a plan. Knock on my door when you're ready."

He kissed me again, and we parted in the hall-way. I hurried to my room to prepare for what I hoped would be a wonderful night. Just after I showered, Daddy called to tell me they were on their way.

"Your young man arrived safely?"

"Yes, Daddy. We're just dressing to meet you and Lucille for cocktails."

"That's very good, Semantha. Lucille has gone ahead and made a reservation at Melvyn's for us all tonight."

"Oh, no, Daddy," I said. "Mrs. Dobson has made an extra special dinner, lobster Alfredo. I asked her to prepare something Italian because Ethan loves Italian food, and she came up with that. I thought it was a very good suggestion, so I told her to go ahead."

"Really?"

"She's doing a special dessert as well."

"Oh?"

I heard him mumbling to Lucille.

"Well, this is a surprise, Semantha."

"I'm sorry, Daddy. I was too occupied to tell you, but I thought it would be all right."

"Yes, yes, it's fine. I'm looking forward to it," he said. "See you soon."

I could tell from the little strain in his voice at the end that Lucille wasn't happy and had let him know it. Lately, she had been more critical of Mrs. Dobson's cooking. If she brought up my planning for dinner without first consulting her, I would remind her that she wanted me to take more responsibility in the house. That was just what I had done. I probably should have told them earlier, but that shouldn't upset them. Nevertheless, I felt my balloon of happiness lose some air. Worrying about upsetting Lucille had become more important than worrying about upsetting Daddy, because he was so tuned in to her every smile and grimace. I felt more like a ballerina dancing on a thinly frozen lake.

Thinking about it, about how much more complicated life at the Heavenstone estate had become, put me a bit of a daze, and I moved at a snail's pace, completely losing track of time. I had just started fixing my hair when there was a gentle knock on my door. I was still wrapped in a towel after showering and hadn't even chosen what to wear.

"Yes?"

Ethan peeked in.

"Oh, sorry. I forgot how much longer women need," he said, smiling.

"No, it's my fault. I've been moving too slowly. I'll be right with you," I said, moving to my vanity table.

"Mind if I come in and watch?"

"I'm just about to put on a little lipstick, that's all."

"Anything you do interests me, Semantha, no matter how small it might seem to you or anyone else. Didn't you ever hear the words in that song?" he asked, and then sang, "Little things mean a lot . . ."

I loved the way his eyes and his words quickened my heart and filled me with a wonderful sense of warmth, washing away the sting of nervous tension.

"Come in, silly. Don't sing in my doorway."

He came in, closed the door softly behind him, and stood behind me, looking at me in the mirror. With his eyes so fixed on me, it was hard to keep my hand steady as I worked my lipstick over my trembling lips.

"What?" I asked, seeing his expression change rapidly from impish joy to serious concern.

"My not contacting you right before your graduation and afterward was inexcusable, I know," he said in a voice just above a whisper, "but I hope you believe me when I say that all through the turmoil with my father, I kept thinking of you, seeing your face, hearing your voice. Maybe it was a good thing, because it kept me together enough to be a strength for my mother."

He put his hand gently on my right shoulder. I lowered the hairbrush and looked at him through the mirror as well.

"Really, why didn't you call, Ethan, so I would understand why you couldn't be there?"

He shook his head and lifted his hand from my shoulder. "That was the contradiction, the irony, I suppose. I wanted to call you, but I thought it would be inappropriate for me to be thinking of you and me during this critical time. I imagined my mother asking me whom I was calling and the expression on her face when I told her. I realize now how silly that was of me. She probably would have been understanding. Sometimes I act like such an ass."

"No, no. What you're saying makes sense now. You were thinking of your parents first. That was right. I'm not upset about it. I understand. If the roles had been reversed, I probably would have behaved the same way."

"Actually, it only made things worse. I was terrified of writing or calling you afterward. I never expected you would forgive me. I did behave like a horse's ass those last days, especially in the motel."

"I'm not so sure I would have behaved any differently had I been in your shoes and had such a story sprung on me like that."

"You're so good, Semantha, so forgiving."

He leaned forward to replace his fingers on my shoulder with a kiss instead. I closed my eyes to drink in and hold the wonderful electric pleasure it sent through my body, and then I felt him kiss my neck. I didn't open my eyes until I felt him slip the towel down and off my breasts. He cupped them, and I turned to bring my lips to his. He lifted me gently under my arms, and the towel fell off completely. We kissed again. He whispered my name, and then we heard voices. Lucille was on the stairway and was calling down some orders to Mrs. Dobson. I quickly picked up the towel and wrapped it around me.

"They're back," I said. "I'd better hurry."

"I should sneak back to my room," he said, and started for the door, but before he got to it, there was a knock, and without my saying anything, Lucille opened it and stepped in, stopping instantly when she saw Ethan. I held my breath, but instead of looking shocked, she smiled.

"Oh. I'm sorry. I didn't mean to interrupt anything. I just wanted to let you know we were back and see where you were in your preparations for dinner. Your father had to make an important phone call. Naturally."

Ethan turned to me like someone sinking in quicksand hoping to be rescued.

"This is Ethan Hunter, Lucille. We were just getting ready ourselves."

"Yes," she said. "I assumed that's who you were. I'm very happy to meet you," she said, extending her hand to Ethan. I hadn't realized until then that whenever Lucille held her hand out to someone, she turned her palm down as if she expected him or her to kiss her ring. Ethan gently and quickly shook her hand.

"Me, too. I mean, happy to meet you. I'm sorry for my dumbfounded look. I guess I'm still quite taken with the Heavenstone estate. It's all so . . ."

"Overwhelming?" she offered, shifting her eyes toward me wrapped in my towel.

"Yes, exactly."

"Don't feel embarrassed. I can't imagine anyone who comes here for the first time being anything but overwhelmed. Did you have a good trip?"

"Terrific. Everything was on time." He turned to me. "I'll just return to my room and wait for you, Semantha," he said, fumbling for a smooth exit.

"Don't be silly," Lucille said, reaching out to seize his left arm. "Go right down to Mr. Heavenstone's office and introduce yourself to Semantha's father. He should be finished with his phone call by now. You men need time together without us flitting about you like moths drawn to candles," she said, giving him one of her deepest, warmest smiles.

He looked to me for a reaction.

"Yes, that's a good idea, Ethan. I need another ten minutes or so."

"Okay," Ethan said. "See you soon." He paused at the door to nod at Lucille. She remained behind, watching him leave, and then turned to me.

"I didn't mean to burst in on you two. I guess I have to wait to hear you say 'enter.' Sorry."

"It's all right, Lucille."

"You didn't tell me how handsome he was. And what a manly, firm demeanor. He handled what could have been an embarrassing situation very well. I've met enough so-called sophisticated young men these days to know he's something special. I'm happy for you, Semantha. Congratulations on your conquest."

Her unexpected burst of compliments stirred mixed feelings. Of course, I was happy to hear her instant approval, but even from the short time I had known Lucille, I sensed this was quite uncharacteristic. From what I had seen of the way she reacted to people, especially people she met for the first time, whether they were salesladies in department stores or waiters in restaurants, there was always a layer of cynicism for them to crack first before she would have a kind word or get off her pedestal. In her philosophy, people, no matter who they were, were to be suspected and doubted first. She had even muttered that she believed respect should be the final gift bestowed on any stranger. And there was never any doubt in my mind that she saw herself treating anyone with respect as a gift bestowed from high above to them.

"I've made no conquest, Lucille. We're not engaged or anything. He's just visiting for a few days." I couldn't help sounding a bit annoyed, even though I wasn't sure why I should.

"Of course you're not engaged, but one look at his face when he looks at you tells me you've made a conquest. Don't be embarrassed. All I'm saying is that he makes a very good first impression. I think you've had enough experience to know it takes time and great caution before you invest in any relationship. At least, I hope you have."

Where I got the nerve to say it I don't know. Maybe it was Cassie's touch, but I held my ground and replied, "You and my father haven't been seeing each other all that long, have you, and you have invested in a long relationship."

She smiled, but not coldly or coyly. It was more like a high school girl's dreamy, soft smile.

"No, not terribly long, but when you reach our

ages and have been through so many emotional battles and journeys, you develop a deeper wisdom. Just like an experienced diamond cutter can tell you almost instantly whether a diamond is worth a great deal or not, your father and I can peel away what's necessary to see what is truly in our hearts, and we've both found gold. I hope you do as well." She turned and went to the door. "I'll see you downstairs, and over the next day or so, I hope to help you to see exactly what you've found. You seem a tad unsure. I only wish to help you build your own self-confidence, Semantha."

My mixed feelings lingered, but now I was thinking that I might have misjudged her again and been unnecessarily harsh when she was only trying to be happy for me. Oh, why did everything have to be so complicated? For a moment, I actually wished I did have Cassie at my side. But then I quickly reminded myself that I had to be my own person now, sink or swim.

I hurried to get ready, afraid that Daddy would frighten or intimidate Ethan so much that he would cut his stay short, but when I started down the stairway, I could hear them both laughing. They were already having cocktails.

"Well, here's our little princess now," Daddy declared when I entered the living room.

He and Ethan were sitting across from each other. Ethan rose. Daddy looked at him with delighted surprise and nodded at me before rising himself.

"White wine, Semantha?"

"Yes, please, Daddy."

He went to the marble bar to open a fresh bottle of Chardonnay, Lucille's favorite.

"You look terrific," Ethan said.

I had decided to wear the strapless aqua blue dress I had worn for Daddy's last birthday party. I expected to hear Daddy say something about it, but he didn't. Mother had once told me that Daddy was as oblivious to what she wore as any stranger might be. He hadn't been that way with Cassie, but she was right when it came to her or to me. "But," she had added, "he never fails to tell me how beautiful I look. It's a standing joke for him to ask me if I have just bought a dress, even though I have worn it two or three times."

I did notice, however, that Daddy never seemed to fail to remark about Lucille's clothes. At least in that regard, his behavior toward a woman other than Cassie had changed, but then again, I wasn't there when he had first begun seeing Mother. Perhaps he had given her as much attention then, too. Cassie, of course, had blamed Mother for Daddy's indifference.

"She lets him take her for granted. She never surprises him," she had said. I should have known back then, sensed how unnatural it was for a daughter to be so critical of her mother, but, like Daddy, I made excuses for her. Cassie was just too intelligent to be anything but objective and honest.

"Let's wait for Lucille before making any sort of toast," Daddy said, handing me my glass of wine. "Now, then, Samantha, you didn't tell me Mr. Hunter was majoring in business and had won his college's coveted future entrepreneur award. How could you overlook something like that?"

"I didn't know about any award," I said, looking at Ethan. "You never mentioned it, or I would have remembered."

"Oh, modest, eh, Ethan?" Daddy said. "Let me give you some quick advice. No one blows your horn better than you do yourself. I don't care whom you hire to promote your business or your career. They just won't have the same passion. There's no shame in being proud of your accomplishments, and more often than not, we have to blast our own headlines."

"You're right," Ethan said. "I see that now, especially in this competitive environment."

"Precisely. Ah, here she is!" Daddy cried. "Ethan, this is—"

"We already met, Teddy," Lucille said.

I was surprised she had gone strapless as well and put on one of her more elegant black satin dresses with a pleated bust. She complemented it with a pair of emerald and diamond earrings and a four-leaf clover emerald and diamond necklace strung on gold.

"Well, look at that," Daddy said. "Lucille's wearing a special gift I gave her. You should be honored, Ethan. Those earrings and necklace marked a little anniversary of ours."

Lucille laughed. "Your father insists on giving me gifts every month to celebrate our first real date," she said.

"I don't blame him," Ethan said.

Lucille's eyes seemed to glitter when she looked at him and gave a little nod of thanks.

"Glass of your white wine?" Daddy said, pouring it.

"Yes, my dear." She moved to the bar.

I stepped closer to Ethan. "Their little anniversary was the first night I met you," I whispered.

"Then I'll have to start giving you a gift, too," he replied.

"Well, then, let's toast the hope that Ethan enjoys his visit," Daddy said, raising his glass.

Lucille held her smile. "I think I can safely say he's already done that," she said.

Ethan blushed and drank rather than speaking.

Our conversations that night both during cocktails and at dinner moved through more topics than ever. I could see that Daddy was quite impressed with how much Ethan knew about the current retail scene, including some favorable and not-so-favorable business tax laws. Whenever the conversation got too dry for her taste, Lucille changed the topic to something to do with their upcoming wedding. Discussion of food and music led to more about the wedding menu and the choices she had made for the orchestra.

"This sounds like the wedding of the century," Ethan remarked.

"To us, it is," Lucille replied. "But you're very nice to say so."

To my surprise, she gave Mrs. Dobson a compliment on the dinner as well, but afterward, she did say that for real lobster Alfredo, we would have to go to Eva's Bistro in Lexington.

After dinner, we went into the den, where Daddy showed Ethan all of his fine electronics, his stereos and high-definition television.

"Not that we have that much time to spend on home entertainment these days," he said.

"It's no one's fault but your own, Teddy," Lucille gently chastised. "You should have better executives on your staff so you would feel more comfortable about assigning responsibilities. You're no different from a president and his cabinet."

"Take note, Ethan," Daddy said. "A good woman sees where her man needs to be strengthened and subtly, perhaps not so subtly sometimes, makes sure that's what happens."

"Maybe that's because we take criticism best from those we love and those who love us," Ethan said, focusing on me when he said it.

"Well said," Daddy replied.

Soon after, Lucille suggested that Ethan and I go for a walk.

"After all, Teddy," she told Daddy, "they don't need to spend all their time with us. I'm sure they have lots of catching up to do."

"Oh, sure, sure. Go on. Show him the pool," Daddy suggested. "All the ground lights are on. Enjoy."

"Thank you, sir," Ethan said, and then looked to me. I rose and led him out.

"My soon-to-be stepmother has a way of taking over everything," I muttered. "Even our agenda."

"Actually, I'm glad she made the suggestion," Ethan whispered. He laughed and hurried us out of the house. "But don't misunderstand me. Your father's a terrific guy. He made me feel comfortable from the moment I met him."

"I'm glad, Ethan."

"I can see why he's so successful. And your future stepmother's quite a nice surprise, too." When I didn't comment, he added, "Don't you like her?"

"What is it they say? The jury's still out."

He laughed and then grew serious, his eyes narrowing and focusing on mine. "No one can replace your mother, I'm sure. That's what your father's going through. It's not easy to marry someone who was happily married but who lost his or her spouse."

"Let's not talk about it right now," I said, maybe too sharply.

He stopped talking, and we just walked until we came to the pool. As Daddy had said, everything was lit up. The water glistened.

"This is beautiful," Ethan said. "This looks like an Olympic-size pool."

"Almost."

"I was on the swimming team in high school, you know."

"No, you didn't mention it, just like you didn't mention your college award."

"Yeah, well, I kind of got caught up in my ambitions and chose not to join any teams at college. I didn't want to take away from my work. I was determined to graduate with honors. How about we take a swim tomorrow before breakfast with your father and future stepmother?"

I laughed at his enthusiasm. "Okay," I said, "but Daddy gets up early."

"And Lucille?"

"Often just as early."

"So, if we miss them, we miss them. We'll see them when we go to Lexington," he said. "I didn't come here to spend time with them, anyway."

I was glad to hear that. For a few moments, I thought he was more intrigued with my father and Lucille and the Heavenstone business than with me.

He flopped onto a chaise and patted the space beside him for me to join him.

"I could sleep out here under the stars tonight if you were with me," he said. "Hey, that way, when we wake up, we could just undress and jump in the pool."

"You're kidding, right?"

"I can dream, can't I?"

He put his arm around me, and I relaxed with my head on his shoulder.

"It's so quiet here," he said. "Where I live, there's so much traffic noise, horns, brakes screeching, and clatter that you don't even want to keep your windows open at night. I'm sure glad I made this trip."

"Me, too."

He turned to kiss me, and then he just stared a moment too long.

"What?"

"I'm really, really sorry for the way I behaved at the motel. It was just such a shock to hear about your horrible experience, made even more horrible because of your sister's involvement."

"It's all right, Ethan. Please stop mentioning it."

"No, it's not all right. It was immature of me, and selfish. I should have had more sympathy and understanding. How often does it come up? I mean, with your father?"

"Never," I said. "He acts as if it never happened."

"So, there's really no contact . . . I mean, what you told me about those cousins and . . ."

"No. They won't even be invited to the wedding."

He nodded. "Well," he said after a long moment. "Then that's how I'll treat it, too, like it never happened."

I know he was saying that to make me feel better, but it didn't. If I told him how I celebrated my daughter's birthday and how often I imagined her crying, he might think differently, but it wasn't something I wanted to share with anyone, not yet and maybe not ever.

We actually fell asleep in each other's arms for a while at the pool, he because of the trip and me because of all the excitement. I also hoped it was because we were so comfortable wrapped up in each other, so comfortable and safe, that we had no fear just drifting from words to thoughts to dreams. He was awake before I was. When I opened my eyes, he was staring at me and smiling.

"How long have you been awake?" I asked.

"A while. I didn't want to wake you. You looked so angelic."

I sat up and ran my fingers through my hair. The few clouds that had been loitering in the sky above had moved on and left the stars undressed.

"It sure is a beautiful night," Ethan said.

"Angel eyes."

"Pardon?"

"That's what my mother called the stars."

"Very nice."

"We should probably go in. It's late, and you have some wild idea about getting up early," I said.

He laughed, stood up, and took my hand.

We walked back silently, and when we entered the house, it was quiet as well. The lights had been turned off in the den. Mrs. Dobson and Doris had long since cleaned up after dinner, and both had gone to bed. There were no lights on down the hallway coming from Daddy's office, so he wasn't up late catching up on some important business.

"Everyone's asleep," I whispered.

We practically tiptoed up the stairway. At my bedroom door, we paused, and Ethan kissed me good night, but he didn't just kiss me and go off. He held me for a few long moments, embracing me as if we had been apart for years or had crossed oceans to be together again. Perhaps in his eyes, coming to the Heavenstone estate was like crossing some sort of ocean, overcoming some deep and wide gap between us. He kissed me again and whispered good night. I watched him start away. He turned and in a louder whisper said, "Wake me when you wake."

"If I don't and you wake first, wake me," I whispered back.

He smiled and went to his room. I couldn't recall a night when I had gone to sleep with a fuller heart and a deeper faith in my dreams to come. No nightmare would dare cross my threshold of happiness, not a sad thought, not a fear, nothing. Sleep would be more like drifting in warm space, waiting for the gentle nudge of morning sunlight to wake me, and never would I be more eager to awaken and greet a new day.

I curled up in my bed and snuggled against my comforter and pillow, scented and soft. Had I been dreaming before I had gone to bed? Was Ethan Hunter really sleeping in the room just across and down the hall from mine? I almost felt it necessary to get up and peek into his room to see if he was truly there. I laughed at myself and then thought only of his eyes, his smile, and his lips on mine. As I had hoped, sleep quickly embraced me and took me prisoner for the night.

I thought I was still dreaming when I heard my name being whispered in my ear. I opened my eyes and saw Ethan kneeling beside my bed. He had one of our Heavenstone emblem guest robes on. My eyelids flickered, and I sat up.

"I heard your father and Lucille go down to breakfast," he said. "I can't believe you slept longer than me."

"I had more dreams to finish," I told him, and he laughed. He sat on the floor and continued to look up at me. "Didn't you sleep well?"

"Oh, sure. That bed's a cloud. I just thought it would be sort of impolite not to join them for breakfast. I don't want your father thinking I'm a goof-off."

"I thought you said you weren't concerned. You were here to see me."

"I know, but I don't like coming off like some playboy or something."

"I won't let him think that. Don't worry."

"We could get dressed and down there before they leave, just to show our faces."

"I'd rather you crawled in here," I said, lifting the blanket.

He smiled, looked at the door, and shook his head. "I'd be too nervous."

"Lucille promised never to walk in without my permission again."

"Later," he insisted, and rose. "Let's do it. Let's get down there before they leave."

I supposed I should be more understanding. To me, Daddy was just Daddy, but to someone outside our family, he was surely a superstar. That was especially true for Ethan now that he had seen firsthand what the Heavenstone family estate was. Reluctantly, I agreed, and he rushed off to dress. I moaned, rose, and scrubbed my face, brushed my hair, and threw on a robe. He returned fully dressed in a pair of slacks and a nice, sparrow-blue shirt.

"You could have gone down in a robe, too," I told him. "Now I'll look like the spoiled one."

"It's all right for you to look like that, but not me. You're the Heavenstone princess."

I know I should have been flattered, but when he said that, it made me wince. All my life, I had been trying not to be a princess in the eyes of my school-mates and especially at Collier, but it did seem impossible. Like some member of royalty, I merely had to ask Daddy for something and it would be at my feet pretty quickly.

"Don't get stuffy on me," I warned. He laughed but looked a little anxious. It was as if he were afraid to do anything that would upset me even in the smallest way. "I'm just kidding, Ethan. Let's go before you have a nervous breakdown and need my therapist."

That brought smiles back to his face, and we giggled our way down the stairs and to the dining room. They were just finishing up, but I have to say Daddy did look pleased that we had come down before they left.

"I assume you both slept well," Lucille said.

"This house could cure insomnia," Ethan told her.

Daddy laughed, and Ethan began asking him just the sorts of questions about some of our artifacts, portraits, and framed documents that he loved. In fact, it was Lucille who reminded him how late it was getting.

"We'll finish the conversation at dinner tonight," he declared. "Lucille has asked our store manager, Richard Erickson, to personally greet and escort you about the store. I understand you're going to lunch with Perry, Semantha?"

"Yes, Daddy."

"Great. I hope you enjoy the day," he said, and then he did something he hadn't done for quite a while. He paused at my chair and waited for me to rise to kiss him good-bye. I looked at Lucille, but I couldn't tell from the expression on her face whether that pleased or annoyed her. It was just that sort of emotionless expression that Cassie had used to call a mask of ice.

And like a mask of ice, it left me with a chill.

And left me with a question. Does it eventually melt away, or does it come and go whenever the truth would be too dangerous to know?

12

Like a Dream

OUR DAY AT one of the Heavenstone Stores turned out to be as educational for me as it was for Ethan. Because I was with him and he knew so many important questions to ask, I learned so much more about Heavenstone Department Stores' operations. Neither Daddy nor Lucille was there in the morning. They were attending some chamber of commerce meeting, but it was clear that Richard Erickson had been given strict orders to devote most of his energies and attention to our tour.

Richard Erickson had been with the store for nearly ten years, but I couldn't recall saying five words to him or him saying five words to me before this. It was clear that he was nervous, however. He was tall and thin, with delicate facial features for a man, including eyelashes girls like Ellie would kill to have. He continually cleared his throat before replying and shifted his light brown eyes from me as if he were afraid of being discovered incompetent. Later, Uncle Perry would reveal that most of the managers in the stores were concerned about Lucille's scrutiny of their work and were just as nervous as Mr.

Erickson, who probably suspected that I might report back to her. Uncle Perry didn't seem critical of Lucille for this, but he didn't seem to approve, either.

"Just from the little I know and have seen of Mr. Heavenstone," Ethan said after he heard Uncle Perry's explanation, "I wouldn't think he would fire anyone who was doing a good job. He strikes me as being what we call a 'bottom-line man.'"

Uncle Perry glanced at me. I saw that small, impish smile invade the corners of his mouth. "A man in love often has cloudy eyes, which could fog up the bottom line," he said. "And my brother is without a doubt a man in love."

Ethan laughed, but I already knew when his laugh was sincere and when it was a response to what was expected. I wanted to lean over at the restaurant table and whisper, "You never have to be subtle or afraid of telling Uncle Perry the truth. There's not a mean bone in his body, and he is no gossip."

Later, Ethan did relax with Uncle Perry when they got into a discussion about his design department and the advertising for the stores. I saw that Uncle Perry was impressed with Ethan's understanding of the various media outlets. He rattled off so many facts and figures someone would think he had spent his last four years of college majoring in the Heavenstone Corporation.

"You have a pretty bright young man here," Uncle Perry told me when Ethan left to go to the bathroom. "Bright and quite good-looking. I spoke for only a minute or so with Teddy this morning, but he seemed quite pleased with him." Then he leaned forward to ask sotto voce, "What does Lucille think of him? Any clue?"

"I'm sure her jury's still out," I said.

He laughed. "I'd hate to have her on a jury judging me, even if I knew I was innocent," he said. "She'd make the defense attorney work his rear off, but I suppose that's a good quality. She is an extraordinary woman, different from your mother, but perhaps just what the doctor ordered for Teddy right now. I can't believe this wedding. It's turning out to be the social event of the year. There are people actually trying to get invited, conniving for an invitation. I can't tell you how many calls I've received from people asking me to do them a favor or promising to do me one if I can deliver."

Ethan returned as Uncle Perry finished what he was saying.

"From what I've heard about it, I don't blame them. I think if I were one of them, I'd try just as hard for an invitation," he said.

Uncle Perry smiled at me. "I don't think you'll have to work that hard to get anyone you want an invite, right, Sam?" He winked. It hadn't occurred to me until that moment to invite Ethan. I suppose I had been thinking he would be back home looking to find some meaningful employment.

Besides, when it came to the wedding, there was something else on my mind. I didn't want to bring it up right now, but my father's agreeing with Lucille to replace Uncle Perry as his best man was still bothering me.

"Maybe it's becoming too much of an event, more like a political event, Uncle Perry."

"What do you mean?"

"Having the senator be my father's best man," I replied. "I'm sure they're not that close."

Ethan's eyebrows rose. I hadn't told him about any of that. "A United States senator?" he asked.

I nodded. "Uncle Perry should be my father's best man."

"Oh, don't worry about it," Uncle Perry said. "I was your father's best man when he married your mother. That meant far more to me than it would this time around."

My eyes glistened with tears. He couldn't have said anything that would have given me more comfort.

"Let's just ride with the tide, Sam. We'll all do just fine," he added, reaching to squeeze my hand. "C'mon, let's get back to my offices. I want to show you where you'd work if you want to have a real job, and I'd like your opinion of a new advertising concept involving the Internet, Ethan."

"Absolutely. I'd be honored," he said.

Uncle Perry gave me a sort of half-smile, one that signaled a note of caution. Ethan was sounding a little too diplomatic. It opened the door to a Cassie-like thought. *Christmas trees, Semantha. Get him to stop trying so hard. Even a blind man could see through the coats of sugar.*

When we stepped into the parking lot, Uncle Perry whistled at my car. "What was it like driving that over here?" he asked Ethan.

"Like I had stepped into some dream machine. We didn't ride; we floated."

We entered Uncle Perry's offices, and he immediately showed Ethan some of his advertising plans for the Internet. Although he was nice about it, Ethan was very critical. He supported all of his criticism with good information, and by the end of the afternoon, he had persuaded Uncle Perry to make changes.

"You do have a pretty bright guy here," Uncle Perry told me when we could speak without Ethan overhearing. "And someone who's not afraid to disagree when he thinks he's right. I wasn't expecting it. I like that."

His review of Ethan made my day, but I couldn't say I was very excited about my prospective area in Uncle Perry's offices. It made me feel a bit claustrophobic. He sensed it and told me to take my time deciding. He promised that no matter what I decided, he would still rely on me for advice. It made me think of Lucille's advice, which was similar, but I didn't tell him that. Maybe I was the one who was being the diplomat now.

Later, when we were alone again, Ethan told me he didn't think I would enjoy spending my time in a small office at one of the stores. He almost parroted Lucille word for word, telling me I should be out among younger people more.

"Maybe you should take your time and enroll in some college classes," he added. "You have a good community college nearby."

I didn't say anything, but there was a part of me that wasn't happy with the suggestion. If I were a young man seeing a girl like me, I wouldn't want her in any environment where she could meet someone else and maybe fall in love with someone else. "Love when it's real and passionate makes you selfish," Mother had once told me. I had been too young then to fully understand what she meant, but I understood it now. You become unreasonably jealous and don't like sharing your loved one with anyone, even for good reason.

I think Ethan saw the disappointment in my face. He quickly added, "As long as it's an all-girl college."

Lucille had thought of everything for us when she and Daddy had planned our day. She had arranged for both of us to freshen up at the store's executive bathrooms and had the head of the men's clothing department arrange for Ethan to be dressed and fitted in something new. The same was done for me in the women's department. It was as if Christmas had arrived early. Because I had never really taken advantage of being my father's daughter at any of our stores, both Ethan and I felt like kids turned loose in a candy store. We rushed up and down the stairs to show each other what we might choose.

Afterward, when Daddy and Lucille met us and Lucille complimented our choices, Ethan said, "I never felt so guilty. I've never taken so much from anyone without somehow earning it."

"Please consider it Mr. Heavenstone's and my graduation present for you, Ethan," Lucille replied.

"Yes, but—"

"Please, don't make a big thing of it," she firmly insisted.

He said no more, but it really did seem to bother him, and I could see that earned him another brownie point with my father. It impressed Daddy enough for him to offer Ethan some of the advice his father had given him.

"Lucille's right. It's our pleasure—but you're right, too, Ethan. Never let yourself get too indebted to anyone. Semantha's grandfather always told me to make sure that whoever gave me a dollar got something worth a dollar from me. Obligations poison your well of independence."

"Absolutely," Ethan replied. "My father's given me similar advice at times."

"Wise man."

"You two worry too much about the small stuff," Lucille half joked.

Afterward, we went to the wonderful, elegant restaurant she had chosen for our dinner. Even I was impressed with how important everyone there made us all seem. I could see Ethan was truly overwhelmed, but he kept his poise, and when Daddy asked him for his opinions on what he had seen at the store, he had a lot to say, much of which seemed to impress Daddy and Lucille as much as it had Uncle Perry.

"It's good to have fresh eyes every once in a while," Lucille said. "People can get too confident in the status quo."

"Absolutely," Daddy said.

I thought that if it were raining and Lucille said the sun was shining, Daddy would agree. Was that the Cassie in me again?

But it had been a wonderful day and evening. Ethan and I were both flying high on the drive home. Daddy and Lucille announced that they were staying at his usual hotel suite in the city because they had some very important early meetings to attend. Plans were made for us all to have dinner the following night, with Lucille choosing the restaurant rather than us eating at home. Nothing had been said about how long Ethan was staying, but we all assumed he wouldn't have come all this way for just three nights. When I asked him when he intended to leave, what day his return airplane ticket was for, he surprised me by telling me he had left it open. He gave me a shy look.

"I wasn't sure how you would feel about me considering how we ended up in Albany. I thought you might be just being polite, but I was willing to take the chance."

"I'm glad you did, Ethan."

He smiled and sped up. Neither of us could wait to get home.

It was late, so I didn't anticipate seeing either Mrs. Dobson or Doris waiting up for us, but when we started up the stairway, I thought I saw Mrs. Dobson peering around a corner. She really was like a grandmother to me, worrying that I was home safely. We paused at my bedroom door. He reached out to embrace me.

"Not here," I said, and continued on to his guest bedroom. He didn't need an explanation. Without a word, he opened the door for me, and I entered. His first kiss was cautious, careful, almost as careful a kiss as a man would give a woman who had a bruised lip. I pulled him back and kissed him so long and hard that it brought a smile of amusement to his face.

"I get the message," he said, laughing, and kissed me again, this time running his lips down my neck and then lifting me to carry me to his bed. I lay there unmoving, watching him undress before he crawled in beside me and started to undress me as well. Neither of us spoke, me worried that I would somehow cause him to lose his passion and desire and him afraid, I'm sure, that he would say something that would stir up my painful memories again. Silence was our best ally right now, and we both knew it.

His kisses and his caresses, our embraces and unrestrained hunger for each other, said it all anyway. Neither of us seemed to think or care about any consequences. There was a rhythm and flow to our lovemaking that forebade the slightest interruption or hesitation. We were almost like two people in a panic, afraid that if we paused, we would be lost to some disaster. Instinct and raw passion seized us. All the while, I kept chanting to myself that this was going to end any doubt, any fear I had about being incapable of loving and making love. I was not ruined after all. I had just as promising a future as any girl my age.

My moans and cries at the right moments gave him more confidence and satisfaction. At one point, he pressed his hands to the bed and lifted himself so he could look down at me and study everything in my face, the hot crimson in my cheeks, the excitement in my eyes, and the wetness on my lips. He dropped his gaze to my breasts and my stomach, and I saw the pleasure in his face. It was as if he were an artist, not a lover, and he had become Pygmalion, the mythological Greek sculptor who fell in love with his own statue. His slight intermission seemed to give him even more sexual energy. We went on until, exhausted and satisfied, we lay beside each other listening to the pounding of our hearts and our wonderful gasps.

"Stay with me tonight," he whispered. "I want to fall asleep with you in my arms."

I snuggled beside him and pressed my cheek to his chest. I could hear his heartbeat slowly normalizing and felt his lips on my forehead. Neither of us spoke. Sleep was like a warm blanket draped over us. When I woke, he was still there beside me, looking into my eyes. We kissed and made love again. Then I hurried out and to my room, at least to make it seem as if I had slept there. I was too embarrassed to face Mrs. Dobson at breakfast with her knowing that I had spent the evening in Ethan's bed. I had no fear of her saying anything or even indicating to me that she knew, but it was enough that I would know she knew.

Ethan got his wish that morning, too. Before we went to breakfast, he insisted we take a dip in the pool. We hurried down and out in our bathing suits and really woke up in the water, splashing each other playfully and then just floating about with me in his arms and my lips just as passionate and demanding of his as his were of mine. Afterward, I had Mrs. Dobson serve us breakfast on the patio so we could remain in our bathing suits and robes. It was turning out to be a perfect day, with just a wisp of a cloud here and there and the breeze a warm caress. The air was perfumed with flowers and freshly cut grass. Ethan sat back and looked at it all with such pleasure in his face he made me see it as if for the first time, too. I told him so, and he smiled.

"Whenever you see something you've seen many times before but now with someone you care deeply for, or love, it does become fresh and new."

"Love?" I asked softly. *Dare we use that word so soon?* I wondered.

He shrugged. "A good test of that is just what you said. When you're in love with someone, you suddenly see everything through her eyes or his. It's as if you share your bodies, your minds, and your very souls."

"That's quite poetic for a business major," I kidded.

He laughed. "You're too clever. No, those aren't my words. I read them but never forgot them in the hope that someday I'd have good reason to use them."

"And now you have?"

"Wouldn't have said them otherwise," he replied, sipping his coffee and focusing his eyes on me. "Am I going too fast?"

"Only if it has an end," I said.

He smiled, rose, and leaned over to kiss me. "Then I'm going too slowly," he whispered.

I did wish I could freeze us forever in the rest of the day. Everything we did, although I had done it before, now seemed special. We went rowing on our lake, and later Mrs. Dobson prepared a picnic lunch for us and we spread a blanket at one of the high spots of the Heavenstone property, enabling us to look out at the forest and rolling hills to the west. We talked for hours, as if we had to reveal as much to each other as possible in the quickest possible time. Exhausted by our own enthusiasm, we once again fell asleep in each other's arms and then walked back to the house slowly, holding hands and moving like two people in a wonderful dream, dreading awakening.

As if we knew we were candles burning at both ends, we agreed to some time alone after which we would get ready to meet my father and Lucille for cocktails and dinner. It wasn't until I looked at the framed picture of me and my mother that Lucille had given me that I thought at all about Cassie. I was too content, too happy, to permit a single dark thought even to show its shadowed face. But I did think of questions to ask her.

Oh, why didn't you let me have a romance like this, enjoy a promise like this, Cassie? Why didn't you love me enough to want happiness for me, too? What had I done to you? How twisted and painful your soul must be, trapped in that iron coffin of envy. You were in it even before you died.

Before she could respond, I rushed to shower and wash my hair and then fill my thoughts only with ways to make myself even more attractive for Ethan. There would be no image in my mirror besides my own, and my ears would shut themselves to any words that did not come from my own lips.

Refreshed and dressed, Ethan and I went down to meet my father and Lucille, who seemed as happy and buoyed by their relationship as Ethan and I were by ours. The music, laughter, and clinking of cocktail glasses gave me the feeling Daddy and Lucille were as young as Ethan and I. We were like two couples double-dating. I couldn't remember Daddy as carefree and silly, and Lucille couldn't have been any nicer to Ethan. Daddy and Lucille had heard some feedback on the way the store's employees had reacted to Ethan and me. I suspected some of it had come from Uncle Perry. It amused them that we had been seen as the prince and princess of Heavenstone. For me, the only sour note was the joy Lucille seemed to take in how much our employees trembled.

"Your father and I think you two should visit every store in the chain," she added. They both laughed. I saw that Ethan enjoyed it, too, but for me, it was as if a wonderful orchestra playing a symphony had hit a sour note.

"Fear isn't the same as respect," I said. My heart skipped a beat. It wasn't something I would say. It was Cassie. She had found an opening through which to poke her head.

Everyone stopped laughing.

"How did you manage to bring up so sensitive and humble a daughter, Teddy?" Lucille asked, her face masked in a cold smile.

Daddy just looked at me. I knew he wanted to say something nice about me, but he was caught between pleasing me and offending Lucille.

"Daddy never looked down on his employees," I said, "but maybe it was also the influence of my mother."

If I had set off a bomb in the room, it wouldn't

have had more of an effect. Lucille turned away and looked at her watch.

"We should think about leaving for the restaurant."

"Absolutely," Daddy said, eager to move on.

Ethan looked from one to the other, resembling a man on a tightrope, afraid to lean in any direction.

"Should we all go in my car?" Daddy asked.

"Why wouldn't we?" Lucille replied for everyone.

When we got into Daddy's car, she seized the moment again, this time turning the conversation to Ethan, using her questions like searchlights on his past. After a while, I thought it was more like a job interview. It continued even at the restaurant. And then, on the way home, she asked him when he intended to leave.

"I'd like to stay longer, but I think I'd better get back tomorrow to see how things are with my father."

"As you should," Lucille said.

I was quiet because he hadn't said this to me, and I couldn't help resenting that he had replied to her without first discussing it with me.

"Well," Lucille continued after the long pause, "of course, it's really Semantha's decision and not ours, but Teddy and I would like to invite you back for our wedding."

"Thank you," Ethan said. He turned to me, and I looked away, tears now coming into my eyes. That had been going to be my surprise tonight after we had gotten home.

No one spoke. They were all waiting for me.

"I already had Ethan's invitation made out and ready to give him tonight," I said.

"Oh, I'm sorry, honey," Lucille said. "I upstaged you. Forgive me, please."

"Semantha is not that kind of a girl," Daddy said. He glanced back at me and flashed a smile.

Suddenly, Cassie was there beside me. I felt her put her hand into mine. She leaned over to whisper in my ear.

"*Being first isn't as important as being right,*" she prompted.

Like some ventriloquist's dummy, I repeated it. Silence can somehow sound like thunder.

Lucille turned and smiled at me. "You're absolutely right, Semantha. That's very true. I am sorry I spoiled your surprise."

"It's not spoiled for me," Ethan said, putting his arm around me to draw me closer to him. When he did that, Cassie disappeared. "If you want me here," he whispered, "I'll come back."

"Of course I want you here."

He kissed me softly, and I leaned against him. No one spoke for the remainder of the trip. Lucille phrased another sort of apology when we entered the house. At this point, mostly for Daddy's sake, I made it sound as if it was all about nothing much and she shouldn't worry. The four of us parted at the top of the stairway. Daddy kissed me good night and said, "Thanks for being understanding."

I watched them go to their bedroom and then caught up with Ethan.

"You can be tough when you want to," he said, and quickly added, "I like that."

"Come in," I said, opening my bedroom door

this time. He followed me in, and I handed him the wedding invitation I had waiting for him on my vanity table. "I was going to give it to you as soon as you told me you were leaving."

"Thanks. I spoke with my mother today after we had come in from our picnic and decided I should get back there for a while. I hate leaving you, so I delayed saying anything."

"I am happy they wanted to invite you, Ethan. I suppose I would have felt uncomfortable about it if I had given you this and then told them and not felt they were pleased about it."

"I'm glad they like me, but how you feel is far more important, Semantha."

He kissed me and then began to move toward making love to me.

I hesitated. "I'm really tired, and you've got a journey tomorrow," I said.

"Sure," he said, and smiled. "It's not like I'll be gone too long." He gave me a quick good-night kiss and then paused at the door. "I'll wake you if you're not up for breakfast."

"I'll be up."

"Sweet dreams," he said.

I was still staring at the door after he closed it. I knew it would only be moments, and I was right.

Cassie was there.

"Nothing is as simple as it seems," she said. *"Especially when it comes to men and Lucille. You can't shut me out, Semantha."*

I didn't argue, but I didn't agree. I went to bed and tried to think only about Ethan and our wonderful time together. I guess I was a lot more tired than I thought. I was asleep only moments after I lowered my head to the pillow, and I slept much later into the morning than I had anticipated. When I woke and saw the time, I shot out of bed, afraid that Ethan had already left. I was nearly dressed and out when he came to my room, laughing.

"How long have you been up?"

"Hours," he said. "I came in to wake you, but you were sleeping so soundly I couldn't do it. I had time anyway, so I joined your father and Lucille for breakfast. I checked on you twice, finished packing, and now I've returned."

"I'm sorry, Ethan."

"It's okay."

From the way he was beaming, I knew there was something more he wanted to tell me.

"What is it?" I said. "You do look like the cat who swallowed the canary."

"Your father offered me a good job at the local Heavenstone Store."

"What sort of job?"

"Assistant manager," he said. "I have to say, I think Lucille had a lot to do with it."

I knew he was waiting for my excited reaction, but it was as though Cassie were replicating herself all over my room. First she was in the right corner nodding, and then she was in the left. She was directly behind Ethan and then next to him.

"Aren't you pleased?"

"Yes, of course I am. When would you start?"

"Right after the wedding," he said. "I'm kind of

excited about it. It's like getting a promotion before you even begin."

"Is it really what you want to do, Ethan?"

"What sort of a question is that? A managerial position in the Heavenstone Corporation? I know at least a dozen MBAs who would die for this."

"Then I'm really happy for you," I said.

He looked at his watch. "I've got to get on the road. My suitcase is in the car. I hate to rush out, but I need to make this early flight. There's a lot for me to do back home now."

I brushed back my hair. "Okay, let's go down."

"Your father and Lucille left a little while ago."

"Of all the mornings for me to oversleep."

"There'll be plenty of mornings for us, Semantha." He took my hand, and we descended the stairway. Mrs. Dobson stepped out of the kitchen when she heard us to tell me she had put up everything fresh for my breakfast.

"I'll be right there," I called back, and followed Ethan out to his rental car.

"I'll be driving back in my own car," he said. He took my hands into his and kissed me softly. "I know things have been difficult for you, Semantha. I hope I can bring some happiness into your life. I know you've brought it into mine."

"Thank you, Ethan. I'm sorry I don't seem as excited as I should. Everything just seems to be happening so fast."

"Tell me about it. My head's spinning."

"Just drive safely, Ethan."

He kissed me again and got into his car. After he

started the engine, he rolled down the window and blew me a kiss. I watched him drive away until his car was out the front gate and gone.

"How much of all that do you believe, Semantha?" Cassie asked.

I didn't reply. I turned and went back inside to eat my breakfast. Daddy called later to tell me he and Lucille had forgotten they were attending a charity event in Lexington. I waited for him to tell me about his hiring Ethan, but he didn't. He just apologized for having to be away another night and day and my having to eat alone. I told him I was fine, and then he was drawn to deal with another important phone call and had to hang up. I wondered if he had ever had a phone call that wasn't important.

The house was so quiet now that Ethan was gone. He had truly come in like a wonderful ray of sunshine, sweeping me up in the warmth. Doris had already gone into the guest bedroom and begun redoing it. It wasn't long before it looked as if no one had been in it.

Later, after I had some lunch, I wandered out to the pool to read. The monotonous sounds of the landscaping machinery droned me into a daze, and I dozed off and on until some heavy dark clouds moved in from the northwest and the breeze grew stronger. I could feel myself sinking into a depression and, like someone falling into a dark, deep well, struggled to grasp and claw at anything that might keep me in the light.

Apparently, some sparrows had built a nest in the eaves of the cabana. Maybe because the breeze was coming from that direction or maybe because they were finally old enough, I heard the pleas of baby birds crying for something to eat. I watched as their mother made frequent trips to and from the nest to feed them. She was tireless, and they were seemingly insatiable. It captured my attention for a while, and then out of it was born a thought I had never dared think.

Instantly, I rose and hurried back to the house to change. Mrs. Dobson heard me going up the stairs and called up to tell me her plans for dinner.

"Oh, don't bother tonight, Mrs. Dobson," I said. "I'm going out."

"Oh? By yourself?"

I smiled. "Yes, Mrs. Dobson, but don't worry."

She nodded, but that didn't mean she wouldn't. I smiled to myself and hurried on to dress. Twenty minutes later, I was down and out to my car. I sat there for a moment hesitating, my fingers trembling before starting the engine. Would I regret doing this? Would Daddy be enraged?

"*Do it*," Cassie said. She was sitting beside me. "*Stop worrying about what everyone else will think. Damn it, Semantha,*" she continued when I still hesitated. "*Haven't I instilled any Heavenstone courage in you at all?*"

I looked at her and then started the car.

"Satisfied?"

"*We'll see,*" she replied, folded her arms across her breasts, and sat back.

I drove away from the house, down the driveway, and out the gate slowly—too slowly for her, I was sure—but as I continued to the highway, I sped up.

"I have no idea what I'm going to do when I get there," I muttered.

"You'll figure it out," she told me. *"With my help, of course."*

Close to an hour later, I turned off the highway and followed a road I had driven many times before in my dreams. It was quite a beautiful rural area, with elaborate farmhouses and corrals. Behind the fenced-in landscapes enclosing lush rolling hills, I saw mares and foals grazing. Some lifted their heads and looked at me cruising by. The spindly-legged colts that scampered at their mothers' sides looked so fresh and new I imagined they weren't more than weeks or months old. Their curiosity about me brought a smile to my otherwise nervous face. It was as if nature was working to bring babies and infants of every kind to mind.

My mind now centered on only one.

I slowed down as I approached my mother's cousin's property. Royce and Shane also had a farm where they raised thoroughbreds. I had never been there, but I had always known exactly where it was. I slowed down and pulled over to a wide, clear area off the road just across from the driveway. I shut off the engine and sat, unsure of what I would do next or why I had even come.

Over the last few years, I had read a number of stories about this exact situation, a situation in which a married couple adopt a teenage girl's child. Most of the adoptive mothers voiced the same fear, that someday, somehow, the biological mother would lay some claim to her child and they would be in some jeopardy of losing the child they had brought up as their own. No matter how much or how well their attorneys reassured them that their written agreements were ironclad, they lived with the nightmare. Some court, some judge, something, would negate it all in favor of the biological mother. What was stronger than blood, after all?

It didn't matter that it wasn't my intention to go there to ask for my daughter back. My presence would surely bring a firestorm of hysterics to my father's doorstep. Right now, the ranch house looked so peaceful, idyllic. My knocking on that door was surely the farthest thing from their minds. And what did I expect would happen when my four-year-old daughter set eyes on me? Did I really believe that there would be some recognition, that she would somehow sense that I was her mother?

"I don't know what I'm doing here, why I came," I muttered.

"*Of course you do. There's a Heavenstone in that house,*" Cassie reminded me. "*And she doesn't even know she is.*"

"I can't do this. Daddy will hate me." I spun on her. "That's what you want, isn't it? You want Daddy to hate me. You're jealous of our new relationship."

She laughed. "*What new relationship? Lucille Bennet shines so brightly in his eyes that he can't see anyone or anything else. You have no one but the child in that house.*"

"I have Ethan," I said

She gave me that condescending Cassie smile.

"I do!"

She shook her head.

"Damn you!"

I had gone to start the car again when I suddenly saw Shane and Royce step out of the house. Royce was holding my daughter's left hand, and Shane was holding her right. I was too far away to see much detail in my daughter's face, but I saw that she had my golden brown hair and it was nearly down to her shoulders. I remembered Daddy telling me that they were naming her Anna.

"That's your flesh and blood. That's a Heaven-stone," Cassie whispered.

I watched them walk off to show my daughter a new colt.

"Get out. Go up there. Pretend you're just visiting. Let her see you. Go on," Cassie urged.

I put my hand on the door handle.

"Do it!"

I tried, but I was too frightened. All I could see was Daddy's red face of rage. Finally, I did start the engine again and started away, hoping they wouldn't look in my direction.

"You're a coward!" Cassie screamed. *"You're an embarrassment to the Heavenstone family. I won't help you anymore. I'll let you fail miserably. Everything in your life is going to go wrong. You're a walking tragedy."*

I drove on, my body shaking so hard I thought I might run off the road. After a while, I calmed, and Cassie was no longer sitting beside me.

She was fuming in her grave.

But her words and threats still echoed in the car.

I had no doubt they would echo in my mind and in my dreams until the day I buried her deeply enough to shut her up forever.

Maybe, though, she was right. Maybe by then it would be too late.

Rehearsal

As DADDY WOULD say, the days remaining before the grand wedding and Ethan's return went like molasses running up a hill. Ethan called me as soon as he reached home and then called every day thereafter, each time talking for nearly a half hour. He even called me periodically from the road when he had begun his journey back to Kentucky so I could be aware of his progress, always ending with something like, "Twelve more hours until touchdown."

At breakfast, two days after Ethan had left the Heavenstone estate, Daddy had finally revealed to me what I already knew: Ethan was coming to work for us.

"I'm quite taken with this young man you've found, Semantha. I think he has great potential." He looked at Lucille, who nodded. It bothered me that he needed her stamp of approval for almost anything he said to me these days. "For now," he continued, still looking at Lucille, "at Lucille's suggestion, we're going to permit him to stay in the guest suite here. I know how difficult it is financially these days for young people to start jobs away from home, and we don't want him wasting time looking for lodging he can afford."

Both looked at me and waited for my response.

"That's very nice," I said in a flat tone of voice, causing Lucille's eyebrows to lift into two quarter-moons. I was suddenly aware that whenever she did that, everything on her face lifted. Her nostrils widened, and her upper lip rose, quivering her chin. Was that a consequence of plastic surgery?

"Nice?" Lucille looked at Daddy and smiled. "You don't have to disguise or contain your excitement about it with us, Semantha. Your father and I agree that you're a young woman now. It's not like we're letting some teenagers run loose or something. Both of you have proven to be very responsible people."

"Everything's happening so fast," I said, by way of explaining my controlled reaction.

"Yes. Well," she said, "when things are right, it's good that they happen fast. However, I assure you that both your father and I have given it all considerable thought. It's in no way an impulsive decision on our part. Are you upset about it? Would you rather we rescinded our offer to Ethan and waited?"

"No, no, of course not. I think it's a wonderful thing you're doing for him," I replied, this time with a great deal of enthusiasm.

"Good. Well, then, that's that."

I said nothing more, and she was eager to get off the topic and return to discussing the wedding and honeymoon plans, barely looking at me and never asking my opinion about anything now. What had happened to her invitation to me to be an integral part of it all as a way of drawing us closer? Had it all been for show, or, as the date drew closer, was she simply far too excited to notice anything else?

Whatever the reason, I soon felt invisible and, in fact, didn't really feel that I existed again in this house until the day Ethan drove through the gate and onto the Heavenstone estate. Work had already begun on construction of the dance floor and the creation and arrangement of the lighting and decorations Lucille had envisioned. Along with the usual grounds workers, dozens more temporary employees were on the property. Sound systems were being tested and refined, and the large tent and smaller tents for specific purposes were being designed and set up. The cabana and some of the other buildings were repainted. More flowers were brought in until there didn't seem to be any area visible to the guests that wasn't brightened. Not a chip, not a crack in any walkway, was left unrepaired.

It seemed there were artisans, caterers, and service people meeting, planning, and rehearsing daily. Lucille assigned one of the Heavenstone Corporation's best secretaries to be her assistant. Along with her wedding planner, the two marched about the house and property with Lucille rattling off thoughts, complaints, and new ideas constantly, her hands flying around her like nervous birds. Everyone jumped when she barked a command or merely looked in his or her direction. It was as if the whole thing were a great puppet show, with Lucille pulling the strings. At least that brought a smile to my face, but nothing as big and as deep as the smile I wore when Ethan finally stepped out of his car and looked up at me waiting on the portico. He had phoned when he was ten minutes away, and I had hurried down to watch him drive in and greet him.

"Man, did I miss you," he said, rushing up the steps. He gathered me up in his arms in a gentle bear hug and kissed me softly. "My parents thought there was something wrong with me, because every once in a while, I would simply drift off and not hear a thing either of them had said. They didn't know that was because I was thinking of you, envisioning you, dreaming of you. There wasn't room in my head for anything or anyone else."

Perhaps there really was a Cassie part of me. What girl wouldn't be thrilled to hear these words from the man she thought she loved and hoped loved her? Yet I couldn't smother the thought that these words sounded too perfect, even rehearsed. Then again, I asked myself, what if they were? What if all during his trip back, or at least the last few hours on the road, he had worked on those words because he wanted them to sound perfect? What was wrong with that, with a man trying as hard as he could to please the woman he loved?

"Is everything all right?" he asked when I didn't burst open like a radiant flower in the sunlight that his smiling face had brought.

"Yes, oh, yes, Ethan. I missed you, too. This place has become so busy with so many people and so much going on that I can't hear myself think. It really is more like an invasion," I said, and he laughed.

"Well, it is the wedding of the century, isn't it?" he asked.

"To Lucille, it is. To me, it's just a hectic, maddening commotion."

He nodded. "I bet. But don't worry. I'm back. I'll help you get away from it all. Let me get my bags. You know, I have a lot more than last time."

"I'll help." I followed him down to the car. A parade of trucks was coming up the driveway, bringing chairs and tables for eighteen hundred people. We paused to watch them park, the men jumping out to unload quickly. They cracked open doors and began piling chairs on carts, orders being shouted in every direction.

"Wow, you're right. This is an invasion," Ethan said. His face lit up. "It's quite exciting."

He handed me the smallest bag and seized the handles of the two large suitcases. Lucille must have been watching us from some window, because we didn't get three steps up before she burst out of the entrance with two of her temporary wedding employees beside her. She muttered some orders and nodded at us. They rushed down to take the bags.

"Welcome back, Ethan," she said. He smiled up at her and quickly hurried to kiss her on both cheeks, something she loved men and even women to do. "Semantha, why don't you show Bob and Steve where to take the bags?" she said. "I need to steal Ethan for ten minutes before you capture all of his attention. Let's go to the office," she told him.

Ethan flashed a smile at me, shrugged, and followed her obediently. I had given Daddy and her only a general idea of when Ethan would arrive, yet she pounced as if she had known the exact moment. It seemed nothing was going on in this house and on this estate without her involvement and control. It was as if she were deciding when we would all eat, sleep, and breathe. Whatever she had for Ethan surely could have waited until he was settled in and we had spent some time together. Fuming, I quickly realized that her two employees were standing there holding Ethan's suitcases and waiting for me to give them instructions.

"Oh, just follow me up the stairs," I said briskly, and marched in and up to Ethan's room. I told them to leave the suitcases next to the bed. They seemed to feel my rage, because they left instantly without glancing at me or saying a word. Then I sat on his bed and pouted like a child until I heard him rushing up the stairway and down the hall.

"There you are," he said.

"What did she want? What could she possibly want from you immediately? What couldn't wait until you settled in after so long a trip?" I demanded, firing all of my questions in one breath. I could feel the crimson heat in my face.

"Oh, she was just nervous about my starting at the store because she's too occupied with everything that's going on here. She had some last-minute instructions," he said, making it all seem innocent and unworthy of my displeasure.

He kissed my cheek and brushed my hair back.

"It could have waited," I insisted. "You're not going to work until after the wedding."

"No. She wants me to start tomorrow. She thinks it's a waste of time for me not to get right in there."

"Tomorrow?"

"I gotta say, she's really rooting for me, hoping I'll be a success. Besides, she wanted to know if I had a tux for the wedding. I didn't realize that I needed one. It's my first real black-tie event. She picked up the phone and immediately ordered Erickson to arrange for my fitting tomorrow morning before anything else. She went on and on about the wedding and the important businesspeople I'll meet. So many dignitaries are attending, too. I had no idea. It's a Who's Who of Kentucky society and then some."

This was exactly what I didn't want, the two of us so caught up in the wedding that we ignored each other. He saw the look on my face and added, "But I told her I just had to get back to you."

I didn't believe him, but I didn't say so. He put his suitcases on the bed and began to unload them. Without another word, I helped him organize and hang up his clothes. He must have been nervous about his decision to accept the offer, because he talked without taking a breath, describing his parents' reactions to his career decision, what he had been doing with the time he had spent at home, the impatience he'd had waiting for his moment of departure, and the weather he'd encountered on the journey.

"I hated the rain because it slowed me down." He finally took a breath and looked at me. "And what have you been doing all this time?"

"Waiting for this wedding to be over," I replied sharply. "It can't end soon enough for me."

"Hold it," he said.

He stopped what he was doing and took my hands into his, leading me back to the settee as if I were his little girl and not his girlfriend. We both sat.

"What?"

"I know what you're going through," he began.

"Do you?"

"Yes, I do. It's understandable. You're upset because your father's swept up in all this and not paying much attention to you. It's natural for you to resent Lucille, too."

"Everyone's my therapist," I said.

"I'm not trying to be a therapist. I'm just trying to reassure you that things will settle down, and besides, I'm here now, and I'll be at your side and taking up your time. I'd rather you not think of anything or anyone else but me, anyway."

"At my side? You're going to work, Ethan. Immediately, it seems, and that will occupy you quite a bit. I'm sure she has a lot more for you to do than you can imagine. Lucille made that pretty clear when she swooped down on you the moment you arrived."

"Yes, I know, but no matter what work they give me, I'll be hurrying back to you at the end of the day, and we'll spend every other waking moment together. Maybe," he said, smiling, "sleeping moments, too. She'd better not try to interfere with that. It would take a crowbar to pry us apart." He sounded a bit like my father. He winked.

I had to smile at his coyness.

"That's better. That's the girl I came rushing back to," he said.

"And not a career with the Heavenstone Corporation?"

"Only if it includes you." My skeptical expression annoyed him. He let go of my hands. "Don't you think I could get a good job elsewhere on my own? There are plenty of retail businesses looking for young, up-and-coming executives, and I have great recommendations from my college teachers and did graduate with honors, Semantha. I'm not in any sort of desperate state. I was still considering returning to college and getting my MBA, too. I have options."

"I know. I'm sorry I said that."

"It's okay." He smiled again. "You're kind of lost in all this, but I'm here now. We're going to have a helluva good time." He got up to complete his unpacking.

Afterward, we went out to look at the work being done in preparation for the wedding. Lucille saw us but marched off with her assistant and the wedding planner, rattling off orders. I saw how impressed Ethan was with everything.

"This is something," he said. "It's one thing to hear about it but another to see it. They probably didn't plan much more at Gettysburg." When I didn't react with any enthusiasm, he added, "Hey, we're going to have a good time at this wedding, too. We'll treat it as a party just for us."

"You mean, as though it were our wedding?"

"Why not?"

I liked that.

"But for now," he continued, "how about we go out to dinner ourselves tonight, or did you want to spend it at home with your father? I know they're heading right out on their honeymoon and—"

"Are you kidding? He and Lucille don't even know I'm at the table."

"Then let's just get out of here, take a ride, and stop somewhere for a quiet dinner," he said. "I'll go up to shower and change."

It was like a transfusion. I felt my happiness and enthusiasm come surging back through my veins and into my heart. We laughed and charged into the house, rushing up the stairway like two people afraid they were going to miss an airplane flight.

He's back, I thought. *He's really back because of me.* He didn't deserve my skepticism and sour face. I felt terrible for having been so negative and immature. He never really got angry about it, either. He was as patient and understanding as my uncle Perry. I was determined to make it up to him, to be more cheerful and more fun.

I was so anxious and excited I was ready before he was and went down to tell Mrs. Dobson we wouldn't be there for dinner. I heard Lucille in the hallway by my father's office and impishly went down to tell her, too. She might soon be the queen, I thought, but I was still the princess. However, I was disappointed in her reaction. I assumed she would want us there to listen attentively to her report to Daddy at dinner. We, especially Ethan, would be her command audience, but I was prepared to say no firmly.

"That's very nice," she said, smiling. "You two should be alone to catch up and make plans. Besides,

you'll both be bored with the endless details of this
wedding. Enjoy." She dismissed me with a wave and
turned back to her assistant. I felt like a blow-up doll
losing air and hurried away.

Ethan was just coming down the stairs.

"I told Mrs. Dobson not to set out places for us
at dinner," I said. "And then I told Lucille we're leaving."

"What for? She's not your dorm mother," Ethan
joked. "From now on, I'm the only one you have to
check in with, understand? And you'd better, too."

"Right, tough guy."

He laughed, and we headed out to my car. Just
as we reached the gate, we saw Daddy driving in. He
stopped and rolled down his window.

"Hey, welcome back, Ethan."

"Thank you, sir."

"Where you guys going?"

"Just for a ride and some dinner."

"Smart. I'd like to jump in with you. The place is
a madhouse."

"We'd love to have you," Ethan said. "Want to
come along?"

"You trying to get me assassinated?" Daddy
quipped. "You look very nice, Semantha," he said.
"Have a good time."

"Thank you, Daddy."

"Your father is such a great guy," Ethan said.
"He deserves to be happy."

I never said he didn't, I thought. *I just don't
know if he will be.*

Ethan asked if there was anywhere in particular

I'd like to go. Almost without realizing it, I directed him to follow the roads that would take us past my cousin's home. Ethan continued to talk about our future, things he'd like to be able to do someday, and places he'd like to visit. This job, this whole new opportunity for him, was like Columbus launching his ships for the New World. His excitement was infectious, but the closer we got to Shane and Royce Norman's home, the more nervous I became. A part of me wanted Ethan to know who lived there, but another part of me feared that he would be so shocked I had taken him there that he would be turned away from me. After all, my memories of his reaction in the motel were still quite vivid. I said nothing as we rode by. I was happy that neither Shane nor Royce was anywhere in sight.

Later, we found an intimate restaurant with a small patio overlooking acres of beautiful prime Kentucky property. We could see the horses grazing near a small pond. It looked like an oil painting, because the clouds were so still and the horses looked so content. Ethan's enthusiasm for his work and for our continued relationship was, as Daddy would say, just what the doctor ordered. We drank wine and had a wonderful dinner. The restaurant had a violin player who went from table to table. At our table, perhaps because he saw how we were holding hands and looking into each other's eyes, he played *"La Vie en Rose."*

"That'll be our song from now on," Ethan said. He leaned forward to kiss me.

Could the day have turned out any better? I did feel swept along but very happy about it. On our way back, we occasionally held hands but said little. For me as well as for him, I suspect, it was like soaking in a warm bath, only our bath was full of love. We weren't home late, but when we arrived, the house was quiet. Every statue looked asleep. The lights were dim, the old grandfather clock barely sounding its ticktock as if it were Heavenstone's slumbering heart.

"They're both probably feeling it," Ethan whispered as we went up the stairway. "I'm sure it's exhausting. They'll really need to get away after this."

I could see that Ethan was fading himself. I knew he was trying to remain energetic for my sake, but I told him to go to sleep and get a good night's rest. He did have a big day tomorrow. Besides, I thought, we were soon to be the master and mistress of this house. Daddy and Lucille would be on their honeymoon. It was no secret that both Ethan and I were thinking we would have a sort of honeymoon ourselves while they were gone.

"Go get ready for bed," I told him. "I'll be in just to say good night."

"Just good night? We'll see about that," he joked, but by the time I got ready and into my nightgown and went to his room, I found him in bed and already in a deep sleep, so deep that when I kissed him good night, he didn't wake. His eyelids didn't even flutter. I fixed his blanket, stood back, and looked at him, at that perfect handsome face, for a few moments to confirm in my own mind that he was really there and that we were really thinking of a life together. Then I turned off his lights and closed his door softly.

To my surprise, when I stepped back into the hallway, I found Lucille standing by my door. She was in her robe and had her face covered in one of her special expensive skin creams. In the hallway light, her face had a yellowish glow, and her eyes seemed more catlike.

"What is it?" I asked. "Something wrong with my father?"

"No, no. He's fine. I think we should talk," she said. "I won't have much time to spend alone with you after tonight. We have all sorts of last-minute preparations tomorrow and then, late in the day, the wedding rehearsal. As you know, your father and I will be gone for ten days immediately after the wedding."

"Talk about what?"

"Your future," she said. She opened my bedroom door for me and stood back.

I looked at her as if I thought she was crazy, but I went into the room. She followed and closed the door behind her.

"My future?"

"You can get into bed," she told me.

How odd, I thought. What was I, her little girl now? Nevertheless, that was just what I did. I was tired, and I did want to go to sleep. Maybe if I closed my eyes, she'd stop talking and leave.

Instead, she stepped closer to the bed, fiddled with my blanket, and smiled.

"I've been meaning to have this conversation with you for days now," she began. "I apologize for taking so long and being so wrapped up in the wedding arrangements. Half the time, I forget to eat lunch, not that I need it. I'm not going to be like so many women as soon as I get married and neglect my figure because I have my man or something. I can assure you of that. You'll never be ashamed to be seen with me."

"What conversation, Lucille?"

"The mother-daughter conversation you should be having. I realize I'll never be what your real mother was to you," she said, nodding at the framed photograph of my mother and me that she had bought me, "but I'm not one to neglect any responsibility. When I marry your father, I take on all his burdens as well as his pleasures, just like the vow dictates. I'll mean it when I say 'I do.'"

"I don't like to think of myself as a burden for my father, Lucille."

"No, I don't mean you're a burden. I meant his responsibilities," she said quickly. Then she smiled. "My, I guess I do have to watch every word with you now. That's good. You're a sharp, alert young lady."

"Really, what is it, Lucille? I'm tired."

"Ethan," she said.

"Ethan?"

"I know I told you that we trust you both to behave as responsible adults, and I'm sure you will, but I didn't want to give you the impression that I was—or rather, that your father and I were—arranging your life for you. If Ethan is indeed the man for you and he continues to develop and mature, fine. If he's not, I don't want you to hesitate in coming to tell me otherwise. Or if you are confused and unsure about everything, please rely on me to help you. In short, I'd like to be your confidante in the same way a mother should be. I don't expect you to throw yourself at me, but I just wanted to be sure you understood that I care about you and welcome being there for you.

"You are very young," she continued. "What is good for the Heavenstone Corporation is not necessarily good for you personally."

"What does that mean?"

"Ethan might be a very good young man to develop at our business, but that does not mean he's being groomed here to be your husband. As I said, if it turns out that he's right for you and you for him . . ."

My God, I thought. *She does see us all as her puppets, especially me perhaps.*

"I don't think I need anyone to tell me who's right for me, Lucille. Thank you for your concern. I am tired now."

She stared a moment and then smiled. "You're just like I was when I was your age, defiant to the end. Be sure you don't do something just for spite, because in the end you spite only yourself." She patted my bed and walked out of my room.

"That's what I call covering your rear end," Cassie said. She was standing by the door. *"That way, Daddy can't blame her for anything you do."*

"I didn't need you to tell me that," I said, and turned on my side so my back would be to her.

"Yes, you did," she replied in her arrogant Heavenstone tone of voice.

I closed my eyes.

"I'll be in your dreams," she threatened.

It made it more difficult for me to fall asleep, but I finally did. When I woke up, it was late, and Ethan had already dressed, had breakfast, and gone to his first day of work and to get his tux. He phoned later in the afternoon to describe what he was doing and how pleasant and cooperative everyone was being. I wanted to ask him what he expected with Lucille being his sponsor, but I thought about it and realized I'd be taking something from him. Maybe the other employees were just as impressed with him. Ethan did have a wonderful personality, and as far as I could tell, he didn't look down on anyone. I was sure his enthusiasm amused them all. He promised to rush home as soon as he could.

In the meantime, Lucille had me try on my maid of honor gown again and inspected it so closely I thought she might send it back for a loose thread. She was satisfied with it all and then began organizing the rehearsal. Her so-called close friends arrived. They did seem nice, especially Claire Dubonnet, who had flown in from Monaco. Even though she worked for the prince, I found her to be more down-to-earth and friendlier than Lucille's other friends, who were all wives of very wealthy businessmen. I learned she had been divorced for five years, but she had a daughter a year older than me who was studying at the Sorbonne in Paris. Although she didn't mean it to, it made me wonder what Lucille's other acquaintances thought about me not attending any college or doing any real work. Did they think I was some sort of

mental invalid or just a spoiled rich girl? Why should
it matter what they thought? I asked myself, to stop
myself from thinking about it.

We all waited as the minister and Lucille's wedding planner conferred about the wedding procession. Daddy seemed nervous, even though it was only
a rehearsal. Uncle Perry, who had arrived and would
be staying at the house, agreed to be the stand-in for
Senator Brice, who couldn't get there until tomorrow.
I kept thinking to myself that tomorrow Uncle Perry
should be exactly where he was tonight, but Lucille
didn't miss an opportunity to refer to the best man as
Senator Brice. She was on top of every decision the
minister and the wedding planner made, even changing the number of steps the flower girls should take.
I watched Daddy closely while the minister sum-
marized the actual ceremony and the vows. Daddy
looked at me only once, but his gaze quickly slid off
my face and back to the minister and Lucille, who
held his hand so tightly anyone would imagine she
was afraid he might turn and run.

Ethan arrived before it ended and watched from
the sidelines. As soon as I could, I hurried over to
him. The orchestra had come to rehearse as well, and
we both listened to some of the music.

"I'm just a last-minute guest, but I feel as nervous as a groom. There is so much being coordinated
here," he said, listening to the wedding planner
review when the champagne would be brought out,
what the waiters and waitresses should be doing
during the ceremony and immediately afterward,
and how the kiosks should be prepared. There were

ushers who had to know exactly where the dignitaries, as Lucille characterized them, would be sitting. A chart with names was prepared on a six-by-four-foot board, and the wedding planner, using a pointer, indicated the various areas for different guests.

"You were right. This is like planning the Normandy invasion," Ethan muttered.

"It's all too big and formal for me," I said. "It makes it seem impersonal. They should have eloped."

Ethan laughed. "Fat chance of Lucille doing something like that."

For the first time, I heard a somewhat disdainful tone in his voice. Maybe he wasn't as mesmerized by her as I had thought.

"Do you like her, Ethan?" I asked him sharply.

He glanced at me and shrugged. "Sure. She's been very nice to me, and she's certainly one of the most capable and intelligent women I've ever met."

"Yes, but would you like her as a stepmother?"

"She'll be okay, Semantha. Don't worry about it."

"I wish you had the opportunity to have met my real mother," I said. "You'd understand."

"Understand what?"

"Why I miss her more than ever right now," I told him. "Why I have a hard time with all this."

He said nothing. We watched some more of the preparation and then went in so he could show me his tux and we could get ready for dinner. I realized it would be the last dinner with the four of us at the table for a good ten days. Lucille reminded me about the Citizen of the Year dinner we were to attend after they had returned from their honeymoon. She said she would see to it that Ethan was included in our party. Now he really looked overwhelmed and even more impressed with her and, especially, my father.

"After the wedding, let's not get so formally dressed for dinner every night," I told him later. "As you can see, we'll have many opportunities to dress formally. Lucille looks determined to include us in every possible event."

"Whatever you want. Just think," he said, holding out his arms. "You'll be the lady of the house, the mistress of Heavenstone. The tiller of this great sailboat will be in your hands, Semantha. Take it wherever you want."

"As long as the wind lets me," I said.

He laughed. "It wouldn't dare do otherwise."

He looked as if he believed it. *How long,* I wondered, *would it take for someone brought to the bosom of the Heavenstone universe to become arrogant enough to think he or she could walk with gods and goddesses?*

"Minutes," Cassie whispered.

I turned sharply.

"What's wrong?" Ethan asked as he opened the door for me.

"Nothing," I said.

I could see Cassie dancing on the grass and then hooking on to the breeze that circled the altar. How I wished I knew as much about our futures as she did, but the price for that was too great.

I hoped I wouldn't pay it.

14

Wedding

I WAS UP with the sunrise on the morning of the wedding. It was as if Cassie had nudged me out of a wishful dream during which we were all young again and Mother was alive and Daddy thought of us as his three precious young women eagerly waiting for him to return from work. I was always the most exuberant, throwing up my arms for his hug. Mother waited nearby to have her welcoming kiss, and Cassie stood smiling as if she were overseeing it all and we were all doing what she had designed.

As soon as the disappointing reality sank in, I rose and went to my window to watch as the great golden eye peered over the horizon timidly, as if it weren't sure it had been invited to the wedding.

"Maybe it just doesn't want this day to happen," Cassie whispered.

"Maybe," I agreed.

The night before, after the rehearsal dinner that included Lucille's father and some cousins as well as her close friends, we all went into the den for after-dinner drinks. Ethan and I spent most of our time talking with Uncle Perry. The conversation wound around to Ethan's new job and how Uncle Perry was acting on some of his suggestions. They both saw that I was bored with the talk, and Uncle Perry began to describe some of his favorite vacations. Claire Dubonnet heard us talking, and she and Uncle Perry discussed southern France and Italy. I saw the way their travels and descriptions excited Ethan.

"Imagine being wealthy enough to go to those places and stay at those hotels," he told me.

I didn't have to imagine it, of course. I was wealthy enough, but I tried to be enthusiastic for his sake. When Daddy announced that he was going to bed because he thought he had a big day tomorrow, everyone laughed. Soon after, the rest of us retired for the night, and the great mansion was quiet. It seemed to be holding its breath in disbelief. Was this really going to happen? Would it have a new mistress?

With the rising sun, the house revived. Along with Doris and Mrs. Dobson, there was a small army of temporary servants crawling over the property like ants. Footsteps echoed everywhere. Doors opened and closed. Waves of new voices rose. Machinery was turned on, and orders were bellowed over the sound system. As Ethan had said during one of his reactions to the preparations, it was like the launching of a great aircraft carrier. I half expected to see Lucille go out there and break a bottle of champagne on a side of the altar.

It was interesting to watch it all, but I didn't feel half the excitement Ethan felt. I think I was more numb than anything else. When the guests began to arrive later in the day, the party atmosphere really

took hold. Lucille had arranged for a bevy of waiters and waitresses to greet each guest with a glass
of champagne that included a floating strawberry.
Women were given stems of roses, and ushers
guided people to the kiosks and cocktails and hors
d'oeuvres. The orchestra began playing, and even if
I had to admit it myself, the machinery of this grand
wedding came to life and began to coordinate with
perfection.

The arrival of the governor and his wife in a helicopter caused a new surge of excitement. He came
with Senator Brice and his wife. Other Kentucky
celebrities and well-known businesspeople began
to stream in afterward. Ethan jokingly said that we
should have had someone at the microphone announcing them the way they did at the royal courts
in Europe.

"Mr. and Mrs. So-and-So, the Earl of Cable Television, or Mr. and Mrs. Jet Set."

I laughed at his imitations, which he was careful
to do out of Lucille's earshot.

The tailor at the Heavenstone Store had done a
wonderful job on his tuxedo. He looked dazzlingly
handsome. Part of his first day had involved going
to a hairstylist, which was something else Lucille had
arranged. I saw how he caught the attention of other
women and felt pangs of jealousy when he nodded
and smiled back at them. I was sure they were all
wondering who he was and how he had come to be
my escort. Maybe I was imagining it, but I thought
the tongues that wagged were all wagging about
us, about me, more than they were about Lucille.

I was sure I heard someone say, "Money can buy anything," but when I turned sharply to look, no one was gazing our way.

Lucille made sure the event was on schedule. Those assigned to collect us for the procession shot out precisely when she had ordered it, and we gathered in the house to get our last-minute instructions. I studied Uncle Perry's face to see if he would finally show some unhappiness about being replaced as best man, but he smiled and winked at me and looked quite relaxed and happy. Outside, the eighteen hundred guests were seated, and the music Lucille had chosen for the procession began. Daddy, Senator Brice—who, at Lucille's request, had come in his military uniform—and the minister walked out first to take their positions at the altar. Daddy turned back before he left, but I wasn't sure he was looking for me.

"*He's not,*" Cassie whispered. "*He can't see anyone but her right now.*"

I said nothing, nor did I turn my head. When it came time for me and the others to walk out, I moved like a robot, my eyes down. I knew where Ethan would be sitting and did turn to look at him. He gave me a thumbs-up, and I finally smiled. Everyone rose when Lucille and her father stepped out to walk down the aisle. *Give the devil her due,* I thought. She looked beautiful and as stately and elegant as the first time I had set eyes on her. I was sure everyone was thinking, *That's what a mistress of Heavenstone should look like.*

The absolute precision of the ceremony was marred by only one thing, and only I knew why. Until that moment, not a single person was out of step, and no one misspoke. The minister's voice cracked sharply and loudly enough for everyone to hear each word. Senator Brice handed Daddy the wedding ring, and when the time came for him to place it on Lucille's finger, his fingers looked as if they trembled, and the ring slipped out and bounced on the ground. There was a hush, a collective gasp. Senator Brice moved quickly to pick it up and hand it to Daddy again. This time, he moved it gracefully onto Lucille's finger.

Only I saw what had really happened.

Cassie was beside Daddy, and when he had extended his hand the first time, she had shaken his arm. After the ring fell, she looked at me and smiled.

Immediately after the ceremony, the partying began. Everyone went to the tables. Lucille had arranged for Ethan to sit with me at the long dais that included her relatives, the governor and his wife, and Senator Brice and his wife. I saw how wide-eyed Ethan was at the sight of all of these important political figures right beside him. He was also drinking quite a bit, which worried me. The only way to slow him down was to get up and dance, and we did so right after Daddy and Lucille had their first dance. To my surprise, before it ended, Lucille's father danced with her, and Daddy beckoned to me.

"Go on," Ethan urged.

I rose and joined him on the dance floor. I hadn't danced with him since I was a little girl.

"Well, what do you think, Semantha? Did Lucille plan a winning affair or what?"

"It's overwhelming, Daddy."

"I hope this is going to be a wonderful new start for all of us," he said. He held me closer, and when we turned, I saw Cassie standing there looking terribly sad. "Not that for one moment I don't wish things had turned out differently for us, Semantha," he continued. "But we can't change what's happened. We've got to go on and be strong." He held me out a bit and looked into my face with his own full of determination. "You're going to be all right. We all will be now. When I get back, we'll be an even closer family."

"Okay, Daddy," I said.

He smiled, and we finished our dance.

"You looked great out there," Ethan said. "Your father's pretty graceful. I only hope I can be half as accomplished and well rounded as he is when I'm his age."

"You're off to a good start," I told him.

He beamed and seemed to grow another inch in height. "I can't fail with a cheerleader like you behind me," he whispered. He kissed me just below the ear and held me tighter as we danced.

We stayed out there until dinner was being served, and I decided Ethan was right after all. We were having a good time. It was a terrific party. I knew I could enjoy it even more if I just didn't think of it so much as my father's wedding. Besides, this was something no daughter wanted to do, dance at her father's wedding. But that was something not easily put aside, especially not if Lucille Bennet had anything to say about it.

The cake-cutting ceremony was as impressive as she had predicted it would be. People were taking pictures with themselves in front of or beside the cake. There were a half-dozen photographers and the film crew working the event. Guests were constantly asked to speak directly into the camera and offer their good wishes. However, for me, listening to all of the well-wishers, one after another, remark about how my father looked ten years younger and so happy was like swallowing sour milk. After a while, no matter how much fun Ethan and I were having, I couldn't wait for the wedding to end.

Ethan had drunk too much and was dozing off from time to time by now, anyway. After the cake ceremony, a parade of people lined up to shake my father's hand and compliment Lucille. It seemed never-ending. The only time Ethan came back to life was when Lucille called to him to meet someone or beckoned him to her side.

"Boy, does she know how to network," he told me, returning. "She introduces me only to people who can be of some benefit to the Heavenstone Stores. I never knew we employed so many attorneys, too."

I smiled to myself at his use of the word "we." Daddy would say he'd become so loyal so quickly that he would take a bullet for the organization. Would he take a bullet for me?

"Don't hold your breath," Cassie whispered. While she was at my side often, I saw her follow Daddy everywhere. She didn't miss a word. I couldn't help but wonder if Lucille would be anywhere near

here if Cassie were alive, but what good did my wondering do now? It only made me more depressed. I drank a little more than I should have, too, and found myself getting tired. Neither Ethan nor I felt much like dancing anymore. All of the noise around me seemed to merge into a low hum. I was sick of smiling, of saying hello and thanking people, many of whom spoke to me only to see how I was reacting.

"There are so many phony smiles," Cassie whispered. *"It's like being at Mardi Gras in a parade of masks."*

I wasn't going to disagree with that. When I saw the first group of guests begin to make their way out to their cars, I sighed with relief. The end was in sight. Finally, the orchestra played its last number, and the remaining guests began to file out. Lucille had given instructions that nothing was to be closed down and no attempt to clean up would begin until all of the guests were gone. It seemed some would never leave, but they finally did, and the cleanup began.

Daddy and Lucille had slipped away to make their final preparations for departure. The limousine would take them to their hotel near the airport, and in the morning, they would catch their flight to connect with their cruise.

When Ethan and I and Uncle Perry went in to go to bed, there was no doubt we would do just that. None of us looked capable of remaining awake another minute. My two best men kissed me good night and sauntered off to their own bedrooms. Ethan looked as if he didn't have the energy to undress and might just fall into the bed in his tux. I barely managed to get myself cleaned up and into my nightgown. When I crawled under the light blanket and laid my head on the pillow, I saw Cassie standing there, her body glowing.

"We buried our mother again tonight," she said. *"Sleep on that."*

I turned my back on her, closed my eyes, and dove into a pool of sleep, welcoming darkness, silence, and amnesia. I didn't open my eyes until noon, and even then, it took twenty more minutes for me to get used to the light and gather enough energy to get myself showered and dressed. Like a sleepwalker, I maneuvered down the hallway and down the stairs. To my surprise, both Ethan and Uncle Perry were already up and dressed and having their late breakfast out on the patio, where they could observe the final cleanup being carried out. They both rose at the sight of me.

"Hey, Sam," Uncle Perry said. "Are you awake?"

"Not yet," I said. Ethan rushed to kiss me good morning and pulled out my chair. Doris was out with fresh coffee and some morning rolls. I told her that would be fine for now.

"Your father called just before they boarded the cruise ship," Uncle Perry said. "He wanted me to tell you he'd call the first chance he got. That was quite an affair last night. No one who attended is going to forget it."

"The wedding to beat all weddings," Ethan said.

I could see Uncle Perry was waiting for me to agree, but I sipped my coffee silently.

"Looks like another beautiful day," he said. "They're almost finished out here. The Heavenstone estate should return to its idyllic state soon."

"Not soon enough," I muttered.

The way Uncle Perry and Ethan glanced at each other told me they had been discussing me.

"Well, you guys enjoy the rest of the day," Uncle Perry said, rising. "I'm heading back."

"I'll be in shortly, too," Ethan told him.

"I don't think you're expected to."

"That's the best time to do what you have to do, when it's unexpected," Ethan told him.

Uncle Perry laughed. "Looks like you've been Heavenstone brainwashed already. All right. If you need anything, anything at all, Sam, you make sure to call me, okay?"

"Thanks, Uncle Perry."

"I'll drop by in a few days nevertheless and invite myself to dinner."

"I'd like that."

He kissed me, shook Ethan's hand, and walked off.

"I really like him," Ethan said. "He's quite different from your father, not as tough, perhaps, but he gives you a chance. Too many people in high positions are so arrogant, so condescending."

"Lucille would say he's not arrogant enough. She finds something wrong or weak with everyone she meets."

"I don't know. My guess is she'll be quite different now."

"How?"

"Not as uptight about everything. She has nothing left to prove. She's there."

"Speaking of that, why do you have to go in today? You heard Uncle Perry. No one expects it."

"I'll just show my face. I sort of promised Lucille I would keep my eyes on things."

"Promised Lucille? Did my father ask you to do that?"

Ethan smiled. "I'm not stupid, Semantha. When Lucille asks you to do something for the corporation, it's pretty much your father asking as well."

I didn't hide my displeasure.

"But I'll be back soon. From the looks of it, you could use some quiet time, anyway. Why don't we plan to meet at the pool late in the afternoon? We'll relax, have a simple dinner, and just curl up together and watch a DVD. How's that sound?"

"Refreshing."

"Good." He finished his coffee, glanced at his watch, and rose. "I'm going up to dress for the office. You staying out here?"

"For now," I said.

He gave me a fatherly peck on the cheek and hurried off.

Doris came out to see if there was anything else I wanted and to clear off some of the dishes. I still had no appetite.

"Where's Mrs. Dobson this morning?" I asked her, realizing I hadn't seen her yet.

"Oh, Mrs. Heavenstone told her to take today off along with her regular day off. She went to visit some friends in Lexington."

"Mrs. Heavenstone?" I muttered, more to myself.

"I guess we call her that now, don't we?"

"Yes, of course, Doris. You should take the day off, too," I said. "We're not doing very much. I certainly don't want an elaborate dinner."

"Oh, I couldn't . . ."

"Yes, you can," I insisted. "With my father and his new wife gone, I'm in charge here," I added, perhaps too sharply. She winced. "You go enjoy yourself and visit friends, too. In fact, you don't have to return tonight."

She looked around as if she were afraid someone else might be listening. "Are you sure?"

"I'm sure, Doris. Mrs. Heavenstone isn't the only one running things here. Go on," I said.

She looked at me with surprise, nodded, and left.

"*Very, very good,*" Cassie whispered. "*Maybe there's some hope for you yet.*"

I continued to sit there, nibbling on a roll and butter and sipping some coffee, until the last of the cleanup was done. Our regular grounds workers swarmed in and in no time had the estate looking close to what it had been before the event. Occasionally, someone looked my way, but it was all really organized and self-run. I didn't have to say a word. Our estate was always well maintained, but it did seem different since Lucille's arrival. It was as if a U.S. Marine drill sergeant had retrained everyone.

Ethan returned in his suit and tie. I told him Mrs. Dobson was gone for the day and night and I had dismissed Doris.

"Then we have this whole place to ourselves?"

"Exactly," I said.

He thought a moment and smiled. "Then I will definitely hurry back."

He kissed me and rushed off. I nearly fell asleep again just listening to the droning of lawn and garden machinery. Doris stopped by to tell me she was leaving. There was a real look of trepidation on her face. It was almost as if she wanted me to put my command in writing so she could prove she hadn't left without permission. In the short time Lucille had been overseeing the estate, she had given Doris and the other employees the sense that she was ubiquitous— she was everywhere and always watching, even when she was off on a honeymoon.

"Have a good time," I told her. I started to clear off what was left on the table.

"Do you want me to do that first?"

"No, Doris, I can do this. I'll be fine. Really. Go on."

She nodded, smiled, and left.

What I wasn't anticipating when I entered the house was the complete stillness. I hadn't heard such silence inside since the days before my mother had died and she, my father, and Cassie were all somewhere else. Strangely, even as a young girl, I had never felt frightened or even alone. Daddy had done such a good job of giving us all the feeling that the house was a living thing and all the relatives captured in portraits and statuary were there in spirit. When I was a very little girl, I would talk to them the way little girls would talk to their dolls. Strangely enough,

Cassie, when she caught me doing that, wouldn't criticize or make fun of me. She'd give me the feeling it was something she had done and might still be doing herself. More than once, she had said, "These icons of our ancestors have more to tell us than most of the so-called living."

I wasn't sure what she meant, but it sounded clearly like permission to imagine conversations and even pretend events.

"Great-aunt Eleanor is having a birthday party today," I'd say to another portrait, and set up a fake cake and candles. If Cassie saw me doing something like that, she'd stop by to give me some real history.

"Great-aunt Eleanor would be one hundred and eighteen," she'd tell me.

"Too many candles for a cake," I'd say, and she'd shake her head and walk away.

Right now, I walked the corridor of ancestors, as we called it, the corridor with portraits on both sides, and asked, "What do you all think of the new Mrs. Heavenstone?"

I didn't need to hear their voices. I could see the displeasure in their eyes.

Later, I did what Ethan suggested and put on my bathing suit and went out to the pool. I swam a little and then fell asleep for a while on a chaise longue. The sound of a door closing woke me, and because of the film of sleep over my eyes, I gazed through what resembled gauze toward the house to see what looked like my father coming out to walk to the pool. I sat up quickly. Why would Daddy be home? I quickly realize he wasn't. It was Ethan, but he was wearing one of my father's dinner jackets with the Heavenstone emblem embossed on the outside left pocket.

"And how is our precious Miss Heavenstone?" he asked as he stepped up to the pool.

I stared at him with a half-smile on my face.

"Where did you get that jacket?"

"My closet, where else?" He leaned down to give me a soft, sweet kiss on my lips and smiled. "If we're to be the master and mistress of Heavenstone, we should act like it, right?"

He sat at my feet on the chaise longue. Then he looked around with scrutinizing eyes and nodded.

"I'd say the place is back up to snuff, wouldn't you, Lucille?"

Lucille? He turned to me, anticipating that I would continue the make-believe.

"No," I said. "I found a tissue on the East Lawn."

He roared. "Well, we'll have to see who was responsible for that area and have him whipped."

"Boiled in oil."

"Skinned alive. Shall we think about dinner?"

"Is it the proper time to think about dinner?"

He looked at his watch. "One minute past the proper time."

"Then we'll think about it," I said.

He leaned forward. "I took the liberty of buying us Chinese take-out. Why don't you go in and dress for dinner, and I'll see to it that everything is warmed up properly?"

"I expected nothing less," I told him, and rose. He stood and held out his arm. I put my hand on it, and the two of us walked in step toward the house, holding our bodies and our heads in an exaggeratedly perfect arrogant royal posture. I did the best I could holding back my laughter, but when we reached the house, it burst forth like water crashing through a dam.

"Now, now," he said. "If you're going to laugh, laugh like a lady."

"Sorry."

I pulled myself in again and headed for the stairway.

"I'll be down shortly," I said. "Please make sure everything is prepared perfectly and I'm not disappointed. Disappointment is forbidden in my presence."

"Yes, Mrs. Heavenstone," he said. He smiled impishly.

I threw him a kiss and hurried up the stairs.

This was going to be fun after all, I thought, and felt a surge of new energy and excitement. I found a dress in my closet closest to one Lucille would wear and pinned my hair up the way she often pinned hers. The devil in me was romping. I went to her and Daddy's bedroom and sorted through some of her jewelry to choose something appropriate, a necklace of pearls and matching pearl earrings in a gold setting. I even found a pearl pinkie ring that fit. Before I left, I thought a moment and then sprayed myself with one of her expensive perfumes. The scent was easy to recognize as hers.

Ethan had the table ready, placing his setting in front of Daddy's chair and mine in front of Lucille's.

When he saw me, he stopped and looked worried for a moment. His eyes shifted as if he were afraid someone would catch us.

"You went whole hog," he finally said.

"Excuse me, but I don't tolerate comparisons to pigs. Angels, goddesses, or wives of powerful politicians, yes, but hogs, no."

He laughed. "Looks like I really started something here."

"Don't play with fire if you're afraid of being burned," I warned. "Are you afraid?"

I had chipped his ego. His shoulders rose, and his posture straightened instantly.

"Absolutely not. Teddy Heavenstone fears nothing and no one. Shall we dine, Mrs. Heavenstone?"

"Of course," I said, and took my seat. He brought out the reheated dishes. "It all smells quite good," I said. "I hope you had the official taster check it out."

"Oh, yes, yes, of course. She lived," he added.

We both laughed. I realized I was really hungry, not having eaten much for breakfast and having forgotten about lunch. We ate. Ethan surprised me again by opening one of Daddy's bottles of expensive French white wine, and then we continued our mimicking, reviewing the wedding just the way we imagined Daddy and Lucille reviewing it. We drank all of the wine and ate most of the food. When I rose and started to clear the table, he seized my left wrist.

"Leave it for the servants," he said. He stood and pulled me closer to him. "This is, after all, our first honeymoon night."

He kissed me and then scooped me up in his arms and carried me up the stairway like Clark Gable in *Gone With the Wind*. At the top, he turned toward our bedrooms, and I stopped him.

"No," I said.

"No?"

"Turn left," I ordered.

He knew what I was thinking and had that frightened look that had flashed on his face when he had first set eyes on me dressed like Lucille, my hair like Lucille's, and wearing her jewelry and perfume.

"Really?"

"It's ours, isn't it? We're the master and mistress of Heavenstone."

He smiled and slowly brought me to Daddy and Lucille's bedroom. For a long moment, he paused in the doorway with me still in his arms and gazed at their grand king-size bed with the new headboard Lucille had designed. The Heavenstone corporate logo had been embossed at the center. The four posts nearly touched the ceiling. Surely no king or queen slept in anything more impressive.

I lifted my head to bring my lips to his. We kissed, and then he smiled and without delay carried me into the room and gently placed me on the bed. Never shifting his eyes from mine even for a moment, he began to undress me and then himself. Before he embraced me again, he kissed me on the tip of my nose and whispered, "Welcome to the family, Mrs. Heavenstone."

When I looked into the nearly wall-size mirror on my right, I saw Cassie. There were two small flames where her eyes should be. Her lips looked painted in blood, and the strain in her neck brought her veins up against her skin, making them look like exposed tree roots.

Of course, she would be enraged, I thought. I was where she had dreamed of being. It didn't matter that Ethan wasn't really Daddy. I was in his bed making love, and she was on a long, invisible leash with the other end firmly tied to her coffin, smothered in darkness.

It's your punishment, I thought.

She had no answer, but I knew her silence wasn't any sort of surrender.

Someday, somehow, she would find the key to her revenge and open the door to more pain for the Heavenstones.

15

Honeymoon's Over

ETHAN AND I so enjoyed role-playing mistress and master of Heavenstone that we continued it on and off during the rest of Daddy and Lucille's honeymoon. They called twice, more to check on me than anything else. I suspected Lucille spoke often to Ethan at work. He went in every day, even on Sunday, just the way Daddy often would. I kept busy with my reading, exercise, and some shopping. A few times, Mrs. Dobson and Doris caught Ethan and me imitating Daddy and Lucille. I saw them smiling and hiding giggles, but neither said anything.

Almost every evening, Ethan and I went for a swim before dinner. It was that special time of day when the sunlight is still warm but not oppressive, when shadows are as refreshing as cool lemonade, and when everything in nature seems content. More often than not, we drew the curiosity of birds perched so still on branches or the roof of the cabana that they looked stuffed. We swam, embraced, kissed, and dozed off next to each other until either he or I would get hungry. Twice the first week, we went out to dinner, and Uncle Perry kept his word and came to dinner toward the end of that week.

Sometimes in the evening, we watched movies in the entertainment center, curling up like an old married couple, our blood not raging and passionate but quiet. Our hearts were content, and I know that I felt safer than ever. Oh, we did make love everywhere on the property, even out at the pool late at night, and we had what anyone would easily call our own special honeymoon.

On cloudy or rainy days, I would wait for him in the living room like some dutiful wife, anxiously looking forward to the sound of his footsteps and the wave of excitement and energy that entered with him.

"And how was your day?" he would ask playfully. Before I could respond, he would begin to review his own, bringing home stories about the store and some of the employees. I quickly saw that he wasn't fond of Richard Erickson. He thought the man wasn't creative enough and wasn't getting the most out of our employees. I listened politely to all of that, but he could see soon enough that the business talk bored me. In that regard, I could never imitate Lucille. I was much more like my mother.

One night, I woke up, realized he wasn't in bed or even in the room, and went looking for him. I found him in Daddy's office, working away on the computer, and asked him what he was doing. I had the sense that this wasn't the first time he had risen in the middle of the night and gone down to Daddy's office to work.

"I'm finishing up a report," he said.

"What report?"

He shifted his eyes as if he was reluctant to tell me and waved away my curiosity. "Just business."

I wouldn't be ignored. "What business could possibly cause you to wake up in the middle of the night and come down here, Ethan?"

"Sometimes I remember things when I'm sleeping, and I'm afraid I might forget them, that's all."

"Like what? What are you doing?" I persisted.

"It's a report I promised Lucille," he finally confessed. "Sort of an efficiency report. All businesses should do it periodically if they are to be well run."

"So, you're like Lucille's spy right now? Is that what you're telling me?"

"I wouldn't call it that, Semantha. It's not for a competitor. It's our own internal evaluation."

"You haven't been here long enough to be doing that, Ethan."

I could see my comment cut him deeply, but I couldn't help resenting the fact that a promise to Lucille was more important than being with me, even if I was asleep.

"Lucille feels I can do it," he replied, as if that was all that needed to be said about it.

"Only my father knows who can and cannot do such a thing," I insisted.

"Well, he must know about it if she asked me to do it, don't you think, Semantha?"

"Maybe."

"It's not a big deal. Don't be so upset. Why would you be so upset, anyway?" He rose and came to me. He took my hands into his and smiled.

"C'mon, don't ruin a perfectly wonderful secret honeymoon."

"You wouldn't work on your honeymoon, would you?" I countered.

His smile faded. "All right. I'll shut down the computer and come up."

"Do what you want," I said, pulling my hands from his and leaving Daddy's office.

He was up and beside me minutes later, kissing me and rambling on and on with one sort of apology after another. Finally, to get some sleep myself, I told him I wasn't upset, just surprised. I'd be fine. He accepted that and went to sleep himself, but it left me with an uneasy feeling. There were new currents running under Heavenstone. I could hear the rumbling, and it kept me awake almost until the morning.

I forgot all of this until the day Daddy and Lucille returned. Ethan didn't do any more work at home the remainder of the time, and the fun we had been having returned. We had just finished dinner when they burst in, both of them with armfuls of gifts for both Ethan and myself. I was surprised that Daddy had not bought anything for Mrs. Dobson and Doris. Before, whenever he returned from a trip bearing gifts, there had always been something for them.

Even though their trip sounded wonderful, we could see how happy they both were to have returned. While Daddy, Ethan, and I sat in the den and listened to his summary of the trip, Lucille went about the mansion and even checked on things outside. Daddy remarked that holding her down was like trying to lasso a comet.

"She dragged me into every department store in every port so we could see how things were being run in different places. At times, I thought we were on a business trip, but that's my Lucille."

My Lucille, I thought. Every new expression, every time he referred to her, made me wince. Not her time here before, or the wedding, or the honeymoon had driven it home as much as Daddy's including her in most references to himself. They were now truly one, and she was beyond any doubt firmly and completely Mrs. Heavenstone, my stepmother.

Neither Ethan nor I had any hint as to what Lucille had been doing or had seen during her tour of the house or the grounds. She said nothing when she returned to the den. She was more interested in what I had been doing, how I had spent my time.

"I'll hear about what Ethan's been doing tomorrow," she said, and turned her attention to me.

It didn't take me long to finish my account of our days. Without comment, she declared that she was tired and did, after all, have a big day back at work tomorrow. She reminded us about the Citizen of the Year award dinner on the weekend and then yawned and stretched. It was a signal to Daddy as well, who rose to go up with her.

Ethan said it was time for him to get to sleep as well. It was as if whatever Lucille decided, she decided for everyone, except me, of course. I was a little tired, but, perhaps to show my independence more than anything, I remained downstairs for another hour watching television. When I went up later and saw that the lights were low and the house was quiet,

I realized our little pretend honeymoon was over and the new regime had begun. I expected some changes would take place, but I had no inkling of how deep and how dramatic those changes would be.

I didn't go down to breakfast with everyone. Ethan came by to tell me he was leaving and was going in with Lucille in her car. He made it sound as if that was some sort of honor.

"Then you won't be back until she comes home today?"

"Yes," he said, looking as if that fact had just occurred to him, too. "Unless your father starts back earlier, which I doubt," he quickly added. "See you later." He gave me a quick peck on the lips and hurried away.

The realization that I would be spending most of my time alone now settled in when I finally did go down for breakfast. Doris had already gone upstairs to clean and restore Daddy and Lucille's bedroom as well as Ethan's. Mrs. Dobson tried to spend time with me, but she had her duties to perform as well and looked more concerned about them than ever.

I pondered my future when I went out to the pool and sat on a chaise. Maybe Ethan was right. Maybe I should enroll in a nearby college, or maybe Uncle Perry was right, and I should go to work in his office. Daddy certainly didn't pressure me to do anything. I could see the concern in his face when I described how uneventful and simple all that I had been doing was, but I could also see that he was afraid of stirring up some sleeping mental problem that would send me rushing back to Dr. Ryan for therapy. More than once, I had heard him tell Lucille, "She'll find herself."

Was I really lost? Where does one begin looking for herself? I had often sat looking at family albums, searching for some clue in my younger face. Sometimes all of us looked like strangers, I thought. Even I looked like a stranger to myself. Mother had used to say she got her identity by being the other half of her marriage and running Heavenstone. She had had great responsibility, but she had loved who and what she was. It identified her. Other women might be identified by their careers, she had said, but she was confident that most weren't as content.

I tried to develop an interest in some sort of career, breezing through descriptions of professions and jobs in a book I suspected Lucille had left lying around for just that purpose. Nothing filled me with any passion or enthusiasm. Maybe that was what Daddy meant by my being lost. I simply didn't care which road I took or where it would lead.

The only place my mind continually directed me was to my cousin's home and my daughter. How, if ever, would I meet her? If I projected myself and her twenty years ahead, would that be when she would learn who I was? Would she have any interest in me then? Would she be angry that she had never been told the truth? Would she think her adopted parents would be terribly hurt if she showed the slightest interest in me? All of it played continuously in my mind, but lately, it was more intense. I was tempted to drive back to the Normans' ranch and once again try to see my daughter.

By mid-afternoon, I was feeling terribly sorry for myself, so much so that I almost missed the sound of someone crying when I returned to the house to change and have some lunch. I paused and listened. It was coming from the kitchen. I went to the door and listened harder. I could hear Mrs. Dobson trying to calm Doris. What terrible thing had happened in her family? I knocked so they would know I was there and entered. Both were sitting at the kitchenette and looked up, surprised. Both had been crying.

"What's wrong, Mrs. Dobson?" I asked. She looked at Doris and then back at me. "What is it?"

"Mrs. Heavenstone just informed us we're terminated."

"Terminated? You mean . . . fired?"

She nodded. "We're being given two months' salary, but we have to leave today."

"That can't be so," I said.

"A messenger from the store just delivered this."

She pushed an envelope on the table in my direction. I stepped forward and pulled the letter out. It was on official Heavenstone stationery. It did not offer any reason for the termination. It merely said, "Your services will no longer be required."

I shook my head in disbelief. "I had no idea."

"Neither did we," Doris said. "Two months' salary is fine, but it's not going to be easy or even possible to get a job as good as this one. And what did we do to deserve this?" she cried, holding her arms up.

"Now, now," Mrs. Dobson said. "There's no point in getting yourself sick over it."

Doris looked down.

"I'm calling my father," I said. "You just wait."

Mrs. Dobson smiled at me as if I were talking about going to Mars.

"I am!" I insisted, and hurried out of the kitchen and down to Daddy's office.

At first, his secretary told me to call back, but I shouted at her that I had to speak with him right now. I was sure they all knew that I had once been in serious therapy. She mumbled and told me to hold on. Moments later, Daddy was on the phone. Through my tears, I told him what Lucille had done and how terrible it was. He was silent.

"She can't do this, Daddy!" I cried when he didn't respond the way I had expected he would.

"Lucille is now in charge of the house, Semantha. You know that I was never really in charge of how the house was run. Your mother handled all that, and now Lucille is the one who does it. She thinks it's best to start fresh. You should understand how she might feel about it. She wants her own stamp on things. We can't deny her that, now, can we?"

"But Mrs. Dobson and Doris have done a wonderful job with Heavenstone. You've said so yourself many times."

"They have, but Lucille wants to do more. She wants us to have a Cordon Bleu chef, and she wants more than one housemaid. She felt Heavenstone wasn't maintained as well as she would have liked while we were away. Now, this is her bailiwick, Semantha, not mine and not yours. I'm making sure both Mrs. Dobson and Doris get excellent recommendations."

"Don't let her do this, Daddy," I pleaded.

"Please be grown-up now, Semantha," he said gruffly. "You shouldn't be focusing on the hired help, anyway. You should be thinking about your own future. I have to get back to my meeting. Don't do anything that would make me ashamed of you," he warned. "I don't want Lucille upset, especially so soon after our wedding. Is that clear? Is it?"

"Crystal," I said, and hung up. For a few moments, I sat there feeling numb. I decided to call Ethan. As soon as he was brought to the phone, I rattled it off, again through my tears.

"There's nothing we can do about it," he said.

"Can't you talk to her, tell her how wonderful they've been while she and Daddy were away?"

"I doubt that would do any good, Semantha. Besides, she might resent my putting my nose in places it doesn't belong. I'm a guest at the house, remember?"

His reluctance and acceptance moved me quickly from sadness to anger.

"You're afraid of her, aren't you? You're afraid of challenging any decision she makes."

"Don't be silly. It's not a matter of my being afraid. It's not my business. I'm an employee here, that's all."

"I thought you were more," I said.

He was quiet a moment. "I am more," he replied. "All right. I'll tell her how upset you are and see what she says. How's that?"

I thought about Daddy's warning. Maybe I would get Ethan into trouble. She had fired Mrs. Dobson and Doris so easily and so quickly. She could certainly do the same to him.

"Forget about it," I said. "My father's the only one who could change this, anyway, and he won't."

"That's true."

There was something in the tone of his voice that stirred another suspicion. How did he know my father wouldn't object to Lucille's action?

"Did she tell you she was going to fire them? Did you know?"

"No, of course not," he said quickly. "That's my point. It has nothing to do with me. This is the first I've heard about it."

"Well, I think it's mean," I said, and hung up.

I hated returning to the kitchen to tell them I had failed. Neither looked surprised, but both were grateful I had tried. I sulked in the living room while they packed their things. Later, when I heard them coming down the hallway, I rushed out. They had ordered a taxi, and it had arrived. Before I could say anything, tears streamed down my face.

"Now, now, Miss Semantha," Mrs. Dobson said. "You don't worry yourself about us. Doris will find suitable new employment, and it's probably time I returned to England anyway. I have some relatives I'd like to see before they or I cash in our chips, as your daddy would say."

I hugged them both, holding on to Mrs. Dobson a little longer.

"I'll write to you," she said. "And you write back and tell me how you're doing, okay?"

"Yes, I will."

"Cheers," she said in the doorway.

The taxi driver came up to help them with their

luggage. I watched as he put it all in the trunk. Doris, looking small and devastated, waved and got in first. Mrs. Dobson turned to me.

"Your dad's a fine man," she said. "Take good care of him."

I nodded. She got into the taxi, and they started away.

"*Now it's just us,*" Cassie said. I turned to see her at my side. She watched the taxi go out the gate and disappear. Then she smiled at me. "*But that's just fine. One day, we'll see her go out that gate for good, too.*"

I nodded and did something I hadn't done since she had died. I reached for her hand.

Two hours later, I was surprised to hear Lucille arrive. I had been up in my room, thinking, when I heard the voices below and hurried out to see what was happening. A tall, dark-haired, stout man carried in two rather large suitcases and stood for a moment looking at everything around him. He stepped forward to gaze into the living room. I watched from the top of the stairway. He wore a white long-sleeved shirt and a pair of black pants.

"This way, Gerad," I heard Lucille call to him, and he moved instantly down the hallway. "We'll get you settled in first and then look over the kitchen. I have some changes in mind, as I'm sure you will as well," she said.

I made my way down the stairway slowly. I could hear their voices in the hallway that led to where Mrs. Dobson and Doris had been. Before I could turn to go in that direction, the doorbell rang. I hesitated and then went to the front door to open it on two women, both with almost identically styled short, light brown hair.

"Hello," the slightly taller one said. "I'm Mia De Stagen, and this is my sister, Catherine."

She waited as if she expected I would know exactly who they were. I saw that they had suitcases, so it wasn't difficult to guess. Before I could respond, however, Lucille came quickly, crying out, *"Willkommen,"* which I knew was German for "Welcome."

"Danke," Mia said.

"Danke," Catherine echoed.

"Please, come in," Lucille told them, glancing sharply at me to step out of the way. I did. "I'll show you to your quarters. Do you need help with your luggage?"

"Oh, no, Madame," Mia said.

"I didn't think so," Lucille said, smiling. "We'll settle you in and then describe your duties. Right down the hall here. Take the first right."

The two moved quickly.

"As soon as I heard these two were available, I pounced," Lucille told me. "They worked for German royalty. Now you'll see how a house like Heavenstone and its inhabitants are properly cared for."

"I saw no problems before," I replied defiantly.

She only smiled. "That's because you've had so little experience with truly elegant living, Semantha. All that's about to change. I'll introduce you to Gerad Bolud, who just happens to have been the chef for Guerin Ambani, the famous French industrialist. Besides enjoying wonderful food, you'll probably pick up some French."

"*Combien merveilleux,*" Cassie whispered in my ear. I had taken French at Collier. I wasn't that good at it, certainly nowhere near as fluent as Cassie had been.

"*Combien merveilleux,*" I repeated.

Lucille laughed. "*Très bien.* Sarcastic in French. You'll enjoy these changes more than you realize," she said, and marched off after the two sisters.

By the time Ethan arrived with Daddy, Lucille had them all organized. Mia was to look after the upstairs, and Catherine the downstairs. Gerad was already preparing our dinner, his best suggestion for so short a preparation time being a skillet-roasted veal chop with wild mushrooms, roasted garlic, and fresh thyme. Our dinners from now on, it seemed, were to be announced and described the way they would be in an expensive restaurant. The De Stagen sisters would serve and would do so in different uniforms.

Ethan came to my room. "How are you doing?" he asked, concerned.

"I met the new household staff," I said. "She's turning Heavenstone into a five-star hotel."

He laughed. "Look, it's her home now."

"It used to be mine, too."

"I'm sure no one's going to change a thing in your room."

"I was never a boarder here, Ethan. This was a home once, a family home."

"It still will be." He shrugged. "Your father has a new life. You have to think about making a new life for yourself, too."

I stared at him a moment, took a deep breath,

and looked away. How could he understand what
Cassie and I knew and understood? This wasn't a
castle or a showcase. Its heritage didn't lie just in its
fame; it had been built with the blood and effort of
my ancestors. It was alive. Lucille would turn it into
a tomb.

There was Cassie in the mirror, shaking her head.

"Okay, Ethan," I said. "I'm all right. Let's not
talk about it anymore right now."

"Good," he said. "I have some other exciting
news to tell you."

He rushed forward, took my hands into his, and
sat us both down on my bed.

"What?"

"Lucille was so impressed with my internal anal-
ysis that she discussed it with your father, and they
called me into his office to tell me that Lucille had
decided to make me her personal assistant, and at a
whopping salary, too."

"Personal assistant?"

"That's right. I'm going to be involved in the
most important and biggest corporate decisions.
For starters, we're going to visit every Heavenstone
Department Store, where I'll be introduced. One of
my chief assignments will be to evaluate each one the
way I did this one. She also wants me to have input
in hiring executive personnel."

"And my father approves of all this?"

"Yes, he does. Aren't you proud of me?"

"You just got out of college. You don't even have
your MBA. Is this normal?"

He laughed. "That's just it. It isn't, but I was

given an opportunity, and I took advantage of it. People do have natural talents and abilities, Semantha. Those who do don't have to follow the same path as those who don't. Your parents, who are pretty sharp people, saw it in me and decided to take advantage of me."

"Parents?"

"Your father and stepmother. They're your parents now, aren't they?"

I looked away. With Mrs. Dobson and Doris gone and Ethan now in awe of Lucille and in debt to her, who would be my ally in this house?

"*I will*," Cassie reminded me.

"Aren't you the least bit happy for me, Semantha? For us?"

"Us?"

"I hope you think of it all that way," he said, holding my hand and looking deeply into my eyes.

"Yes, I think of it that way. I'm also thinking how busy and involved you'll be with Lucille."

"Not so busy that I won't be thinking of you," he said.

"Right," I said dryly.

"It is right. After they promoted me today, my thoughts went immediately to you, to us."

I didn't look back at him. I was sliding into my own dark places. He felt it and shook my hand to get my attention. When I turned back, he got it, fully.

He had begun to slip a ring on my finger.

An engagement ring!

16

Engaged

"I HOPE YOU don't mind," Ethan said. "I went to the Heavenstone jewelry department. I got something of a discount. Ordinarily, I could not afford a diamond this big with this clarity, but I wanted you to have a ring worthy of your finger, a ring worthy of you.

"And don't say it's not the size of it that matters," he added quickly. "I didn't want to be embarrassed, and I certainly don't want you to be embarrassed. I have my pride, too, you know."

I looked at it and then at him. The joy and excitement in his face were instantly replaced with worry and concern because of my controlled reaction. Some might say it was more like no reaction.

"I'm asking you to marry me," he said, as if there were some doubt about what it meant.

When I replied, the words I spoke felt as if they had originated with Cassie. From the day I had returned, I had often heard them echoing throughout Heavenstone. It was as if all of our ancestors captured on that wall of portraits had become a Greek chorus chanting.

"Everything's happening so fast."

He laughed. "Tell me about it. A few weeks ago, I was applying for an assistant floor manager's position at a small department store in my hometown and worrying that I wouldn't even be granted an interview."

"I don't mean just about your career, Ethan. Everything at Heavenstone, my family, my life, too. Before I can catch my breath after one change, there's another and another."

"All for the better, I hope," he said. "But you're right about one thing. I never gave myself to one girl as quickly as I've given myself to you. From the first moment I saw you in that dorm lobby, I knew you were someone special, and I knew I wanted you to be in my life. I thought I saw the same feeling in you, too. I hope that wasn't a mistake."

"No, it wasn't," I said.

"Then this," he said, running his finger over the diamond, "isn't coming too fast. As Lucille says, if it's right, it's never too fast."

"Now you're going to start quoting her?"

He laughed. "You're always quoting your father."

"That's different," I said. "He's a part of Kentucky history. I'm not the only one who quotes him."

"Of course. I was just teasing. I would never put Lucille on the same level as your father."

I thought for a moment, looked at the ring, and then asked, "Does she know about this?"

"The ring? No. I haven't even told your father yet. I was hoping you'd be happy and the two of us would have some fun at dinner tonight. We won't say anything when we first enter the dining room. We'll wait to see how long it takes for one or both of them to notice. How's that sound?"

"That sounds good," I said, happy to hear he hadn't gotten Lucille's or my father's approval first, that this was entirely his doing.

"I will confess that the way you sounded on the phone today sped up my plans. I knew you were terribly unhappy, and I wanted to do something to please you and cheer you up. I wasn't going to wait too many more days, anyway. As soon as they called me into your father's office and promoted me, I felt I could propose to you."

"Our love shouldn't depend on how much money you make or how important you are in the Heavenstone Corporation, Ethan."

"And it doesn't, but it doesn't hurt, either," he said. "Hey, don't blame me for being a bit intimidated by all this. Look at what you're used to having. Any guy would think, *Who am I to assume she'd care enough?*"

"I never flaunted anything."

"You never had to. It flaunts itself. But I do think we see each other now for who we really are, don't you? And that is truly love. Am I right?"

"Yes," I said, smiling. "You can't have love without honesty."

When I looked at the mirror, I saw Cassie dwindling, but I didn't care. This was more important than fighting Lucille over maids and cooks and the running of the house. This was my future, my love.

"Okay," he said, rising. "I'm going to get

showered and dressed for our first so-called gourmet dinner. Let's both wear something special. Lucille will think we're doing it because of the changes she has made, this gourmet chef, and so on, but we'll surprise her. And of course, your father as well."

"Yes," I said. Now it did sound more like fun.

He fixed his eyes on me with that serious, deep look that made my heart skip beats.

"I'll always think of you first, Semantha. I hope you'll always believe that."

He hurried off. I didn't move for a few moments, and then, looking at my ring, feeling a new surge of excitement and energy, I, too, hurried to prepare for the unveiling of our future. Maybe my father and Lucille wouldn't be as quick to approve of it as Ethan obviously thought. Maybe Daddy would say it was a bit too fast and we should wait. Maybe Lucille would be very annoyed with how we had stolen her thunder. None of these possibilities frightened me.

First, it would be a good test of Ethan's sincerity. If Daddy or Lucille told us to put our engagement on hold and he retreated, I would know that their approval, his career, was more important to him than our love and our lives together. Second, I had never looked forward more to shaking up my father than I did at this moment. If he could disregard all prudence to bring Lucille into the Heavenstone world so quickly and firmly, I could do the same with Ethan.

Most important, perhaps, it would truly be declaring our independence. Our lives, what we did now and in the future, would be our decision.

Heavenstone wasn't a puppet theater, and we weren't puppets.

I chose one of my more formal dresses and bedecked myself in my most expensive necklace and earrings. I worked on my hair and my makeup the way I would have if I were about to attend my own debutante ball. When Ethan returned, dressed in a new black suit and tie, he looked at me as if he had lost his breath.

"You're absolutely beautiful," he said.

"You're not so bad yourself. When did you get that suit?"

"Yesterday. Lucille picked it out."

"Lucille? She's picking out your clothes now, too?"

"Oh, she just knew we had some new styles and told me to try it on. I'm wearing it because I thought I looked good in it and you'd like it."

"I do."

He held out his arm. "Okay, then. Shall we make some Heavenstone history tonight?"

"Absolutely, Mr. Hunter." I took his arm.

"I'll tell you why I really proposed," he said as we started for the stairway.

"Why?"

"I want my portrait up on that wall below someday."

He laughed. I laughed, too, but sometimes, as Cassie would say, there is more truth in a jest than you'd expect. Anyway, so what? Why shouldn't he want his portrait on our wall? It wasn't a bad ambition to have. Besides, it was the house. Heavenstone had an undeniably powerful effect on anyone who lived within it.

Cassie was the one who had told me how much influence the house had on us, so she shouldn't be critical of Ethan's half joke.

Daddy and Lucille were already at the table when we arrived. Mia was pouring Daddy some red wine from a bottle she had wrapped in white cloth, taking great care not to permit a drop to escape.

"Ah, you two are in for a treat tonight," Daddy said. He smelled the wine, looked at it in the light, and then sipped it. Mia stood by with the bottle, just like a waitress in a restaurant, waiting to see if Daddy approved. He nodded, and she poured Lucille a glass. "Our new chef suggested this French wine for tonight," Daddy explained, more to Ethan than to me.

"A real chef knows what's appropriate to drink with certain food," Lucille added.

Mia hurried around to pour us each a glass. Ethan gazed at me with a half-smile on his face. Neither Daddy nor Lucille had made a comment on how formally we were dressed, and neither had yet seen my ring. I deliberately lifted my wineglass with my left hand so the ring would be quite visible, glittering in the light of the chandelier, but just at that moment, our new chef, Gerad Bolud, appeared. Lucille introduced him to us. He nodded and began to describe our four-course dinner. He had managed to prepare a French onion soup, which he said was a bit rushed but should be fine.

"Gerad didn't even unpack his things," Lucille explained. "He went right to work on tonight's dinner." She beamed as proudly as an artist next to her painting. He bowed again and returned to the kitchen. Lucille had successfully turned our meal into a show.

Catherine appeared with a tray carrying our salads. Mia helped her serve them. Unlike our usual salad, this one contained fruit. I had to admit to myself that it was delicious. Daddy was so involved with his bread, wine, and salad that he still had not noticed my ring. Ethan kept throwing me impish little grins, while Lucille continued to describe Gerad Bolud's background, emphasizing how lucky we were to have captured him before someone else could do so. She wanted us to understand and be impressed with how in demand he was and how she had found out about him and outmaneuvered everyone else, using some of her best connections. Daddy couldn't have given her more compliments.

Finally, when the soup was brought out and we all had begun to eat it, Daddy paused, lowered his spoon, and leaned forward.

"What is that ring I see, Semantha?" he asked.

Lucille looked up. I held my breath.

"It's an engagement ring," Lucille said. "Isn't that an engagement ring?"

"Yes," I said.

"I gave it to her tonight," Ethan said. "We wanted to surprise you both."

"Surprise? I'll say," Daddy said.

For a long moment, no one spoke. *Here it comes,* I thought, *the fatherly advice or Lucille's wisdom.* At the very least, I expected to hear her ask, *"Isn't this a bit quick?"* or, *"Shouldn't you first have discussed this with Mr. Heavenstone?"*

"Well," she began instead, "we seem to have quite a bit to celebrate tonight."

She looked at Daddy. He digested all that was happening in front of him and then slowly nodded and smiled and lifted his wineglass.

"Congratulations to you both," he said.

Ethan reached for my hand. I looked at Lucille. She lifted her glass as well.

"Just think," she declared, "so soon after our wedding, we'll be planning another. Have you two decided on a date?"

"No," Ethan said. "I thought it best to look at our calendars together. I know there is so much going on for the Heavenstone Corporation, that new construction you were discussing, new personnel . . ."

"Well, you don't plan a wedding like this in a few weeks, anyway. Semantha already has a good idea what goes into the planning of a well-run wedding, don't you, Semantha?"

Since Ethan and I hadn't discussed it, I was reluctant to say anything, but there was one thing I didn't need much discussion to decide, and I thought I'd make that clear right then and there, right at the start.

"I don't want a wedding like yours."

She recoiled with surprise.

"I want a small family affair."

Lucille stared at me a moment. "I see," she said. She wore an incredulous half-smile that quickly evaporated as she looked at the rest of her soup. "I'm sure you'll change your mind when all this settles in," she said without looking at me.

"I'm sure I won't," I replied, and looked at Ethan. He tried smiling, but his eyes were two pools of fear. The surprise was veering off like a plane that had lost its tail end.

No one else spoke. Mia returned and took away our soup bowls. Moments later, Chef Gerad came in himself with the tray of entrées. He was proud of his creation and stood back to watch us taste the veal chop. Everyone, even I, who was still quite upset about the dismissal of Mrs. Dobson and Doris, had to admit it was delicious. Daddy once again congratulated Lucille for getting us Gerad.

The two De Stagen sisters hovered behind us during the entire meal, ready to jump and pour more wine or pass something on the table. Dishes and glasses were removed as soon as they were no longer required. I looked to see if anyone else was bothered by their intensity, but no one was. When Mrs. Dobson and Doris were there, dinner had still felt like a homemade meal in a home. This dinner gave me the feeling that I had been transported to an elegant and expensive French restaurant. I half expected to see Daddy get the bill and pull out his credit card. I almost said so but thought it would only upset him. Later, however, I did tell Ethan how I felt.

"You'll get used to it," he said.

"I don't want to get used to it. I don't want to be on a stage when I eat dinner. Next thing you know, we'll be given a book of etiquette to study."

I saw a slight smile on his lips.

"You don't have that book, do you, Ethan?"

"A little fairy put it on my dresser when I first arrived."

"I wonder who that was," I said, and shook my head.

"You weren't serious about our wedding, were you?" he asked.

"Yes, why?"

"Oh, you don't want to do that, Semantha. A father gets so much pleasure from making his daughter's wedding. Your dad surely wants to enjoy it, too, don't you think?"

"I don't know," I said. I hadn't thought of it from that viewpoint.

"Well, just give it some more thought, okay?"

I nodded, but I had a Cassie thought. Was it really my father he was thinking of, or was he thinking of himself and what an impression he would be making on his family and his friends? I hated having such a thought about him and shook it out as soon as it occurred.

In the days that followed, I didn't have much time to think about it, anyway. We went to Daddy's award dinner, which was quite impressive. There were television and newspaper people all over us the whole time. When we returned home, there was too much going on in the house to think about much else.

Lucille apparently had decided to make some significant decorative changes, which included some of the upstairs, but not yet my wing. I learned about it as it happened. What surprised me was how deep some of the changes were. Not only were walls repainted and floors redone, but furniture was replaced. With something else happening every day, it was hard to catch my breath and ask about what had been done.

What shocked me most of all was Daddy's acquiescence. For all of my life, the furnishings and decor of Heavenstone had been sacrosanct. Mother had been permitted to make only the smallest of changes compared with what Lucille was doing, which included a total revamping of the kitchen to make it "a first-class gourmet kitchen." The old furniture was relegated to the attic, which was rapidly becoming the Heavenstone historic cemetery.

Of course, I complained to Ethan, who told me it was only natural for a woman to want to put her own stamp of identity on her home.

"You would do the same thing," he said, which put a new thought in my head, especially now that I saw what Lucille was doing and Daddy was letting her do.

"Maybe you're right. After we're married, we'll have our own home. I suppose we should start thinking about it."

He looked at me strangely. "Our own home? You mean, you'd want to move out of Heavenstone?"

"It's not my home now. You just said so. It's Lucille's."

"But it's so big. Four families could live here without ever seeing each other."

"Don't you want your own home, Ethan?"

He thought a moment and nodded. "Yes, you're

right," he said. "I just never thought you'd want to move."

"I didn't until now," I told him.

We didn't discuss it again for a while. Instead, the conversation returned to the subject of our wedding. Lucille had suggested some dates. Ethan didn't come right out and say she was basically deciding when we would get married, but I read between the lines when he talked about his work and what was being planned.

"We can get married here," I said as a form of compromise, "but I don't want hundreds of strangers. As I said at dinner when we announced our engagement, let's just have our families."

He didn't argue, but I knew he was discussing it with both Lucille and my father. Finally, Daddy brought it up at dinner one night. When he spoke, Lucille kept her eyes on her plate and pursed her lips and listened.

"We have so many close friends who would like to share in our happiness," Daddy began. "We don't have to have a wedding as big as Lucille's and mine was, but we could have a modest affair."

"Modest? I'm sure you'll have trouble cutting down on the list, Daddy. Look how hard it was for you with your own wedding."

"You just let me worry about that, Semantha."

Lucille glanced at me and then looked at Daddy. "If it's really making her that uncomfortable even to think about it, Teddy . . ."

"It is," I said quickly.

"Then maybe she should have a few more

sessions with Dr. Ryan," she added. "She's still avoiding socializing."

I felt the blood rise up my neck and into my cheeks. "I have to go to therapy because I don't want my wedding to become a social-political event like yours?"

"Semantha!" Daddy shouted. "That's an inappropriate thing to say."

I looked at Ethan, who was looking down, and then I rose and left the dining room.

"*Good,*" Cassie said, and led me out of the house.

I was halfway to the pool before I heard Ethan call to me. He ran to catch up.

"Hey, hold up," he said, taking my right arm at the elbow. "Why did you get so upset?"

"You're kidding. Why did I get so upset?"

He shook his head.

"Lucille basically just said that if I don't want a big wedding, I need mental help, and you wonder why I got so upset?"

He nodded and walked along slowly. "It's just how she thinks. She can't imagine any young woman not wanting a big wedding with all the trimmings."

"I'm not Lucille, and just because she can't imagine it doesn't mean there's something wrong with me, does it?"

"Of course not. Your father wouldn't send you to a therapist for that. He just told her so in no uncertain terms after you left."

I paused. "Did he?"

"Yes. He feels terrible. I could see. He told me to

tell you that he didn't mean to cause us any concern, and if you want to have a small family event, fine."

"Well, why didn't he say so at the table?"

Ethan shrugged. "I imagine, like any parent, he was worried you weren't thinking it out fully, but he doesn't want to see you upset. He's very happy with how things have been going."

"I wish he'd tell me that sometimes."

"I'm sure he will. Right now, he thinks you have eyes and ears for no one else but me. Probably because that's the way he is with Lucille. He thinks we're just as much in love. Well, I have news for him."

"What?"

"We're more in love." He turned me to him. "Right?"

"I hope so," I said.

"I know so," he replied, and kissed me. I saw Cassie standing behind him, shaking her head. "Anyway," he continued, walking me along, "under the circumstances, with our wedding being a small family affair, I suggest we get married within a month. Lucille just admitted that because it's such an intimate affair, the preparation time wouldn't be that long. They went off to check on some dates for us. We can have invitations out in a few days. Gerad will prepare a wonderful wedding dinner, and Lucille thinks Mia and Catherine can handle our small reception." He emphasized "small."

"It will have more meaning for us, Ethan, if we just have the people we love and who love us."

"I understand. I'm not upset, and now, neither

are they. There'll be plenty of time afterward for elaborate social events at Heavenstone."

His understanding tone helped me calm down. I rested my head against his shoulder.

"You are more sensible than I am."

"I'm here for you. That's what matters the most." He kissed me on the forehead, and we settled on a chaise longue. I didn't see Cassie, but I felt certain she wasn't far away. She was probably very disappointed, having expected my leaving the dinner table to be the beginning of some big fight with Lucille.

"My sister would never have liked Lucille," I said.

"How do you know?"

"I know."

"From what I hear about her, especially from your father, she wasn't so different from Lucille. She was intelligent, determined, and very protective of Heavenstone. They'd probably agree about many things."

"No. They wouldn't agree about anything."

"Well, that isn't important now," he said. "She's not the one who has to coexist with Lucille. You are, and you'll do just fine."

I didn't like the sound of the word "coexist."

"I meant what I said about moving out of here, Ethan. If we're going to get married that soon, we should begin to look for a new home."

He was thoughtful for a while before speaking. "Well," he said, "let's not pile it on them tonight. We'll break the news in a day or so, okay?"

"Okay."

He held me, but it was as if he weren't there. His thoughts were so far off.

"Let's go back in," I said. The sky was overcast, and it wasn't as pleasant as most of the nights we had spent out there.

We rose and started back toward the house. Cassie was waiting at the door. She said nothing, but followed us in. I knew she was waiting for an opportunity, waiting until I was alone. Ethan wanted us to join Daddy and Lucille in the den.

"*They'll gang up on you,*" Cassie whispered. "*They're not giving you a chance to think.*"

"You go on ahead," I told him. "I'll be down in a while."

I headed up the stairway, Cassie right behind me. We went into my room and I closed the door. I could feel her rage.

"*How dare you?*" she asked.

"What?"

"*I heard what you said. How dare you give up Heavenstone, surrender to that woman? Get married and then find your own home? What are you, some common, average person looking forward to a life in oblivion? Don't you realize what you'd be turning your back on if you did such a thing? Go down and look into the face of every Heavenstone on the wall of portraits. See if there is one coward among them.*"

"I can't live here with her. She won't have Ethan only at work; she'll run our lives through him here. Look at the influence she has on Daddy already. If he can't stand up to her, what do you think Ethan would do?"

"*Then maybe he's not the one for you. You can decide that later. You are moving too quickly, or should I say you are being moved too quickly? You're so pathetic sometimes with that mealy-mouth look, that desperation for someone to love you. You've always been this way, no matter how I tried to change you, to protect you.*

"*You go right back downstairs and make it clear to them that you're in charge of your own destiny and what will be the destiny of Heavenstone. The very idea of Lucille determining your wedding date . . . doesn't that make you sick?*"

"Yes. But what will I say?"

"*Simple. You want time to let everything settle in. You're still not sure about what you want to do career-wise. It was Lucille who talked you out of joining Uncle Perry, wasn't it? Not only is she deciding what you'll eat here and what you will and will not do every day, she's laying out your entire future. It's ridiculous to think you could find an adequate new home that quickly, anyway. Ethan knows that. He'll 'yes' you to death so you're happy and she's happy. Well, take control. Think of yourself as me for a change.*

"*Go on. Straighten your shoulders. Firm up your voice. Claim your birthright,*" she ordered. "*Daddy will respect you more.*"

"Will he?"

"*He respected me, didn't he? He still does. Ethan told you how he talked about me.*"

"Will you be there with me?"

"*Of course. I'm with you forever,*" she said.

I picked up my picture of Mother and myself, pressed it to my heart, put it back, and started out. Cassie was there in the hallway. She walked alongside me and was right behind me as I descended.

I heard Daddy, Lucille, and Ethan laughing in the den. They all had drinks and turned to me as I entered.

"Well, feeling a bit better, Semantha?" Daddy asked.

"Yes, Daddy, thank you."

"Would you like an after-dinner drink? We're all trying this port wine Senator Brice sent over yesterday."

"It's terrific," Ethan said.

"Thank you. I would."

Lucille studied me closely as I approached the bar. She sensed something different. Ethan simply held his smile, frozen like a man halfway across on a tightrope.

Daddy poured my drink.

"Well, now, what should we drink to?" he asked, raising his glass.

"The Heavenstones," I said. He smiled. Everyone sipped the port. "And my decisions," I added.

Ethan looked worried. He started to shake his head, afraid I was going to announce our moving out.

"What decisions?" Lucille asked.

"For one, I'd like to think more about the wedding. Maybe I spoke too quickly. I might want a bigger affair, so I don't want to rush it just to meet an available date."

Both Lucille and Ethan looked speechless.

Daddy smiled. "That's very wise," he said.

"And second, after we're married, we'll be setting up our lives together, and we'd obviously want
to stay at Heavenstone."

I looked at Ethan, whose eyebrows rose. He
smiled.

"Of course you would," Daddy said, now looking even happier. "I wouldn't hear otherwise."

"So, I think I should lay claim to the west wing,"
I continued. "We'll need guest rooms for our guests
occasionally, and those rooms, the powder room, and
what could easily be an upstairs den for us should
not be touched. I think there should only be very
minor changes, especially in what was once Cassie's
room."

For a moment, you could hear a pin drop. Ethan
looked as if he was holding his breath.

"That's a very sensible, wise thought," Daddy
said. He turned to Lucille. "Isn't it?"

Lucille looked as if she had a mouthful of sour
milk. The smile that finally emerged was as cold as
the smile on death's face, I was sure. "Yes, that would
be fine," she said, as if she were the one who made
the final decision. I certainly wasn't going to thank
her.

"I didn't think I'd like port," I said, drinking
some more. "It's very good."

Daddy laughed. "I never knew a Heavenstone
who didn't like it. My father had a glass of port every
night before he went to bed."

Lucille put her glass on the bar and turned to
Daddy. "Speaking of bed, I think I'll go up now,
Teddy."

"Right. I'm coming. We're off to Louisville to-morrow. Big chamber of commerce luncheon event at which we're special guests," he explained. He stopped to kiss me good night and then hurried after Lucille.

"Well, well, you're certainly full of surprises," Ethan said. "I know they were pleased with your decision about the wedding. Of course, I regret having to wait longer to make you Mrs. Hunter, but under the circumstances, it's a good plan. And I'm happy you decided we should stay here."

"Lucille wasn't exactly pleased about that."

"I don't know. I think she was just tired. What got you to change your mind?"

"My sister," I said.

"Your sister?" He held his smile. "I don't understand."

"Cassie was always the sensible one. I just thought about what she would do."

"Sensible?" He shook his head. "I know your father said she was intelligent and always concerned about the family, but after what you said she did to you, I'm not sure I'd conclude she was sensible."

I didn't reply. I turned my back on him and put my glass on the bar.

"Well, none of that really matters now. I guess I'll go up, too," he said. "Lucille left a list a mile long for me to follow up on tomorrow while they're away." He came up to me and put his arms around my waist. Then he kissed me on the back of the neck. "Going up?"

"Not yet," I said, still not turning around. "But

don't worry about me. You go on. You need your rest if you want to keep up with her."

He laughed and let go of me. "She does have endless energy. Half the time, she forgets to eat lunch. Okay, but you get some rest, too. Emotional events wear you down."

I turned to him, and he kissed me good night.

"Everything's going to be great now. You'll see," he said. "I'm proud of you."

I watched him leave, and then I looked at Cassie, who had been standing off to the right the whole time.

She was smiling.

"Everything will be great now," she said. *"But he has no idea why."*

Family Planning

SOMETIMES DURING THE weeks that followed, I wondered if I had really gotten the better of Lucille. Perhaps Cassie hadn't given me the right advice, after all. Like a swimmer caught in a current, Lucille realized it was wiser to swim with it than against it. Only by swimming faster than the current could she maintain her precious control.

Because I had implied that I might agree to a big wedding, she immediately began to plan it. Soon, there wasn't a dinner at home that didn't include some brochure, some new wedding idea, or some new design she had discovered for an altar. She agreed that it wasn't necessary for our wedding to be as big as hers and Daddy's, but there were at least five hundred people who should be invited.

"Five hundred people is not outrageous," she said before I could object.

"No, it's not," Daddy agreed.

I didn't object, and that soon led to a listing and discussion of names, almost all of whom I had no knowledge of. They were, in Lucille's terms, "the core of our business relationships."

Ethan had already given her his list of relatives and some friends from home he'd like to see invited. But that was only twenty names. I had no close girl-friends to ask to be my bridesmaids. Lucille's solution was to suggest that I have some of the company's most important young female employees.

"They'll all be honored, and it will enhance the wedding to have a half-dozen or so," she said. Of course, Daddy agreed.

Most of the time, I simply listened to the discussion without commenting. However, one night after dinner, I asked Ethan to do me a favor regarding our wedding.

"Anything," he said. "What?"

"Ask my uncle Perry to be your best man."

"Really?" He held his smile. He wasn't stupid. He knew what I was doing. I was showing Lucille just how wrong she had been to replace Uncle Perry with Senator Brice. "He's not really my best friend. I was thinking of George Samuels from back home. George and I were very close in high school and never lost touch with each other. You'll like George."

"Uncle Perry is my best friend," I said. "In time, he'll become yours as well, but if he's mine now, he's yours now, too."

He nodded, seeing how firmly I wanted this. "Okay. I'll ask him."

"Thank you."

"We'll have to settle on a date, then," he warned.

"That's fine. You decide," I said.

I knew he would run right to Lucille and Daddy and determine the date with them. They concluded that we could hold the wedding in about three months. Now that it was more than just a small family affair, Lucille announced that she and I would explore a few hotels. She determined which ones to consider. I couldn't disagree, because she was more familiar with all of that than I could ever be. In fact, I told her to make the choice herself.

"What? It's your wedding," she said, really taken by surprise. "You should be the one making the choice."

It's my wedding, I thought, *but you've taken it over.*

"I trust you to make the right decision," I said.

She smiled. "Well, I'm happy to see you have that much faith in me, Semantha."

"I certainly do when it comes to something like this," I said, and she looked very pleased.

It was really Cassie's strategy. Ever since Lucille and I had had that little tiff at dinner and I had insisted that she not touch my wing of Heavenstone, Lucille was more aloof, suspecting not only that I didn't like her but that I would try to cause some break in her relationship with Daddy.

"Are you absolutely sure you want me to handle this all by myself?" she asked.

"I saw how well you planned your own wedding. I'm not the least bit worried."

"Well, would you like some help choosing your gown?"

"Give her an inch, and she'll take a foot," Cassie whispered.

"Of course I do," I said.

As far as Daddy and Ethan were concerned, when they heard about all of this, the thin wall of ice that had formed between Lucille and me rapidly melted.

"Good. Let's take some time and do that this weekend, then," she said, lowering her voice as if someone could overhear us. "I have a secret. I'm not crazy about the wedding dresses at our stores. I haven't gotten into the problems with that designer yet, but I have a specialty store for us to visit in Lexington, and they'll do an extra-special job for me."

"Thank you," I said, and our day was planned. My cooperation and willingness to have her do what any mother of the bride would do filled her with such an air of joy that she seemed to float through Heavenstone. Her new trust in me was palpable. She had nothing but smiles for me.

When we drove in my car to the wedding-gown store, Lucille even apologized for the comment she had made at dinner when discussion about the size of my wedding had first occurred.

"I didn't mean it to be mean," she said. "I am concerned about you and want you to have a successful relationship and marriage. Ethan is going to rise quickly in our executive ranks. You'll be attending many social functions, and I'm sure you will be an enormous asset to him. There's no reason for you to be shy about meeting people, either.

"You'll soon realize that half the people you meet, especially some of the women, are not half as bright as you are, believe me, and I'll be there often to help you with anyone or anything. As my father would say, you can take that to the bank."

She laughed and held her smile. I was driving and had barely spoken or changed expression.

"I see significant growth in you already, Semantha," she continued.

Cassie had used to say some people abhor silence the way nature abhors a vacuum. Lucille had to have conversation.

"I do want us to be great friends," she added when my silence continued.

"Of course," I said.

She didn't ask, but I saw in her face that she wasn't sure if I meant *Of course you do* or *Of course we will be*. That was a Cassie trick. When she wanted to be ambiguous, she could be, and trying to determine what she meant by looking at her did no good. Her face was a Broadway billboard flashing expressions on and off so quickly you weren't sure what you had just seen.

At Lucille's choice for a wedding-gown store, I tried on a half-dozen different styles before Lucille warmed to one. When I considered it objectively, I had to confess it was a beautiful dress, and it did, as she said, complement my figure. We went through the accessories and then had a late lunch at a restaurant she frequented often. Everyone working there knew her, and a number of other customers stopped by our table to say hello. She identified most of them by the fame of their families or their family businesses. "She belongs to Altman Jewelry," she would say, nodding at a woman who had just visited with us, or "He's the principal shareholder of Frontier National." Or "That was Miss Kentucky Scaffold. Her father's company somehow wins government bid after government bid."

Later, when I described my day to Ethan, I told him, "Lucille doesn't really know people; she knows businesses. It's like looking for people's telephone numbers in the yellow pages rather than the white pages."

He laughed. "Sometimes you do come out with a good one," he said. "You're a delightful surprise, Semantha. I'm happy you're getting along better with Lucille. By the way, she's done us another favor."

"Oh? What now?"

"Our honeymoon."

"Don't tell me she's paying for it."

"No, but remember her friend from Monaco, Claire Dubonnet? The woman who works for the prince?"

"Yes, of course."

"Lucille contacted her for us, and she's arranged for us to stay at Hotel de Paris in an upgrade. Not a bad choice for a honeymoon, huh?"

"It sounds wonderful," I said. "But shouldn't we be the ones deciding where to go on our honeymoon?"

"It's just a suggestion," he said, holding up his hand. "If you have other ideas . . ."

"Do you?"

"Not any that would beat this," he said. "As your father says, no sense in looking a gift horse in the mouth."

"Okay, then, that's where we'll go," I told him.

With the plans for our wedding going well, my

gown and accessories taken care of, and our honeymoon set, the atmosphere of harmony continued at
Heavenstone. Daddy seemed more relaxed. Lucille
certainly was, and Ethan was practically floating
as high as she was. Occasionally, I would look for
Cassie in the middle of it all and find her here and
there, sitting quietly, pondering.

"Am I doing everything right?" I asked her.

"*For now,*" she said. "*The second shoe has yet
to drop.*"

"How will I know when it has?"

"*Oh, you'll know. Don't worry. You'll know.*"

Lucille determined that the ideal venue for our
wedding would be the Hotel Glory, which was only
twenty miles from Heavenstone. She took me to see
the ballroom and meet with the special-occasions
manager to review the menu. Once I had let her decide on the site of our wedding, she went forward
and made all of the other arrangements as well,
including ordering the flowers, choosing the invitations, and settling on the band. She brought every
choice to me, and I stamped it with my approval
without comment. Ordinarily, she would have been
very happy to see me being so continually cooperative and appreciative, but my attitude, which I'm sure
to her bordered on indifference, began to irk her.

Finally, she came right out and said, "You don't
seem as excited by all this as I would expect. You do
want to get married, don't you, Semantha?"

"Oh, yes, of course," I said. "Ethan and I love
each other very much. I guess I'm looking forward to
our marriage more than I am to our wedding. After

all, a wedding is just a big party that lasts for a few hours and then gets pressed into albums."

She held her mouth slightly open and looked speechless. Finally realizing it, she said, "From how your father describes your sister Cassie, I would think that would be something she would have said, something she would have believed. I thought you were different."

"Really? How?" I was really curious about how Daddy had described the two of us.

"More feminine, more into being a woman. For most women, their wedding day is one of the most important days of their lives."

"Oh, I don't mean to say it isn't important. I'm just trying to be sensible and grounded, Lucille. In a way, I'm trying to be more like you."

"Me?" She thought a moment. I could see she wasn't sure if I was giving her a compliment or not. She smiled. "I'm glad you're being sensible, but you can let go sometimes and just have fun, too."

"I will," I promised.

She nodded, but I could see she wasn't quite sure now what to make of me.

"Perfect," Cassie whispered. *"You have her off-balance. You're chipping away at that Great Wall of Confidence she wraps around herself."*

I knew this was true, because Lucille was discussing me more and more with Ethan, especially after this last conversation about our wedding. I realized it because he continually asked me about the wedding preparations, looking for a sign of unhappiness.

"If there's something Lucille did or is doing that you don't like, please tell me," he said.

"Everything's fine, Ethan. As long as Uncle Perry is your best man, that is."

"Yes, he's agreed."

"Then don't worry," I told him, but he wore the same suspicious and uncertain expression Lucille now wore.

Only Daddy seemed unaffected by my complacency. He ascribed it to my realization that Lucille was a unique, bright woman and thought it was very wise of me to seek her counsel, especially when it came to planning a wedding.

"My father told me the wisest man is one who knows when he needs advice and where to go for it. People are like tools. You choose the right one for the right job. I'm really proud of you, Semantha."

"Thank you, Daddy."

"I keep thinking that we've turned a page. We're all off to a wonderful new beginning. I do feel ten years younger, and the proof is that there is no new proposal, no matter how ambitious it might seem, that frightens me. I'm a real Heavenstone again. And so are you."

"*If I didn't know you don't buy into all that, I'd be worried,*" Cassie whispered. "*Just keep smiling. Our time will come.*"

And smile was what I did. There were no arguments, no disagreements. Even Uncle Perry was convinced that we were all heading toward better times. Daddy was roaring about with his new energy. Lucille was making some very wise decisions and not alienating the employees the way he had feared she might. And Ethan was gaining everyone's respect.

To cap it off, Uncle Perry told me I was beginning to look like the future mistress of Heavenstone should.

Behind him, behind everyone who complimented the four of us now, stood Cassie, wearing that sly smile, and behind that smile, her clever, conniving mind was molding a plan. We would take back our heritage and our history and, most of all, control of our destiny. No one, least of all Lucille, should have come into our world thinking otherwise. I could feel Cassie's confidence inside me. It was like the old days when she had been my strength, my spine, and I felt very safe.

The first time I worried a little about that safety came when Ethan shocked me with a proposal. We had just finished another of Gerad's gourmet dinners, all of us drinking more wine than usual. Daddy and Lucille went off to talk about some business projects in his office. Considering what they had consumed, I wondered how they could discuss anything intelligently. I was feeling a little tipsy myself, and Ethan's face was so flushed that someone might think he had just come in from an afternoon of intense sunbathing. He took my hand and led me to the den. I could see he had something on his mind. He looked like a little boy planning to raid a cookie jar.

"I have an idea," he began. "It's something I know will please your father very much and something we'll probably be doing anyway."

"And what's that?"

"I think we should plan right now on your getting pregnant as soon as possible. I mean, it's not something we have to wait until we are actually married before we plan. Anyway, what difference will two more months make? Of course, the hope is that our firstborn will be a boy we can name Asa. He won't be Asa Heavenstone, he'll be Asa Hunter—but your father will still have his grandson."

"I wasn't planning on getting pregnant that fast after we were married, Ethan."

The whole idea seemed terrifying—and for reasons Ethan wouldn't understand.

"But you did plan on us having children, right?"

"Yes, in time," I said.

"Well, you're not exactly going to sacrifice a career or anything when you become a mother," he said.

I was sure that he wouldn't have been so blunt if it hadn't been for the wine. Nevertheless, I recoiled.

"That's not the only reason a woman might wait. I'm not exactly closing in on the end of my child-bearing years."

"I didn't mean to imply anything negative," he said. "I just thought . . . well . . ." He looked at me harder. "You're not afraid to have children now because of what happened to you, are you?"

"Don't start talking therapy, Ethan," I warned.

"No, no, I don't mean to even suggest such a thing. I just want you to know I'm here for you and want to help you get over anything you have to get over."

"I don't have to get over anything. What is this rush to have children?"

"It's not meant to be a rush. I just thought it would be something wonderful for all of us. I'm not saying it would even happen that quickly. I know you've been on your birth control pills, and it could take months after you stop because of how a woman's body readjusts, but—"

"What, are you doing research about it?"

"A little," he said, smiling. "My Boy Scout background. Always be prepared. Anyway, I know a woman could have to wait about two or three months or more after she stops the pill and returns to her normal menstrual cycle before she conceives, so the sooner you stop taking it, the better the chances of our having a baby within the first year or so of our marriage. That wouldn't be so terrible, would it? Just imagine. When our children are older and on their own, we'll still be relatively young."

"That's true," I said, but I was thinking more about my daughter. I'd only be in my thirties when she was a teenager. I could literally be a grandmother in my thirties.

"Sure. It makes sense for us. I know the room we should fix up as a nursery," he added quickly. "It's the one right next to yours, the smaller guest room. Lucille even suggested we have an access door made from your room, which will become ours, to this nursery."

"Lucille suggested? You discussed this with her first?"

"She was just talking one day about the future and planning, and she came up with the idea."

"What else did she suggest about our future and how we should conduct our lives?"

He held up both hands as if he were trying to

keep a wall from toppling. "Now, don't get upset. It was an innocent suggestion. She's not trying to run anyone's life. She's a woman with great experience and insight. We might as well take advantage of her."

"As long as we're taking advantage of her and she's not taking advantage of us."

He laughed. "How could she do that?"

"Maybe he's not as bright as you think," Cassie whispered. *"I'm a little worried about how eagerly and how much he confides in her. Don't say too much more right now."*

"Okay," I told him. "I'll put all this in my bank account of ideas."

He missed my sarcasm, smiled, and kissed me. "Then you'll stop taking birth control pills?"

I nodded, and he was satisfied, but the whole discussion made me uneasy. We talked no more about it, but the frequency with which Ethan came to my bedroom to make love made me think about it. He made sure to know when my period was supposed to come again and counted days, telling me when I was ovulating. I tried to be as enthusiastic as he was, but it was difficult.

Was I wrong to question why he wanted children so early? Was I so reluctant and skeptical because of my own emotional and psychological wounds? In my mind, I still had not found closure and accepted the fact that I had a daughter who would never know me. True, I didn't hear the cry of a baby as much anymore, but I didn't stop thinking about her, about all of it. I even wondered if Porter Andrew Hall, the father of our daughter, ever thought about her, ever had the same curiosity about her that I did.

I imagined myself meeting him one day by accident and him being cordial and apologetic. I knew that he had gotten married and had a family of his own. Daddy would never mention his name, but I had come across it reading the social news. He had become a lawyer and lived in the suburbs of Lexington. Daddy could have destroyed him but had decided in the end just to drive him out of our business and bury the rest of it forever.

But we would meet in this imagined scenario, and he would ask me if I knew anything at all about our daughter. "Did you ever see her?" he would wonder.

Of course, I would tell him no and then ask him if he had ever tried.

"Once," he would say. "I drove out there and parked across from their house and waited to see if I could get a glimpse of her."

"I've done the same," I would confess.

He'd nod in understanding. "I never saw her," he would say, "and then I thought I, of all people, have no right to be here and quickly drove away. Well, it's nice seeing you, though, seeing you're all right."

"Am I?"

His smile would dwindle, and my imagined scenario popped like a bubble.

If I did give birth to another child, I thought, would I look at him or her and always think of my lost daughter?

So, despite what I had told Ethan, I did not stop

taking my birth control pills. Cassie wouldn't let me, anyway. When Ethan asked me ten days before our wedding if I had gotten my period, I had to tell him yes to cover up my deception.

"Don't be discouraged," he said. "As I told you, it's very common for a woman who's been on the pill as long as you have to have some difficulty conceiving quickly. But," he added, brightening, "we're going to have quite a romantic honeymoon, and if I have my calendar planning right, you'll be in a prime time."

He was so excited about the possibility that I almost confessed, but I didn't. I smiled and let it all seem possible. As the days before our wedding ticked down, the excitement seemed to make every sound, every voice in Heavenstone, louder, drowning out any other thought. The moment Daddy, Lucille, and Ethan returned home, the chatter began. Our pictures were, of course, in all of the social columns. Preparations were made for Ethan's parents, who would fly in two days before the wedding so he could show them our estate and the department store. Lucille helped with the arrangements, providing the Heavenstone limousine to pick them up at the airport. She then turned her attention to my wardrobe, because she claimed I didn't have quite the fashion for the French Riviera.

"You're going to where the world's most glamorous and wealthiest people gather to have fun. The women you'll meet will be very sophisticated. I'm going to lend you some of my best jewelry," she continued, "but we need to dress you up a bit. You don't mind my telling you this, do you?"

"Oh, no, I don't mind," I said. I wanted to add, *I don't care,* but more for Daddy's and Ethan's sakes, I didn't add a word. I smiled and went along with her, permitting her to choose clothing, shoes, and accessories. By the time we were finished outfitting me for my honeymoon, there was no room in my suitcases for anything but the new things.

Ethan thought it was all very amusing but never stopped telling me how grateful I should be and how lucky we both were to have someone like Lucille to advise us. Half the time, I wasn't sure if he was saying these things for my benefit or hers.

"Tell me," I asked him one night while we lay together in my bed after making love, "do you ever disagree with Lucille? I don't mean have out-and-out arguments with her, but do you ever tell her you don't think so or you don't believe that, whatever?"

He shrugged. "I avoid any of that. If I don't agree with her, I'm silent, or I change the subject."

"You don't think that's cowardice?"

"Cowardice? Hell, no. Hey," he said with a smirk, "I see the way she has your father twisted around her finger, Semantha. Believe me, anyone who crosses Lucille Bennet Heavenstone will get the boot, and you know where."

"She wouldn't dare fire you or even try to now," I said.

"Yeah, maybe not, but she would definitely make sure I didn't move an inch further in the corporation. It's easier just to let her think she's right about everything. Besides, I don't see you arguing so much with her anymore. What's the point of it, anyway? It's better to have harmony if we're going to be a family, don't you think?"

"As long as you don't surrender your self-respect, Ethan," I said as soon as Cassie had whispered it. I saw him wince as if I had burned him.

He rose, his mood darkening. "Self-respect is overrated," he muttered, and put on his robe. Then he paused, turned, and smiled at me. "As long as I have your respect, I'm fine."

"Do I have yours?"

"It comes hand in hand with my love," he said, pasted a kiss on my lips, and started out. "My parents are coming tomorrow. I'd better get some rest. My mother loves to ask questions, so be prepared. She's a question machine."

"Ethan!" I cried out before he reached the door. I felt a small panic fluttering under my heart.

"What?"

"What do they know? I mean, about my past . . ."

"Nothing," he said. He smiled again. "Relax. You have no past. You have only a future with me. Sleep tight," he said, and left.

"That," Cassie said, *"is the dumbest thing I've ever heard and something that causes me real concern. You have no past? You? You're a Heavenstone. We are the past. We have the heritage. Does he think a few wedding vows will change any of that?"*

"He was only trying to make me feel better."

"That's like telling the passengers on the Titanic *they're in for a refreshing swim. Christmas trees."*

I turned my back on her.

She's just jealous, I thought. I hoped.

Can't she ever be wrong?

She had the final word before I brought down the shades on the windows of my mind and curled into the darkness to sleep.

"I may have made some unintentional mistakes, Semantha, but I've never been wrong about people.

"Never."

18

Games

ETHAN'S MOTHER WAS nowhere near the busybody he had suggested she was. Perhaps she was intimidated by the sight and size of Heavenstone and the grounds workers she saw on arrival. Lucille had designed some major landscape changes, especially bordering the gate and driveway.

Daddy liked Ethan's father. Although he had no wealthy client who came close to us, he knew how to behave around someone like Daddy. They were both on the same page when it came to business interests, the government, and taxes and at times sounded like echo chambers. No mention was made of Ethan's father's relatively recent heart problems. I thought he looked rather healthy and robust. I asked him how he was feeling, and he simply said, "Wonderful."

When I mentioned it to Ethan, he smiled and nodded. "My mother hates hearing or talking about it," he warned.

Lucille was cordial to both of Ethan's parents, but I saw how she almost immediately climbed back onto her high horse and spoke as if she resided in the clouds. Ethan's mother clearly was afraid to interrupt her, offer an opinion, or ask her a question. She spent most of her time nodding and heaping compliments.

All of Ethan's other relatives and friends were staying at the Glory, where we held the rehearsal and the rehearsal dinner. Everyone was impressed with the hotel and the arrangements. Although the rehearsal dinner was Ethan's parents' event, Lucille was on top of it, and Ethan's mother was not eager to challenge or even offer a counteropinion about anything.

On the morning of my wedding day, Daddy did something he hadn't done for some time. He came to my bedroom before I had risen. When I heard the knock, I assumed it was Ethan. As soon as Daddy entered, I sat up quickly. He smiled and sat on my bed to take my hand.

"I'm more excited about your wedding than I was about mine and Lucille's, even though it was an affair few will ever forget and we had a lot of big shots. When I first heard you were going with someone at school, I admit I was very nervous, but you selected a fine young man. I wanted you to know I couldn't be happier for you, Semantha."

He leaned over to kiss my cheek and then patted my hand and stood. For a long moment, he stared at the picture of me and my mother.

"She would have been quite pleased," he said. "We'll both be thinking about her when you take your vows."

He sounded so sad I nearly burst into tears. I saw

Cassie sitting by my desk, her head down. Daddy clapped his hands, the way he often did when he was going to make a definite decision.

"But we won't be sad for even a moment today. Today is a happy, happy day. I'm proud of you."

He nodded and headed out.

"Proud of you? For what?" Cassie asked, looking up, her eyes cold, steely gray, and sharp. *"For getting married?"*

"Probably for doing something normal," I muttered. "After what has been done to me, that's an accomplishment," I added as sharply as I could.

She looked away and then disappeared as quickly as she had appeared.

I rose slowly to start my wedding day. A year ago, such a day had seemed more like an impossible dream. Certainly, my roommate, Ellie, would never have imagined it would come so quickly for me, and most certainly not before hers. I wondered what had become of her and how surprised she would be if she heard about me. All of those girls would be surprised. Look at what had become of the girl they had derided as Norma Bates.

All day long, I kept telling myself I should be happier and more excited. There was so much going on around me, and all of it was because of me. I was the center of attention, not Cassie, not Daddy, and not Lucille, but Lucille remained at the forefront of everything. She had written out the schedule determining when we would leave Heavenstone for the hotel, when we were to take the family photos, and when each step in the ceremony would occur. Ethan went off early to spend his day with his family and friends. Lucille had booked a room for him to use. Was there anything she didn't think of?

Late in the morning, Uncle Perry stopped by to see me.

"Knock knock," he said, stepping into my open doorway. I was at my vanity table toying with some other way to wear my hair. "Hey, Sam."

"Hi, Uncle Perry."

"Preparations, preparations," he said, looking at my dress spread out on my bed. "So? Excited?"

"Yes, now that it's really happening."

"Oh, it's happening." He winked. "I know you had a lot to do with my being Ethan's best man," he said. "I hope I live up to the privilege."

"For us, there was no other choice, Uncle Perry. You'll always be the closest friend we have."

He, too, looked at my mother's photo. "How happy she would be today," he said. "I'm proud of you, too, Sam." Then he laughed. "Your father's about as nervous as I've seen him."

He wished me luck and went off to see Daddy. Lucille was at the hotel overseeing last-minute tasks and corrections.

Just after lunch, I had a surprise phone call. Mrs. Dobson called me from London. She had read about my wedding and wanted to wish me good luck and happiness. Hearing her voice brought tears immediately. She told me she was doing just fine, having acquired another position in another posh house. "Not as posh as Heavenstone, mind you, but pretty posh."

"I'm glad, Mrs. Dobson. I do miss you. I hope someday we'll meet again."

"I had a strong feeling you and that young man would come to something. I'm sure sometime in the future, you'll be traveling and set down in London. When you do, you can ring me up. I'll send you my new number and address."

"I surely will," I said.

"You stay healthy and happy," she said.

It broke my heart to hear the line go dead and realize she wouldn't be there at my wedding. When I had suggested finding out where she was and inviting her, Daddy had looked upset and said, "She's back in England, Semantha. It would be inordinately expensive for someone in her bracket to attend this affair. It would be unfair to invite her."

"*And a slap in the face for Lucille,*" Cassie had muttered, but I didn't say it.

Now I felt terrible that I hadn't insisted we send her an invitation. She could have declined, but at least she would have known I hadn't forgotten her and never would. It was the one sad note to an otherwise exciting day, but I didn't let anyone know about it, especially Daddy, who I could see was beaming with pride and happiness.

Our wedding was truly a micro version of Daddy and Lucille's. *Give the devil her due,* I kept thinking as it went along without the slightest problem. The ceremony was beautiful, and the reception was wonderful. Ethan's friends and cousins really enjoyed themselves. We all danced until we could barely stand, and then Ethan and I, according to the way

Lucille had planned it, made our departure in the Heavenstone limousine, which took us to the airport hotel, where we spent the rest of the night before our flight to Nice, France. Both of us were exhausted and went right to sleep. We even slept through most of the flight.

Thanks again to Lucille, every little detail of our trip was addressed. A car waited for us in Nice, and we were driven to Monaco and the Hotel de Paris, where we were led to a large, plush suite. A basket of fruit and a bottle of champagne were waiting for us, sent by Claire Dubonnet, Lucille's friend. In the card, she wished us a wonderful stay and said we should call in the impossible event of our being bored.

Ethan decided we should spend the day resting and adjusting to the jet lag. We'd order in and, despite the wonderful weather and the temptation of touring, stay in bed.

"After all," he said, "I promised a romantic honeymoon, and this is where it all starts."

Talk about things happening fast. How could I have felt more swept away? We made love, ate, slept, and made love. When I woke again, Ethan was up and showering. I called to him, and he poked his head out of the bathroom.

"You up to going out?" he asked.

I looked at the clock. "It's nine. Where are we going?"

"To the world-famous Monte Carlo casino, of course. Lucille gave us a side gift."

"What?"

"Five thousand dollars to gamble. It's probably peanuts to most of the people down there, but it's a start. Put on something sexy. When we drive up, you'll see dozens of paparazzi waiting to snap pictures of anyone who might just be famous. When they see you, they'll think they've got a find."

"I doubt it."

"Well, get dressed, anyway. It's fun, and we're here to have fun, aren't we?"

He returned to shaving, and I rose. When I thought about what I should wear, I appreciated the choices Lucille had made for me. I put on a black strapless dress and took out the jewelry she had lent me. While I showered, Ethan put on his tuxedo. He kept rushing me along.

"You're the one making me self-conscious about my appearance," I said. "It's not like we're going to a show and might miss the opening curtain."

"Believe me, you'll see this is a great show."

Finally, I was ready, and we arrived at the casino close to ten-thirty. How long would we stay? I wondered. It was just as Ethan had described. Dozens of photographers lined the entrance, snapping our pictures as we hurried into Le Grand Casino, as it was known. It also housed the Grand Theatre de Monte Carlo and the headquarters of the Ballet de Monte Carlo. I was surprised when we were asked to show our passports in order to enter.

"Why?" I asked Ethan.

"Citizens of Monaco are forbidden to enter the gaming rooms," he said as we gaped at the elaborate and glamorous structure with its rococo turrets, green copper cupolas, and gold chandeliers. "Even the royal family is forbidden and uses a side entrance to attend the theater." He paid our entrance fee.

The sight of so many elegantly dressed women with dazzling jewels and the elegantly dressed men was impressive. Ethan was obviously very excited.

"I never thought I'd be here so quickly in my life," he muttered as he looked around, "but I dreamed of it. C'mon," he said after we took a glass of champagne. "I want to start with craps. Just think of me as James Bond."

"I don't know anything about playing craps," I said as he exchanged money for chips.

"I played it a lot in high school. This will be a bit more formal."

We stood on the sidelines to watch a little. Ethan quickly explained what was going on. I listened, surprised at how much he knew and how anxious he was to get into the game. Before long, he was the shooter and began to toss the dice. When he won the first time, I knew he would be there for a while, so while he played, I walked around to look at more of the casino, watch some of the other people, and see some of the other ways they were gambling. Other rooms required entrance fees, and one room was for the very wealthy to play poker. I wandered back to where Ethan was, saw that he was still quite involved, and strolled toward the rear.

A tall, thin man standing by a doorway thought I wanted to exit and opened it for me.

"S'il vous plaît," he said, nodding and bowing slightly.

"Merci," I said, nodding.

I stepped out onto a terrace that was above beautiful well-lit gardens. As I looked out, the tall man stepped up beside me.

"First time here?" he asked.

I turned and looked at him as he lit a cigarette.

"Yes. How did you know?"

"You have that wide-eyed look American tourists wear the first time. Are you with family?"

"I'm on my honeymoon," I said.

"Oh." He widened his smile. "You don't want to watch your new husband gamble?"

"Not all night," I said, and he laughed.

"You see those lights out there?" He pointed with his cigarette.

"Yes."

"That's Bordighera, Italy."

"Really? I didn't realize we were so close to Italy."

"Everywhere in Europe, you're close to another country," he said. "You should go see it if you can tear your husband away from the casino."

"Oh, I will," I said. "Thank you."

He bowed. *"Bonne chance, madame,"* he said. He put out his cigarette and went back into the casino. I looked out at the night and the lights of Bordighera. It was beautiful there, and it did fill me with new hope. I was anxious to get out and tour. I had read about everything and wanted especially to go to the palace and see Princess Grace's tomb.

When I returned to the casino, I saw Ethan had left the craps table and was at roulette.

"Did you win?" I asked.

He showed me his pile of chips, his face lit up like a Christmas tree. "Ten thousand dollars! I was up fifteen and lost five, so I decided to move to something else."

"Why don't we quit while we're ahead?" I suggested.

"Quit? We just got here."

"A man showed me the lights of Bordighera, Italy. You can see it from the terrace."

"That's nice." He watched the roulette wheel, and when it stopped, he clapped his hands. "We're on a streak."

I watched for a while. He lost and then won again and again. I could see pulling him away was not going to be easy, but I was actually bored and wandered about again. I looked for the tall gentleman but didn't see him. When it was close to midnight, I returned to Ethan, who immediately told me we were up twenty-two thousand dollars.

"I'm getting tired," I said. "And we want to get up early to see things, don't we?"

"Sure, sure, but I'm not that tired. We slept so much today. Tell you what," he said peeling off some euros. "Take a taxi back and get into bed. I'll be there in about an hour or so, okay?"

It wasn't okay, but I took the money. This was Lucille's fault, I thought. If she hadn't given him that five thousand dollars, he wouldn't be in there. A little annoyed but too tired to argue, I took the taxi and returned to our suite. I tried to stay up, but when I lay down, my eyelids shut like automatic steel prison doors, and in moments I was asleep.

Because I hadn't shut the curtains tightly enough, the morning sunlight burst like an egg on my face and woke me. I moaned and then remembered I had fallen asleep before Ethan had returned. Feeling guilty, I turned to apologize and was shocked to see that he had not gotten into bed.

"Ethan?"

I looked toward the bathroom. The door was open, but I heard nothing, and there was no sign of him in the suite. There wasn't a note anywhere, either, to indicate that he had gone out for something. I rose, got into my slippers, and went into the bathroom to be sure he wasn't there. He wasn't. I decided to shower and get dressed. Before I came out, I heard the door of the suite open.

"Ethan?"

I grabbed a towel and wrapped it around myself. When I stepped out, Ethan was on the bed, still fully clothed, his eyes closed.

"What happened to you? Where were you?" I asked.

He groaned.

"Ethan?"

He opened his right eye and then put his hand over his forehead, pressing his fingers to his temples.

"I had a little too much to drink. Crying in my beer, so to speak."

"What are you talking about? Where were you?"

"I was at the casino, winning and winning, and then suddenly losing and losing. I lost it all," he said. "And then some."

"What do you mean, 'and then some'?"

"I couldn't believe I had hit such a run of bad luck."

He turned over onto his side. I shook him.

"What does 'and then some' mean?"

He didn't answer.

"Ethan?"

"Another twenty thousand dollars," he muttered.

"Twenty thousand! Where did you get that?"

Again, he was quiet.

"Ethan?"

"Our wedding gifts," he said, then groaned and turned on his stomach.

"What? You gambled away wedding money besides what Lucille gave you?"

He lifted his hand and dropped it. "Let me sleep a little," he said.

I stepped back as if the bed were about to burst into flames. It was as if another person had gotten into Ethan's body. Where was the responsible, loving young man I had married? If Daddy heard about this, he'd be very angry, I thought. I plopped into a chair and stared at his unmoving body. The longer I looked at him, the angrier I became. I decided to finish dressing and go down to the restaurant to get myself some breakfast. He didn't move or make a sound the whole time. I glanced at him once, decided it would be a waste of effort to try to get him up, and slammed the door behind me.

While I was looking at the menu, I sensed someone standing just behind me and to my left.

Ethan, I thought happily, but when I turned and
looked up, I saw the thin, tall, elegant man I had met
at the casino.

He smiled and nodded. "Why is it," he asked,
"that every time I see you on your honeymoon,
you're alone?"

"My husband is sleeping off a night of disaster,"
I replied.

"I see. The dangers of temptation. Well, would
you like some company?" He gestured at the seat
across from me.

His question took me by complete surprise. I
fumbled for a moment and then said, "Yes."

I will always wonder why I said yes to a stranger
in a different country. I didn't even know his name,
and he didn't know mine, but there was something in
his face, some soft, vulnerable look, that stepped over
any fear I felt. He sat, smiled, glanced at the menu,
and signaled the waitress. He ordered café au lait and
a croissant with jam.

He looked at my plate of eggs and bacon, a roll,
cheese, and coffee, and laughed.

"American breakfast. We French favor what we
call *petit dejeuner.* Where are you from?"

"Kentucky."

"Ah, the Bluegrass State, no?"

"Yes."

"You have horses, too?"

"Not on our property, but my father owns
some."

"Some?"

"Some," I said. Cassie always told me not to sound too wealthy to strangers.

"My name is Henri Beaumont," he said, extending his hand across the table.

"Semantha Heaven . . . Semantha Hunter."

"*Enchanté,*" he said.

"I took some French in high school, but I don't speak it fluently enough to try."

"Very wise. And college? You didn't continue with a language?"

I laughed. "I'm not that old. I haven't even started going to college, much less graduated from one."

"Ah, a child bride."

"*Peut-être,*" I said, remembering that it meant "maybe." He laughed again.

The waitress brought his coffee and croissant.

"How long did you stay last night?" he asked.

"Not too much longer after I saw you. You left?"

"Oh, no. I was on a break. I'm a blackjack dealer. You know how to play blackjack?"

"Yes, but I don't gamble or play cards."

I smiled to myself, remembering how much Cassie had hated board games and cards. Mother had tried to get us to play gin rummy with her, but Cassie wouldn't.

"Simply killing time with worthless amusement is the same as lying in a grave," she had told us. To her, nothing had been as sinful as wasting time when she could be reading or doing something she considered worthwhile.

"And this new husband of yours, he does?"

"Not before this. At least, not with me, not as long as I've known him," I said mournfully.

Henri picked up on my tone and look. "He lost a lot . . . you said a 'disaster'?"

"Yes."

"I'm sorry. Maybe it's a painful lesson, and from now on he'll be different."

"I hope so."

He smiled and nodded. "I have a daughter who should be about your age now," he said.

"Should be? Don't you know if she is?"

"Unfortunately, I haven't seen her since she was two. My wife couldn't tolerate this life."

"Oh, I'm sorry."

He shrugged. "I don't blame her, but she moved as far away from me as she could. She lives in Tahiti and is remarried."

"I'm sorry."

"Whenever I see a pretty young woman like yourself, I think of my daughter. Being with you makes me feel as if I'm with her. I can imagine, at least. You understand?"

"Yes," I said. "You've been a blackjack dealer for a long time, then?"

"A long time. It's not so bad for me. I like to watch the people who gamble. Some say prayers. Some have good-luck charms, and some have their own mathematical methods. Too many think they'll find some answer, some happiness, something to fill a hole in their lives, if they win big. And then there are those who are, like your husband, I imagine, caught up in the excitement. Don't tell anyone I told you, but it's a dangerous place."

"Yes, it is," I said. "And beautiful, too. I read about the architecture."

"Beauty without innocence is dangerous too often. You understand?"

"I think so."

"You're young. Even if you don't understand now, you will."

I put down my silverware and looked at my watch. "I'd better get back up to our suite and get my husband moving."

"Yes, good luck with that," he said. "Try to get to Italy. There's good shopping. I get most of my clothes and shoes there."

"I will."

I looked for the waitress.

"Oh, please. Let me pay the bill," he said. "You've given me great pleasure, and besides, let a casino employee pick up a tab now. That's only, how do you say, poetic justice?"

"*Merci.*" I stood up but paused. "Don't you ever write or try to call your daughter?"

"I used to, but my angry ex-wife is not . . . how should I put it? Cooperative. This," he added, "is my hole in my life, but I don't fill it with false hope."

"Keep trying," I said. "I'm sure she's worth the effort. *Au revoir.*"

He smiled. "*Au revoir.*"

As I walked away, I thought to myself that I hadn't just met Henri Beaumont by accident. Cassie had sent him my way.

She was afraid that after marrying Ethan, I would stop thinking about my daughter.

Even here, thousands of miles from her grave, she was beside me. I was, after all, her resurrection, the only way she could come back to life.

Shutting her out would be like killing her again.

19

A Visit

ETHAN SLEPT AWAY the entire morning. I sat in the suite's living room and watched some television, bitterly thinking that this was some way to spend a honeymoon. Finally, he rose, apologized, and went to take a shower. When he dressed and came out, he saw I was still angry, and he kept apologizing.

"I'll make it up to you," he promised. He got on his knees and kissed my hand, begging forgiveness. "I'm such an idiot. Here," he said, handing me a flower from the vase on the table. "Give me twenty lashes."

I couldn't help but finally laugh. What else could I do but forgive him?

"Good," he said, leaping to his feet. "Let's go somewhere beautiful and have lunch."

"What about a car?"

"Lucille's travel agent made all the arrangements. We should have had a car delivered by now. The desk will have the keys."

He was right. The car was waiting. I wanted to say that someday we'd have to do everything for ourselves and not depend on Lucille, but I was afraid to add any unpleasant thoughts or tone now. We would finally have a real honeymoon.

At lunch, I told him about the Frenchman I had met at the casino and at breakfast, Henri Beaumont. He didn't seem to think much of it and didn't pick up on anything when I talked about Beaumont missing his daughter.

"He called it the hole in his life."

"Don't worry. That won't happen to us," Ethan promised. "In fact, in fifty years, we'll return to Monaco to celebrate a golden anniversary."

"But you won't go to the casino."

"No," he said. He raised his hand. "I'm cured. The only thing I'll gamble on from here on is the weather."

We had been directed to a beautiful restaurant up in a place called Eze that looked out over the ocean. It was like walking into a fantasy. The cobblestone streets, the quaint shops, and the scenery held our attention most of the day. Late in the afternoon, we drove back to the hotel and went to the pool, where we had cocktails and both dozed off. Claire Dubonnet had left a list of restaurants for us to try for dinner. One was at another hotel, La Reserve in Beaulieu-sur-Mer. Once again, we sat out on a patio and looked at the ocean.

It was a wonderful dinner, during which Ethan once again apologized for his actions and vowed to work harder at making our marriage a success. When he added "as successful as your father and Lucille's marriage," I felt my stomach tighten.

"Actually, my father's marriage to my mother

was far more successful a marriage. They were as devoted to each other as any two people could be. They weren't tied together by our business or wealth, but only by their love."

"Well, then, that's the way we'll be," Ethan said quickly, but I thought he glanced at me oddly as he drank his port. Maybe he thought I was jumping on everything he said too quickly; maybe I was too sensitive. It wasn't my intention to drive him away or cause him to worry every minute he was with me. I tried to be more pleasant and relaxed, and it worked. As soon as we were back in our suite, he wanted to make love.

"We have to make love every night, even during the afternoon if we can," he said, reminding me about my time for ovulation.

"When you talk about all that, you sound more like a fertility doctor," I said, gently teasing. "It's not romantic, Ethan."

Once again, he unleashed one apology after another. We made love, but I couldn't help thinking about my deception. My mother would never have kept such a secret from my father, I thought. If I really loved him and he really loved me, I should be able to tell him the truth.

But I didn't. Something kept me from doing it, kept me acting as if I wanted to be pregnant as much as he wanted me to be.

We spent the rest of our days touring and shopping. We did get to Italy and bought much more than we should have. A good deal of it we sent ahead. I thought he spent a lot more time than necessary searching for a special gift for Lucille.

"She's done so much for us," he said when he saw I was getting annoyed. "We've got to find something different, something unusual. What do you buy for someone who has everything?"

Eventually, he settled on a beautiful and unique necklace an artisan had created. We bought it in a village called Saint-Paul De Vence, where we had a wonderful lunch and visited the shops. For our last night, Ethan thought we should call Claire Dubonnet and invite her to dine with us. Maybe it was selfish of me, but I wanted the last night to be more special, to be just us. As it turned out, when she met us at one of the restaurants in Monaco that she had suggested, the conversation centered around Lucille and the times she had spent with her. When I glanced at Ethan as she spoke, I thought he looked entranced. It was as if he were hearing about experiences someone had had with a major political figure or celebrity.

She told us she hoped to visit Lucille sometime next year.

"Maybe we'll have another surprise for you by then," Ethan said, reaching for my hand.

"Oh? Are you expecting?" she asked.

I knew what she was thinking. So many of the guests at our wedding had looked as if they were thinking and gossiping about the same thing, that we had gotten married so quickly because I was pregnant.

She looked surprised when Ethan answered quickly for me. "No, not yet, but hopefully soon."

"Well, I wish you luck," she said. "Lucille told me how much your father would love to have a grandson."

"We'll keep trying until he does," Ethan vowed, which drove an icy sword of guilt through my heart.

I argued with myself about stopping the birth control pills, but later, when I had to take one, I did. I was behaving like someone addicted, but my addiction wasn't drug-related. It was fear, and I knew it. Maybe I would return to my therapist, I thought. The debate raged in my mind on and off during our trip home.

Ethan had sent home Lucille's gift, along with so many other things we had bought. He was both surprised and delighted to see her wearing it when we arrived at Heavenstone in time for dinner.

She and Daddy were anxious to hear all about our trip.

"Thank you so much for this," Lucille said, indicating the necklace when we sat at the table. "How did you find something so unique?"

"Semantha spotted it," Ethan said quickly.

Lucille smiled and kissed me on the cheek. "Claire's already called me," she told us, "and described you both as glowing. Sometimes a woman glows from something quite significant in her life." She looked quickly from me to Ethan. I saw him shake his head ever so slightly. She pursed her lips and went on to ask us other questions. When she asked about Le Grand Casino, both of us looked down quickly. That brought laughter.

"Lost, then?" she asked. I looked at Ethan and then at Daddy, who seemed more interested in his rack of lamb.

"I'm afraid so," Ethan said.

"Well, like most things in life, you win some, you lose some. Right, Teddy?"

"What? Oh. Yes, yes. This is absolutely fabulous. I haven't had better in any restaurant," he said. "We have a jewel in the kitchen."

Lucille beamed and patted his arm. "You deserve no less, Teddy, and I'll make sure it continues."

"She's looking after me in every way possible," he declared, and leaned over to kiss her. "Take note, Semantha. Nothing's changed when it comes to men and women. One way or another, the way to a man's heart is through his stomach."

They laughed. Ethan looked grateful that there were no other questions about his gambling, and then he went on to describe some of our touring. The trip and the jet lag began to catch up with me, and I started drifting off. Daddy was the first to see it.

"Semantha has that glassy, far-off look. Don't worry about the time difference," he said. "You sleep until you're back to yourself. Same for you, Ethan."

"Oh, no, sir. I'm anxious to get back to work. I'll be up and at it with you two tomorrow."

"Well, I'd probably be the same way," Daddy told him.

He couldn't have made him happier. Any way Ethan could be like my father was obviously an accomplishment. Any daughter who loved her father as much as I did should be happy to see that in her husband, I thought, but something about it bothered me.

I sat thinking about it for a moment until I heard Cassie whisper, *"Maybe he's trying too hard. Maybe he's stroking Daddy's ego just to get what he wants. Maybe he's a phony."*

I had a terrific urge to rage back at her but held myself in check, knowing full well what such an outburst at the table would do to the rest of them. *I'll deal with her later,* I thought.

"I am tired," I confessed, surrendering my knife and fork. "I'm even too tired to finish eating."

"Don't worry about it," Daddy said.

"No, dear, go get your rest," Lucille added. "I'm sure Ethan will follow shortly."

"I will, only I'm with Dad here," he said, calling my father 'Dad' for the first time. "I'm not leaving any of this rack of lamb."

Daddy nodded and laughed.

I stood up so abruptly and ungracefully, swaying for a moment and having to put my hand on the table to stop the room from spinning, that everyone turned to me.

"You all right?" Daddy asked.

I took a deep breath. "Fine. Just tired. I'll see you all . . . when I see you all," I said.

I felt their silence behind me as I walked out of the dining room and to the stairs. Cassie was waiting for me at the foot.

"You're losing it," she said as I turned to go up.

"Losing what?"

"The battle," she replied.

I hurried up ahead of her. Even though I did it, I knew that slamming the door in her face wouldn't matter. She didn't speak, however. She simply sat there watching me prepare for bed. She rose and walked over to the bed when I slipped under my blanket. I kept my eyes closed, but I could feel her staring down at me.

"I don't want to hear any more about it right now," I said. "And I want you to stay out of my dreams." I opened my eyes and glared up at her.

"*Your dreams are simply the truths you don't want to face. You were always cowardly, Semantha.*"

"I was not!" I cried. "You were the cowardly one. You did the cowardly deeds!"

I wanted to say more but suddenly realized that Ethan had quietly opened the door and was standing there gaping at me.

"Who are you talking to?" he asked.

"What?"

Cassie smiled.

"Oh, was I talking? I fell asleep so quickly. I must have been dreaming," I said.

"And how," he replied, closing the door. "Are you all right? You looked like you were going to faint at the table."

"Yes, I'm fine. I'm just exhausted."

"I'm just too hyper," he said. "I'm going to change into something more comfortable and talk to your parents for a while longer."

"She's not my parent," I corrected.

He shrugged and smiled. "A stepmother is still a parent."

"Not for me," I said. "I had only one mother. Lucille is my father's wife. She is not my mother."

"All right. Don't get upset. It will keep you up. Get some sleep."

He went to his closet.

Cassie stood there, nodding with that self-satisfied smirk on her face.

I turned my back on her and closed my eyes tightly. I lunged at the darkness, embraced it, and fell asleep rather quickly. When the darkness brightened and fell back, I saw myself walking slowly toward my cousin's house. My daughter was outside playing in a sandbox and talking to a small doll. She was pretending to be the doll's mother.

"I won't forget you," she told her doll. "Never, never, never."

Then she looked up at me and asked, "Who are you?"

"I'm your mother," I told her.

She shook her head. "No, you're not," she said.

"Yes, I am," I told her, drawing closer.

"No, you're not!" she screamed, then grabbed her doll and ran back to the house.

"Wait!" I shouted after her. She didn't turn around. I began to sob.

"Semantha," I heard. I felt myself being shaken. "Semantha."

I opened my eyes and turned to see Ethan leaning over me.

"What?"

"I just got into bed and heard you crying." He touched my cheek. "Tears. You were really crying," he said. "Why?"

For a moment, I was very confused. What time was it? How long had I been sleeping? It took me another moment to realize we were home and not still in Monaco.

"I don't know," I said. "Bad dream, maybe."

"Oh. Do you remember it?"

"No."

"That's good. Who wants to remember bad dreams?" He kissed my cheek. "You're just overtired. Me, too. Good night," he said, and turned away.

For a while, I just lay there looking up at the darkness.

"You've got to go get her and bring her home," Cassie whispered, *"before it's too late."*

I closed my eyes again. By the time I woke up, Ethan was long gone. I had slept so deeply I had not heard him get up and get dressed, and he hadn't attempted to wake me. It had not been a restful sleep for me. I wasn't rested, but I rose, showered, and dressed and went down to get some breakfast.

No matter how I tried to distract myself, I couldn't get my dream out of my mind. I could feel Cassie hovering over me, sticking close to me, following me everywhere I went. I went all over the house, then outside for a long walk, and then back up to our bedroom. She even followed me into the bathroom. Her voice was echoing. I put my hands over my ears.

"Christmas trees!" she cried. *"She has Heavenstone blood, and she'll never know it."*

By early afternoon, I felt as if I would go wild and run through the house screaming, which would surely frighten the De Stagen sisters to death, as well as Gerad. Ethan called to see how I was doing, but I didn't speak to him. I let the answering machine pick up. He said he would call again later. Finally, feeling as if I had ants crawling up and down inside my stomach, I rushed out of the house, got into my car, and drove to the Normans' ranch.

I parked on the road just a little ways down from their driveway and got out. Walking toward the house made me feel I had entered my dream. I half expected to see my daughter playing outside with her doll in that sandbox. At first, I saw no one, and then off to the right, I saw Royce Norman returning from one of the horse corrals. My daughter held her hand and walked beside her, and in her arms she carried a doll similar to the one that had been in the dream.

Royce slowed down as she saw me approaching. Instinctively, perhaps, she pulled my daughter closer to her.

"Hello," I said.

"What are you doing here?" she asked sharply. It occurred to me that I might have been in her nightmares, that she might have often dreamed I would come.

"I wanted to see her," I replied, nodding at my daughter.

"You were not supposed to come here . . . ever," she told me. She knelt down and scooped my daughter into her arms. "Please leave this instant."

"She's my daughter," I said.

"No, she's not. Not anymore, not ever. Now, get off our property. I'm calling my husband, and he'll be calling your father."

"Anyone looking at her could see she's a Heavenstone," I said. I felt a little like a puppet, mouthing

Cassie's words. "You're deceiving yourself if you think otherwise."

Despite how Royce was attacking me, my daughter kept her eyes on me. *She's fascinated with me,* I thought. *Yes, Cassie's right. She knows who I am. In her heart, she knows. The bond of blood is too strong to be denied by any legal papers or courts.*

"Couldn't I just hold her, talk to her for a few minutes?"

"Are you crazy? Get out!" Royce shouted, and ran past me toward the house.

I didn't run after her. I stood watching, expecting my daughter to turn around and look back at me. She did, and that made me smile. I lifted my hand to wave. Royce bounded up the steps and rushed into the house, slamming the door. I heard her lock it as well.

"*What hysteria,*" Cassie said. "*I can't imagine a woman like that bringing up a Heavenstone. She'll probably get away from this place as soon as she's able. We've got to do something.*"

Yes, I thought. *We've got to do something.* There were many cases concerning women who mistakenly gave away their children and then got them back.

"*And few had the power and financial stability of the Heavenstones,*" Cassie reminded me. "*You're married now, too.*"

Yes, yes, I continued to think as I walked away. I didn't quite reach my car before I heard another vehicle racing down the road. The driver hit his brakes, and the tires squealed as he pulled up alongside me. It was Shane Norman. He leaped out.

"It *is* you," he said, standing with his hands on his hips. His face was flushed and his eyes were wide with disbelief. "Why did you come here? Why did you frighten Royce like that?"

"I didn't frighten her. I came quietly and asked only to see and speak to my daughter."

"Anna is not your daughter, and you were specifically forbidden to make any direct contact until she was eighteen. It's written clearly in black and white. Does your father know you're here?"

He stepped closer, threateningly.

"She's my daughter," I said, turning away and walking to my car. He didn't follow. He stood back watching me. I opened my door, and then I turned back to him and said, "She's got Heavenstone blood. She'll always be my daughter."

"You're crazy!" he shouted. "You stay away, or I'll call the police."

I got into the car and started the engine.

"You did well," Cassie said. *"Don't worry. We'll win in the end."*

I drove home. The emotional roller coaster exhausted me. I went directly to the bedroom to lie down. Not long afterward, the phone rang, and I heard Daddy leave his message. It was curt, full of rage.

"Call me immediately, Semantha. Immediately!"

"Ignore him," Cassie said. *"He'll calm down."*

He didn't. I remained in bed for the rest of the day, dozing on and off, but much later, when I heard his familiar footsteps pounding on the hallway's tile floor, I braced myself. He didn't knock. He burst in and stood there for a moment. Then he closed the door softly and approached the bed.

"Why did you do that? You frightened them both, and after all these years."

"I just wanted to see her, to hear her voice. She looks a lot like me—like Mother, in fact."

He simply stared down at me for a few moments. Maybe he realized I was right, I thought hopefully, but that wasn't it.

"What got into you? To do such a thing now, especially? You've just recently gotten married, started yourself off on a whole new life. To bring back that mess, that horror, now? Ethan's beside himself with worry. Lucille is calming him."

"If he really loves me, he should understand," I said. My lips began to tremble. Tears glistened in my eyes. "You should understand, too. You're my father. You should know me better than anyone can. You should feel my pain, too."

He bristled. "What nonsense is this? What pain, Semantha? We solved a horrendous situation. You were so young. Your entire life could have been ruined, and we found a wonderful couple who could and wanted to raise her well. Besides, you violated a legal agreement. They have the right to sue us. At the least, they could get a court order forbidding you to come anywhere near that property and that child, and something like that could make the newspapers and television. You'd be putting not only us into a scandal but the Normans and the little girl!"

Cassie whispered in my ear.

"That's Lucille talking and not you," I said.

He looked as if he would explode. His shoulders swelled, and his cheeks puffed as his eyes widened. I couldn't remember ever seeing him this enraged, and I was sure neither could Cassie.

"How could you say such a terrible thing? Lucille talking? Why, all that woman is doing right now is calming down your new husband, pleading with him to be understanding. Yes, she's worried about the Heavenstone name, but that's important for you and Ethan as well as for us. You should thank your lucky stars we have someone like her here now, someone who can think coolly. As a matter of fact, it was Lucille who went to the phone and called the Normans. She's the one who got them calmed down, too. I was far too angry to speak to anyone.

"This is a betrayal of me, of what I did for you," he continued. "Why would you even think of going there without first discussing it with me? Cassie would never have done such a thing."

"Cassie would never? Cassie told me to do it," I said.

He blinked rapidly and wiped his forehead. "What? What did you say?"

"Cassie told me to do it. She said my daughter has Heavenstone blood and will never be anything but a Heavenstone. One way or another, she'll come back to us."

"Cassie was gone by the time you gave birth. She knew nothing of the arrangements, Semantha. You're not making any sense. I don't know what's gotten into you or who put such ideas into your head, but you had better put a stop to this right now. And another thing," he said "I'm going to arrange for you to see Dr. Ryan again. You obviously should continue with your therapist."

"That's Lucille talking again," I said.

He glared at me and then walked out and slammed the door behind him.

"*Well,*" Cassie said, "*from that reaction, you can readily see we are almost too late.*"

Even so, I couldn't help but sob. Ever since I could remember, I had hated Daddy's being angry at me. He never had to punish me. All he had to do was show he was upset, and that was punishment enough for a daughter who so craved her father's love. When anger was as intense as his was, forgiveness cowered in a corner, too frightened even to show its face. It was like waiting for the fallout of a nuclear explosion to pass.

"*Get a hold of yourself,*" Cassie snapped.

I took deep breaths and started to get out of bed when the door opened again. This time, it was Ethan. He closed the door and looked at me with what I thought was worry more than anger or confusion.

"What made you do such a thing?" he asked.

"I've never stopped thinking about her, Ethan. No matter how you or anyone would like it to be, a woman can't have her child growing inside her and then cut herself off completely from her."

"But . . . according to your own words, she was the result of a date rape. And besides, your father had solved the situation for you. Why would you dredge up all that now? We're going to have our own child soon. You'll be a mother again. There must be hundreds, thousands of young girls who were like you and who were grateful someone had found a way for them to go on and have a normal young life. I don't know," he said, pacing. "Maybe your father's right. You probably should go back into therapy now."

"Therapy won't change anything."

"Yesterday wasn't the first time I heard you talking to yourself or someone else who wasn't here, Semantha. You need a little help. I'm not the only one who's heard you doing that, either."

He plopped onto the cushioned chair.

"What do you mean? Who else?"

"Your roommate told me about your conversations with no one else in the room."

"When?"

"After I met you," he said. "She called me. I knew she was only trying to keep me from seeing you. She was jealous. So I disregarded anything she told me. That's really why I was so upset with what happened at the motel."

"And why you didn't come to my graduation? It really had nothing to do with your father's illness, then?"

"Partly," he admitted. "Look. I love you. I just think you need some more therapy. It's no big deal. Half the country is in therapy, and the other half needs it."

"Who told you that—Lucille?"

He shook his head. "I don't know why you're on her case so much, Semantha. That's probably another topic for your therapy, but the truth is, Lucille has been in your corner from the start. I wouldn't even be here if it weren't for her."

"What does that mean?"

"Nothing," he said, and immediately took on the look of someone who had stepped into quicksand.

"No. You wouldn't have said it if you didn't think you had a reason to say it. Why did you say that?"

"Look," he said, standing. "This discussion is just getting us deeper and deeper into a mud hole. Let's just calm down and do what we can to restore things. We're off to a wonderful new start."

He started for the door.

"I'll go back down and tell your father and Lucille that we had a good conversation and you're seriously considering returning to therapy. You take a hot shower or something, get dressed, and we'll have another one of our wonderful gourmet dinners and get everyone settled. What's done is done, but it's over with, and that should be that."

"Wait!" I said, standing and walking to him. "If you were so worried about my mental health, about being with someone like me, why did you finally write to me?"

"I told you. I felt guilty about my behavior, about ignoring you . . . what difference does any of that make now? We fell in love, didn't we? We have a wonderful future. Why dredge up the troubled past? That's why everyone's so upset with what you did today."

I knew what Cassie was going to whisper, even before she did.

"It was Lucille, wasn't it? Lucille contacted you and told you to write to me."

"Stop this!" he pleaded. "If you really love your father, you'll stop this."

Then, before I could ask or say another thing, he turned and went out the door. I stood there looking at the closed door, my heart pounding like a fist on the inside of my chest. I gasped to catch my breath.

Cassie had arranged for me to have a baby.

Lucille had arranged for me to have a husband.

Nothing's changed. And nothing will, until I change it. I turned to see her sitting on my bed.

"All of this began with you," I said. "It's your fault. You have to help me."

She smiled with glee. *"Why do you think I've come back?"*

20

Cassie

DADDY AND ETHAN looked shaken at dinner, even somewhat frightened. Neither looked at me very much, and both tried to keep the conversation focused on business issues at the Heavenstone Corporation. Lucille, however, was as cool and collected as ever. If anything, she was ingratiating toward me, complimenting me on my hair and my dress, which was, after all, one of the dresses she'd had me buy for my honeymoon. There was also a tone in her voice that made me feel as if she was handling me, keeping me from going stark raving mad. Every once in a while, she glanced at Daddy to see if he was appreciating how clever she was with me. He was obviously happy she was the one doing it and not he.

Ethan, on the other hand, looked as if he was holding his breath every time I spoke, especially when I spoke to Lucille. But I wasn't going to do anything outlandish. Cassie's advice was to behave as if nothing at all had occurred, so as not to give them an opportunity to dismiss me as emotionally unstable. If that happened, there would be no question that

Daddy would ask Dr. Ryan to put me on medication and see me on a regular basis again.

After dinner, Daddy and Lucille went to the den to have their usual after-dinner drinks and perhaps watch some television. Ethan suggested that he and I take a walk, as if fresh air would clear our heads of the cobwebs of twisted thoughts and fears that had come out of nowhere like a common cold.

"We'll join you later," he told them. "Feeling better?" he asked me moments after we had stepped out.

"Yes."

"Good. What do you say we go out tomorrow night for dinner? I was going to introduce you to one of our executives and his wife, but maybe we'll leave that for another time and just have a quiet dinner together."

"Yes, maybe I'll meet them next time," I said.

I could feel him stealing glances at me as we strolled through the garden. My silence was unnerving him, but I had nothing I wanted to say. It was as if we were parallel to each other on tightropes, afraid to turn our heads and look at each other because we might fall. I sensed he was trying to be careful about anything he said now. In truth, I was as well.

"Your father and I were talking about naming a new horse he bought Sam. He thought your uncle would like that, too. Wouldn't that be fun? Having a horse named after you? I'm actually surprised he has never done it."

"He had a horse named Cassie Girl, named after my sister."

"Well, now it's your turn."

"As long as no one blames me for not being a winner. Cassie Girl was a winner."

"Of course, no one would. Don't be silly." He took my arm and stopped walking. "Look, Semantha, I'm sorry if I did or said anything to disturb you before. I know you had a little relapse of sorts, and right now, you're a little fragile, so you're seeing everything from the dark side. I'm hoping I can change that. I hope you believe me.

"Anyway," he continued when I remained silent, "I'm more convinced than ever that the best thing that could happen to us would be for you to get pregnant. Nothing binds two people as much as their children. Maybe that would help put your past unhappiness further behind you as well."

He waited anxiously for my response, but I had none.

"I'm a little cold suddenly," I said, embracing myself.

"Yes, I thought it would be warmer. Okay, let's go back inside. Do you want to be with your father and Lucille or—"

"Let's just go up and watch television in our own suite, Ethan."

"Sure. I'll just let them know," he said, and went right to the den after we entered.

"*He's probably telling them you're under control,*" Cassie said.

"I am," I replied, and went upstairs.

When I entered our suite, the phone was ringing. It was Uncle Perry.

"How are you, Sam?" he asked. "I understand you've had quite a day."

"I'm all right, Uncle Perry."

"You know, if you need someone to talk to, I'm here for you."

"I know."

"Your father can be a bull in a china shop."

"It's all right," I assured him. "I'm fine. We're fine."

"You sure?"

"Yes."

"All right. I'll see you soon," he promised.

Ethan didn't come up for nearly half an hour. I distracted myself watching a movie, but when he finally came up, he tried again to start a conversation about having children.

When I didn't respond, he said, "I guess this is important to me because I was an only child. I'd like us to have four, at least. What about you?"

"I don't know."

"You'd want some sons to get to grow up and become executives in the Heavenstone Corporation, right?"

"*Of course,*" Cassie whispered.

"Not necessarily," I said.

"What? Why not?" he asked with an incredulous smile.

"The business was always more important to Cassie than it was to me. I wouldn't force my children to work in the corporation. Suppose one of them wanted to be a doctor or an actor or something?"

He laughed. "No one growing up here could avoid becoming a part of the Heavenstone Corporation."

"I did," I said.

"I thought you were going to work for your uncle."

"But I didn't, did I? Actually, Lucille talked me out of it. And then you did as well. Remember?"

He was quiet, and we didn't talk about the corporation or having children any more that night. Despite how everyone had acted at dinner and afterward, I knew my having visited my daughter was still quite shocking. I had even heard it in Uncle Perry's voice when he had called.

I imagined he and Daddy had some conversations about me over the next few days. I was sure Uncle Perry took my side of things and probably persuaded Daddy to wait before getting me back into formal therapy again. He never mentioned it. In fact, as Ethan had hoped, my visiting the Normans wasn't mentioned again, either. Ethan and I had our dinners out. He was as sensitive and caring as could be the first night and tried to repeat the warm, romantic times we'd had in Monaco.

The second time, we did meet the executive he had mentioned, Charles Duncan, and his wife, Sandra. They had two children: a boy, age five, and a girl, age four. Sandra was a stay-at-home mother, who had gone to college and majored in English, intending to become a teacher. She said she had made the choice to be with her children during their younger years and expected to go into teaching when they were older.

Although Sandra was very nice, I had the feeling Ethan had wanted me to meet her so I would be more enthusiastic about having children. I even thought he had discussed it with Charles beforehand and encouraged them to be upbeat about their family life. All the way home, he raved about how wonderful their marriage was and how he had high hopes that ours would be as good. He urged me to get friendlier with Sandra, too.

"You need friends, Semantha. You have to get out and about so you can look to the future and not dwell on the past."

When you had a past like mine, how did you not dwell on it? I wondered.

My dreams, Cassie's whispers, and my unhappy memories continued to dominate my days during the weeks and months that followed. Ethan tried to get me to go out more often, but I always came up with some excuse to avoid it. Twice, Lucille—the second time with more authority and sternness—advised me to socialize more and stop being such a homebody. "You have a husband who needs you at his side," she said.

A few times, perhaps hoping to get me jealous or something, she accompanied Ethan to a business social event and then raved about how flattered she was when strangers assumed she was his wife. Even Daddy began urging me more intently to socialize. "Enjoy your life more, Semantha," he said. "Take advantage of your wonderful opportunities."

I was sure that it was mostly for my benefit when he and Lucille insisted that Ethan and I accompany them on some dinner dates. I made one excuse or another to avoid it. After a while, they stopped pressuring me and tried a new tactic. They spent most of the time at dinner or anyplace else we were all together talking about how wonderful the event had been that I hadn't attended. I sat quietly listening. Their conversations became solely three-way, and gradually it was as if I weren't there or had become invisible.

I knew Lucille was beginning to be more persistent in urging my father to get me back into therapy. However, unlike with most of the things she asked him to do, he held back. I did overhear him telling her, "If she doesn't want to do it, Lucille, it won't be of any value. It's not like we can have her committed. This has to be voluntary. She has to believe she needs to do it; otherwise, it will be a waste of time and money."

Cassie was very pleased about that. Finally, there was something significant over which Daddy and Lucille disagreed. She attributed it to my becoming more and more like her. *"You've got backbone now. You don't let everyone take advantage of you, use you. You're becoming more and more of a Heavenstone."*

Yes, I thought. *I am becoming more like her. It's true.* I thought I could even see it in the faces of the Heavenstone ancestors on the wall of portraits whenever I walked past them. Oddly enough, even though everyone was treating me as if I were as fragile as bone china, I felt stronger. I think Daddy saw it in my face as well. I detected something different in the way he looked at me.

"He's seeing me in you," Cassie whispered. *"That's good. We're winning."*

Yes, I thought again, and then, maybe just out of some instinct that had been resurrected within me, I turned one day in the upstairs corridor and entered Cassie's room. The room had never been touched or changed in any way. The maids had been told to dust it periodically, but nothing had been taken out of it or moved to the attic. It was as if everyone knew Cassie really was still there. Daddy wanted the room kept that way, and for some reason, this was one thing Lucille never challenged. It was easier simply to keep the door closed.

Entering the room now brought back a flood of memories, very early ones from when we had been much closer as sisters. Often, when I was young, I would sit beside her or on the floor while she paraded about giving one of her Cassie lectures about school and other kids my age, but mostly she had preached about what was expected of us as Heavenstones. I had been quite in awe of her back then, and even at that young age, I had sensed how much Daddy and other adults respected her. I couldn't help but want to be like her in so many ways.

I went to her closet and opened it to look at her clothing. Mother had dressed me so differently. My hair had always been longer, and I did much more with makeup. That was not to say that Cassie had been unattractive. She had many striking features, and boys who didn't know anything about her had been drawn to her at first. She had Mother's eyes and healthy-looking, rich light-brown hair. She had been more full-figured than I would be at her age, and quite a bit taller.

Sifting through her clothes, I came upon a dark

blue skirt she had worn often. It had a gold hem. I plucked it out and put it against me. Instead of falling mid-leg, it was closer to ankle-length, but our waists weren't that different. I took off my skirt and put it on. Then I sifted through her clothes again until I found the top she had often worn with this skirt. It was a lighter blue, short-sleeved, with a V-neck. I took off my top and put it on. It was more loose and baggy than any top most girls would wear, but not clownish.

When I looked at myself in the mirror, I saw Cassie slip into my body. My hands went right to my hair, and then, without the slightest hesitation, I opened the top drawer of her vanity table and found her scissors. My memory of Cassie's hair was still quite vivid. She wouldn't wear it much longer than to the bottom of her earlobe. I began to cut my hair. Once I started, there was no choice but to finish. I snipped and snipped, doing what I thought was a rather good job of keeping the ends even. My hair fell around me in clumps. I brushed the strands off my top and stood back to look at myself.

Cassie's face faded in and out of mine. My heart was pounding. *This will surprise Daddy,* I thought, *but he will surely like it.* Despite Mother's continuous suggestions for her hair, her clothes, and her makeup, Cassie had never altered anything, and most important of all, Daddy had never urged her to follow Mother's suggestions and never complained about her appearance. I knew he was still unhappy with me for visiting the Normans, even though he didn't mention it anymore. I wanted to please him. If he saw what was Cassie in me, he would surely think about the good times, when there had been far more love in Heaven-stone, and smiles and laughter had been more at home.

This will change everything, I thought, *and he will be more my father than Lucille's husband.* What had once been a strong family, a Heavenstone family, would return in its full glory.

"Yes," Cassie whispered, *"yes."*

Ethan was home before Daddy and Lucille. He found me sitting in the living room reading one of Cassie's favorite books. I didn't realize how long he had been standing there when I looked up from the pages. The sight of me surprised him so much that he was speechless.

"Oh, hi," I said.

"What did you do to your hair?"

"Just cut it," I said, bringing my hands to it and fluffing it a bit.

"Yourself? You cut your own hair?"

"It wasn't that hard."

"It wasn't hard, but it's not a professional job by any means, Semantha. You're going to have to go to a salon and have it fixed."

"I don't need to do that," I said.

"Jesus." He flopped onto the chair across from me. "And what are you wearing?" he asked with a grimace.

"Just an ordinary skirt and top. Nothing terribly special," I said.

"Kind of blah for you," he said. "It doesn't look like it fits you, either."

"I don't think it's so blah. It fits all right."

"Whatever." He leaned forward. "Have you

been keeping track of things, the date? Anything to report?"

"No," I said.

"You had a period, then?"

"Yes."

"Damn. I don't know. Maybe we should see one of those fertility doctors."

I didn't reply. I dropped my gaze back to the pages.

"Lucille and your father won't be home for dinner tonight."

"Oh?"

"It's the chamber of commerce event. Remember? I wanted us to go, but you didn't want to."

"Well, why didn't you go anyway?"

"I don't think your father likes you being home alone so much, Semantha. I don't think he likes me going about like a bachelor, either."

"What about Lucille?"

"Lucille's not happy, either. They're both concerned about you, and of course, so am I."

"I'm sorry," I said. "Everyone should just stop worrying." I looked at the book again. "I'm not into all that. Cassie never liked socializing with business-people. She called it swimming with baby sharks. They all want something from us."

"That's not entirely true, and you're not Cassie."

I continued to read.

"You're sure you had a period, right?" he asked.

I looked up and smiled. "It's not something you need to guess about, Ethan."

He nodded, slapped the arms of the chair, and stood.

"I'm going up to change. What's Gerad making for dinner?"

"Tonight's Gerad's and the De Stagen sisters' night off. He prepared some sort of casserole with a fancy name. It just has to be warmed. There's a salad for us as well. I'll take care of it. If you don't like the casserole, I can make something else."

"I'm sure what Gerad prepared is great. Okay. See you in a while," he said, and left.

"He doesn't believe we can do it," Cassie whispered. *"He should have been here when there was no one but us. Daddy doesn't say it, but the meals Mother and I made were just as wonderful."*

Yes, I thought. Even better because we had been more like a real family then, and our conversation at the dinner table had rarely involved business. We would talk about ourselves or our home. It had never felt the way it did now, more like a corporate meeting.

I looked at my watch, closed the book, and went off to the kitchen to get dinner together. I was actually happy to do it whenever I could. It made me feel more like I belonged again and helped resurrect happy moments.

Just after I put the casserole into the oven, I heard Ethan scream my name. I listened. As he came down the stairway, he continued to call out for me. I checked the temperature on the stove and went out to the hallway as he reached the bottom of the stairs and turned. He had something in his right hand and was waving it. When I drew closer, I realized what it was.

"You're still on these birth control pills, aren't you?" he asked.

I stopped walking. He approached slowly, his eyes wide with amazement and anger.

"You went through my things?"

"It was lying out on your vanity table."

I didn't remember leaving it there. Had Cassie done that?

"Well? Are you still using these?"

"Yes," I admitted.

"Yes? Why? *Why?*" he shouted. "Why did you pretend you weren't? All this time, Semantha, I've been talking about our having a child, and you've never said a word. You let me go on and on while you knew you were preventing it from happening. Why?"

"We're not ready yet."

I looked just past him at Cassie, who nodded.

"We're not? I'm certainly more than ready. Why aren't we ready yet? It's not a question of being able to afford children, and if you're worried about caring for an infant or being bogged down, we certainly would have help."

"There are things that have to be done yet."

"What things? What are you talking about?"

"Heavenstone has to be restored," I said. Cassie smiled and nodded. "The family has to be restored."

"What?" He took a step back as if I had something contagious. "I don't understand what you're saying." He shook his head. "You're not making any sense." He looked at the birth control pills in his hand and then at me. "Lucille's right. You need to return to serious therapy, Semantha. This makes me sick."

"If you loved me, really loved me, you would understand," I said.

"Try me. Explain it to me."

"She's manipulating us, changing everything. Maybe you don't even realize how much she controls you."

"Who? Lucille?"

"What did she promise you, Ethan? What did she tell you she'd do for you if you returned to me?"

"That's crazy, Semantha. You know I fell in love with you, and you did fall in love with me, didn't you? She couldn't control that, could she?" He nodded. "You're suffering from serious paranoia now. And look at what you've done to yourself, chopping off your hair. And this," he said, waving the birth control pills. "This, while all along deceiving me."

He stared at me, his anger receding, his face relaxing as the rage left his eyes.

"I shouldn't yell at you. I'm sorry. I'm sorry this is happening, but I'm not losing hope and my faith in you. I love you too much. We'll get you the help you need, and we'll start again. It will be all right. I do understand and I forgive you."

He put the birth control pills in his pocket and stepped forward to embrace me.

"We'll talk about it all later," he said, and kissed my forehead the way a father would kiss his daughter.

"Go pick out a bottle of wine and take it to the dining room," I told him. "We'll bring in our salads."

"We? I thought the De Stagens were off."

I smiled at him as if he were being silly and returned to the kitchen. While I was working in the kitchen, he obviously went to a phone to call my father and Lucille. Whatever he told them caused them to make their excuses and rush to come home. I saw by the way he was checking his watch and listening that he anticipated their arrival shortly. What puzzled me at first was that Cassie left the room almost as soon as he had entered.

He smiled at me, but I could see he was quite nervous. He didn't seem to know what he was eating and drinking. I ate slowly, enjoying every morsel.

"Don't you like your salad?" I asked, seeing how he was picking at it.

"Oh, yes, it's fine." He smiled and gestured at me with his fork. "That skirt and blouse."

"Yes?"

"They're your sister's clothes, aren't they? I've never seen them in your closet."

"Yes, they are. We share things."

"Shared?"

"Always. Not that my clothes would ever fit her and not that she liked them. We couldn't share shoes, of course, but I wore her leather coat sometimes."

"Why did you put that on now, Semantha?"

I thought about it. It was a good question. "I think I wanted to feel closer to her right now."

"So, you've forgiven her for what she did to you?"

"I've always understood it without forgiving her, but I think my father's forgiven her. That's why I wanted to see my daughter, wanted her to know me."

"But now you understand that he doesn't want that, right? It would create other problems."

"We'll see."

"What does that mean, 'we'll see'? You're not going to go back there, are you?"

"No, not now," I said.

He looked at his watch.

"There's a light chiffon lemon cake for dessert."

"Good."

He returned to eating, now smiling at me almost every time we looked at each other. His growing nervousness almost made me laugh.

"I'm all right, Ethan," I said. "Don't worry."

"Yes, you are all right, and you will be all right. We'll take care of you, Semantha. I do love you."

"I hope so," I said. "Just be patient. Everything will be fine."

He raised his eyebrows because I was talking to him as if he was the one who needed therapy. That almost made him laugh. He ate more vigorously and then helped me clean up the dishes. I prepared some coffee and brought it out with the cake. He was pacing in the dining room now and looking at his watch. He smiled at me and said he'd be right back. I watched him go out and hurry down the hallway to Daddy's office. When he returned this time, he looked very concerned.

I cut the cake and put a piece on his plate. Then I poured his coffee. He thanked me but didn't start eating or drinking any coffee.

"Are you okay?" I asked.

"Huh? Oh, yes. Fine," he said, and lifted his fork.

When the phone rang, he leaped out of his seat and rushed into the kitchen, mumbling that he'd get it and I should relax. I sipped some coffee and tried the cake. It was delicious. Nothing Gerad made wasn't, but I hated giving Lucille any credit. That was probably unfair to Gerad. It wasn't his fault that he had been brought in to replace Mrs. Dobson.

Before Ethan returned, Cassie entered the dining room.

"Where were you?" I asked.

"I just couldn't stand the pathetic way you were defending yourself when he confronted you with the pills, making it seem as if he were the aggrieved party. Poor Ethan, poor, poor Ethan, isn't getting what he wants as quickly as he wants it. Christmas trees."

She popped out of sight the moment Ethan came back from the kitchen. His face was pale.

"What's wrong, Ethan?"

"I've got . . . we've got to leave immediately for the hospital," he said.

"What? Why?"

He considered me a moment, looking as if he was afraid to say another thing, afraid of what it would do to me.

"Tell me."

"We've got to go to the hospital. Get your coat. Your father and Lucille have been in a car accident."

I turned to see Cassie in the corner.

She was smiling.

21

Accident

BY THE TIME we arrived at the hospital, Uncle Perry had already spoken with the doctors. He greeted us at the emergency-room entrance. He was distracted for a moment when he saw what I had done with my hair and what I was wearing, but he turned quickly to Ethan.

"Teddy's left arm is broken just below the elbow. It's already in a cast," he said. "The left side of his face was badly bruised, and his earlobe needed stitches. The driver's door and window were bashed on impact, but if you saw the car, you'd wonder how anyone lived."

"What about Lucille?" Ethan asked.

"Don't know the extent of her injuries yet. She wasn't wearing her seat belt, apparently."

"Do we know exactly how this happened?" Ethan asked.

"I spoke with the traffic officer who was on the site. Apparently, a truck moved into Teddy's lane around a curve and slammed into the driver's side of his car, sending it careening over the edge of the road, where it turned over a few times before landing upright. Fortunately, the truck driver didn't flee the scene. He called for help immediately."

"Where's Daddy?" I asked.

"He's in one of the examination rooms in emergency, Sam."

"Can we see him?"

"Yes," he said. "He's conscious. C'mon."

Ethan reached for my hand, and we followed him through the lobby to a corridor. The emergency-room doctor and a nurse were standing in the hallway talking softly just outside the examination room. They turned as we approached, and Uncle Perry introduced us.

"This is Mr. Heavenstone's son-in-law, Ethan Hunter," Uncle Perry said. "And this is his daughter, Semantha."

"Dr. Morris," the doctor said. "He's resting comfortably now. X-rays show a slight concussion. His left arm was broken. We didn't see any tear in his shoulder, but it's taken a hard blow and twisting. Fortunately, he had his seat belt on and didn't get thrown about during the rollover, or he would have had far worse injuries, maybe fatal."

I glanced through the door and saw Daddy dressed in a hospital gown and lying on a gurney. I could see his eyes had already begun to turn black and blue.

Ethan nodded, looked at me, and then, holding his breath, asked, "Any more news about Mrs. Heavenstone?"

"Well, as I've told your uncle, apparently, she wasn't wearing her seat belt. She's suffered some severe head injuries, I'm afraid. She's in intensive care. Dr. Neuberger has been called in to examine her. He's our top neurological surgeon."

"She's unconscious?"

"Oh, yes. They may or may not have decided to operate by now. I'll call up for you," he added, and looked at me with great sympathy. "Sorry," he said.

"She's not my actual mother," I said. The moment I said it, Ethan released his grip on my hand and gave me a severe look of disapproval.

"Does Mr. Heavenstone know the extent of Mrs. Heavenstone's injuries?" Ethan asked.

"He knows as much as we know at the moment, yes. You can go in to see him," he added, glanced again at me, and then walked off with the nurse.

Ethan, Uncle Perry, and I entered Daddy's room slowly. He had his eyes closed.

"Ethan and Sam are here, Ted."

"Hey, Dad," Ethan said softly.

Daddy opened his eyes. He looked at him and shook his head.

"What a horrible mess," he said. Then he turned to me and for a moment looked terribly confused.

"Hi, Daddy."

"Semantha?"

"I'm sorry you were in a terrible accident, but I'm glad you'll be all right."

He simply stared at me and then looked at Ethan, who nodded at the silent thoughts that passed between them.

"I should have waited and not called you," Ethan said. "I'm sorry."

"No, it's not your fault. We weren't going that fast. The driver of that truck told the investigating officer that something blinded him, a flash of light. They're checking to be sure he wasn't drinking. I saw no flash of light. We nearly missed going head-on. Who knows? Maybe that would have been better. You know about Lucille?"

"We don't know any details. Dr. Morris is calling up for us."

"Good," Daddy said. He looked at me again.

"Why did you cut your hair like that, Semantha?"

"I felt I needed to," I said. He closed his eyes. "Do your injuries hurt?"

"Yes," he said. "They're not giving me anything strong for pain just yet because of my concussion. I'm such a fool. Lucille wanted us to use the limousine, but I decided to drive us. I don't know why," he said. "I don't know why. I usually worry about having too much to drink. What was in my head?"

Cassie, I thought. *Cassie whispered to you. She was in your head.*

"It doesn't sound like you could have prevented the accident, but why wasn't Lucille wearing her seat belt?" Ethan asked him.

"She was, but the clasp must have snapped open under pressure, so they think she wasn't wearing it, but the car beeps when someone doesn't put his or her belt on, so I know she was. I guess that doesn't make any difference now." He grimaced with pain.

"Take it easy, Teddy," Uncle Perry told him. He turned to Ethan. "Maybe we should let him rest."

Ethan nodded and then, out of the corner of his eye, saw Dr. Morris standing in the hallway. The doctor gestured for Ethan to step out.

"Let me see what's happening with Lucille," Ethan said.

"Yes, go on," Uncle Perry said. He put his arm around me. We both looked at Daddy. "Everything will be all right, Sam. He's going to be fine."

I nodded. Uncle Perry looked into the hallway. Ethan was now beckoning to him.

"I'll be right back," he told me.

I moved closer to Daddy and took his hand. He opened his eyes and looked at me again.

"Those aren't your clothes. Those are Cassie's clothes, aren't they? Why are you wearing Cassie's clothes?"

"I felt a need to be close to her," I said.

"So you tried to make your hair look like her hair, too?"

"Yes. Cassie is still with me, Daddy," I said. "I've been trying to tell you that."

He just stared at me a moment and then closed his eyes.

"She's here with you, too, Daddy."

He shook his head and then opened his eyes when Ethan and Uncle Perry returned with the doctor.

"It's not good, Dad," Ethan said. "There's too much brain damage. She's already on life support."

"I've made some calls and sent for another opinion, Ted," Uncle Perry said, "but this neurologist has a very good reputation."

Daddy groaned, closed and opened his eyes. The doctor stepped up to the bed and began explaining it all in more detail, describing the areas of the brain that were injured. I backed away slowly and then saw that Cassie was in the hallway. I looked at Ethan and Uncle Perry, who were paying close attention to what the doctor was saying, and I went out to her. There was no one else in the hallway.

"You did this," I said. "You caused that flash of light, didn't you? You caused the truck driver to hit them."

I couldn't depend on you. The way you were going would soon cause you to lose all credibility. Tomorrow you would have been committed, and Lucille would have become Queen of Heavenstone. Now there's nothing to fear.

"But you could have hurt Daddy even more. Look how injured he is."

"I had to make it look good, didn't I?" she said. *"He'll be fine now."*

"What are you doing?" Ethan asked, coming out to me. His eyes were open wide. He looked up and down the hall as if he had missed someone. "Why did you come out here?"

"I hate to see Daddy in pain and so sad. He was sadder when my mother died, of course," I quickly added, "and also when Cassie died."

"This is a devastating tragedy, Semantha. He's

lost a second chance for happiness, and he was happy, very happy."

"We'll make him happy again," I said. I looked for Cassie, but she was gone.

"Your uncle and I are taking your father up to Lucille. She's in the ICU. They're bringing us a wheelchair. Then we'll be taking him home. The family doctor's been notified and will be at the house—Dr. Moffet. He's bringing a nurse to stay with your father tonight. She'll be sure he's made comfortable."

"Yes, Dr. Moffet," I said, smiling. "Good."

"Maybe it's best that you wait in the lobby and not go up with us to see Lucille," he suggested.

"That's fine, yes. I'll wait in the lobby."

He returned to Daddy's bedside, and I found my way to the lobby. It was very crowded, but there was an open seat next to a thin African American lady with stark white hair who was just staring blankly. She glanced at me when I sat.

"My father was in a car accident," I said.

"Sorry. My granddaughter has epilepsy. She had a bad seizure. My daughter's with her. It's the third time we've been here this month."

"How terrible."

"Yes. Everything's more horrible when it happens to little people."

She turned away and continued staring at the floor. She had the look of someone who wasn't hearing or seeing anything, but after another few moments, she turned back to me.

"How is your father? Hurt bad?"

"Banged up, broken arm, and a slight concussion, but he was lucky."

"He was by himself?"

"No. My stepmother was with him," I said. "She has severe head injuries. She may not live."

"Oh, I'm sorry."

"It wasn't my father's fault," I said. "A truck swiped the side of his car, and he was forced off the road."

"Oh."

"But it wasn't the truck driver's fault, either."

She looked at me strangely and then returned to staring ahead.

I looked around to see if Cassie would reappear, but she seemed to be gone. When she had said, *"Now there's nothing to fear,"* she made it sound as if she was saying good-bye. Surely, she wanted to be sure that Daddy was really all right, that everything would be. I closed my eyes and rested my head against the wall behind me. The sound of conversations became a low murmur. I felt a tightness in my body loosen until I was very relaxed. Somehow I fell asleep.

I woke when Ethan shook my shoulder.

"Hey," he said. "You all right?"

For a few seconds, I couldn't remember where I was. Then it all came crashing back. The woman who had been sitting beside me was gone and replaced by a teenage boy who had a bandage around his head. There was a large bloodstain on the bandage. There seemed to be quite a few more people waiting as well.

"We're taking your father home now, Semantha. Uncle Perry is getting him into the car. Let's go," he urged.

"What about Lucille?" I asked as I stood.

"They won't do anything until tomorrow, after the doctor your uncle sent for arrives and examines her and evaluates the tests and pictures they've taken. Come on."

He held his arm out for me, and we left the lobby and stepped into the parking lot. A nurse was helping Uncle Perry guide Daddy comfortably into the car.

"Okay," Uncle Perry said as we approached. "I'll follow you guys. Dr. Moffet and the nurse should be there when we arrive."

We got in, and I turned to look at Daddy lying there with a pillow behind his head and a light blanket. His eyes were closed.

"Are you comfortable, Dad?" Ethan asked.

"Yeah, I'm fine. This is unreal," he said without opening his eyes. "This is a nightmare."

"That it is," Ethan said. He started the engine and drove out slowly.

"Maybe it's all been a nightmare," I said. I think I was talking mostly to myself. "Maybe I'll wake up, and Mother will still be alive, and so will Cassie."

Daddy moaned.

Ethan glanced at him in the rearview mirror and then at me. I thought I could read his thoughts.

Look at this rich and powerful family, broken, in great physical and emotional pain. Money can do only so much for you in this world. It really can't buy

*you love, and without love, you can't have happiness,
no matter how big your bank account.*

We drove on in silence. Dr. Moffet and the
nurse he had brought were waiting for us when we
arrived. Uncle Perry was right behind us. While he
and Ethan helped get Daddy up to his room, I went
to the kitchen to finish cleaning up from our dinner. The De Stagens wouldn't be back until morning, but I thought I heard Gerad moving about
down by his room. I left the kitchen to see. I heard
his music, Edith Piaf, and for a moment remembered when Ethan and I had heard her *"La Vie en
Rose"* and vowed to make it our love song. These
songs Gerad was playing, however, were different
and seemed appropriately sad. I knocked on his
door.

"Just a moment, *s'il vous plaît*," he said, and
opened the door after he had put on his robe. "Ah,
yes?"

"I'm sorry to bother you," I said, "but I thought
you should know my father and Lucille were in a
very bad car accident tonight."

"No."

"Yes, and Lucille is not coming home."

His face seemed to sink inside his skull for a moment. "What are you saying, please?"

"She had very serious head injuries, and they are
not holding out much hope. My father is upstairs
with our doctor, a private-duty nurse, my uncle,
and my husband. My father has a broken arm and a
slight concussion. We'll have to send up his breakfast
in the morning."

He stood speechless.

"I'm sorry," I said, "but everything is going to change here now."

I turned and walked away. He stepped out to look after me, perhaps to be sure he wasn't dreaming, too. I met Ethan and Uncle Perry in the hallway, talking. The way they both looked at me as I approached convinced me that they had been talking about me and not about Daddy.

"How are you doing, Sam?" Uncle Perry asked.

"Okay," I said. "Is Dr. Moffet with Daddy?"

"Yes."

"He's more than our doctor. He's an old friend," I said.

"The nurse's name is Lila Millard. She says she'll be fine sleeping on the sofa in the bedroom suite. I'll be back in the morning. You're going to the office, right?" he asked Ethan.

"Yes. I'll get what I can organized and join you at the hospital."

"I'm sure Teddy will insist on going back, too," Uncle Perry said. He looked at me for a long moment before speaking. "You should get some rest now, Sam. It's going to be a difficult few days."

"She'll be okay," Ethan told him, and looked at me. "You want to go up to say good night to your father now and then go to bed yourself, honey. You look pretty tired."

"Do I? Okay," I said.

Uncle Perry hugged me and whispered, "I'm going to spend more time with you, Sam. I promise."

"That'll be nice," I told him.

He kissed my cheek, nodded at Ethan, and left.

"You won't wear your sister's clothes tomorrow, will you, Semantha?"

"No, I don't have to."

"You don't have to? Why did you have to now?"

I just smiled at him.

"Will you let me send for a stylist to repair what you've done to your hair?"

"I can go to the salon myself, Ethan," I said. "Stop worrying about me so much."

I started for the stairway. He hurried to catch up and take my arm to make me pause.

"Don't let your father feel or think you're happy about Lucille, Semantha. That would be a terrible, terrible mistake."

"I think I know how to talk to my father, Ethan. I love my father, and he loves me. I wouldn't do anything to hurt him or bring him more sorrow."

"All right," he said. "I'm going to sleep. Your uncle is right. It's going to be a very difficult few days ahead."

He walked past me and up the stairs. I followed slowly and then turned to Daddy's bedroom. Dr. Moffet was just leaving.

"Ah, Semantha, another tragedy befalls Heavenstone. I'm sorry," he said.

"The Heavenstone family is used to tragedy and knows how to overcome it," I said. I was sure I was repeating something Cassie had said, perhaps even to him after Mother's death.

"Yes. Well, best to take each day as it comes." He patted me on the arm and continued out.

I smiled to myself. Old Dr. Moffet, oblivious to the obvious things sometimes but with microscope eyes when it came to analyzing illness. Were we all doctors that way, oblivious to the obvious, too narrowly focused? I waited to hear Cassie's response, but there was nothing but silence.

"Where are you?" I called down the hallway. Then I went to Daddy's bedroom. The nurse was taking his blood pressure. She looked up as I entered. Daddy was lying there with his eyes closed.

"He's exhausted," she said. "Just a few minutes."

I ignored her just as Cassie would and went right to Daddy's side.

"You're home and in your own bed, Daddy," I said, taking his hand.

He opened his eyes and looked at me. "We're going to lose our Lucille," he said. His lips quivered.

"We'll be fine, Daddy. We have each other."

"She was good for us, Semantha, for all of us."

Tears came to my eyes, not for Lucille but for Daddy, who was suffering from grief already.

"Take my advice and cherish one another, Semantha. Snap out of your doldrums or whatever is wrong with you, and enjoy your husband and your marriage. I'm depending on you more than ever now."

"I will, Daddy. I promise," I said.

"You'd better let him rest," the nurse said. She was practically hovering over me.

"Good night, Daddy. I'll be here as soon as I wake up," I said, and kissed him. He held my hand longer, held it as if he never wanted to let it go.

Daddy's back, I thought. I didn't need Cassie to tell me.

Ethan was already in bed when I entered our bedroom. I moved about as quietly as I could. When I was in the bathroom, I looked at myself in the mirror and admitted to myself that I had made a terrible mess of my hair. I would call the salon first thing after breakfast. I was confident they'd fit me in. Everyone in this community would hear about Daddy's accident. It would be breaking news on television and radio.

When I crawled under the blanket, I expected Ethan would turn to talk to me, but he was apparently in a deep sleep already. I didn't want to wake him, but I couldn't fall asleep quickly. I lay there staring up into the darkness. Flashing on the ceiling were scenes from the past, mostly happy scenes, memories of Mother and me taking a walk or cleaning house together. It was easy to picture her smiling; she had done it so often.

Cassie had used to say Mother behaved more like an innocent, unsophisticated young girl. She'd had so much faith in people and had a stubborn insistence on believing things would turn out all right.

"Our mother lives in a Santa Claus world," Cassie would say. "She thinks ice on the road is a layer of diamonds, most crime is accidental, and death is a commercial interruption. Happiness will always survive and return."

"I like that, Cassie. I want to be the same way and believe in the same things."

"You would. If you're not careful, you'll end up just like her, a prisoner of delusion."

"A happy prisoner, though."

"Christmas trees. Talking to you is like talking to the wall."

"You said these walls have ears," I would remind her.

"Ancestral ears. Heavenstone is history. Oh, forget it," she would say. "You're giving me a headache."

Like two conspirators, Mother and I would smile after Cassie had said something unpleasant.

"She's too smart to be sour forever," Mother would tell me. In time, I had to admit to myself that was a delusion.

The pictures on the ceiling began to diminish as I grew more tired. I didn't want to fall asleep without seeing or hearing Cassie, but I couldn't wait much longer. *Maybe she'll be in my dreams,* I thought, and finally closed my eyes.

She wasn't. In fact, I slept more like someone under anesthesia. One moment, it was dark, and the next, it was light. Ethan was already up and gone. I sprang out of bed, rushed to get on some clothes, and hurried down to Daddy's bedroom. I was shocked to see Mia De Stagen remaking Daddy's empty bed.

"Where's my father?" I asked. She paused, her face full of sorrow.

"He went to the hospital with your husband." She reached into her apron to pluck out a tissue to dab her eyes. "Mrs. Heavenstone is very bad. He went to say good-bye, I'm afraid."

"Where's the nurse?"

"She went with them to look after your father."

"Why didn't anyone wake me?"

She had no answer, of course. I went down to get some coffee and then went to the phone and called Ethan on his cell phone. He didn't answer, so I left a message that I was surprised he hadn't woken me and that after breakfast, I intended to go to the salon. I told him to call me on my cell phone. Then I called the salon and made an appointment.

Gerad waited in the kitchen for orders. I was surprised that I had a big appetite and asked him to prepare one of his famous omelettes. Like most people awash in sorrow, he was grateful for something to do. Catherine De Stagen was the same way and hovered about me at the dining-room table, practically lunging to get me the pepper when I started to reach for it. She wore the same mask of sorrow Mia wore. It was hard for me to believe they were so emotionally tied to Lucille, but maybe they were. Maybe she was the sort of employer they admired, or maybe they wondered now if they would be retained much longer.

Ethan had still not called me before I left for the salon. I kept expecting him to as I sat in the chair and my stylist began to repair my chop job. She didn't pursue how my hair had come to be so badly mangled once I told her I had gone overboard trying to do it myself. She didn't ask why. I thought she did a remarkably good job of rescuing it. I didn't look like Cassie or myself, but it was an interesting new look for me. Ethan would be happy, I thought. Just toward the end, my phone finally rang.

"It's over," he began. "There was nothing the doctor your uncle brought in could do that would have made any sort of difference. Your father made the decision to cut off the life support."

"How is he?"

"Devastated. He's with your uncle and the minister. Where are you?"

"Finishing up in the salon. You'll love what she's done."

"Good. I've got to go help with the funeral planning. We want to take as much of this off your father's shoulders as we can."

"Okay," I said. "Should I come there or go home?"

"Go home. I'm sure we'll be headed that way soon. Are you all right, Semantha?" I could feel the tension in his voice. He was surely holding his breath.

"I'm fine, Ethan. Everything's okay. Don't worry about me now."

"That's good, Semantha. I need you to be strong. Now you sound like a real Heavenstone."

I nearly laughed. "Of course. That's who I've been and always will be, Ethan. And Ethan?"

"Yes?"

"I didn't take any birth control pills, and I won't anymore," I said.

He was silent so long that I thought he might have hung up. "That's good," he finally said.

I arrived at Heavenstone before they did and

waited nervously for Daddy. I paced and stood by one of the windows in the living room that faced the front and finally saw the limousine coming up the driveway. I rushed to the front door and out onto the portico as Ethan helped Daddy out. I noticed the nurse wasn't with them. Daddy looked up at me. I hurried down to him and embraced him.

While I had been waiting for him, I thought about Mother and how she would greet him and behave. Something she either had said or surely would say kept repeating itself in my mind: "Your happiness should never depend on someone else's unhappiness, Semantha. Daddy is truly in pain."

"I'm so sorry, Daddy," I said. "I know how happy you were."

"Thank you, honey," he said, and kissed me.

Along with Ethan, I helped him up the stairs.

"Where's your nurse?"

"I don't need someone hovering over me. I'll be all right. People get around with broken arms and slight concussions."

"Especially Heavenstones," I said, and he nodded.

He looked at me. "Glad you had your hair fixed," he said, "and you're wearing your own clothes."

"I'm sorry, Daddy. I didn't mean to upset you."

He nodded. When we entered the house, he insisted on going to his office instead of up to his bedroom.

"I can rest there as well, and there are things we just have to get done," he told Ethan.

We accompanied him to the office. He sat behind his desk and for a moment just stared ahead. He reminded me of the African American lady in the emergency room, stunned by her sadness and fear.

"You're sure you don't want to lie down for a while, Daddy?"

"I'm okay. I'll lie down in a little while." He picked up the phone and began to make his calls.

Ethan looked at me and gestured for us to leave.

"I'll look in on him in a moment or so," he told me as we left the office. "It's better for him to keep busy." He paused. "You're right. I like this new hair-style on you."

"Thank you."

"Let's get some lunch," he suggested.

Again, Gerad was more than happy to accommodate us, as were both De Stagens. Ethan told them to bring my father something to eat.

"This funeral is going to seem as big as their wedding," Ethan told me.

He had to give Lucille one last compliment, one that I might very well have sincerely given her myself.

"Fortunately for your father, we discovered she had thought out and planned for everything," he told me. "I guess it's logical that someone who was so in control of her life would be sure to be in control of her death. It's like some road map all laid out to follow. There's nothing for us to do but bear witness and comfort your father."

I didn't need Cassie beside me to whisper the right thing to say.

"I've done that before," I said.

He nodded and reached for my hand.

We sat there listening to the sound of silence that had seized Heavenstone and held us hypnotized.

Epilogue

ETHAN WAS RIGHT about Lucille's funeral. It ran like a Swiss clock, and the number of people who wanted to attend was so great that he, with Daddy overseeing him, had to create a preferred guest list. There were actually people at the church door checking off names. They set up speakers for the crowd that gathered outside the church, and of course, anyone who wanted to could attend at the cemetery.

It was the cemetery decision more than anything else Lucille had done that won my respect. She had not changed her desire to be buried alongside her first husband. Daddy would lie next to Mother. I was sure that set some tongues wagging, but I could just imagine Lucille staring them down with that condescending expression that said, "How dare you question one of my decisions?"

There was a seemingly endless parade of sympathetic mourners at Heavenstone during the days that followed. Gerad and the De Stagens worked harder than ever. Ethan was right alongside Daddy and Uncle Perry, greeting people and thanking them for their condolences. I wasn't as out front as they were, but there was no hiding. In an ironic way, Lucille's funeral and the aftermath did more to bring me out in public than anything she had tried. Daddy actually complimented me, telling me he was proud of the way I was conducting myself. Both Ethan and Uncle Perry followed up with their compliments as well. In the end, there were the four of us, sitting quietly together, all feeling as if we had just been through a great battle.

Daddy proudly rattled off some of the messages he had received from high government officials and important businesspeople, as well as journalists and television personalities from our area. After we had heard most of it, Uncle Perry said Lucille had impressed many people and was highly respected.

"Maybe there's just a curse on Heavenstone wives," Daddy said. "Our grandmother died at an early age."

"I won't have that problem," Uncle Perry muttered. It was just a thought that had come to him, but after he said it, he looked up at us as if he had blurted out something terrible. It was the first time Daddy had laughed for days.

"You will if they legalize gay marriage," Daddy quipped, and Uncle Perry's face turned into a ripe apple. Ethan smiled, and I thought to myself that Cassie would have enjoyed this.

As soon as Daddy was able to get around more comfortably, he was back at his office. Sometimes Ethan would drive him, and sometimes he would use the Heavenstone limousine. I decided to drive over and drop in on Daddy and Ethan from time to time.

I saw how much it pleased them, as well as Uncle Perry. He spent almost every weekend with us during the months that followed.

Daddy kept Gerad and the De Stagens working for us, and Heavenstone was basically run the way it had been before Lucille's death. Of course, some of the changes Lucille had envisioned and planned were not continued. To me, it was as if the grand old house released a deeply held breath. The faces on the ancestors in the corridor of portraits looked pleased. There was only one set of eyes that followed me with nervous interest, the eyes of Asa Heavenstone.

A number of times, I thought I saw Cassie floating through rooms and hallways. I waited anxiously for her whispers, but they didn't come. Just before summer, I learned I was finally pregnant. Ethan and Daddy took me out to celebrate, but they wouldn't let me drink anything alcoholic. They became nervous Nellies, hovering over me, nagging me about lifting anything too heavy. When I reached my fourth month, both forbade me to drive. Daddy assigned the limousine to me, and the poor driver had to hang about waiting for me to want to go here or there.

Almost the day after my pregnancy was confirmed, work began on the nursery to be right beside our bedroom, just the way Lucille had suggested. Ethan and I moved to one of the guest bedrooms while the carpenters created an adjoining door. For as long as I could, I resisted learning whether I was going to give birth to a boy or a girl. My memories of Mother finding out she was having a boy and the joy that followed were too vivid. That joy had made the tragedy much greater, I thought, and I was fearful. Ethan finally talked me into it, using the choices for furniture and the color of the nursery walls as a reason.

I knew both of them were holding their breath, and when the doctor announced I was going to have a boy, it could have been New Year's Eve. Someone might have thought I was giving birth to the new Messiah or at least some holy child. If the two of them had been nags before, they were now insane with protecting me. Daddy even thought aloud about hiring a nurse to be with me during the last trimester.

I was sure he was sending Uncle Perry to Heavenstone more often just to keep an eye on me. He began to have lunch with me twice a week and to take my walks with me. All the while, I looked for signs of Cassie, but I didn't even see her ghostlike image floating through rooms or hallways anymore. Sometimes I would burst into her bedroom and stand there looking at everything as if I expected to see some proof that she was there, but nothing ever changed.

One afternoon, while we were having lunch, Uncle Perry fixed his gaze on me with an intensity I recognized as the preface to some very serious comment or question. Cassie had used to call it his "tell" and claimed he was too obvious ever to be subtle or clever. I had told her he was refreshing because he wasn't conniving, and of course she had thought that was a weakness.

"When you're obvious, you're vulnerable," she

had said. I packed it away with some of her other words of wisdom that, despite their value, were still annoying to me.

"I'm sure you know, Sam, that your father and your husband would rather pretend that there was nothing wrong with you during the weeks and even months before Lucille's tragic death. You said and did things that recommended you for continued therapy. I'm happy to see that's all changed, but I worry for you, and ironically, I'm now the Heavenstone brother who refuses to bury his head in the sand."

"You mean when I tried to see my daughter?"

"That and other things, Sam. How do you feel about not seeing or spending any time with her?"

"I understand why the Normans were so fearful. They've invested their love in her and she in them. It would be cruel to do anything to ruin that relationship."

"Very good. I'm proud of you for saying that. Someday, maybe when she's much older, they'll tell her the truth, and then you two might meet."

"I think so."

"But something else obsessed you. I felt it often whenever I visited and you acted as if our conversations were being recorded or something, and certainly when you had a little breakdown of sorts and cut your hair and began dressing like Cassie. Is that over?"

I hesitated to answer. Was it?

"She's not here anymore," I finally admitted. "I don't hear her voice."

"I'm not surprised," he said. "When she was

alive, she was in your head far too much. She never let you be yourself."

"She was afraid for Heavenstone."

"No, I think she was afraid for herself, afraid she was wrong about most things. When she engineered your first pregnancy, she was completing her mission to take you over completely. In her mind, you were having her baby, right?"

"Yes," I said.

"And that's why you went to the Normans' home. You thought that was what Cassie would want."

"Partly. I was curious, Uncle Perry. It's only natural."

"Is she gone now, Semantha?"

"I don't know," I admitted.

He nodded and then brightened and stood up. "Let's take a ride."

"A ride? Where to?"

"Just take a ride," he said. "Trust me."

He went out to his car and drove through the gate, neither of us talking. As we drove along, I realized where he was going. Suddenly, I did hear Cassie again.

"No," she was whispering. "*Turn back*," she was telling me. "*Tell him no.*"

It took all my strength to defy her, but I did. I said nothing. Her whispers grew more and more frantic, and when we drove through the entrance to the cemetery, she was screaming. Uncle Perry looked at me a number of times. I saw how worried he was, but I held my breath.

Finally, I had to put my hands over my ears. He parked and quickly got out of the car to go around and open my door.

"Come on, Sam. You've got to."

I let him guide me out and held on to his arm as we walked up the path until we reached Cassie's grave. For a moment, the two of us stood there silently staring at the tombstone.

"Bury her again," Uncle Perry said. "Go on, Sam. Do it."

He let go of me. I stepped forward and then fell to my knees and spread my arms as I lowered myself to embrace the earth. The grass was cool against my cheek.

"Good-bye, Cassie," I whispered. "I don't hate you, but I don't need you anymore."

Her whispering stopped.

Uncle Perry helped me to my feet. I brushed off my clothes, and we started out.

Far off in the distance in the direction of Heavenstone, the clouds began to part to reveal the bluest of blue sky.

And I felt like a child opening a gift and discovering she had been given herself.

Finally and forever.

Forbidden Sister

Virginia Andrews

Now available from
Simon & Schuster

Turn the page for a preview
of the thrilling first installment
in a brand new series

Prologue

My mother wasn't supposed to have me. She wasn't supposed to get pregnant again.

Nearly nine years before I was born, she gave birth to my sister, Roxy. Her pregnancy with Roxy was very difficult, and when my mother's water broke and she was rushed to the hospital, Roxy resisted coming into the world. My mother says she fought being born. An emergency cesarean was conducted, and my mother nearly died. She fell into a coma for almost three days, and after she regained consciousness, the first thing her doctor told her was to never get pregnant again.

When I first heard and understood this story, I immediately thought that I must have been an accident. Why else would they have had another child after so many years had passed? She and Papa surely had agreed with the doctor that it was dangerous for her to get pregnant again. Mama could see that thought and concern in my face whenever we talked about it, and she always assured me that I wasn't a mistake.

"Your father wanted you even more than I did," she told me, but just thinking about it made me wonder about children who are planned and those who are not. Do parents treat children they didn't plan any differently from the way they treat the planned ones? Do they love them any less?

I know there are single mothers who give away their children immediately because they can't manage them or they don't want to begin a loving relationship they know will not last. Some don't want to set eyes on them. When their children find out that they were given away, do they think about the fact that their mothers really didn't want them to be born? How could they help but think about it? That certainly can't be helpful to their self-confidence.

Despite my mother's assurances, I couldn't help wondering. If I weren't planned, was my soul floating around somewhere minding its own business and then suddenly plucked out of a cloud of souls and ordered to get into my body as it was forming in Mama's womb? Was birth an even bigger surprise for unplanned babies? Maybe that was what really happened in Roxy's case. Maybe she wasn't planned, and that was why she resisted.

Wondering about myself always led me to wonder about Roxy. What sort of a shock was it for her when she first heard she was going to have a sister, after having been an only child all those years? She must have known Mama wasn't supposed to have me. Did she feel very special because of that? Did she see herself as their precious golden child, the only one Mama and Papa could have? And then, when Mama told her about her new pregnancy, did Roxy pout and sulk, thinking she would have to share our parents' attention and love? Share her throne? Was she worried that she would have to help take care of me and that it would cut into her fun time? Although I didn't know how she felt about me for some time, from the little I remember about her, I had the impression that I was at least an inconvenience to her. Maybe my being born was the real reason Roxy became so rebellious.

My mother told me that my father believed her complications in giving birth to Roxy were God's first warning about her. However, despite her difficult birth, there was nothing physically wrong with Roxy. She began exceptionally beautiful and is to this day, but according to Mama, even when Roxy was an infant, she was headstrong and rebellious. She ate when she wanted to eat, no matter what my mother prepared for her or how she tried to get her to eat, and she slept when she wanted to sleep. Rocking her or singing to her didn't work. My mother told me my father would get into a rage about it. Finally, he insisted she take Roxy to the doctor. She did, but the doctor concluded that there was absolutely nothing wrong with Roxy. My father ordered her to find another doctor. The result was the same.

Roxy's tantrums continued until my mother finally gave in and slept when Roxy wanted to sleep. She even ate when Roxy wanted to eat, leaving my father to eat alone often.

"If I didn't eat with her, she wouldn't eat, or she'd take hours to do so," my mother said. "Your father thought she was being spiteful even when she was an infant."

According to how my mother described all this to me, Roxy's tantrums spread to everything she did and everything that was done with her or for her. My father complained to my mother that he couldn't pick Roxy up or kiss her unless she wanted him to do so at that moment. If he tried to do otherwise, she wailed and flailed about "like a fish out of water." My mother didn't disagree with that description. She said Roxy would even hold her breath and stiffen her body into stone until she got her way. Her face would turn pink and then crimson.

"As red as a polished apple! I had no doubt that

she would die before she would give in or get what she wanted."

I was always told that fathers and daughters could have a special relationship, because daughters often see their fathers as perfect, and fathers see their daughters as little princesses. My mother assured me that nothing was farther from the truth when it came to Roxy and my father.

"*Mon dieu.* I swear sometimes your father would look at Roxy with such fire in his eyes that I thought he'd burn down the house," my mother said.

Although she was French, my mother was fluent in English as a child, and after years and years of living in America, she usually reverted to French with my father and me only when she became emotional or wanted to stress something. Of course, I learned to speak French because of her. She knew that teaching it to me when I was young was the best way to get me fluent in the language.

"Your sister would look right back at him defiantly and never flinch. He was always the first to give up, to look away. And if he ever spanked her or slapped her, she would never cry.

"Once, when she was fourteen and came home after two o'clock in the morning when she wasn't even supposed to go out, he took his belt to her," my mother continued. "I had to pull him off her, practically claw his arm to get him to stop. You know how big your father's hands are and how powerful he can be, especially when he's very angry. Roxy didn't cry and never said a word. She simply went to her room as if she had walked right through him.

"She defied him continually, breaking every rule he set down, until he gave up and threw her out of the house. You were just six and really the ideal child in his eyes, *une enfant parfait*. Why waste his time on a hopeless cause, he would say, when he could spend his time and energy on you instead? He was always afraid she'd be a bad influence on you, contaminate you with her nasty and stubborn ways.

"Your sister didn't cry or beg to stay. She packed her bags, took the little savings she had, and went out into the world as if she had never expected to do anything different. She didn't even look to me to intercede on her behalf. I don't think she ever respected me as a woman or as her mother, because I wouldn't stand up to your father the way she would. Sometimes she wouldn't even let me touch her. The moment I put my hand out to stroke her hair or caress her face, she recoiled like a frightened bird.

"Maybe your father hoped she would finally learn a good lesson and return, begging him to let her back into our home and family and promising to behave. But if he did have that expectation, he was very good at keeping it secret. After she left, he avoided mentioning her name to me, and if I talked about her, he would get up and leave the room. If I did so at dinner, he would get up and go out to eat, and if I mentioned her when we were in bed, he would go out to the living room to sleep.

"So I gave up trying to change his mind. Sometimes I went out looking for her, taking you with me, but this is a very big city. Paris is a bigger city, but more people live here in New York. It was probably as difficult as looking for a needle in a haystack."

"Didn't you call the police, try to get her face on milk cartons or something?"

"Your father wouldn't hear of it for the first few

months. Later, there were newspaper stories and a magazine article about lost girls, and your sister was featured. Nothing came of it. I used to go to other neighborhoods and walk and walk, hoping to come upon her, especially on her birthday, but it wasn't until five years later that your father revealed that he had seen her. He told me only because he thought it proved he was right to throw her out.

"He was at a dinner meeting with some of his associates at the investment bank. After it had ended, one of them told him he had a special after-dinner date. They walked out together, and a stretch limousine pulled up. The man winked at your father and went to the limousine. The chauffeur opened the door, and your father saw a very attractive and expensively dressed young woman inside the limousine. At first, he didn't recognize her, but after a few moments, he realized it was Roxy. He said she looked years older than she was and that she glared out at him with the same defiance he had seen in her face when she was only five.

"Later, he found out she was a high-priced call girl. She even had a fancy name, Fleur du Coeur, which you know means 'Flower of the Heart.' That's how rich men would ask for her when they called the escort service.

"*Mon dieu, mon dieu!* It broke my heart to hear all of that, but I didn't cry in front of him."

Even now, talking about it brought tears to her eyes, however.

My mother told me more about Roxy after my father had passed away. I was devastated by my father's death, but now that he was no longer there to stop it, I wanted to hear as much as I could about my forbidden sister, the sister whose existence I could never acknowledge.

I had no trouble pretending I was an only child. Since the day Roxy had left, I was living that way anyway. My father had taken all of her pictures off the walls and shelves and dressers. He had burned most of them. Mama was able to hide a few, but anything else Roxy had left behind was dumped down the garbage chute. It was truly as if he thought he could erase all traces of her existence. He never even acknowledged her birthday. Looking at the calendar, he would do little more than blink.

He didn't know it, but I still had a charm bracelet Roxy had given me. It had a wonderful variety of charms that included the Eiffel Tower, a fan, a pair of dancing shoes, and a dream catcher. My mother's brother had given it to her when my parents and she were in France visiting, and she gave it to me. I never wore it in front of my father for fear that he would seize it and throw it away, too.

Of course, I could never mention her name in front of my father when he was alive, and I didn't dare ask him any questions about her. My mother was the one who told me almost all I knew about Roxy after she had left. She said that once my father had seen Roxy in the limousine, he had tried to learn more about her, despite himself. He found out that she lived in a fancy hotel on the East Side, the Hotel Beaux-Arts. I had overheard them talking about it. The Beaux-Arts was small but very expensive. Most of the rooms were suites and some were full apartments. My mother said that my father was impressed with how expensive it was.

"The way he spoke about her back then made me think that he was impressed with how much money she was making. Before I could even think he had softened his attitude about her, he added that she was nothing more than a high-priced prostitute," she said.

She didn't want to tell me all of this, but it was as if it had all been boiling inside her and she finally had the chance to get it out. I knew that she went off afterward to cry in private. I was conflicted about asking her questions because I saw how painful it was for her to tell these things to me. I rarely heard my parents speak about Roxy, and I knew I couldn't ask my mother any questions about her in front of Papa. If I did ask when he wasn't home, my mother would avoid answering or answer quickly, as if she expected the very walls would betray her and whisper to my father.

However, the questions were there like weeds, undaunted, invulnerable, and as defiant as Roxy.

What did she look like now?

What was her life really like?

Was she happy? Did she have everything she wanted?

Was she sad about losing her family?

Mostly, I wanted to know if she ever thought about me. It suddenly occurred to me one day that Roxy might have believed that my father risked my mother's life to have me just so he could ignore her. He was that disgusted with her. Surely, if Roxy thought that, she could have come to hate me.

Did she still hate me?

The answers were out there, just waiting for me. They taunted me and haunted me.

I had no doubt, however, that I would eventually get to know them.

What I wondered was, would I be sorry when I did get to know them?

Would they change my life?

And maybe most important of all, would I hate my sister as much as my father had?

1

My father was always the first to rise in the morning, even on weekends. He was never quiet about it, either. All three bedrooms in our town house just off Madison Avenue on East 81st Street in New York were upstairs. It was a relatively new building in the neighborhood, and Papa often complained about the workmanship and how the builders had cut corners to make more money. He said the older structures on the street were far more solid, even though ours cost more. Our walls were thinner, as were the framing and the floors.

Consequently, I could hear him close drawers, start his shower, close cabinets, and even talk to Mama, especially if their bedroom door was open. The cacophony of sounds he made was his rendition of Army reveille. Of course, being the son of an Army general, he actually had heard it most of his young life. His family had often lived that close to the barracks, depending on where his father had been stationed, especially when they were overseas. When I commented about it once, Mama said the volume of the noise he made after he got up in the morning was a holdover from the days when Roxy lived with us. Her bedroom was on the other side of theirs. She would never wake up for school on her own, so Papa would be sure to make all this noise to get her up much earlier than was necessary. No matter what Mama said, he was stubborn about it. Maybe Roxy had inherited that obstinacy from him. Who could be more inflexible when he had made up his mind than my father?

Even though he basically had defied his own father's wishes and chosen a business career rather than a military one as his older brother, Orman, had, Papa still believed in military discipline. Disobeying an order in our house could lead to the equivalent of being court-martialed. At least, that was how it felt to me, and I'm sure it had felt that way to Roxy, especially when he told her to leave the house. To her it must have been like a dishonorable discharge. Perhaps, despite what Papa said, she had felt some shame. I imagined she would have, even though I couldn't remember her that well anymore. After all, it was now a little more than nine years since I had last seen her or heard her voice.

I often wondered if she had seen me and secretly watched me growing up. During these years, did she hide somewhere nearby and wait for a glimpse of either my mother or me? One of the first things I used to do when I stepped out, and often still do, was to look across the street, searching for someone Roxy's age standing behind a car or off to the side of a building, watching for any sight of us. Even if I didn't see her, I couldn't help but wonder if she followed me to school.

Sometimes I would pretend she was, and I would stop suddenly and turn to catch her. People behind me would look annoyed or frightened. Whenever I walked in the city, whether to school or to the store or just to meet friends, I would scan the faces of any young woman who would be about Roxy's age. I often studied some young woman's face so hard she flashed anger back at me, and I quickly looked away and sped up.

One of the first things my parents had taught me about walking the streets of New York was never to make too much eye contact with strangers. I supposed Roxy would be like a complete stranger to me now. I even had trouble recalling the sound of her voice, but I did sneak looks at the pictures of her that Mama had hidden every chance I had.

I believed that Roxy would be as curious about me as I was about her. Why shouldn't she be? Although I feared it, it was hard for me to accept that she hated Mama and me because of what Papa had done to her. Despite his stern ways, it was also hard for me to believe she hated him. Maybe it was difficult only because I didn't want to believe it. I didn't even want to think that someone with whom I shared so much DNA could be that bad, that immoral. Or did it mean that somewhere deep inside me there was a strain of evil that would someday rise to the surface, too? How would it show itself? What emotions, lusts, and desires did we share?

Having an older sister who had become so infamous to my parents naturally made me worry about myself. When I suggested such a thing to Mama once, she looked at me with pain in her eyes. I know the pain was there, because, like me, she didn't want to believe Roxy was so wicked and sinful or as evil as Papa made her out to be. Then she softened her look and told me to think of Cain and Abel in the Bible. Abel wasn't evil because Cain was. Abel was good.

"Besides, we must not believe that evil is stronger than good, Emmie. You're my perfect daughter, my *fille parfaite, n'est-ce pas?*"

"*Oui,* Mama," I would say whenever she asked me that, but I didn't believe I was as perfect as Mama or Papa thought I was. Who could be?

Yes, I kept my room neat, made my bed, helped Mama with house chores, shopped for her, came home when my parents told me I must, never smoked or drank alcohol with my classmates, not even a beer, and refused to try any drugs or pot any classmate offered. Mama believed in letting me drink wine at dinner, even when I was barely ten, and I drank some vodka to celebrate things occasionally, but that was the way she had been brought up in France, and Papa thought it was just fine.

"The best training ground for most things is your home," he would tell me. My friends at school, especially the ones who knew how strict my father could be, didn't know what to make of that. He sounded so lenient, but I knew that his leniency didn't go any farther than our front door. Sometimes, especially when I left our house, I felt as if I were walking around with an invisible leash and collar around my neck.

Rules rained down around me everywhere I looked, not just in my home. Our school, which was a private school, didn't tolerate sexy clothing or any body piercing, not that I wanted to do that. Our teachers even criticized some girls for wearing too much makeup. It was far more serious for my classmates to violate rules than it was for students in a public school, because, unlike in a public school, they wouldn't simply be suspended. They'd be thrown out, and all of their tuition money would be forfeited. What they did after school the moment they left the property was another thing, however. Buttons were undone, rings were put in noses, and cigarettes came out of hidden places. Students puffed defiantly. Suddenly, their mouths were full of profanity, words they would be afraid even to whisper in the school's hallways. It was as if all of the pent-up nasty behavior was bursting at the seams. They were far from goody-goodies, so why shouldn't I wonder if I was, too?

I probably wouldn't be attending a strict private school if it weren't for Roxy. She had been going to a public school, had been suspended for smoking and for cheating on a test, and, worst of all, was nearly arrested and expelled for smoking a joint in the girls' room. It was one of the better public schools in New York, too, but according to what I gleaned from Mama, Roxy never had better than barely passing grades.

The only thing she excelled at was speaking French, thanks to Mama. But even with that skill, she got in trouble. She would say nasty things in French to her teachers under her breath or even aloud, and when some of them went to the language teacher for translations, Roxy ended up in the principal's office, and Mama would have to come to school. She tried to keep as much of it as she could hidden from Papa, but often there was just too much to hide, and whatever he did learn was way more than enough to rile him and send him into a rage.

Mama could get away with hiding much of it, because Papa was dedicated to his work at the investment firm. He was up early to deal with the stock market and then always working late into the afternoon with financial planning and other meetings. Mama said that her having to call him at work because of something Roxy had done was like the president having to use the famous red phone or something. I had no doubt that Mama trembled whenever she had to tell him about something very bad Roxy had done in school. She said he was so furious that he could barely speak whenever he had to leave work to attend a meeting because of something she had done.

"It got so that your sister wouldn't even pretend to feel remorseful about something she had done. She would just look at him with that silent defiance, just as she would when he would rattle the whole house to get her out of bed in the morning."

Even though Papa got up earlier than I would have to on weekday mornings, I was used to rising and having breakfast with him and Mama. She was always up to make his breakfast. I would spend the extra morning time studying for a test or reading. Whenever I did anything that was the opposite of what Roxy would have done, such as be at breakfast with him, I could see the satisfaction in Papa's face. I used to think, and still do, that he was letting out an anxious breath, always half expecting that I would somehow turn out to be like Roxy. No matter how well I did in school, how polite I was to his and Mama's friends, or how much I helped Mama, he couldn't help fearing that I would wake up one day and be like my sister.

It was as if he had two different kinds of daughters. One was Dr. Jekyll, and the other was Miss Hyde, only he wasn't sure if Miss Hyde would also emerge in me.

"So what's on for today?" Papa asked. It was the same question he asked me every day at breakfast.

Anyone who thought that he asked it out of habit would be wrong, however. He really wanted to know what I had to do and, especially, what I wanted to do. My route to and from school was to follow Madison Avenue north for five blocks and then turn west for another block. I could do it blindfolded by now. If I had any plans to diverge from the route, especially during nice weather like what we were having this particular fall, and go somewhere after school, I would have to tell him. He even wanted to know when I would take my lunch and eat it with some friends in Central Park. The school let us do that. Even many of our teachers did it, but doing something spontaneously was very difficult.

Maybe because of how angry Papa would get about Roxy if Mama slipped and brought up her name, I tried extra hard to please him. To get him to smile at me, laugh at something I had said or done, and kiss me when he hugged me was very important to me. Although I didn't come out and say it, earning this reaction from him was like telling him that I wasn't and never would be like Roxy. Nothing made me feel warmer and happier than when he used Mama's French to call me his *fille parfaite*. Maybe hearing him say that I was a perfect daughter in French made it even more special.

Sometimes I would imagine that Roxy was standing there beside me in the house, scowling and sneering whenever Papa said that. I knew what sibling rivalry was, how friends of mine competed with their sisters or brothers for their parents' affection and approval. As strange as it might sound, even though my sister was gone from our home and our lives, I still felt sibling rivalry. Perhaps I was competing with a ghost. My visions of her were as vague as that, but I still felt that I was always being measured against her. Was my French as good as hers? Was I as pretty?

Other girls and boys my age might have older brothers or sisters to look up to and try to emulate. I had a sister, a secret sister always to be better than. It wasn't difficult for me to outdo her in every way except misbehavior, but nothing I could do or say really stopped my parents from thinking about her. I knew that was true, regardless of what Papa pretended or how furious and red his face would become at the mere suggestion of her.

Roxy was there; she would always be there, haunting us all. Keeping her bedroom door shut, throwing out her things, removing her pictures from the shelves and the mantel, ignoring her birthday, and forbidding the sound of her name didn't stop her voice from echoing somewhere in the house. Whenever I saw Papa stop what he was doing or look up from what he was reading and stare blankly at a corner or at a chair, I had the feeling he was seeing Roxy. I know Mama did. It got so I recognized those moments when she would pause no matter what she was doing and just stare at something. I would say nothing. Afterward, she often went off to cry in secret.

"If it doesn't rain, we're going to the park for lunch, and then after school, I'm going to Chastity Morgan's house to study for our unit exam in social studies," I told Papa at breakfast. His whole body was at attention, waiting for my response.

"Just you and Chastity?" he asked, his dark brown eyebrows lifted in anticipation of my answer.

Even though Papa was never in the Army, he kept his dark brown hair as short as a soldier's hair and had a soldier's posture, with his shoulders back and his back straight. He had a GI Joe shave every morning and wore spit-polished shoes. He was a little taller than six feet and tried to keep himself physically fit. He would walk as much as he could and avoid taxicabs whenever possible, but his job was sedentary. Despite his efforts, he had slowly gained weight over the years, until his doctor warned him about his blood pressure and cholesterol. He tried to watch his diet, but Mama was French and cooked with sauces he loved. It did him no good to try to pass the blame onto her, either, because she was ready to point out how the French were thinner and healthier because they didn't ask for seconds as he would often do.

Except for that and the topic of my sister, my parents rarely argued. If anyone complained, it was Mama about herself. I thought it was an odd complaint.

"I'm too devoted to that man," she would mutter. "But I can't help it."

I wondered if that was true. Could you love someone too much? What was too much? From what I saw in the lives of my classmates, especially when I visited them at their homes, their parents could use love inoculations, affection booster shots. Chastity Morgan's parents were like that. Eating dinner in their dining room was like eating at a restaurant. Their conversation was mostly directed to their maid. I was there when Chastity's father sent food back to be cooked longer or complained about being given food that was too cool. I half expected him to leave a tip at his plate before he left the table.

Most of the time at these dinners, her mother would talk to Chastity and me without saying more than two words to Chastity's father. Her father often read a paper at the dinner table, too. My father would have him face a firing squad for doing something like that.

When Chastity came to my house for dinner, the

contrast was so great it almost brought tears to her eyes. Both of my parents made her feel like part of our family. Papa directed a great deal of conversation her way. However, I wished he wouldn't, because his conversation was mostly interrogation. Maybe Chastity wasn't aware of it as much as I was, but he was looking to see if she would be a bad influence on me, even though we had been best friends for two years, and she was the only one at school who knew I had an older sister. I had even told her where Roxy lived and what Roxy did.

I didn't do that because I was proud of Roxy. I did it because I wanted company when I eventually went to spy on Roxy, and I knew this would excite Chastity. She and I had been talking about it for weeks, and I had decided that I was finally ready to do it. She understood that it required lots of planning. I just couldn't go hanging around the hotel for hours and hours. My parents, especially my father, would want to know where I had been and what I had been doing. I needed a solid alibi, and telling my father that I was going to Chastity's house to study would suffice.